STANLEY WEINBAUM RESURRECTED

The Short Stories of Stanley Weinbaum

By Stanley Weinbaum
Edited by Greg Fowlkes

STANLEY WEINBAUM RESURRECTED

The Short Stories of Stanley Weinbaum

© 2011 Resurrected Press
www.ResurrectedPress.com

Published by Resurrected Press

This classic book was handcrafted by Resurrected Press. Resurrected Press is dedicated to bringing high quality classic books back to the readers who enjoy them. These are not scanned versions of the originals, but, rather, quality checked and edited books meant to be enjoyed!

Please visit ResurrectedPress.com to view our entire catalogue!

ISBN 13: 978-1-935774-99-0

Printed in the United States of America

FOREWORD

From his first published story, "A Martian Odyssey," it was obvious that Stanley Grauman Weinbaum was something new and different. Up until that time most science fiction stories, especially those in the pulp magazines, were little more than adventure stories with a change of locale to some planet or moon that really wasn't that different than a Terrestrial desert or jungle. Aliens, if they were present, were merely monsters, there for the hero to vanquish before getting the girl.

With "A Martian Odyssey" and its sequel, "Valley of Dreams," Weinbaum changed science fiction forever. In these two stories of the first Martian expedition, his explores come in contact with Tweel, half bird, half plant, but completely alien. Instead of a monster, Tweel is friendly, even helpful, in his own very unique way, helping the expedition survive and learn about the planet and the Martians.

In many ways, it was Weinbaum that put the science in science fiction. At the University of Wisconsin he had studied chemical engineering before changing his major to English. He was knowledgeable about many areas of chemistry, physics, mathematics and biology, and his stories are infused with what for the time were scientifically accurate concepts.

Each of the stories he wrote during his too short career was centered on some particular scientific fact or theory that had struck his fancy. In the prescient "Shifting Seas" he examined what would happen if the Gulf Stream was diverted so that it no longer warmed Europe. The resultant ecological catastrophe and resulting political crisis brings all too clear the dangers in climate change. His story, "Proteus Island," has an experiment with radiation induced mutation running amok in a manner that predates any number of 1950's science fiction movies using the same concept.

He took great delight in inventing alien worlds populated by bizarre life forms. Once he had decided on a premise, he would rigorously examine how this would actually affect the environment his heroes and heroines inhabited. The Venus described in "Parasite Planet" is tidally locked on the sun, with one side baking in eternal day while the other is a frozen wasteland in perpetual darkness, while the border between the two hemispheres is an unstable zone where the plants and animals compete to survive. In "Redemption Cairn" he describes the moon Europa as having valleys with breathable air while the intervening mountains extend above the atmosphere. His hero must devise a way to cross from one valley to the next using only local resources. "The Lotus Eaters," "The Planet of Doubt," "Flight on Titan" and "The Mad Moon" all feature strange creatures in exotic environments. In "Red Peri" the heroes must deal with carbon eating crystals and space pirates, but having to face the vacuum of space without a spacesuit is the real heart of the story.

     While his stories have plenty of the action typical of the period, it was the science and ideas that were the core of his stories. This was a concept that was to become common during the "Golden Age" of science fiction starting with the editorship of Astounding under John Campbell, but as Isaac Asimov put it, Weinbaum was writing "perfect Campbellian stories before John Campbell." The idea of taking a concept and exploring the consequences was a major innovation in the genre and set the tone for much of what came after.

     As an example, in the set of humorous stories featuring Dixon Wells and the slightly mad Professor Manderpootz, the professor invents a number of gadgets that Dixon then tries out. In "Worlds of If" the device allows him to explore an alternative world where he takes a rocket plane that crashes, in "The Ideal" the machine realizes an image of the ideal example of a word the user contemplates, and in "The Point of View" the device allows the user to see the world from the point of view of another person. Of course, in each case, the result is unexpected, Dixon falls in love with a woman only to have her marry someone else, and a nice little moral is expounded.

     The story, "Pygmalions's Spectacles," has the hero try a device which immerses him in a dream world where he falls in love with a beautiful woman. When he awakes, he finds it was all an illusion. In "Adaptive Ultimate" a woman is given an experimental medical treatment which heightens her ability to adapt to fight off her disease. The unintended consequence is that she becomes invulnerable and beyond control.

The tragedy is that less than eighteen months after his first story was published, Stanley Weinbaum was dead from lung cancer. We shall never know what he might have written had he lived. While much of the science that he based his stories on is now, seventy-five years later, now dated, we are indebted to him for the idea that science fiction should be based on real science. Even if the science is dated, the stories still maintain their ability to entertain reader.

Resurrected Press has gathered in this volume all of the short fiction Weinbaum wrote in his short career. Several stories have been omitted because they were finished after his death by others. This was done, not because of any defect in those stories, but because they do not, completely, reflect the character of the author. We think that this collection represents an important facet in the history of science fiction. Beyond that, the stories are entertaining and and I hope you will enjoy them as much as I have.

Greg Fowlkes
Editor-In-Chief
Resurrected Press
www.ResurrectedPress.com

Other Resurrected Press Science Fiction

TABLE OF CONTENTS

THE STORIES OF TWEEL

A Martian Odyssey

Originally Published in *Wonder Stories*
July 1934

A Martian Odyssey

Jarvis stretched himself as luxuriously as he could in the cramped general quarters of the *Ares*.

"Air you can breathe!" he exulted. "It feels as thick as soup after the thin stuff out there!" He nodded at the Martian landscape stretching flat and desolate in the light of the nearer moon, beyond the glass of the port.

The other three stared at him sympathetically—Putz, the engineer, Leroy, the biologist, and Harrison, the astronomer and captain of the expedition. Dick Jarvis was chemist of the famous crew, the *Ares* expedition, first human beings to set foot on the mysterious neighbor of the earth, the planet Mars. This, of course, was in the old days, less than twenty years after the mad American Doheny perfected the atomic blast at the cost of his life, and only a decade after the equally mad Cardoza rode on it to the moon. They were true pioneers, these four of the *Ares*. Except for a half-dozen moon expeditions and the ill-fated de Lancey flight aimed at the seductive orb of Venus, they were the first men to feel other gravity than earth's, and certainly the first successful crew to leave the earth-moon system. And they deserved that success when one considers the difficulties and discomforts—the months spent in acclimatization chambers back on earth, learning to breathe the air as tenuous as that of Mars, the challenging of the void in the tiny rocket driven by the cranky reaction motors of the twenty-first century, and mostly the facing of an absolutely unknown world.

Jarvis stretched and fingered the raw and peeling tip of his frost-bitten nose. He sighed again contentedly.

"Well," exploded Harrison abruptly, "are we going to hear what happened? You set out all shipshape in an auxiliary rocket, we don't get a peep for ten days, and finally Putz here picks you out of a lunatic ant-heap with a freak ostrich as your pal! Spill it, man!"

"Speel?" queried Leroy perplexedly. "Speel what?"

"He means '*spiel*'," explained Putz soberly. "It iss to tell."

Jarvis met Harrison's amused glance without the shadow of a smile. "That's right, Karl," he said in grave agreement with Putz. "*Ich spiel es!*" He grunted comfortably and began.

"According to orders," he said, "I watched Karl here take off toward the North, and then I got into my flying sweat-box and headed South. You'll remember, Cap—we had orders not to land, but just scout about for points of interest. I set the two cameras clicking and buzzed along, riding pretty high—about two thousand feet—for a couple of reasons. First, it gave the cameras a greater field, and second, the under-jets travel so far in this half-vacuum they call air here that they stir up dust if you move low."

"We know all that from Putz," grunted Harrison. "I wish you'd saved the films, though. They'd have paid the cost of this junket; remember how the public mobbed the first moon pictures?"

"The films are safe," retorted Jarvis. "Well," he resumed, "as I said, I buzzed along at a pretty good clip; just as we figured, the wings haven't much lift in this air at less than a hundred miles per hour, and even then I had to use the under-jets.

"So, with the speed and the altitude and the blurring caused by the under-jets, the seeing wasn't any too good. I could see enough, though, to distinguish that what I sailed over was just more of this grey plain that we'd been examining the whole week since our landing—same blobby growths and the same eternal carpet of crawling little plant-animals, or biopods, as Leroy calls them. So I sailed along, calling back my position every hour as instructed, and not knowing whether you heard me."

"I did!" snapped Harrison.

"A hundred and fifty miles south," continued Jarvis imperturbably, "the surface changed to a sort of low plateau, nothing but desert and orange-tinted sand. I figured that we were right in our guess, then, and this grey plain we dropped on was really the Mare Cimmerium which would make my orange desert the region called Xanthus. If I were right, I ought to hit another grey plain, the Mare Chronium in another couple of hundred miles, and then another orange desert, Thyle I or II. And so I did."

"Putz verified our position a week and a half ago!" grumbled the captain. "Let's get to the point."

"Coming!" remarked Jarvis. "Twenty miles into Thyle—believe it or not—I crossed a canal!"

"Putz photographed a hundred! Let's hear something new!"

"And did he also see a city?"

"Twenty of 'em, if you call those heaps of mud cities!"

"Well," observed Jarvis, "from here on I'll be telling a few things Putz didn't see!" He rubbed his tingling nose, and continued. "I knew that I had sixteen hours of daylight at this season, so eight hours—eight hundred miles—from here, I decided to turn back. I was still over Thyle, whether I or II I'm not sure, not more than twenty-five miles into it. And right there, Putz's pet motor quit!"

"Quit? How?" Putz was solicitous.

"The atomic blast got weak. I started losing altitude right away, and suddenly there I was with a thump right in the middle of Thyle! Smashed my nose on the window, too!" He rubbed the injured member ruefully.

"Did you maybe try vashing der combustion chamber mit acid sulphuric?" inquired Putz. "Sometimes der lead giffs a secondary radiation—"

"Naw!" said Jarvis disgustedly. "I wouldn't try that, of course—not more than ten times! Besides, the bump flattened the landing gear and busted off the under-jets. Suppose I got the thing working—what then? Ten miles with the blast coming right out of the bottom and I'd have melted the floor from under me!" He rubbed his nose again. "Lucky for me a pound only weighs seven ounces here, or I'd have been mashed flat!"

"I could have fixed!" ejaculated the engineer. "I bet it vas not serious."

"Probably not," agreed Jarvis sarcastically. "Only it wouldn't fly. Nothing serious, but I had my choice of waiting to be picked up or trying to walk back—eight hundred miles, and perhaps twenty days before we had to leave! Forty miles a day! Well," he concluded, "I chose to walk. Just as much chance of being picked up, and it kept me busy."

"We'd have found you," said Harrison.

"No doubt. Anyway, I rigged up a harness from some seat straps, and put the water tank on my back, took a cartridge belt and revolver, and some iron rations, and started out."

"Water tank!" exclaimed the little biologist, Leroy. "She weigh one-quarter ton!"

"Wasn't full. Weighed about two hundred and fifty pounds earth-weight, which is eighty-five here. Then, besides, my own personal two hundred and ten pounds is only seventy on Mars, so, tank and all, I grossed a hundred and fifty-five, or fifty-five pounds less than my everyday earth-weight. I figured on that when I undertook the forty-mile daily stroll. Oh—of course I took a thermo-skin sleeping bag for these wintry Martian nights.

"Off I went, bouncing along pretty quickly. Eight hours of daylight meant twenty miles or more. It got tiresome, of course—plugging along over a soft sand desert with nothing to see, not even Leroy's crawling biopods. But an hour or so brought me to the canal—just a dry ditch about four hundred feet wide, and straight as a railroad on its own company map.

"There'd been water in it sometime, though. The ditch was covered with what looked like a nice green lawn. Only, as I approached, the lawn moved out of my way!"

"Eh?" said Leroy.

"Yeah, it was a relative of your biopods. I caught one—a little grass-like blade about as long as my finger, with two thin, stemmy legs."

"He is where?" Leroy was eager.

"He is let go! I had to move, so I plowed along with the walking grass opening in front and closing behind. And then I was out on the orange desert of Thyle again.

"I plugged steadily along, cussing the sand that made going so tiresome, and, incidentally, cussing that cranky motor of yours, Karl. It was just before twilight that I reached the edge of Thyle, and looked down over the gray Mare Chronium. And I knew there was seventy-five miles of *that* to be walked over, and then a couple of hundred miles of that Xanthus desert, and about as much more Mare Cimmerium. Was I pleased? I started cussing you fellows for not picking me up!"

"We were trying, you sap!" said Harrison.

"That didn't help. Well, I figured I might as well use what was left of daylight in getting down the cliff that bounded Thyle. I found an easy place, and down I went. Mare Chronium was just the same sort of place as this—crazy leafless plants and a bunch of crawlers; I gave it a glance and hauled out my sleeping bag. Up to that time, you know, I hadn't seen anything worth worrying about on this half-dead world—nothing dangerous, that is."

"Did you?" queried Harrison.

"*Did I!* You'll hear about it when I come to it. Well, I was just about to turn in when suddenly I heard the wildest sort of shenanigans!"

"Vot iss shenanigans?" inquired Putz.

"He says, 'Je ne sais quoi,'" explained Leroy. "It is to say, 'I don't know what.'"

"That's right," agreed Jarvis. "I didn't know what, so I sneaked over to find out. There was a racket like a flock of crows eating a bunch of canaries—whistles, cackles, caws, trills, and what have you. I rounded a clump of stumps, and there was Tweel!"

"Tweel?" said Harrison, and "Tveel?" said Leroy and Putz.

"That freak ostrich," explained the narrator. "At least, Tweel is as near as I can pronounce it without sputtering. He called it something like 'Trrrweerrlll.'"

"What was he doing?" asked the Captain.

"He was being eaten! And squealing, of course, as any one would."

"Eaten! By what?"

"I found out later. All I could see then was a bunch of black ropy arms tangled around what looked like, as Putz described it to you, an ostrich. I wasn't going to interfere, naturally; if both creatures were dangerous, I'd have one less to worry about.

"But the bird-like thing was putting up a good battle, dealing vicious blows with an eighteen-inch beak, between screeches. And besides, I caught a glimpse or two of what was on the end of those arms!" Jarvis shuddered. "But the clincher was when I noticed a little black bag or case hung about the neck of the bird-thing! It was intelligent! That or tame, I assumed. Anyway, it clinched my decision. I pulled out my automatic and fired into what I could see of its antagonist.

"There was a flurry of tentacles and a spurt of black corruption, and then the thing, with a disgusting sucking noise, pulled itself and its arms into a hole in the ground. The other let out a series of clacks, staggered around on legs about as thick as golf sticks, and turned suddenly to face me. I held my weapon ready, and the two of us stared at each other.

"The Martian wasn't a bird, really. It wasn't even bird-like, except just at first glance. It had a beak all right, and a few feathery appendages, but the beak wasn't really a beak. It was somewhat flexible; I could see the tip bend slowly from side to side; it was almost like a cross between a beak and a trunk. It had four-toed feet, and four fingered things—hands, you'd have to call them, and a little roundish body, and a long neck ending in a tiny head—and that beak. It stood an inch or so taller than I, and—well, Putz saw it!"

The engineer nodded. "*Ja!* I saw!"

Jarvis continued. "So—we stared at each other. Finally the creature went into a series of clackings and twitterings and held out its hands toward me, empty. I took that as a gesture of friendship."

"Perhaps," suggested Harrison, "it looked at that nose of yours and thought you were its brother!"

"Huh! You can be funny without talking! Anyway, I put up my gun and said 'Aw, don't mention it,' or something of the sort, and the thing came over and we were pals.

"By that time, the sun was pretty low and I knew that I'd better build a fire or get into my thermo-skin. I decided on the fire. I picked a spot at the base of the Thyle cliff, where the rock could reflect a little heat on my back. I started breaking off chunks of this desiccated Martian vegetation, and my companion caught the idea and brought in an armful. I reached for a match, but the Martian fished into his pouch and brought out something that looked like a glowing coal; one touch of it, and the fire was blazing—and you all know what a job we have starting a fire in this atmosphere!

"And that bag of his!" continued the narrator. "That was a manufactured article, my friends; press an end and she popped open—press the middle and she sealed so perfectly you couldn't see the line. Better than zippers.

"Well, we stared at the fire a while and I decided to attempt some sort of communication with the Martian. I pointed at myself and said 'Dick'; he caught the drift immediately, stretched a bony claw at me and repeated 'Tick.' Then I pointed at him, and he gave that whistle I called Tweel; I can't imitate his accent. Things were going smoothly; to emphasize the names, I repeated 'Dick,' and then, pointing at him, 'Tweel.'

"There we stuck! He gave some clacks that sounded negative, and said something like 'P-p-p-proot.' And that was just the beginning; I was always 'Tick,' but as for him—part of the time he was 'Tweel,' and part of the time he was 'P-p-p-proot,' and part of the time he was sixteen other noises!

"We just couldn't connect. I tried 'rock,' and I tried 'star,' and 'tree,' and 'fire,' and Lord knows what else, and try as I would, I couldn't get a single word! Nothing was the same for two successive minutes, and if that's a language, I'm an alchemist! Finally I gave it up and called him Tweel, and that seemed to do.

"But Tweel hung on to some of my words. He remembered a couple of them, which I suppose is a great achievement if you're used to a language you have to make up as you go along. But I couldn't get the hang of his talk; either I missed some subtle point or we just didn't *think* alike—and I rather believe the latter view.

"I've other reasons for believing that. After a while I gave up the language business, and tried mathematics. I scratched two plus two equals four on the ground, and demonstrated it with pebbles. Again Tweel caught the idea, and informed me that three plus three equals six. Once more we seemed to be getting somewhere.

"So, knowing that Tweel had at least a grammar school education, I drew a circle for the sun, pointing first at it, and then at the last glow of the sun. Then I sketched in Mercury, and Venus, and Mother Earth, and Mars, and finally, pointing to Mars, I swept my hand around in a sort of inclusive gesture to indicate that Mars was our current environment. I was working up to putting over the idea that my home was on the earth.

"Tweel understood my diagram all right. He poked his beak at it, and with a great deal of trilling and clucking, he added Deimos and Phobos to Mars, and then sketched in the earth's moon!

"Do you see what that proves? It proves that Tweel's race uses telescopes—that they're civilized!"

"Does not!" snapped Harrison. "The moon is visible from here as a fifth magnitude star. They could see its revolution with the naked eye."

"The moon, yes!" said Jarvis. "You've missed my point. Mercury isn't visible! And Tweel knew of Mercury because he placed the Moon at the *third* planet, not the second. If he didn't know Mercury, he'd put the earth second, and Mars third, instead of fourth! See?"

"Humph!" said Harrison.

"Anyway," proceeded Jarvis, "I went on with my lesson. Things were going smoothly, and it looked as if I could put the idea over. I pointed at the earth on my diagram, and then at myself, and then, to clinch it, I pointed to myself and then to the earth itself shining bright green almost at the zenith.

"Tweel set up such an excited clacking that I was certain he understood. He jumped up and down, and suddenly he pointed at himself and then at the sky, and then at himself and at the sky again. He pointed at his middle and then at Arcturus, at his head and then at Spica, at his feet and then at half a dozen stars, while I just gaped at him. Then, all of a sudden, he gave a tremendous leap. Man, what a hop! He shot straight up into the starlight, seventy-five feet if an inch! I saw him silhouetted against the sky, saw him turn and come down at me head first, and land smack on his beak like a javelin! There he stuck square in the center of my sun-circle in the sand—a bull's eye!"

"Nuts!" observed the captain. "Plain nuts!"

"That's what I thought, too! I just stared at him open-mouthed while he pulled his head out of the sand and stood up. Then I figured he'd missed my point, and I went through the whole blamed rigamarole again, and it ended the same way, with Tweel on his nose in the middle of my picture!"

"Maybe it's a religious rite," suggested Harrison.

"Maybe," said Jarvis dubiously. "Well, there we were. We could exchange ideas up to a certain point, and then—blooey! Something in us was different, unrelated; I don't doubt that Tweel thought me just as screwy as I thought him. Our minds simply looked at the world from different viewpoints, and perhaps his viewpoint is as true as ours. But—we couldn't get together, that's all. Yet, in spite of all difficulties, I *liked* Tweel, and I have a queer certainty that he liked me."

"Nuts!" repeated the captain. "Just daffy!"

"Yeah? Wait and see. A couple of times I've thought that perhaps we—" He paused, and then resumed his narrative.

"Anyway, I finally gave it up, and got into my thermo-skin to sleep. The fire hadn't kept me any too warm, but that damned sleeping bag did. Got stuffy five minutes after I closed myself in. I opened it a little and bingo! Some eighty-below-zero air hit my nose, and that's when I got this pleasant little frostbite to add to the bump I acquired during the crash of my rocket.

"I don't know what Tweel made of my sleeping. He sat around, but when I woke up, he was gone. I'd just crawled out of my bag, though, when I heard some twittering, and there he came, sailing down from that three-story Thyle cliff to alight on his beak beside me. I pointed to myself and toward the north, and he pointed at himself and toward the south, but when I loaded up and started away, he came along.

"Man, how he traveled! A hundred and fifty feet at a jump, sailing through the air stretched out like a spear, and landing on his beak. He seemed surprised at my plodding, but after a few moments he fell in beside me, only every few minutes he'd go into one of his leaps, and stick his nose into the sand a block ahead of me. Then he'd come shooting back at me; it made me nervous at first to see that beak of his coming at me like a spear, but he always ended in the sand at my side.

"So the two of us plugged along across the Mare Chronium. Same sort of place as this—same crazy plants and same little green biopods growing in the sand, or crawling out of your way. We talked—not that we understood each other, you know, but just for company. I sang songs, and I suspect Tweel did too; at least, some of his trillings and twitterings had a subtle sort of rhythm.

"Then, for variety, Tweel would display his smattering of English words. He'd point to an outcropping and say 'rock,' and point to a pebble and say it again; or he'd touch my arm and say 'Tick,' and then repeat it. He seemed terrifically amused that the same word meant the same thing twice in succession, or that the same word could apply to two different objects. It set me wondering if perhaps his language wasn't like the primitive speech of some earth people—you know, Captain, like the Negritoes, for instance, who haven't any generic words. No word for food or water or man—words for good food and bad food, or rain water and sea water, or strong man and weak man—but no names for general classes. They're too primitive to understand that rain water and sea water are just different aspects of the same thing. But that wasn't the case with Tweel; it was just that we were somehow mysteriously different—our minds were alien to each other. And yet—we *liked* each other!"

"Looney, that's all," remarked Harrison. "That's why you two were so fond of each other."

"Well, I like *you!*" countered Jarvis wickedly. "Anyway," he resumed, "don't get the idea that there was anything screwy about Tweel. In fact, I'm not so sure but that he couldn't teach our highly praised human intelligence a trick or two. Oh, he wasn't an intellectual superman, I guess; but don't overlook the point that he managed to understand a little of my mental workings, and I never even got a glimmering of his."

"Because he didn't have any!" suggested the captain, while Putz and Leroy blinked attentively.

"You can judge of that when I'm through," said Jarvis. "Well, we plugged along across the Mare Chronium all that day, and all the next. Mare Chronium—Sea of Time! Say, I was willing to agree with Schiaparelli's name by the end of that march! Just that grey, endless plain of weird plants, and never a sign of any other life. It was so monotonous that I was even glad to see the desert of Xanthus toward the evening of the second day.

"I was fair worn out, but Tweel seemed as fresh as ever, for all I never saw him drink or eat. I think he could have crossed the Mare Chronium in a couple of hours with those block-long nose dives of his, but he stuck along with me. I offered him some water once or twice; he took the cup from me and sucked the liquid into his beak, and then carefully squirted it all back into the cup and gravely returned it.

"Just as we sighted Xanthus, or the cliffs that bounded it, one of those nasty sand clouds blew along, not as bad as the one we had here, but mean to travel against. I pulled the transparent flap of my thermo-skin bag across my face and managed pretty well, and I noticed that Tweel used some feathery appendages growing like a mustache at the base of his beak to cover his nostrils, and some similar fuzz to shield his eyes."

"He is a desert creature!" ejaculated the little biologist, Leroy.

"Huh? Why?"

"He drink no water—he is adapt' for sand storm—"

"Proves nothing! There's not enough water to waste any where on this desiccated pill called Mars. We'd call all of it desert on earth, you know." He paused. "Anyway, after the sand storm blew over, a little wind kept blowing in our faces, not strong enough to stir the sand. But suddenly things came drifting along from the Xanthus cliffs—small, transparent spheres, for all the world like glass tennis balls! But light—they were almost light enough to float even in this thin air—empty, too; at least, I cracked open a couple and nothing came out but a bad smell. I asked Tweel about them, but all he said was 'No, no, no,' which I took to mean that he knew nothing about them. So they went bouncing by like tumbleweeds, or like soap bubbles, and we plugged on toward Xanthus. Tweel pointed at one of the crystal balls once and said 'rock,' but I was too tired to argue with him. Later I discovered what he meant.

"We came to the bottom of the Xanthus cliffs finally, when there wasn't much daylight left. I decided to sleep on the plateau if possible; anything dangerous, I reasoned, would be more likely to prowl through the vegetation of the Mare Chronium than the sand of Xanthus. Not that I'd seen a single sign of menace, except the rope-armed black thing that had trapped Tweel, and apparently that didn't prowl at all, but lured its victims within reach. It couldn't lure me while I slept, especially as Tweel didn't seem to sleep at all, but simply sat patiently around all night. I wondered how the creature had managed to trap Tweel, but there wasn't any way of asking him. I found that out too, later; it's devilish!

"However, we were ambling around the base of the Xanthus barrier looking for an easy spot to climb. At least, I was. Tweel could have leaped it easily, for the cliffs were lower than Thyle— perhaps sixty feet. I found a place and started up, swearing at the water tank strapped to my back—it didn't bother me except when climbing—and suddenly I heard a sound that I thought I recognized!

"You know how deceptive sounds are in this thin air. A shot sounds like the pop of a cork. But this sound was the drone of a rocket, and sure enough, there went our second auxiliary about ten miles to westward, between me and the sunset!"

"Vas me!" said Putz. "I hunt for you."

"Yeah; I knew that, but what good did it do me? I hung on to the cliff and yelled and waved with one hand. Tweel saw it too, and set up a trilling and twittering, leaping to the top of the barrier and then high into the air. And while I watched, the machine droned on into the shadows to the south.

"I scrambled to the top of the cliff. Tweel was still pointing and trilling excitedly, shooting up toward the sky and coming down head-on to stick upside down on his beak in the sand. I pointed toward the south and at myself, and he said, 'Yes—Yes—Yes'; but somehow I gathered that he thought the flying thing was a relative of mine, probably a parent. Perhaps I did his intellect an injustice; I think now that I did.

"I was bitterly disappointed by the failure to attract attention. I pulled out my thermo-skin bag and crawled into it, as the night chill was already apparent. Tweel stuck his beak into the sand and drew up his legs and arms and looked for all the world like one of those leafless shrubs out there. I think he stayed that way all night."

"Protective mimicry!" ejaculated Leroy. "See? He is desert creature!"

"In the morning," resumed Jarvis, "we started off again. We hadn't gone a hundred yards into Xanthus when I saw something queer! This is one thing Putz didn't photograph, I'll wager!

"There was a line of little pyramids—tiny ones, not more than six inches high, stretching across Xanthus as far as I could see! Little buildings made of pygmy bricks, they were, hollow inside and truncated, or at least broken at the top and empty. I pointed at them and said 'What?' to Tweel, but he gave some negative twitters to indicate, I suppose, that he didn't know. So off we went, following the row of pyramids because they ran north, and I was going north.

"Man, we trailed that line for hours! After a while, I noticed another queer thing: they were getting larger. Same number of bricks in each one, but the bricks were larger.

"By noon they were shoulder high. I looked into a couple—all just the same, broken at the top and empty. I examined a brick or two as well; they were silica, and old as creation itself!"

"How you know?" asked Leroy.

"They were weathered—edges rounded. Silica doesn't weather easily even on earth, and in this climate—!"

"How old you think?"

"Fifty thousand—a hundred thousand years. How can I tell? The little ones we saw in the morning were older—perhaps ten times as old. Crumbling. How old would that make *them*? Half a million years? Who knows?" Jarvis paused a moment. "Well," he resumed, "we followed the line. Tweel pointed at them and said 'rock' once or twice, but he'd done that many times before. Besides, he was more or less right about these.

"I tried questioning him. I pointed at a pyramid and asked 'People?' and indicated the two of us. He set up a negative sort of clucking and said, 'No, no, no. No one-one-two. No two-two-four,' meanwhile rubbing his stomach. I just stared at him and he went through the business again. 'No one-one-two. No two-two-four.' I just gaped at him."

"That proves it!" exclaimed Harrison. "Nuts!"

"You think so?" queried Jarvis sardonically. "Well, I figured it out different! 'No one-one-two!' You don't get it, of course, do you?"

"Nope—nor do you!"

"I think I do! Tweel was using the few English words he knew to put over a very complex idea. What, let me ask, does mathematics make you think of?"

"Why—of astronomy. Or—or logic!"

"That's it! 'No one-one-two!' Tweel was telling me that the builders of the pyramids weren't people—or that they weren't intelligent, that they weren't reasoning creatures! Get it?"

"Huh! I'll be damned!"

"You probably will."

"Why," put in Leroy, "he rub his belly?"

"Why? Because, my dear biologist, that's where his brains are! Not in his tiny head—in his middle!"

"*C'est* impossible!"

"Not on Mars, it isn't! This flora and fauna aren't earthly; your biopods prove that!" Jarvis grinned and took up his narrative. "Anyway, we plugged along across Xanthus and in about the middle of the afternoon, something else queer happened. The pyramids ended."

"Ended!"

"Yeah; the queer part was that the last one—and now they were ten-footers—was capped! See? Whatever built it was still inside; we'd trailed 'em from their half-million-year-old origin to the present.

"Tweel and I noticed it about the same time. I yanked out my automatic (I had a clip of Boland explosive bullets in it) and Tweel, quick as a sleight-of-hand trick, snapped a queer little glass revolver out of his bag. It was much like our weapons, except that the grip was larger to accommodate his four-taloned hand. And we held our weapons ready while we sneaked up along the lines of empty pyramids.

"Tweel saw the movement first. The top tiers of bricks were heaving, shaking, and suddenly slid down the sides with a thin crash. And then—something—something was coming out!

"A long, silvery-grey arm appeared, dragging after it an armored body. Armored, I mean, with scales, silver-grey and dull-shining. The arm heaved the body out of the hole; the beast crashed to the sand.

"It was a nondescript creature—body like a big grey cask, arm and a sort of mouth-hole at one end; stiff, pointed tail at the other—and that's all. No other limbs, no eyes, ears, nose— nothing! The thing dragged itself a few yards, inserted its pointed tail in the sand, pushed itself upright, and just sat.

"Tweel and I watched it for ten minutes before it moved. Then, with a creaking and rustling like—oh, like crumpling stiff paper—its arm moved to the mouth-hole and out came a brick! The arm placed the brick carefully on the ground, and the thing was still again.

"Another ten minutes—another brick. Just one of Nature's bricklayers. I was about to slip away and move on when Tweel pointed at the thing and said 'rock'! I went 'huh?' and he said it again. Then, to the accompaniment of some of his trilling, he said, 'No—no—,' and gave two or three whistling breaths.

"Well, I got his meaning, for a wonder! I said, 'No breath?' and demonstrated the word. Tweel was ecstatic; he said, 'Yes, yes, yes! No, no, no breet!' Then he gave a leap and sailed out to land on his nose about one pace from the monster!

"I was startled, you can imagine! The arm was going up for a brick, and I expected to see Tweel caught and mangled, but— nothing happened! Tweel pounded on the creature, and the arm took the brick and placed it neatly beside the first. Tweel rapped on its body again, and said 'rock,' and I got up nerve enough to take a look myself.

"Tweel was right again. The creature was rock, and it didn't breathe!"

"How you know?" snapped Leroy, his black eyes blazing interest.

"Because I'm a chemist. The beast was made of silica! There must have been pure silicon in the sand, and it lived on that. Get it? We, and Tweel, and those plants out there, and even the biopods are *carbon* life; this thing lived by a different set of chemical reactions. It was silicon life!"

"*La vie silicieuse!*" shouted Leroy. "I have suspect, and now it is proof! I must go see! *Il faut que je—*"

"All right! All right!" said Jarvis. "You can go see. Anyhow, there the thing was, alive and yet not alive, moving every ten minutes, and then only to remove a brick. Those bricks were its waste matter. See, Frenchy? We're carbon, and our waste is carbon dioxide, and this thing is silicon, and *its* waste is silicon dioxide—silica. But silica is a solid, hence the bricks. And it builds itself in, and when it is covered, it moves over to a fresh place to start over. No wonder it creaked! A living creature half a million years old!"

"How you know how old?" Leroy was frantic.

"We trailed its pyramids from the beginning, didn't we? If this weren't the original pyramid builder, the series would have ended somewhere before we found him, wouldn't it?—ended and started over with the small ones. That's simple enough, isn't it?

"But he reproduces, or tries to. Before the third brick came out, there was a little rustle and out popped a whole stream of those little crystal balls. They're his spores, or eggs, or seeds—call 'em what you want. They went bouncing by across Xanthus just as they'd bounced by us back in the Mare Chronium. I've a hunch how they work, too—this is for your information, Leroy. I think the crystal shell of silica is no more than a protective covering, like an eggshell, and that the active principle is the smell inside. It's some sort of gas that attacks silicon, and if the shell is broken near a supply of that element, some reaction starts that ultimately develops into a beast like that one."

"You should try!" exclaimed the little Frenchman. "We must break one to see!"

"Yeah? Well, I did. I smashed a couple against the sand. Would you like to come back in about ten thousand years to see if I planted some pyramid monsters? You'd most likely be able to tell by that time!" Jarvis paused and drew a deep breath. "Lord! That queer creature! Do you picture it? Blind, deaf, nerveless, brainless—just a mechanism, and yet—immortal! Bound to go on making bricks, building pyramids, as long as silicon and oxygen exist, and even afterwards it'll just stop. It won't be dead. If the accidents of a million years bring it its food again, there it'll be, ready to run again, while brains and civilizations are part of the past. A queer beast—yet I met a stranger one!"

"If you did, it must have been in your dreams!" growled Harrison.

"You're right!" said Jarvis soberly. "In a way, you're right. The dream-beast! That's the best name for it—and it's the most fiendish, terrifying creation one could imagine! More dangerous than a lion, more insidious than a snake!"

"Tell me!" begged Leroy. "I must go see!"

"Not *this* devil!" He paused again. "Well," he resumed, "Tweel and I left the pyramid creature and plowed along through Xanthus. I was tired and a little disheartened by Putz's failure to pick me up, and Tweel's trilling got on my nerves, as did his flying nosedives. So I just strode along without a word, hour after hour across that monotonous desert.

"Toward mid-afternoon we came in sight of a low dark line on the horizon. I knew what it was. It was a canal; I'd crossed it in the rocket and it meant that we were just one-third of the way across Xanthus. Pleasant thought, wasn't it? And still, I was keeping up to schedule.

"We approached the canal slowly; I remembered that this one was bordered by a wide fringe of vegetation and that Mud-heap City was on it.

"I was tired, as I said. I kept thinking of a good hot meal, and then from that I jumped to reflections of how nice and home-like even Borneo would seem after this crazy planet, and from that, to thoughts of little old New York, and then to thinking about a girl I know there—Fancy Long. Know her?"

"Vision entertainer," said Harrison. "I've tuned her in. Nice blonde—dances and sings on the *Yerba Mate* hour."

"That's her," said Jarvis ungrammatically. "I know her pretty well—just friends, get me?—though she came down to see us off in the *Ares*. Well, I was thinking about her, feeling pretty lonesome, and all the time we were approaching that line of rubbery plants.

"And then—I said, 'What 'n Hell!' and stared. And there she was—Fancy Long, standing plain as day under one of those crack-brained trees, and smiling and waving just the way I remembered her when we left!"

"Now you're nuts, too!" observed the captain.

"Boy, I almost agreed with you! I stared and pinched myself and closed my eyes and then stared again—and every time, there was Fancy Long smiling and waving! Tweel saw something, too; he was trilling and clucking away, but I scarcely heard him. I was bounding toward her over the sand, too amazed even to ask myself questions.

"I wasn't twenty feet from her when Tweel caught me with one of his flying leaps. He grabbed my arm, yelling, 'No—no—no!' in his squeaky voice. I tried to shake him off—he was as light as if he were built of bamboo—but he dug his claws in and yelled. And finally some sort of sanity returned to me and I stopped less than ten feet from her. There she stood, looking as solid as Putz's head!"

"Vot?" said the engineer.

"She smiled and waved, and waved and smiled, and I stood there dumb as Leroy, while Tweel squeaked and chattered. I *knew* it couldn't be real, yet—there she was!

"Finally I said, 'Fancy! Fancy Long!' She just kept on smiling and waving, but looking as real as if I hadn't left her thirty-seven million miles away.

"Tweel had his glass pistol out, pointing it at her. I grabbed his arm, but he tried to push me away. He pointed at her and said, 'No breet! No breet!' and I understood that he meant that the Fancy Long thing wasn't alive. Man, my head was whirling!

"Still, it gave me the jitters to see him pointing his weapon at her. I don't know why I stood there watching him take careful aim, but I did. Then he squeezed the handle of his weapon; there was a little puff of steam, and Fancy Long was gone! And in her place was one of those writhing, black, rope-armed horrors like the one I'd saved Tweel from!

"The dream-beast! I stood there dizzy, watching it die while Tweel trilled and whistled. Finally he touched my arm, pointed at the twisting thing, and said, 'You one-one-two, he one-one-two.' After he'd repeated it eight or ten times, I got it. Do any of you?"

"*Oui!*" shrilled Leroy. "*Moi—je le comprends!* He mean you think of something, the beast he know, and you see it! *Un chien*—a hungry dog, he would see the big bone with meat! Or smell it—not?"

"Right!" said Jarvis. "The dream-beast uses its victim's longings and desires to trap its prey. The bird at nesting season would see its mate, the fox, prowling for its own prey, would see a helpless rabbit!"

"How he do?" queried Leroy.

"How do I know? How does a snake back on earth charm a bird into its very jaws? And aren't there deep-sea fish that lure their victims into their mouths? Lord!" Jarvis shuddered. "Do you see how insidious the monster is? We're warned now—but henceforth we can't trust even our eyes. You might see me—I might see one of you—and back of it may be nothing but another of those black horrors!"

"How'd your friend know?" asked the captain abruptly.

"Tweel? I wonder! Perhaps he was thinking of something that couldn't possibly have interested me, and when I started to run, he realized that I saw something different and was warned. Or perhaps the dream-beast can only project a single vision, and Tweel saw what I saw—or nothing. I couldn't ask him. But it's just another proof that his intelligence is equal to ours or greater."

"He's daffy, I tell you!" said Harrison. "What makes you think his intellect ranks with the human?"

"Plenty of things! First, the pyramid-beast. He hadn't seen one before; he said as much. Yet he recognized it as a dead-alive automaton of silicon."

"He could have heard of it," objected Harrison. "He lives around here, you know."

"Well how about the language? I couldn't pick up a single idea of his and he learned six or seven words of mine. And do you realize what complex ideas he put over with no more than those six or seven words? The pyramid-monster—the dream-beast! In a single phrase he told me that one was a harmless automaton and the other a deadly hypnotist. What about that?"

"Huh!" said the captain.

"*Huh* if you wish! Could you have done it knowing only six words of English? Could you go even further, as Tweel did, and tell me that another creature was of a sort of intelligence so different from ours that understanding was impossible—even more impossible than that between Tweel and me?"

"Eh? What was that?"

"Later. The point I'm making is that Tweel and his race are worthy of our friendship. Somewhere on Mars—and you'll find I'm right—is a civilization and culture equal to ours, and maybe more than equal. And communication is possible between them and us; Tweel proves that. It may take years of patient trial, for their minds are alien, but less alien than the next minds we encountered—if they *are* minds."

"The next ones? What next ones?"

"The people of the mud cities along the canals." Jarvis frowned, then resumed his narrative. "I thought the dream-beast and the silicon-monster were the strangest beings conceivable, but I was wrong. These creatures are still more alien, less understandable than either and far less comprehensible than Tweel, with whom friendship is possible, and even, by patience and concentration, the exchange of ideas.

"Well," he continued, "we left the dream-beast dying, dragging itself back into its hole, and we moved toward the canal. There was a carpet of that queer walking-grass scampering out of our way, and when we reached the bank, there was a yellow trickle of water flowing. The mound city I'd noticed from the rocket was a mile or so to the right and I was curious enough to want to take a look at it.

"It had seemed deserted from my previous glimpse of it, and if any creatures were lurking in it—well, Tweel and I were both armed. And by the way, that crystal weapon of Tweel's was an interesting device; I took a look at it after the dream-beast episode. It fired a little glass splinter, poisoned, I suppose, and I guess it held at least a hundred of 'em to a load. The propellent was steam—just plain steam!"

"Shteam!" echoed Putz. "From vot come, shteam?"

"From water, of course! You could see the water through the transparent handle and about a gill of another liquid, thick and yellowish. When Tweel squeezed the handle—there was no trigger—a drop of water and a drop of the yellow stuff squirted into the firing chamber, and the water vaporized—pop!—like that. It's not so difficult; I think we could develop the same principle. Concentrated sulphuric acid will heat water almost to boiling, and so will quicklime, and there's potassium and sodium—

"Of course, his weapon hadn't the range of mine, but it wasn't so bad in this thin air, and it *did* hold as many shots as a cowboy's gun in a Western movie. It was effective, too, at least against Martian life; I tried it out, aiming at one of the crazy plants, and darned if the plant didn't wither up and fall apart! That's why I think the glass splinters were poisoned.

"Anyway, we trudged along toward the mud-heap city and I began to wonder whether the city builders dug the canals. I pointed to the city and then at the canal, and Tweel said 'No—no—no!' and gestured toward the south. I took it to mean that some other race had created the canal system, perhaps Tweel's people. I don't know; maybe there's still another intelligent race on the planet, or a dozen others. Mars is a queer little world.

"A hundred yards from the city we crossed a sort of road—just a hard-packed mud trail, and then, all of a sudden, along came one of the mound builders!

"Man, talk about fantastic beings! It looked rather like a barrel trotting along on four legs with four other arms or tentacles. It had no head, just body and members and a row of eyes completely around it. The top end of the barrel-body was a diaphragm stretched as tight as a drum head, and that was all. It was pushing a little coppery cart and tore right past us like the proverbial bat out of Hell. It didn't even notice us, although I thought the eyes on my side shifted a little as it passed.

"A moment later another came along, pushing another empty cart. Same thing—it just scooted past us. Well, I wasn't going to be ignored by a bunch of barrels playing train, so when the third one approached, I planted myself in the way—ready to jump, of course, if the thing didn't stop.

"But it did. It stopped and set up a sort of drumming from the diaphragm on top. And I held out both hands and said, 'We are friends!' And what do you suppose the thing did?"

"Said, 'Pleased to meet you,' I'll bet!" suggested Harrison.

"I couldn't have been more surprised if it had! It drummed on its diaphragm, and then suddenly boomed out, 'We are v-r-r-riends!' and gave its pushcart a vicious poke at me! I jumped aside, and away it went while I stared dumbly after it.

"A minute later another one came hurrying along. This one didn't pause, but simply drummed out, 'We are v-r-r-riends!' and scurried by. How did it learn the phrase? Were all of the creatures in some sort of communication with each other? Were they all parts of some central organism? I don't know, though I think Tweel does.

"Anyway, the creatures went sailing past us, every one greeting us with the same statement. It got to be funny; I never thought to find so many friends on this God-forsaken ball! Finally I made a puzzled gesture to Tweel; I guess he understood, for he said, 'One-one-two—yes!—two-two-four—no!' Get it?"

"Sure," said Harrison, "It's a Martian nursery rhyme."

"Yeah! Well, I was getting used to Tweel's symbolism, and I figured it out this way. 'One-one-two—yes!' The creatures were intelligent. 'Two-two-four—no!' Their intelligence was not of our order, but something different and beyond the logic of two and two is four. Maybe I missed his meaning. Perhaps he meant that their minds were of low degree, able to figure out the simple things—'One-one-two—yes!'—but not more difficult things— 'Two-two-four—no!' But I think from what we saw later that he meant the other.

"After a few moments, the creatures came rushing back— first one, then another. Their pushcarts were full of stones, sand, chunks of rubbery plants, and such rubbish as that. They droned out their friendly greeting, which didn't really sound so friendly, and dashed on. The third one I assumed to be my first acquaintance and I decided to have another chat with him. I stepped into his path again and waited.

"Up he came, booming out his 'We are v-r-r-riends' and stopped. I looked at him; four or five of his eyes looked at me. He tried his password again and gave a shove on his cart, but I stood firm. And then the—the dashed creature reached out one of his arms, and two finger-like nippers tweaked my nose!"

"Haw!" roared Harrison. "Maybe the things have a sense of beauty!"

"Laugh!" grumbled Jarvis. "I'd already had a nasty bump and a mean frostbite on that nose. Anyway, I yelled 'Ouch!' and jumped aside and the creature dashed away; but from then on, their greeting was 'We are v-r-r-riends! Ouch!' Queer beasts!

"Tweel and I followed the road squarely up to the nearest mound. The creatures were coming and going, paying us not the slightest attention, fetching their loads of rubbish. The road simply dived into an opening, and slanted down like an old mine, and in and out darted the barrel-people, greeting us with their eternal phrase.

"I looked in; there was a light somewhere below, and I was curious to see it. It didn't look like a flame or torch, you understand, but more like a civilized light, and I thought that I might get some clue as to the creatures' development. So in I went and Tweel tagged along, not without a few trills and twitters, however.

"The light was curious; it sputtered and flared like an old arc light, but came from a single black rod set in the wall of the corridor. It was electric, beyond doubt. The creatures were fairly civilized, apparently.

"Then I saw another light shining on something that glittered and I went on to look at that, but it was only a heap of shiny sand. I turned toward the entrance to leave, and the Devil take me if it wasn't gone!

"I suppose the corridor had curved, or I'd stepped into a side passage. Anyway, I walked back in that direction I thought we'd come, and all I saw was more dimlit corridor. The place was a labyrinth! There was nothing but twisting passages running every way, lit by occasional lights, and now and then a creature running by, sometimes with a pushcart, sometimes without.

"Well, I wasn't much worried at first. Tweel and I had only come a few steps from the entrance. But every move we made after that seemed to get us in deeper. Finally I tried following one of the creatures with an empty cart, thinking that he'd be going out for his rubbish, but he ran around aimlessly, into one passage and out another. When he started dashing around a pillar like one of these Japanese waltzing mice, I gave up, dumped my water tank on the floor, and sat down.

"Tweel was as lost as I. I pointed up and he said 'No—no—no!' in a sort of helpless trill. And we couldn't get any help from the natives. They paid no attention at all, except to assure us they were friends—ouch!

"Lord! I don't know how many hours or days we wandered around there! I slept twice from sheer exhaustion; Tweel never seemed to need sleep. We tried following only the upward corridors, but they'd run uphill a ways and then curve downwards. The temperature in that damned ant hill was constant; you couldn't tell night from day and after my first sleep I didn't know whether I'd slept one hour or thirteen, so I couldn't tell from my watch whether it was midnight or noon.

"We saw plenty of strange things. There were machines running in some of the corridors, but they didn't seem to be doing anything—just wheels turning. And several times I saw two barrel-beasts with a little one growing between them, joined to both."

"Parthenogenesis!" exulted Leroy. "Parthenogenesis by budding like *les tulipes*!"

"If you say so, Frenchy," agreed Jarvis. "The things never noticed us at all, except, as I say, to greet us with 'We are v-r-r-riends! Ouch!' They seemed to have no home-life of any sort, but just scurried around with their pushcarts, bringing in rubbish. And finally I discovered what they did with it.

"We'd had a little luck with a corridor, one that slanted upwards for a great distance. I was feeling that we ought to be close to the surface when suddenly the passage debouched into a domed chamber, the only one we'd seen. And man!—I felt like dancing when I saw what looked like daylight through a crevice in the roof.

"There was a—a sort of machine in the chamber, just an enormous wheel that turned slowly, and one of the creatures was in the act of dumping his rubbish below it. The wheel ground it with a crunch—sand, stones, plants, all into powder that sifted away somewhere. While we watched, others filed in, repeating the process, and that seemed to be all. No rhyme nor reason to the whole thing—but that's characteristic of this crazy planet. And there was another fact that's almost too bizarre to believe.

"One of the creatures, having dumped his load, pushed his cart aside with a crash and calmly shoved himself under the wheel! I watched him being crushed, too stupefied to make a sound, and a moment later, another followed him! They were perfectly methodical about it, too; one of the cartless creatures took the abandoned pushcart.

"Tweel didn't seem surprised; I pointed out the next suicide to him, and he just gave the most human-like shrug imaginable, as much as to say, 'What can I do about it?' He must have known more or less about these creatures.

"Then I saw something else. There was something beyond the wheel, something shining on a sort of low pedestal. I walked over; there was a little crystal about the size of an egg, fluorescing to beat Tophet. The light from it stung my hands and face, almost like a static discharge, and then I noticed another funny thing. Remember that wart I had on my left thumb? Look!" Jarvis extended his hand. "It dried up and fell off—just like that! And my abused nose—say, the pain went out of it like magic! The thing had the property of hard x-rays or gamma radiations, only more so; it destroyed diseased tissue and left healthy tissue unharmed!

"I was thinking what a present *that'd* be to take back to Mother Earth when a lot of racket interrupted. We dashed back to the other side of the wheel in time to see one of the pushcarts ground up. Some suicide had been careless, it seems.

"Then suddenly the creatures were booming and drumming all around us and their noise was decidedly menacing. A crowd of them advanced toward us; we backed out of what I thought was the passage we'd entered by, and they came rumbling after us, some pushing carts and some not. Crazy brutes! There was a whole chorus of 'We are v-r-r-riends! Ouch!' I didn't like the 'ouch'; it was rather suggestive.

"Tweel had his glass gun out and I dumped my water tank for greater freedom and got mine. We backed up the corridor with the barrel-beasts following—about twenty of them. Queer thing—the ones coming in with loaded carts moved past us inches away without a sign.

"Tweel must have noticed that. Suddenly, he snatched out that glowing coal cigar-lighter of his and touched a cart-load of plant limbs. Puff! The whole load was burning—and the crazy beast pushing it went right along without a change of pace! It created some disturbance among our 'V-r-r-riends,' however—and then I noticed the smoke eddying and swirling past us, and sure enough, there was the entrance!

"I grabbed Tweel and out we dashed and after us our twenty pursuers. The daylight felt like Heaven, though I saw at first glance that the sun was all but set, and that was bad, since I couldn't live outside my thermo-skin bag in a Martian night—at least, without a fire.

"And things got worse in a hurry. They cornered us in an angle between two mounds, and there we stood. I hadn't fired nor had Tweel; there wasn't any use in irritating the brutes. They stopped a little distance away and began their booming about friendship and ouches.

"Then things got still worse! A barrel-brute came out with a pushcart and they all grabbed into it and came out with handfuls of foot-long copper darts—sharp-looking ones—and all of a sudden one sailed past my ear—zing! And it was shoot or die then.

"We were doing pretty well for a while. We picked off the ones next to the pushcart and managed to keep the darts at a minimum, but suddenly there was a thunderous booming of 'v-r-r-riends' and 'ouches,' and a whole army of 'em came out of their hole.

"Man! We were through and I knew it! Then I realized that Tweel wasn't. He could have leaped the mound behind us as easily as not. He was staying for me!

"Say, I could have cried if there'd been time! I'd liked Tweel from the first, but whether I'd have had gratitude to do what he was doing—suppose I *had* saved him from the first dream-beast—he'd done as much for me, hadn't he? I grabbed his arm, and said 'Tweel,' and pointed up, and he understood. He said, 'No—no—no, Tick!' and popped away with his glass pistol.

"What could I do? I'd be a goner anyway when the sun set, but I couldn't explain that to him. I said, 'Thanks, Tweel. You're a man!' and felt that I wasn't paying him any compliment at all. A man! There are mighty few men who'd do that.

"So I went 'bang' with my gun and Tweel went 'puff' with his, and the barrels were throwing darts and getting ready to rush us, and booming about being friends. I had given up hope. Then suddenly an angel dropped right down from Heaven in the shape of Putz, with his under-jets blasting the barrels into very small pieces!

"Wow! I let out a yell and dashed for the rocket; Putz opened the door and in I went, laughing and crying and shouting! It was a moment or so before I remembered Tweel; I looked around in time to see him rising in one of his nosedives over the mound and away.

"I had a devil of a job arguing Putz into following! By the time we got the rocket aloft, darkness was down; you know how it comes here—like turning off a light. We sailed out over the desert and put down once or twice. I yelled 'Tweel!' and yelled it a hundred times, I guess. We couldn't find him; he could travel like the wind and all I got—or else I imagined it—was a faint trilling and twittering drifting out of the south. He'd gone, and damn it! I wish—I wish he hadn't!"

The four men of the *Ares* were silent—even the sardonic Harrison. At last little Leroy broke the stillness.

"I should like to see," he murmured.

"Yeah," said Harrison. "And the wart-cure. Too bad you missed that; it might be the cancer cure they've been hunting for a century and a half."

"Oh, that!" muttered Jarvis gloomily. "That's what started the fight!" He drew a glistening object from his pocket.

"Here it is."

Valley of Dreams

Originally Published in *Wonder Stories*
November 1934

Valley of Dreams

Captain Harrison of the *Ares* expedition turned away from the little telescope in the bow of the rocket. "Two weeks more, at the most," he remarked. "Mars only retrogrades for seventy days in all, relative to the earth, and we've got to be homeward bound during that period, or wait a year and a half for old Mother Earth to go around the sun and catch up with us again. How'd you like to spend a winter here?"

Dick Jarvis, chemist of the party, shivered as he looked up from his notebook. "I'd just as soon spend it in a liquid air tank!" he averred. "These eighty-below zero summer nights are plenty for me."

"Well," mused the captain, "the first successful Martian expedition ought to be home long before then."

"Successful if we get home," corrected Jarvis. "I don't trust these cranky rockets—not since the auxiliary dumped me in the middle of Thyle last week. Walking back from a rocket ride is a new sensation to me."

"Which reminds me," returned Harrison, "that we've got to recover your films. They're important if we're to pull this trip out of the red. Remember how the public mobbed the first moon pictures? Our shots ought to pack 'em to the doors. And the broadcast rights, too; we might show a profit for the Academy."

"What interests me," countered Jarvis, "is a personal profit. A book, for instance; exploration books are always popular. *Martian Deserts*—how's that for a title?"

"Lousy!" grunted the captain. "Sounds like a cook-book for desserts. You'd have to call it 'Love Life of a Martian,' or something like that."

Jarvis chuckled. "Anyway," he said, "if we once get back home, I'm going to grab what profit there is, and never, never, get any farther from the earth than a good stratosphere plane'll take me. I've learned to appreciate the planet after plowing over this dried-up pill we're on now."

"I'll lay you odds you'll be back here year after next," grinned the Captain. "You'll want to visit your pal—that trick ostrich."

"Tweel?" The other's tone sobered. "I wish I hadn't lost him, at that. He was a good scout. I'd never have survived the dream-beast but for him. And that battle with the push-cart things—I never even had a chance to thank him."

"A pair of lunatics, you two," observed Harrison. He squinted through the port at the gray gloom of the Mare Cimmerium. "There comes the sun." He paused. "Listen, Dick—you and Leroy take the other auxiliary rocket and go out and salvage those films."

Jarvis stared. "Me and Leroy?" he echoed ungrammatically. "Why not me and Putz? An engineer would have some chance of getting us there and back if the rocket goes bad on us."

The captain nodded toward the stern, whence issued at that moment a medley of blows and guttural expletives. "Putz is going over the insides of the *Ares*," he announced. "He'll have his hands full until we leave, because I want every bolt inspected. It's too late for repairs once we cast off."

"And if Leroy and I crack up? That's our last auxiliary."

"Pick up another ostrich and walk back," suggested Harrison gruffly. Then he smiled. "If you have trouble, we'll hunt you out in the *Ares*," he finished. "Those films are important." He turned. "Leroy!"

The dapper little biologist appeared, his face questioning.

"You and Jarvis are off to salvage the auxiliary," the Captain said. "Everything's ready and you'd better start now. Call back at half-hour intervals; I'll be listening."

Leroy's eyes glistened. "Perhaps we land for specimens—no?" he queried.

"Land if you want to. This golf ball seems safe enough."

"Except for the dream-beast," muttered Jarvis with a faint shudder. He frowned suddenly. "Say, as long as we're going that way, suppose I have a look for Tweel's home! He must live off there somewhere, and he's the most important thing we've seen on Mars."

Harrison hesitated. "If I thought you could keep out of trouble," he muttered. "All right," he decided. "Have a look. There's food and water aboard the auxiliary; you can take a couple of days. But keep in touch with me, you saps!"

Jarvis and Leroy went through the airlock out to the grey plain. The thin air, still scarcely warmed by the rising sun, bit flesh and lung like needles, and they gasped with a sense of suffocation. They dropped to a sitting posture, waiting for their bodies, trained by months in acclimatization chambers back on earth, to accommodate themselves to the tenuous air. Leroy's face, as always, turned a smothered blue, and Jarvis heard his own breath rasping and rattling in his throat. But in five minutes, the discomfort passed; they rose and entered the little auxiliary rocket that rested beside the black hull of the *Ares*.

The under-jets roared out their fiery atomic blast; dirt and bits of shattered biopods spun away in a cloud as the rocket rose. Harrison watched the projectile trail its flaming way into the south, then turned back to his work.

It was four days before he saw the rocket again. Just at evening, as the sun dropped behind the horizon with the suddenness of a candle falling into the sea, the auxiliary flashed out of the southern heavens, easing gently down on the flaming wings of the under-jets. Jarvis and Leroy emerged, passed through the swiftly gathering dusk, and faced him in the light of the *Ares*. He surveyed the two; Jarvis was tattered and scratched, but apparently in better condition than Leroy, whose dapperness was completely lost. The little biologist was pale as the nearer moon that glowed outside; one arm was bandaged in thermo-skin and his clothes hung in veritable rags. But it was his eyes that struck Harrison most strangely; to one who lived these many weary days with the diminutive Frenchman, there was something queer about them. They were frightened, plainly enough, and that was odd, since Leroy was no coward or he'd never have been one of the four chosen by the Academy for the first Martian expedition. But the fear in his eyes was more understandable than that other expression, that queer fixity of gaze like one in a trance, or like a person in an ecstasy. "Like a chap who's seen Heaven and Hell together," Harrison expressed it to himself. He was yet to discover how right he was.

He assumed a gruffness as the weary pair sat down. "You're a fine looking couple!" he growled. "I should've known better than to let you wander off alone." He paused. "Is your arm all right, Leroy? Need any treatment?"

Jarvis answered. "It's all right—just gashed. No danger of infection here, I guess; Leroy says there aren't any microbes on Mars."

"Well," exploded the Captain, "Let's hear it, then! Your radio reports sounded screwy. 'Escaped from Paradise!' Huh!"

"I didn't want to give details on the radio," said Jarvis soberly. "You'd have thought we'd gone loony."

"I think so, anyway."

"*Moi aussi!*" muttered Leroy. "I too!"

"Shall I begin at the beginning?" queried the chemist. "Our early reports were pretty nearly complete." He stared at Putz, who had come in silently, his face and hands blackened with carbon, and seated himself beside Harrison.

"At the beginning," the Captain decided.

"Well," began Jarvis, "we got started all right, and flew due south along the meridian of the *Ares*, same course I'd followed last week. I was getting used to this narrow horizon, so I didn't feel so much like being cooped under a big bowl, but one does keep overestimating distances. Something four miles away looks eight when you're used to terrestrial curvature, and that makes you guess its size just four times too large. A little hill looks like a mountain until you're almost over it."

"I know that," grunted Harrison.

"Yes, but Leroy didn't, and I spent our first couple of hours trying to explain it to him. By the time he understood (if he does yet) we were past Cimmerium and over that Xanthus desert, and then we crossed the canal with the mud city and the barrel-shaped citizens and the place where Tweel had shot the dream-beast. And nothing would do for Pierre here but that we put down so he could practice his biology on the remains. So we did.

"The thing was still there. No sign of decay; couldn't be, of course, without bacterial forms of life, and Leroy says that Mars is as sterile as an operating table."

"*Comme le coeur d'une fileuse,*" corrected the little biologist, who was beginning to regain a trace of his usual energy. "Like an old maid's heart!"

"However," resumed Jarvis, "about a hundred of the little grey-green biopods had fastened onto the thing and were growing and branching. Leroy found a stick and knocked 'em off, and each branch broke away and became a biopod crawling around with the others. So he poked around at the creature, while I looked away from it; even dead, that rope-armed devil gave me the creeps. And then came the surprise; the thing was part plant!"

"*C'est vrai!*" confirmed the biologist. "It's true!"

"It was a big cousin of the biopods," continued Jarvis. "Leroy was quite excited; he figures that all Martian life is of that sort—neither plant nor animal. Life here never differentiated, he says; everything has both natures in it, even the barrel-creatures—even Tweel! I think he's right, especially when I recall how Tweel rested, sticking his beak in the ground and staying that way all night. I never saw him eat or drink, either; perhaps his beak was more in the nature of a root, and he got his nourishment that way."

"Sounds nutty to me," observed Harrison.

"Well," continued Jarvis, "we broke up a few of the other growths and they acted the same way—the pieces crawled around, only much slower than the biopods, and then stuck themselves in the ground. Then Leroy had to catch a sample of the walking grass, and we were ready to leave when a parade of the barrel-creatures rushed by with their push-carts. They hadn't forgotten me, either; they all drummed out, 'We are v-r-r-iends—ouch!' just as they had before. Leroy wanted to shoot one and cut it up, but I remembered the battle Tweel and I had had with them, and vetoed the idea. But he did hit on a possible explanation as to what they did with all the rubbish they gathered."

"Made mud-pies, I guess," grunted the captain.

"More or less," agreed Jarvis. "They use it for food, Leroy thinks. If they're part vegetable, you see, that's what they'd want—soil with organic remains in it to make it fertile. That's why they ground up sand and biopods and other growths all together. See?"

"Dimly," countered Harrison. "How about the suicides?"

"Leroy had a hunch there, too. The suicides jump into the grinder when the mixture has too much sand and gravel; they throw themselves in to adjust the proportions."

"Rats!" said Harrison disgustedly. "Why couldn't they bring in some extra branches from outside?"

"Because suicide is easier. You've got to remember that these creatures can't be judged by earthly standards; they probably don't feel pain, and they haven't got what we'd call individuality.

Any intelligence they have is the property of the whole community—like an ant-heap. That's it! Ants are willing to die for their ant-hill; so are these creatures."

"So are men," observed the captain, "if it comes to that."

"Yes, but men aren't exactly eager. It takes some emotion like patriotism to work 'em to the point of dying for their country; these things do it all in the day's work." He paused.

"Well, we took some pictures of the dream-beast and the barrel-creatures, and then we started along. We sailed over Xanthus, keeping as close to the meridian of the *Ares* as we could, and pretty soon we crossed the trail of the pyramid-builder. So we circled back to let Leroy take a look at it, and when we found it, we landed. The thing had completed just two rows of bricks since Tweel and I left it, and there it was, breathing in silicon and breathing out bricks as if it had eternity to do it in—which it has. Leroy wanted to dissect it with a Boland explosive bullet, but I thought that anything that had lived for ten million years was entitled to the respect due old age, so I talked him out of it. He peeped into the hole on top of it and nearly got beaned by the arm coming up with a brick, and then he chipped off a few pieces of it, which didn't disturb the creature a bit. He found the place I'd chipped, tried to see if there was any sign of healing, and decided he could tell better in two or three thousand years. So we took a few shots of it and sailed on.

"Mid afternoon we located the wreck of my rocket. Not a thing disturbed; we picked up my films and tried to decide what next. I wanted to find Tweel if possible; I figured from the fact of his pointing south that he lived somewhere near Thyle. We plotted our route and judged that the desert we were in now was Thyle II; Thyle I should be east of us. So, on a hunch, we decided to have a look at Thyle I, and away we buzzed."

"*Der* motors?" queried Putz, breaking his long silence.

"For a wonder, we had no trouble, Karl. Your blast worked perfectly. So we hummed along, pretty high to get a wider view, I'd say about fifty thousand feet. Thyle II spread out like an orange carpet, and after a while we came to the grey branch of the Mare Chronium that bounded it. That was narrow; we crossed it in half an hour, and there was Thyle I—same orange-hued desert as its mate. We veered south, toward the Mare

Australe, and followed the edge of the desert. And toward sunset we spotted it."

"Shpotted?" echoed Putz. "Vot vas shpotted?"

"The desert was spotted—with buildings! Not one of the mud cities of the canals, although a canal went through it. From the map we figured the canal was a continuation of the one Schiaparelli called Ascanius.

"We were probably too high to be visible to any inhabitants of the city, but also too high for a good look at it, even with the glasses. However, it was nearly sunset, anyway, so we didn't plan on dropping in. We circled the place; the canal went out into the Mare Australe, and there, glittering in the south, was the melting polar ice-cap! The canal drained it; we could distinguish the sparkle of water in it. Off to the southeast, just at the edge of the Mare Australe, was a valley—the first irregularity I'd seen on Mars except the cliffs that bounded Xanthus and Thyle II. We flew over the valley—" Jarvis paused suddenly and shuddered; Leroy, whose color had begun to return, seemed to pale. The chemist resumed, "Well, the valley looked all right—then! Just a gray waste, probably full of crawlers like the others.

"We circled back over the city; say, I want to tell you that place was—well, gigantic! It was colossal; at first I thought the size was due to that illusion I spoke of—you know, the nearness of the horizon—but it wasn't that. We sailed right over it, and you've never seen anything like it!

"But the sun dropped out of sight right then. I knew we were pretty far south—latitude 60—but I didn't know just how much night we'd have."

Harrison glanced at a Schiaparelli chart. "About 60—eh?" he said. "Close to what corresponds to the Antarctic circle. You'd have about four hours of night at this season. Three months from now you'd have none at all."

"Three months!" echoed Jarvis, surprised. Then he grinned. "Right! I forget the seasons here are twice as long as ours. Well, we sailed out into the desert about twenty miles, which put the city below the horizon in case we overslept, and there we spent the night.

"You're right about the length of it. We had about four hours of darkness which left us fairly rested. We ate breakfast, called our location to you, and started over to have a look at the city.

"We sailed toward it from the east and it loomed up ahead of us like a range of mountains. Lord, what a city! Not that New York mightn't have higher buildings, or Chicago cover more ground, but for sheer mass, those structures were in a class by themselves. Gargantuan!

"There was a queer look about the place, though. You know how a terrestrial city sprawls out, a nimbus of suburbs, a ring of residential sections, factory districts, parks, highways. There was none of that here; the city rose out of the desert as abruptly as a cliff. Only a few little sand mounds marked the division, and then the walls of those gigantic structures.

"The architecture was strange, too. There were lots of devices that are impossible back home, such as set-backs in reverse, so that a building with a small base could spread out as it rose. That would be a valuable trick in New York, where land is almost priceless, but to do it, you'd have to transfer Martian gravitation there!

"Well, since you can't very well land a rocket in a city street, we put down right next to the canal side of the city, took our small cameras and revolvers, and started for a gap in the wall of masonry. We weren't ten feet from the rocket when we both saw the explanation for a lot of the queerness.

"The city was in ruin! Abandoned, deserted, dead as Babylon! Or at least, so it looked to us then, with its empty streets which, if they had been paved, were now deep under sand."

"A ruin, eh?" commented Harrison. "How old?"

"How could we tell?" countered Jarvis. "The next expedition to this golf ball ought to carry an archeologist—and a philologist, too, as we found out later. But it's a devil of a job to estimate the age of anything here; things weather so slowly that most of the buildings might have been put up yesterday. No rainfall, no earthquakes, no vegetation is here to spread cracks with its roots—nothing. The only aging factors here are the erosion of the wind—and that's negligible in this atmosphere—and the cracks caused by changing temperature. And one other agent—meteorites. They must crash down occasionally on the city, judging from the thinness of the air, and the fact that we've seen four strike ground right here near the *Ares.*"

"Seven," corrected the captain. "Three dropped while you were gone."

"Well, damage by meteorites must be slow, anyway. Big ones would be as rare here as on earth, because big ones get through in spite of the atmosphere, and those buildings could sustain a lot of little ones. My guess at the city's age—and it may be wrong by a big percentage—would be fifteen thousand years. Even that's thousands of years older than any human civilization; fifteen thousand years ago was the Late Stone Age in the history of mankind.

"So Leroy and I crept up to those tremendous buildings feeling like pygmies, sort of awe-struck, and talking in whispers. I tell you, it was ghostly walking down that dead and deserted street, and every time we passed through a shadow, we shivered, and not just because shadows are cold on Mars. We felt like intruders, as if the great race that had built the place might resent our presence even across a hundred and fifty centuries. The place was as quiet as a grave, but we kept imagining things and peeping down the dark lanes between buildings and looking over our shoulders. Most of the structures were windowless, but when we did see an opening in those vast walls, we couldn't look away, expecting to see some horror peering out of it.

"Then we passed an edifice with an open arch; the doors were there, but blocked open by sand. I got up nerve enough to take a look inside, and then, of course, we discovered we'd forgotten to take our flashes. But we eased a few feet into the darkness and the passage debouched into a colossal hall. Far above us a little crack let in a pallid ray of daylight, not nearly enough to light the place; I couldn't even see if the hall rose clear to the distant roof. But I know the place was enormous; I said something to Leroy and a million thin echoes came slipping back to us out of the darkness. And after that, we began to hear other sounds— slithering rustling noises, and whispers, and sounds like suppressed breathing—and something black and silent passed between us and that far-away crevice of light.

"Then we saw three little greenish spots of luminosity in the dusk to our left. We stood staring at them, and suddenly they all shifted at once. Leroy yelled '*Ce sont des yeux!*' and they were! They were eyes!

"Well, we stood frozen for a moment, while Leroy's yell reverberated back and forth between the distant walls, and the echoes repeated the words in queer, thin voices. There were mumblings and mutterings and whisperings and sounds like strange soft laughter, and then the three-eyed thing moved again. Then we broke for the door!

"We felt better out in the sunlight; we looked at each other sheepishly, but neither of us suggested another look at the buildings inside—though we *did* see the place later, and that was queer, too—but you'll hear about it when I come to it. We just loosened our revolvers and crept on along that ghostly street.

"The street curved and twisted and subdivided. I kept careful note of our directions, since we couldn't risk getting lost in that gigantic maze. Without our thermo-skin bags, night would finish us, even if what lurked in the ruins didn't. By and by, I noticed that we were veering back toward the canal, the buildings ended and there were only a few dozen ragged stone huts which looked as though they might have been built of debris from the city. I was just beginning to feel a bit disappointed at finding no trace of Tweel's people here when we rounded a corner and there he was!

"I yelled 'Tweel!' but he just stared, and then I realized that he wasn't Tweel, but another Martian of his sort. Tweel's feathery appendages were more orange hued and he stood several inches taller than this one. Leroy was sputtering in excitement, and the Martian kept his vicious beak directed at us, so I stepped forward as peace-maker. I said 'Tweel?' very questioningly, but there was no result. I tried it a dozen times, and we finally had to give it up; we couldn't connect.

"Leroy and I walked toward the huts, and the Martian followed us. Twice he was joined by others, and each time I tried yelling 'Tweel' at them but they just stared at us. So we ambled on with the three trailing us, and then it suddenly occurred to me that my Martian accent might be at fault. I faced the group and tried trilling it out the way Tweel himself did: 'T-r-r-rwee-r-rl!' Like that.

"And that worked! One of them spun his head around a full ninety degrees, and screeched 'T-r-r-rweee-r-rl!' and a moment later, like an arrow from a bow, Tweel came sailing over the nearer huts to land on his beak in front of me!

"Man, we were glad to see each other! Tweel set up a twittering and chirping like a farm in summer and went sailing up and coming down on his beak, and I would have grabbed his hands, only he wouldn't keep still long enough.

"The other Martians and Leroy just stared, and after a while, Tweel stopped bouncing, and there we were. We couldn't talk to each other any more than we could before, so after I'd said 'Tweel' a couple of times and he'd said 'Tick,' we were more or less helpless. However, it was only mid-morning, and it seemed important to learn all we could about Tweel and the city, so I suggested that he guide us around the place if he weren't busy. I put over the idea by pointing back at the buildings and then at him and us.

"Well, apparently he wasn't too busy, for he set off with us, leading the way with one of his hundred and fifty-foot nosedives that set Leroy gasping. When we caught up, he said something like 'one, one, two—two, two, four—no, no—yes, yes—rock—no breet!' That didn't seem to mean anything; perhaps he was just letting Leroy know that he could speak English, or perhaps he was merely running over his vocabulary to refresh his memory.

"Anyway, he showed us around. He had a light of sorts in his black pouch, good enough for small rooms, but simply lost in some of the colossal caverns we went through. Nine out of ten buildings meant absolutely nothing to us—just vast empty chambers, full of shadows and rustlings and echoes. I couldn't imagine their use; they didn't seem suitable for living quarters, or even for commercial purposes—trade and so forth; they might have been all right as power-houses, but what could have been the purpose of a whole city full? And where were the remains of the machinery?

"The place was a mystery. Sometimes Tweel would show us through a hall that would have housed an ocean-liner, and he'd seem to swell with pride—and we couldn't make a damn thing of it! As a display of architectural power, the city was colossal; as anything else it was just nutty!

"But we did see one thing that registered. We came to that same building Leroy and I had entered earlier—the one with the three eyes in it. Well, we were a little shaky about going in there, but Tweel twittered and trilled and kept saying, 'Yes, yes, yes!' so we followed him, staring nervously about for the thing that had watched us. However, that hall was just like the others, full of murmurs and slithering noises and shadowy things slipping away into corners. If the three-eyed creature were still there, it must have slunk away with the others.

"Tweel led us along the wall; his light showed a series of little alcoves, and in the first of these we ran into a puzzling thing—a very weird thing. As the light flashed into the alcove, I saw first just an empty space, and then, squatting on the floor, I saw—it! A little creature about as big as a large rat, it was, gray and huddled and evidently startled by our appearance. It had the queerest, most devilish little face!—pointed ears or horns and satanic eyes that seemed to sparkle with a sort of fiendish intelligence.

"Tweel saw it, too, and let out a screech of anger, and the creature rose on two pencil-thin legs and scuttled off with a half-terrified, half defiant squeak. It darted past us into the darkness too quickly even for Tweel, and as it ran, something waved on its body like the fluttering of a cape. Tweel screeched angrily at it and set up a shrill hullabaloo that sounded like genuine rage.

"But the thing was gone, and then I noticed the weirdest of imaginable details. Where it had squatted on the floor was—a book! It had been hunched over a book!

"I took a step forward; sure enough, there was some sort of inscription on the pages—wavy white lines like a seismograph record on black sheets like the material of Tweel's pouch. Tweel fumed and whistled in wrath, picked up the volume and slammed it into place on a shelf full of others. Leroy and I stared dumbfounded at each other.

"Had the little thing with the fiendish face been reading? Or was it simply eating the pages, getting physical nourishment rather than mental? Or had the whole thing been accidental?

"If the creature were some rat-like pest that destroyed books, Tweel's rage was understandable, but why should he try to prevent an intelligent being, even though of an alien race, from *reading*—if it *was* reading? I don't know; I did notice that the book was entirely undamaged, nor did I see a damaged book among any that we handled. But I have an odd hunch that if we knew the secret of the little cape-clothed imp, we'd know the mystery of the vast abandoned city and of the decay of Martian culture.

"Well, Tweel quieted down after a while and led us completely around that tremendous hall. It had been a library, I think; at least, there were thousands upon thousands of those queer black-paged volumes printed in wavy lines of white. There were pictures, too, in some; and some of these showed Tweel's people. That's a point, of course; it indicated that his race built the city and printed the books. I don't think the greatest philologist on earth will ever translate one line of those records; they were made by minds too different from ours.

"Tweel could read them, naturally. He twittered off a few lines, and then I took a few of the books, with his permission; he said 'no, no!' to some and 'yes, yes!' to others. Perhaps he kept back the ones his people needed, or perhaps he let me take the ones he thought we'd understand most easily. I don't know; the books are outside there in the rocket.

"Then he held that dim torch of his toward the walls, and they were pictured. Lord, what pictures! They stretched up and up into the blackness of the roof, mysterious and gigantic. I couldn't make much of the first wall; it seemed to be a portrayal of a great assembly of Tweel's people. Perhaps it was meant to symbolize Society or Government. But the next wall was more obvious; it showed creatures at work on a colossal machine of some sort, and that would be Industry or Science. The back wall had corroded away in part, from what we could see, I suspected the scene was meant to portray Art, but it was on the fourth wall that we got a shock that nearly dazed us.

"I think the symbol was Exploration or Discovery. This wall was a little plainer, because the moving beam of daylight from that crack lit up the higher surface and Tweel's torch illuminated the lower. We made out a giant seated figure, one of the beaked Martians like Tweel, but with every limb suggesting heaviness, weariness. The arms dropped inertly on the chair, the thin neck bent and the beak rested on the body, as if the creature could scarcely bear its own weight. And before it was a queer kneeling figure, and at sight of it, Leroy and I almost reeled against each other. It was, apparently, a man!"

"A man!" bellowed Harrison. "A man you say?"

"I said apparently," retorted Jarvis. "The artist had exaggerated the nose almost to the length of Tweel's beak, but the figure had black shoulder-length hair, and instead of the Martian four, there were *five* fingers on its outstretched hand! It was kneeling as if in worship of the Martian, and on the ground was what looked like a pottery bowl full of some food as an offering. Well! Leroy and I thought we'd gone screwy!"

"And Putz and I think so, too!" roared the captain.

"Maybe we all have," replied Jarvis, with a faint grin at the pale face of the little Frenchman, who returned it in silence. "Anyway," he continued, "Tweel was squeaking and pointing at the figure, and saying 'Tick! Tick!' so he recognized the resemblance—and never mind any cracks about my nose!" he warned the captain. "It was Leroy who made the important comment; he looked at the Martian and said 'Thoth! The god Thoth!'"

"*Oui!*" confirmed the biologist. "*Comme l'Egypte!*"

"Yeah," said Jarvis. "Like the Egyptian ibis-headed god—the one with the beak. Well, no sooner did Tweel hear the name Thoth than he set up a clamor of twittering and squeaking. He pointed at himself and said 'Thoth! Thoth!' and then waved his arm all around and repeated it. Of course he often did queer things, but we both thought we understood what he meant. He was trying to tell us that his race called themselves Thoth. Do you see what I'm getting at?"

"I see, all right," said Harrison. "You think the Martians paid a visit to the earth, and the Egyptians remembered it in their mythology. Well, you're off, then; there wasn't any Egyptian civilization fifteen thousand years ago."

"Wrong!" grinned Jarvis. "It's too bad we *haven't* an archeologist with us, but Leroy tells me that there was a stone-age culture in Egypt then, the pre-dynastic civilization."

"Well, even so, what of it?"

"Plenty! Everything in that picture proves my point. The attitude of the Martian, heavy and weary—that's the unnatural strain of terrestrial gravitation. The name Thoth; Leroy tells me Thoth was the Egyptian god of philosophy and the inventor of *writing*! Get that? They must have picked up the idea from watching the Martian take notes. It's too much for coincidence that Thoth should be beaked and ibis-headed, and that the beaked Martians call themselves Thoth."

"Well, I'll be hanged! But what about the nose on the Egyptian? Do you mean to tell me that stone-age Egyptians had longer noses than ordinary men?"

"Of course not! It's just that the Martians very naturally cast their paintings in Martianized form. Don't human beings tend to relate everything to themselves? That's why dugongs and manatees started the mermaid myths—sailors thought they saw human features on the beasts. So the Martian artist, drawing either from descriptions or imperfect photographs, naturally exaggerated the size of the human nose to a degree that looked normal to him. Or anyway, that's my theory."

"Well, it'll do as a theory," grunted Harrison. "What I want to hear is why you two got back here looking like a couple of year-before-last bird's nests."

Jarvis shuddered again, and cast another glance at Leroy. The little biologist was recovering some of his accustomed poise, but he returned the glance with an echo of the chemist's shudder.

"We'll get to that," resumed the latter. "Meanwhile I'll stick to Tweel and his people. We spent the better part of three days with them, as you know. I can't give every detail, but I'll summarize the important facts and give our conclusions, which may not be worth an inflated franc. It's hard to judge this dried-up world by earthly standards.

"We took pictures of everything possible; I even tried to photograph that gigantic mural in the library, but unless Tweel's lamp was unusually rich in actinic rays, I don't suppose it'll show. And that's a pity, since it's undoubtedly the most interesting object we've found on Mars, at least from a human viewpoint.

"Tweel was a very courteous host. He took us to all the points of interest—even the new water-works."

Putz's eyes brightened at the word. "Vater-vorks?" he echoed. "For vot?"

"For the canal, naturally. They have to build up a head of water to drive it through; that's obvious." He looked at the captain. "You told me yourself that to drive water from the polar caps of Mars to the equator was equivalent to forcing it up a twenty-mile hill, because Mars is flattened at the poles and bulges at the equator just like the earth."

"That's true," agreed Harrison.

"Well," resumed Jarvis, "this city was one of the relay stations to boost the flow. Their power plant was the only one of the giant buildings that seemed to serve any useful purpose, and that was worth seeing. I wish you'd seen it, Karl; you'll have to make what you can from our pictures. It's a sun-power plant!"

Harrison and Putz stared. "Sun-power!" grunted the captain. "That's primitive!" And the engineer added an emphatic "*Ja!*" of agreement.

"Not as primitive as all that," corrected Jarvis. "The sunlight focused on a queer cylinder in the center of a big concave mirror, and they drew an electric current from it. The juice worked the pumps."

"A t'ermocouple!" ejaculated Putz.

"That sounds reasonable; you can judge by the pictures. But the power-plant had some queer things about it. The queerest was that the machinery was tended, not by Tweel's people, but by some of the barrel-shaped creatures like the ones in Xanthus!" He gazed around at the faces of his auditors; there was no comment.

"Get it?" he resumed. At their silence, he proceeded, "I see you don't. Leroy figured it out, but whether rightly or wrongly, I don't know. He thinks that the barrels and Tweel's race have a reciprocal arrangement like—well, like bees and flowers on earth. The flowers give honey for the bees; the bees carry the pollen for the flowers. See? The barrels tend the works and Tweel's people build the canal system. The Xanthus city must have been a boosting station; that explains the mysterious machines I saw. And Leroy believes further that it isn't an intelligent arrangement—not on the part of the barrels, at least—but that it's been done for so many thousands of generations that it's become instinctive—a tropism—just like the actions of ants and bees. The creatures have been bred to it!"

"Nuts!" observed Harrison. "Let's hear you explain the reason for that big empty city, then."

"Sure. Tweel's civilization is decadent, that's the reason. It's a dying race, and out of all the millions that must once have lived there, Tweel's couple of hundred companions are the remnant. They're an outpost, left to tend the source of the water at the polar cap; probably there are still a few respectable cities left somewhere on the canal system, most likely near the tropics. It's the last gasp of a race—and a race that reached a higher peak of culture than Man!"

"Huh?" said Harrison. "Then why are they dying? Lack of water?"

"I don't think so," responded the chemist. "If my guess at the city's age is right, fifteen thousand years wouldn't make enough difference in the water supply—nor a hundred thousand, for that matter. It's something else, though the water's doubtless a factor."

"*Das wasser*," cut in Putz. "Vere goes dot?"

"Even a chemist knows that!" scoffed Jarvis. "At least on earth. Here I'm not so sure, but on earth, every time there's a lightning flash, it electrolyzes some water vapor into hydrogen and oxygen, and then the hydrogen escapes into space, because terrestrial gravitation won't hold it permanently. And every time there's an earthquake, some water is lost to the interior. Slow—but damned certain." He turned to Harrison. "Right, Cap?"

"Right," conceded the captain. "But here, of course—no earthquakes, no thunderstorms—the loss must be very slow. Then why is the race dying?"

"The sun-power plant answers that," countered Jarvis. "Lack of fuel! Lack of power! No oil left, no coal left—if Mars ever had a Carboniferous Age—and no water-power—just the driblets of energy they can get from the sun. That's why they're dying."

"With the limitless energy of the atom?" exploded Harrison.

"They don't know about atomic energy. Probably never did. Must have used some other principle in their space-ship."

"Then," snapped the captain, "what makes you rate their intelligence above the human? We've finally cracked open the atom!"

"Sure we have. We had a clue, didn't we? Radium and uranium. Do you think we'd ever have learned how without those elements? We'd never even have suspected that atomic energy existed!"

"Well? Haven't they—?"

"No, they haven't. You've told me yourself that Mars has only 73 percent of the earth's density. Even a chemist can see that that means a lack of heavy metals—no osmium, no uranium, no radium. They didn't have the clue."

"Even so, that doesn't prove they're more advanced than we are. If they were *more* advanced, they'd have discovered it anyway."

"Maybe," conceded Jarvis. "I'm not claiming that we don't surpass them in some ways. But in others, they're far ahead of us."

"In what, for instance?"

"Well—socially, for one thing."

"Huh? How do you mean?"

Jarvis glanced in turn at each of the three that faced him. He hesitated. "I wonder how you chaps will take this," he muttered. "Naturally, everybody likes his own system best." He frowned. "Look here—on the earth we have three types of society, haven't we? And there's a member of each type right here. Putz lives under a dictatorship—an autocracy. Leroy's a citizen of the Sixth Commune in France. Harrison and I are Americans, members of a democracy. There you are—autocracy, democracy, communism—the three types of terrestrial societies. Tweel's people have a different system from any of us."

"Different? What is it?"

"The one no earthly nation has tried. Anarchy!"

"Anarchy!" the captain and Putz burst out together.

"That's right."

"But—" Harrison was sputtering. "What do you mean—they're ahead of us? Anarchy! Bah!"

"All right—bah!" retorted Jarvis. "I'm not saying it would work for us, or for any race of men. But it works for them."

"But—anarchy!" The captain was indignant.

"Well, when you come right down to it," argued Jarvis defensively, "anarchy is the ideal form of government, if it works. Emerson said that the best government was that which governs least, and so did Wendell Phillips, and I think George Washington. And you can't have any form of government which governs less than anarchy, which is no government at all!"

The captain was sputtering. "But—it's unnatural! Even savage tribes have their chiefs! Even a pack of wolves has its leader!"

"Well," retorted Jarvis defiantly, "that only proves that government is a primitive device, doesn't it? With a perfect race you wouldn't need it at all; government is a confession of weakness, isn't it? It's a confession that part of the people won't cooperate with the rest and that you need laws to restrain those individuals which a psychologist calls anti-social. If there were no anti-social persons—criminals and such—you wouldn't need laws or police, would you?"

"But government! You'd need government! How about public works—wars—taxes?"

"No wars on Mars, in spite of being named after the War God. No point in wars here; the population is too thin and too scattered, and besides, it takes the help of every single community to keep the canal system functioning. No taxes because, apparently, all individuals cooperate in building public works. No competition to cause trouble, because anybody can help himself to anything. As I said, with a perfect race government is entirely unnecessary."

"And do you consider the Martians a perfect race?" asked the captain grimly.

"Not at all! But they've existed so much longer than man that they're evolved, socially at least, to the point where they don't need government. They work together, that's all." Jarvis paused. "Queer, isn't it—as if Mother Nature were carrying on two experiments, one at home and one on Mars. On earth it's trial of an emotional, highly competitive race in a world of plenty; here it's the trial of a quiet, friendly race on a desert, unproductive, and inhospitable world. Everything here makes for cooperation. Why, there isn't even the factor that causes so much trouble at home—sex!"

"Huh?"

"Yeah: Tweel's people reproduce just like the barrels in the mud cities; two individuals grow a third one between them. Another proof of Leroy's theory that Martian life is neither animal nor vegetable. Besides, Tweel was a good enough host to let him poke down his beak and twiddle his feathers, and the examination convinced Leroy."

"*Oui*," confirmed the biologist. "It is true."

"But anarchy!" grumbled Harrison disgustedly. "It would show up on a dizzy, half-dead pill like Mars!"

"It'll be a good many centuries before you'll have to worry about it on earth," grinned Jarvis. He resumed his narrative.

"Well, we wandered through that sepulchral city, taking pictures of everything. And then—" Jarvis paused and shuddered—"then I took a notion to have a look at that valley we'd spotted from the rocket. I don't know why. But when we tried to steer Tweel in that direction, he set up such a squawking and screeching that I thought he'd gone batty."

"If possible!" jeered Harrison.

"So we started over there without him; he kept wailing and screaming, 'No-no-no! Tick!' but that made us the more curious. He sailed over our heads and stuck on his beak, and went through a dozen other antics, but we ploughed on, and finally he gave up and trudged disconsolately along with us.

"The valley wasn't more than a mile southeast of the city. Tweel could have covered the distance in twenty jumps, but he lagged and loitered and kept pointing back at the city and wailing 'No—no—no!' Then he'd sail up into the air and zip down on his beak directly in front of us, and we'd have to walk around him. I'd seen him do lots of crazy things before, of course; I was used to them, but it was as plain as print that he didn't want us to see that valley."

"Why?" queried Harrison.

"You asked why we came back like tramps," said Jarvis with a faint shudder. "You'll learn. We plugged along up a low rocky hill that bounded it, and as we neared the top, Tweel said, 'No breet', Tick! No breet'!' Well, those were the words he used to describe the silicon monster; they were also the words he had used to tell me that the image of Fancy Long, the one that had almost lured me to the dream-beast, wasn't real. I remembered that, but it meant nothing to me—then!

"Right after that, Tweel said, 'You one-one-two, he one-one-two,' and then I began to see. That was the phrase he had used to explain the dream-beast to tell me that what I thought, the creature thought—to tell me how the thing lured its victims by their own desires. So I warned Leroy; it seemed to me that even the dream-beast couldn't be dangerous if we were warned and expecting it. Well, I was wrong!

"As we reached the crest, Tweel spun his head completely around, so his feet were forward but his eyes looked backward, as if he feared to gaze into the valley. Leroy and I stared out over it, just a gray waste like this around us, with the gleam of the south polar cap far beyond its southern rim. That's what it was one second; the next it was—Paradise!"

"What?" exclaimed the captain.

Jarvis turned to Leroy. "Can you describe it?" he asked.

The biologist waved helpless hands, "*C'est impossible!*" he whispered. "*Il me rend muet!*"

"It strikes me dumb, too," muttered Jarvis. "I don't know how to tell it; I'm a chemist, not a poet. Paradise is as good a word as I can think of, and that's not at all right. It was Paradise and Hell in one!"

"Will you talk sense?" growled Harrison.

"As much of it as makes sense. I tell you, one moment we were looking at a grey valley covered with blobby plants, and the next—Lord! You can't imagine that next moment! How would you like to see all your dreams made real? Every desire you'd ever had gratified? Everything you'd ever wanted there for the taking?"

"I'd like it fine!" said the captain.

"You're welcome, then!—not only your noble desires, remember! Every good impulse, yes—but also every nasty little wish, every vicious thought, everything you'd ever desired, good or bad! The dream-beasts are marvelous salesmen, but they lack the moral sense!"

"The dream-beasts?"

"Yes. It was a valley of them. Hundreds, I suppose, maybe thousands. Enough, at any rate, to spread out a complete picture of your desires, even all the forgotten ones that must have been drawn out of the subconscious. A Paradise—of sorts! I saw a dozen Fancy Longs, in every costume I'd ever admired on her, and some I must have imagined. I saw every beautiful woman I've ever known, and all of them pleading for my attention. I saw every lovely place I'd ever wanted to be, all packed queerly into that little valley. And I saw—other things." He shook his head soberly. "It wasn't all exactly pretty. Lord! How much of the beast is left in us! I suppose if every man alive could have one look at that weird valley, and could see just once what nastiness is hidden in him—well, the world might gain by it. I thanked heaven afterwards that Leroy—and even Tweel—saw their own pictures and not mine!"

Jarvis paused again, then resumed, "I turned dizzy with a sort of ecstasy. I closed my eyes—and with eyes closed, I still saw the whole thing! That beautiful, evil, devilish panorama was in my mind, not my eyes. That's how those fiends work—through the mind. I knew it was the dream-beasts; I didn't need Tweel's wail of 'No breet'! No breet'!' But—*I couldn't keep away!* I knew it was death beckoning, but it was worth it for one moment with the vision."

"Which particular vision?" asked Harrison dryly.

Jarvis flushed. "No matter," he said. "But beside me I heard Leroy's cry of 'Yvonne! Yvonne!' and I knew he was trapped like myself. I fought for sanity; I kept telling myself to stop, and all the time I was rushing headlong into the snare!

"Then something tripped me. Tweel! He had come leaping from behind; as I crashed down I saw him flash over me straight toward—toward what I'd been running to, with his vicious beak pointed right at her heart!"

"Oh!" nodded the captain. "*Her* heart!"

"Never mind that. When I scrambled up, that particular image was gone, and Tweel was in a twist of black ropey arms, just as when I first saw him. He'd missed a vital point in the beast's anatomy, but was jabbing away desperately with his beak.

"Somehow, the spell had lifted, or partially lifted. I wasn't five feet from Tweel, and it took a terrific struggle, but I managed to raise my revolver and put a Boland shell into the beast. Out came a spurt of horrible black corruption, drenching Tweel and me—and I guess the sickening smell of it helped to destroy the illusion of that valley of beauty. Anyway, we managed to get Leroy away from the devil that had him, and the three of us staggered to the ridge and over. I had presence of mind enough to raise my camera over the crest and take a shot of the valley, but I'll bet it shows nothing but gray waste and writhing horrors. What we saw was with our minds, not our eyes."

Jarvis paused and shuddered. "The brute half poisoned Leroy," he continued. "We dragged ourselves back to the auxiliary, called you, and did what we could to treat ourselves. Leroy took a long dose of the cognac that we had with us; we didn't dare try anything of Tweel's because his metabolism is so different from ours that what cured him might kill us. But the cognac seemed to work, and so, after I'd done one other thing I wanted to do, we came back here—and that's all."

"All, is it?" queried Harrison. "So you've solved all the mysteries of Mars, eh?"

"Not by a damned sight!" retorted Jarvis. "Plenty of unanswered questions are left."

"*Ja!*" snapped Putz. "Der evaporation—dot iss shtopped how?"

"In the canals? I wondered about that, too; in those thousands of miles, and against this low air-pressure, you'd think they'd lose a lot. But the answer's simple; they float a skin of oil on the water."

Putz nodded, but Harrison cut in. "Here's a puzzler. With only coal and oil—just combustion or electric power—where'd they get the energy to build a planet-wide canal system, thousands and thousands of miles of 'em? Think of the job we had cutting the Panama Canal to sea level, and then answer that!"

"Easy!" grinned Jarvis. "Martian gravity and Martian air—that's the answer. Figure it out: First, the dirt they dug only weighed a third its earth-weight. Second, a steam engine here expands against ten pounds per square inch less air pressure than on earth. Third, they could build the engine three times as large here with no greater internal weight. And fourth, the whole planet's nearly level. Right, Putz?"

The engineer nodded. "*Ja!* Der shteam—engine—it iss *sieben-und zwanzig*—twenty-seven times so effective here."

"Well, there *does* go the last mystery then," mused Harrison.

"Yeah?" queried Jarvis sardonically. "You answer these, then. What was the nature of that vast empty city? Why do the Martians *need* canals, since we never saw them eat or drink? Did they really visit the earth before the dawn of history, and, if not atomic energy, what powered their ship? Since Tweel's race seems to need little or no water, are they merely operating the canals for some higher creature that does? *Are* there other intelligences on Mars? If not, what was the demon-faced imp we saw with the book? There are a few mysteries for you!"

"I know one or two more!" growled Harrison, glaring suddenly at little Leroy. "You and your visions! 'Yvonne!' eh? Your wife's name is Marie, isn't it?"

The little biologist turned crimson. "*Oui,*" he admitted unhappily. He turned pleading eyes on the captain. "Please," he said. "In Paris *tout le monde*—everybody he think differently of those things—no?" He twisted uncomfortably. "Please, you will not tell Marie, *n'est-ce pas?*"

Harrison chuckled. "None of my business," he said. "One more question, Jarvis. What was the one other thing you did before returning here?"

Jarvis looked diffident. "Oh—that." He hesitated. "Well I sort of felt we owed Tweel a lot, so after some trouble, we coaxed him into the rocket and sailed him out to the wreck of the first one, over on Thyle II. Then," he finished apologetically, "I showed him the atomic blast, got it working—and gave it to him!"

"You *what?*" roared the Captain. "You turned something as powerful as that over to an alien race—maybe some day as an enemy race?"

"Yes, I did," said Jarvis. "Look here," he argued defensively. "This lousy, dried-up pill of a desert called Mars'll never support much human population. The Sahara desert is just as good a field for imperialism, and a lot closer to home. So we'll never find Tweel's race enemies. The only value we'll find here is commercial trade with the Martians. Then why shouldn't I give Tweel a chance for survival? With atomic energy, they can run their canal system a hundred per cent instead of only one out of five, as Putz's observations showed. They can repopulate those ghostly cities; they can resume their arts and industries; they can trade with the nations of the earth—and I'll bet they can teach us a few things," he paused, "if they can figure out the atomic blast, and I'll lay odds they can. They're no fools, Tweel and his ostrich-faced Martians!"

THE STORIES
OF
PROFESSOR
MANDERPOOTZ

THE WORLDS OF IF

ORIGINALLY PUBLISHED IN *WONDER STORIES*
AUGUST 1935

THE WORLDS OF IF

I stopped on the way to the Staten Island Airport to call up, and that was a mistake, doubtless, since I had a chance of making it otherwise. But the office was affable. "We'll hold the ship five minutes for you," the clerk said. "That's the best we can do."

So I rushed back to my taxi and we spun off to the third level and sped across the Staten bridge like a comet treading a steel rainbow. I had to be in Moscow by evening, by eight o'clock, in fact, for the opening of bids on the Ural Tunnel. The Government required the personal presence of an agent of each bidder, but the firm should have known better than to send me, Dixon Wells, even though the N. J. Wells Corporation is, so to speak, my father. I have a—well, an undeserved reputation for being late to everything; something always comes up to prevent me from getting anywhere on time. It's never my fault; this time it was a chance encounter with my old physics professor, old Haskel van Manderpootz. I couldn't very well just say hello and good-bye to him; I'd been a favorite of his back in the college days of 2014.

I missed the airliner, of course. I was still on the Staten Bridge when I heard the roar of the catapult and the Soviet rocket *Baikal* hummed over us like a tracer bullet with a long tail of flame.

We got the contract anyway; the firm wired our man in Beirut and he flew up to Moscow, but it didn't help my reputation. However, I felt a great deal better when I saw the evening papers; the *Baikal*, flying at the north edge of the eastbound lane to avoid a storm, had locked wings with a British fruitship and all but a hundred of her five hundred passengers were lost. I had almost become "the late Mr. Wells" in a grimmer sense.

I'd made an engagement for the following week with old van Manderpootz. It seems he'd transferred to N.Y.U. as head of the department of Newer Physics—that is, of Relativity. He deserved it; the old chap was a genius if ever there was one, and even now, eight years out of college, I remember more from his course than from half a dozen calculus, steam and gas, mechanics, and other hazards on the path to an engineer's education. So on Tuesday night I dropped in an hour or so late, to tell the truth, since I'd forgotten about the engagement until mid-evening.

He was reading in a room as disorderly as ever. "Humph!" he grunted. "Time changes everything but habit, I see. You were a good student, Dick, but I seem to recall that you always arrived in class toward the middle of the lecture."

"I had a course in East Hall just before," I explained. "I couldn't seem to make it in time."

"Well, it's time you learned to be on time," he growled. Then his eyes twinkled. "Time!" he ejaculated. "The most fascinating word in the language. Here we've used it five times (there goes the sixth time—and the seventh!) in the first minute of conversation; each of us understands the other, yet science is just beginning to learn its meaning. Science? I mean that *I* am beginning to learn."

I sat down. "You and science are synonymous," I grinned. "Aren't you one of the world's outstanding physicists?"

"One of them!" he snorted. "One of them, eh! And who are the others?"

"Oh, Corveille and Hastings and Shrimski—"

"Bah! Would you mention them in the same breath with the name of van Manderpootz? A pack of jackals, eating the crumbs of ideas that drop from my feast of thoughts! Had you gone back into the last century, now—had you mentioned Einstein and de Sitter—there, perhaps, are names worthy to rank with (or just below) van Manderpootz!"

I grinned again in amusement. "Einstein was considered pretty good, wasn't he?" I remarked. "After all, he was the first to tie time and space to the laboratory. Before him they were just philosophical concepts."

"He didn't!" rasped the professor. "Perhaps, in a dim, primitive fashion, he showed the way, but I—*I*, van Manderpootz—am the first to seize time, drag it into my laboratory, and perform an experiment on it."

"Indeed? And what sort of experiment?"

"What experiment, other than simple measurement, is it possible to perform?" he snapped.

"Why—I don't know. To travel in it?"

"Exactly."

"Like these time-machines that are so popular in the current magazines? To go into the future or the past?"

"Bah! Many bahs! The future or the past—pfui! It needs no van Manderpootz to see the fallacy in that. Einstein showed us that much."

"How? It's conceivable, isn't it?"

"Conceivable? And you, Dixon Wells, studied under van Manderpootz!" He grew red with emotion, then grimly calm. "Listen to me. You know how time varies with the speed of a system—Einstein's relativity."

"Yes."

"Very well. Now suppose then that the great engineer Dixon Wells invents a machine capable of traveling very fast, enormously fast, nine-tenths as fast as light. Do you follow? Good. You then fuel this miracle ship for a little jaunt of a half million miles, which, since mass (and with it inertia) increases according to the Einstein formula with increasing speed, takes all the fuel in the world. But you solve that. You use atomic energy. Then, since at nine-tenths light-speed, your ship weighs about as much as the sun, you disintegrate North America to give you sufficient motive power. You start off at that speed, a hundred and sixty-eight thousand miles per second, and you travel for two hundred and four thousand miles. The acceleration has now crushed you to death, but you have penetrated the future." He paused, grinning sardonically. "Haven't you?"

"Yes."

"And how far?"

I hesitated.

"Use your Einstein formula!" he screeched. "How far? I'll tell you. *One second!*" He grinned triumphantly. "That's how possible it is to travel into the future. And as for the past—in the first place, you'd have to exceed light-speed, which immediately entails the use of more than an infinite number of horsepowers. We'll assume that the great engineer Dixon Wells solves that little problem too, even though the energy out-put of the whole universe is not an infinite number of horsepowers. Then he applies this more than infinite power to travel at two hundred and four thousand miles per second for *ten* seconds. He has then penetrated the past. How far?"

Again I hesitated.

"I'll tell you. *One second!*" He glared at me. "Now all you have to do is to design such a machine, and then van Manderpootz will admit the possibility of traveling into the future—for a limited number of seconds. As for the past, I have just explained that all the energy in the universe is insufficient for that."

"But," I stammered, "you just said that you—"

"I did *not* say anything about traveling into either future or past, which I have just demonstrated to you to be impossible—a practical impossibility in the one case and an absolute one in the other."

"Then how *do* you travel in time?"

"Not even van Manderpootz can perform the impossible," said the professor, now faintly jovial. He tapped a thick pad of typewriter paper on the table beside him. "See, Dick, this is the world, the universe." He swept a finger down it. "It is long in time, and"—sweeping his hand across it—"it is broad in space, but"—now jabbing his finger against its center—"it is very thin in the fourth dimension. Van Manderpootz takes always the shortest, the most logical course. I do not travel along time, into past or future. No. Me, I travel across time, sideways!"

I gulped. "Sideways into time! What's there?"

"What would naturally be there?" he snorted. "Ahead is the future; behind is the past. Those are real, the worlds of past and future. What worlds are neither past nor future, but contemporary and yet—extemporal—existing, as it were, in time parallel to our time?"

I shook my head.

"Idiot!" he snapped. "The conditional worlds, of course! The worlds of 'if.' Ahead are the worlds to be; behind are the worlds that were; to either side are the worlds that might have been—the worlds of 'if!'"

"Eh?" I was puzzled. "Do you mean that you can see what will happen if I do such and such?"

"No!" he snorted. "My machine does not reveal the past nor predict the future. It will show, as I told you, the conditional worlds. You might express it, by 'if I had done such and such, so and so would have happened.' The worlds of the subjunctive mode."

"Now how the devil does it do that?"

"Simple, for van Manderpootz! I use polarized light, polarized not in the horizontal or vertical planes, but in the direction of the fourth dimension—an easy matter. One uses Iceland spar under colossal pressures, that is all. And since the worlds are very thin in the direction of the fourth dimension, the thickness of a single light wave, though it be but millionths of an inch, is sufficient. A considerable improvement over time-traveling in past or future, with its impossible velocities and ridiculous distances!"

"But—are those—worlds of 'if'—real?"

"Real? What is real? They are real, perhaps, in the sense that two is a real number as opposed to $\sqrt{2}$, which is imaginary. They are the worlds that would have been *if*— Do you see?"

I nodded. "Dimly. You could see, for instance, what New York would have been like if England had won the Revolution instead of the Colonies."

"That's the principle, true enough, but you couldn't see that on the machine. Part of it, you see, is a Horsten psychomat (stolen from one of my ideas, by the way) and you, the user, become part of the device. Your own mind is necessary to furnish the background. For instance, if George Washington could have used the mechanism after the signing of peace, he could have seen what you suggest. We can't. You can't even see what would have happened if I hadn't invented the thing, but *I* can. Do you understand?"

"Of course. You mean the background has to rest in the past experiences of the user."

"You're growing brilliant," he scoffed. "Yes. The device will show ten hours of what would have happened *if*—condensed, of course, as in a movie, to half an hour's actual time."

"Say, that sounds interesting!"

"You'd like to see it? Is there anything you'd like to find out? Any choice you'd alter?"

"I'll say—a thousand of 'em. I'd like to know what would have happened if I'd sold out my stocks in 2009 instead of '10. I was a millionaire in my own right then, but I was a little—well, a little late in liquidating."

"As usual," remarked van Manderpootz. "Let's go over to the laboratory then."

The professor's quarters were but a block from the campus. He ushered me into the Physics Building, and thence into his own research laboratory, much like the one I had visited during my courses under him. The device—he called it his "subjunctivisor," since it operated in hypothetical worlds— occupied the entire center table. Most of it was merely a Horsten psychomat, but glittering crystalline and glassy was the prism of Iceland spar, the polarizing agent that was the heart of the instrument.

Van Manderpootz pointed to the headpiece. "Put it on," he said, and I sat staring at the screen of the psychomat. I suppose everyone is familiar with the Horsten psychomat; it was as much a fad a few years ago as the ouija board a century back. Yet it isn't just a toy; sometimes, much as the ouija board, it's a real aid to memory. A maze of vague and colored shadows is caused to drift slowly across the screen, and one watches them, meanwhile visualizing whatever scene or circumstances he is trying to remember. He turns a knob that alters the arrangement of lights and shadows, and when, by chance, the design corresponds to his mental picture—presto! There is his scene re-created under his eyes. Of course his own mind adds the details. All the screen actually shows are these tinted blobs of light and shadow, but the thing can be amazingly real. I've seen occasions when I could have sworn the psychomat showed pictures almost as sharp and detailed as reality itself; the illusion is sometimes as startling as that.

Van Manderpootz switched on the light, and the play of shadows began. "Now recall the circumstances of, say, a half-year after the market crash. Turn the knob until the picture clears, then stop. At that point I direct the light of the subjunctivisor upon the screen, and you have nothing to do but watch."

I did as directed. Momentary pictures formed and vanished. The inchoate sounds of the device hummed like distant voices, but without the added suggestion of the picture, they meant nothing. My own face flashed and dissolved and then, finally, I had it. There was a picture of myself sitting in an ill-defined room; that was all. I released the knob and gestured.

A click followed. The light dimmed, then brightened. The picture cleared, and amazingly, another figure emerged, a woman. I recognized her; it was Whimsy White, erstwhile star of television and premiere of the "Vision Varieties of '09." She was changed on that picture, but I recognized her.

I'll say I did! I'd been trailing her all through the boom years of '07 to '10, trying to marry her, while old N. J. raved and ranted and threatened to leave everything to the Society for Rehabilitation of the Gobi Desert. I think those threats were what kept her from accepting me, but after I took my own money and ran it up to a couple of million in that crazy market of '08 and '09, she softened.

Temporarily, that is. When the crash of the spring of '10 came and bounced me back on my father and into the firm of N. J. Wells, her favor dropped a dozen points to the market's one. In February we were engaged, in April we were hardly speaking. In May they sold me out. I'd been late again.

And now, there she was on the psychomat screen, obviously plumping out, and not nearly so pretty as memory had pictured her. She was staring at me with an expression of enmity, and I was glaring back. The buzzes became voices.

"You nit-wit!" she snapped. "You can't bury me out here. I want to go back to New York, where there's a little life. I'm bored with you and your golf."

"And I'm bored with you and your whole dizzy crowd."

"At least they're *alive*. You're a walking corpse. Just because you were lucky enough to gamble yourself into the money, you think you're a tin god."

"Well, I *don't* think *you're* Cleopatra! Those friends of yours—they trail after you because you give parties and spend money—*my* money."

"Better than spending it to knock a white walnut along a mountainside!"

"Indeed? You ought to try it, Marie." (That was her real name.) "It might help your figure—though I doubt if anything could!"

She glared in rage and—well, that was a painful half hour. I won't give all the details, but I was glad when the screen dissolved into meaningless colored clouds.

"Whew!" I said, staring at Van Manderpootz, who had been reading.

"You liked it?"

"Liked it! Say, I guess I was lucky to be cleaned out. I won't regret it from now on."

"That," said the professor grandly, "is van Manderpootz's great contribution to human happiness. 'Of all sad words of tongue or pen, the saddest are these: It might have been!' True no longer, my friend Dick. Van Manderpootz has shown that the proper reading is, 'It might have been—worse!'"

*   *   *   *   *

It was very late when I returned home, and as a result, very late when I rose, and equally late when I got to the office. My father was unnecessarily worked up about it, but he exaggerated when he said I'd never been on time. He forgets the occasions when he's awakened me and dragged me down with him. Nor was it necessary to refer so sarcastically to my missing the *Baikal*; I reminded him of the wrecking of the liner, and he responded very heartlessly that if I'd been aboard, the rocket would have been late, and so would have missed colliding with the British fruitship. It was likewise superfluous for him to mention that when he and I had tried to snatch a few weeks of golfing in the mountains, even the spring had been late. I had nothing to do with that.

"Dixon," he concluded, "you have no conception whatever of time. None whatever."

The conversation with van Manderpootz recurred to me. I was impelled to ask, "And have you, sir?"

"I have," he said grimly. "I most assuredly have. Time," he said oracularly, "is money."

You can't argue with a viewpoint like that.

But those aspersions of his rankled, especially that about the *Baikal*. Tardy I might be, but it was hardly conceivable that my presence aboard the rocket could have averted the catastrophe. It irritated me; in a way, it made me responsible for the deaths of those unrescued hundreds among the passengers and crew, and I didn't like the thought.

Of course, if they'd waited an extra five minutes for me, or if I'd been on time and they'd left on schedule instead of five minutes late, or if—*if!*

If! The word called up van Manderpootz and his subjunctivisor—the worlds of "if," the weird, unreal worlds that existed beside reality, neither past nor future, but contemporary, yet extemporal. Somewhere among their ghostly infinities existed one that represented the world that would have been had I made the liner. I had only to call up Haskel van Manderpootz, make an appointment, and then—find out.

Yet it wasn't an easy decision. Suppose—just suppose that I found myself responsible—not legally responsible, certainly; there'd be no question of criminal negligence, or anything of that sort—not even morally responsible, because I couldn't possibly have anticipated that my presence or absence could weigh so heavily in the scales of life and death, nor could I have known in which direction the scales would tip. Just—responsible; that was all. Yet I hated to find out.

I hated equally not finding out. Uncertainty has its pangs too, quite as painful as those of remorse. It might be less nerve-racking to know myself responsible than to wonder, to waste thoughts in vain doubts and futile reproaches. So I seized the visiphone, dialed the number of the University, and at length gazed on the broad, humorous, intelligent features of van Manderpootz, dragged from a morning lecture by my call.

*   *   *   *   *

I was all but prompt for the appointment the following evening, and might actually have been on time but for an unreasonable traffic officer who insisted on booking me for speeding. At any rate, van Manderpootz was impressed.

"Well!" he rumbled. "I almost missed you, Dixon. I was just going over to the club, since I didn't expect you for an hour. You're only ten minutes late."

I ignored this. "Professor, I want to use your—uh—your subjunctivisor."

"Eh? Oh, yes. You're lucky, then. I was just about to dismantle it."

"Dismantle it! Why?"

"It has served its purpose. It has given birth to an idea far more important than itself. I shall need the space it occupies."

"But what *is* the idea, if it's not too presumptuous of me to ask?"

"It is not too presumptuous. You and the world which awaits it so eagerly may both know, but you hear it from the lips of the author. It is nothing less than the autobiography of van Manderpootz!" He paused impressively.

I gaped. "Your autobiography?"

"Yes. The world, though perhaps unaware, is crying for it. I shall detail my life, my work. I shall reveal myself as the man responsible for the three years' duration of the Pacific War of 2004."

"You?"

"None other. Had I not been a loyal Netherlands subject at that time, and therefore neutral, the forces of Asia would have been crushed in three months instead of three years. The subjunctivisor tells me so; I would have invented a calculator to forecast the chances of every engagement; van Manderpootz would have removed the hit or miss element in the conduct of war." He frowned solemnly. "There is my idea. The autobiography of van Manderpootz. What do you think of it?"

I recovered my thoughts. "It's—uh—it's colossal!" I said vehemently. "I'll buy a copy myself. Several copies. I'll send 'em to my friends."

"I," said van Manderpootz expansively, "shall autograph your copy for you. It will be priceless. I shall write in some fitting phrase, perhaps something like *Magnificus sed non superbus.* 'Great but not proud!' That well described van Manderpootz, who despite his greatness is simple, modest, and unassuming. Don't you agree?"

"Perfectly! A very apt description of you. But—couldn't I see your subjunctivisor before it's dismantled to make way for the greater work?"

"Ah! You wish to find out something?"

"Yes, professor. Do you remember the *Baikal* disaster of a week or two ago? I was to have taken that liner to Moscow. I just missed it." I related the circumstances.

"Humph!" he grunted. "You wish to discover what would have happened had you caught it, eh? Well, I see several possibilities. Among the world of 'if' is the one that would have been real if you had been on time, the one that depended on the vessel waiting for your actual arrival, and the one that hung on your arriving within the five minutes they actually waited. In which are you interested?"

"Oh—the last one." That seemed the likeliest. After all, it was too much to expect that Dixon Wells could ever be on time, and as to the second possibility—well, they *hadn't* waited for me, and that in a way removed the weight of responsibility.

"Come on," rumbled van Manderpootz. I followed him across to the Physics Building and into his littered laboratory. The device still stood on the table and I took my place before it, staring at the screen of the Horsten psychomat. The clouds wavered and shifted as I sought to impress my memories on their suggestive shapes, to read into them some picture of that vanished morning.

Then I had it. I made out the vista from the Staten Bridge, and was speeding across the giant span toward the airport. I waved a signal to van Manderpootz, the thing clicked, and the subjunctivisor was on.

The grassless clay of the field appeared. It is a curious thing about the psychomat that you see only through the eyes of your image on the screen. It lends a strange reality to the working of the toy; I suppose a sort of self-hypnosis is partly responsible.

I was rushing over the ground toward the glittering, silver-winged projectile that was the *Baikal*. A glowering officer waved me on, and I dashed up the slant of the gangplank and into the ship; the port dropped and I heard a long "Whew!" of relief.

"Sit down!" barked the officer, gesturing toward an unoccupied seat. I fell into it; the ship quivered under the thrust of the catapult, grated harshly into motion, and then was flung bodily into the air. The blasts roared instantly, then settled to a more muffled throbbing, and I watched Staten Island drop down and slide back beneath me. The giant rocket was under way.

"Whew!" I breathed again. "Made it!" I caught an amused glance from my right. I was in an aisle seat; there was no one to my left, so I turned to the eyes that had flashed, glanced, and froze staring.

It was a girl. Perhaps she wasn't actually as lovely as she looked to me; after all, I was seeing her through the half-visionary screen of a psychomat. I've told myself since that she *couldn't* have been as pretty as she seemed, that it was due to my own imagination filling in the details. I don't know; I remember only that I stared at curiously lovely silver-blue eyes and velvety brown hair, and a small amused mouth, and an impudent nose. I kept staring until she flushed.

"I'm sorry," I said quickly. "I—was startled."

There's a friendly atmosphere aboard a trans-oceanic rocket. The passengers are forced into a crowded intimacy for anywhere from seven to twelve hours, and there isn't much room for moving about. Generally, one strikes up an acquaintance with his neighbors; introductions aren't at all necessary, and the custom is simply to speak to anybody you choose—something like an all-day trip on the railroad trains of the last century, I suppose. You make friends for the duration of the journey, and then, nine times out of ten, you never hear of your traveling companions again.

The girl smiled. "Are you the individual responsible for the delay in starting?"

I admitted it. "I seem to be chronically late. Even watches lose time as soon as I wear them."

She laughed. "Your responsibilities can't be very heavy."

Well, they weren't of course, though it's surprising how many clubs, caddies, and chorus girls have depended on me at various times for appreciable portions of their incomes. But somehow I didn't feel like mentioning those things to the silvery-eyed girl.

We talked. Her name, it developed, was Joanna Caldwell, and she was going as far as Paris. She was an artist, or hoped to be one day, and of course there is no place in the world that can supply both training and inspiration like Paris. So it was there she was bound for a year of study, and despite her demurely humorous lips and laughing eyes, I could see that the business was of vast importance to her. I gathered that she had worked hard for the year in Paris, had scraped and saved for three years as fashion illustrator for some woman's magazine, though she couldn't have been many months over twenty-one. Her painting meant a great deal to her, and I could understand it. I'd felt that way about polo once.

So you see, we were sympathetic spirits from the beginning. I knew that she liked me, and it was obvious that she didn't connect Dixon Wells with the N. J. Wells Corporation. And as for me—well, after that first glance into her cool silver eyes, I simply didn't care to look anywhere else. The hours seemed to drip away like minutes while I watched her.

You know how those things go. Suddenly I was calling her Joanna and she was calling me Dick, and it seemed as if we'd been doing just that all our lives. I'd decided to stop over in Paris on my way back from Moscow, and I'd secured her promise to let me see her. She was different, I tell you; she was nothing like the calculating Whimsy White, and still less like the dancing, simpering, giddy youngsters one meets around at social affairs. She was just Joanna, cool and humorous, yet sympathetic and serious, and as pretty as a Majolica figurine.

We could scarcely realize it when the steward passed along to take orders for luncheon. Four hours out? It seemed like forty minutes. And we had a pleasant feeling of intimacy in the discovery that both of us liked lobster salad and detested oysters. It was another bond; I told her whimsically that it was an omen, nor did she object to considering it so.

Afterwards we walked along the narrow aisle to the glassed-in observation room up forward. It was almost too crowded for entry, but we didn't mind that at all, as it forced us to sit very close together. We stayed long after both of us had begun to notice the stuffiness of the air.

It was just after we had returned to our seats that the catastrophe occurred. There was no warning save a sudden lurch, the result, I suppose, of the pilot's futile last-minute attempt to swerve—just that and then a grinding crash and a terrible sensation of spinning, and after that a chorus of shrieks that were like the sounds of battle.

It *was* battle. Five hundred people were picking themselves up from the floor, were trampling each other, milling around, being cast helplessly down as the great rocket-plane, its left wing but a broken stub, circled downward toward the Atlantic.

The shouts of officers sounded and a loudspeaker blared. "Be calm," it kept repeating, and then, "There has been a collision. We have contacted a surface ship. There is no danger— There is no danger—"

I struggled up from the debris of shattered seats. Joanna was gone; just as I found her crumpled between the rows, the ship struck the water with a jar that set everything crashing again. The speaker blared, "Put on the cork belts under the seats. The life-belts are under the seats."

I dragged a belt loose and snapped it around Joanna, then donned one myself. The crowd was surging forward now, and the tail end of the ship began to drop. There was water behind us, sloshing in the darkness as the lights went out. An officer came sliding by, stooped, and fastened a belt about an unconscious woman ahead of us. "You all right?" he yelled, and passed on without waiting for an answer.

The speaker must have been cut on to a battery circuit. "And get as far away as possible," it ordered suddenly. "Jump from the forward port and get as far away as possible. A ship is standing by. You will be picked up. Jump from the—". It went dead again.

I got Joanna untangled from the wreckage. She was pale; her silvery eyes were closed. I started dragging her slowly and painfully toward the forward port, and the slant of the floor increased until it was like the slide of a ski-jump. The officer passed again. "Can you handle her?" he asked, and again dashed away.

I was getting there. The crowd around the port looked smaller, or was it simply huddling closer? Then suddenly, a wail of fear and despair went up, and there was a roar of water. The observation room walls had given. I saw the green surge of waves, and a billowing deluge rushed down upon us. I had been late again.

That was all. I raised shocked and frightened eyes from the subjunctivisor to face van Manderpootz, who was scribbling on the edge of the table.

"Well?" he asked.

I shuddered. "Horrible!" I murmured. "We—I guess we wouldn't have been among the survivors."

"We, eh? *We?*" His eyes twinkled.

I did not enlighten him. I thanked him, bade him good-night, and went dolorously home.

*   *   *   *   *

Even my father noticed something queer about me. The day I got to the office only five minutes late, he called me in for some anxious questioning as to my health. I couldn't tell him anything, of course. How could I explain that I'd been late once too often, and had fallen in love with a girl two weeks after she was dead?

The thought drove me nearly crazy. Joanna! Joanna with her silvery eyes now lay somewhere at the bottom of the Atlantic. I went around half dazed, scarcely speaking. One night I actually lacked the energy to go home and sat smoking in my father's big overstuffed chair in his private office until I finally dozed off. The next morning, when old N. J. entered and found me there before him, he turned pale as paper, staggered, and gasped, "My heart!" It took a lot of explaining to convince him that I wasn't early at the office but just very late going home.

At last I felt that I couldn't stand it. I had to do something—anything at all. I thought finally of the subjunctivisor. I could see—yes, I could see what would have transpired if the ship hadn't been wrecked! I could trace out that weird, unreal romance hidden somewhere in the worlds of "if". I could, perhaps, wring a somber, vicarious joy from the things that might have been. I could see Joanna once more!

It was late afternoon when I rushed over to van Manderpootz's quarters. He wasn't there; I encountered him finally in the hall of the Physics Building.

"Dick!" he exclaimed. "Are you sick?"

"Sick? No. Not physically. Professor. I've got to use your subjunctivisor again. I've *got* to!"

"Eh? Oh—that toy. You're too late, Dick. I've dismantled it. I have a better use for the space."

I gave a miserable groan and was tempted to damn the autobiography of the great van Manderpootz. A gleam of sympathy showed in his eyes, and he took my arm, dragging me into the little office adjoining his laboratory.

"Tell me," he commanded.

I did. I guess I made the tragedy plain enough, for his heavy brows knit in a frown of pity. "Not even van Manderpootz can bring back the dead," he murmured. "I'm sorry, Dick. Take your mind from the affair. Even were my subjunctivisor available, I wouldn't permit you to use it. That would be but to turn the knife in the wound." He paused. "Find something else to occupy your mind. Do as van Manderpootz does. Find forgetfulness in work."

"Yes," I responded dully. "But who'd want to read my autobiography? That's all right for you."

"Autobiography? Oh! I remember. No, I have abandoned that. History itself will record the life and works of van Manderpootz. Now I am engaged in a far grander project."

"Indeed?" I was utterly, gloomily disinterested.

"Yes. Gogli has been here, Gogli the sculptor. He is to make a bust of me. What better legacy can I leave to the world than a bust of van Manderpootz, sculptured from life? Perhaps I shall present it to the city, perhaps to the university. I would have given it to the Royal Society if they had been a little more receptive, if they—if—*if!*" The last in a shout.

"Huh?"

"*If!*" cried van Manderpootz. "What you saw in the subjunctivisor was what would have happened *if* you had caught the ship!"

"I know that."

"But something quite different might really have happened! Don't you see? She—she— Where are those old newspapers?"

He was pawing through a pile of them. He flourished one finally. "Here! Here are the survivors!"

Like letters of flame, Joanna Caldwell's name leaped out at me. There was even a little paragraph about it, as I saw once my reeling brain permitted me to read:

"At least a score of survivors owe their lives to the bravery of twenty-eight-year-old Navigator Orris Hope, who patrolled both aisles during the panic, lacing life-belts on the injured and helpless, and carrying many to the port. He remained on the sinking liner until the last, finally fighting his way to the surface through the broken walls of the observation room. Among those who owe their lives to the young officer are: Patrick Owensby,

New York City; Mrs. Campbell Warren, Boston; Miss Joanna Caldwell, New York City—"

I suppose my shout of joy was heard over in the Administration Building, blocks away. I didn't care; if van Manderpootz hadn't been armored in stubby whiskers, I'd have kissed him. Perhaps I did anyway; I can't be sure of my actions during those chaotic minutes in the professor's tiny office.

At last I calmed. "I can look her up!" I gloated. "She must have landed with the other survivors, and they were all on that British tramp freighter the *Osgood*, that docked here last week. She must be in New York—and if she's gone over to Paris, I'll find out and follow her!"

Well, it's a queer ending. She was in New York, but—you see, Dixon Wells had, so to speak, known Joanna Caldwell by means of the professor's subjunctivisor, but Joanna had never known Dixon Wells. What the ending might have been if—*if*— But it wasn't; she had married Orris Hope, the young officer who had rescued her. I was late again.

THE IDEAL

ORIGINALLY PUBLISHED IN *WONDER STORIES*
SEPTEMBER 1935

THE IDEAL

"This," said the Franciscan, "is my Automaton, who at the proper time will speak, answer whatsoever question I may ask, and reveal all secret knowledge to me." He smiled as he laid his hand affectionately on the iron skull that topped the pedestal.

The youth gazed open-mouthed, first at the head and then at the Friar. "But it's iron!" he whispered. "The head is iron, good father."

"Iron without, skill within, my son," said Roger Bacon. "It will speak, at the proper time and in its own manner, for so have I made it. A clever man can twist the devil's arts to God's ends, thereby cheating the fiend—Sst! There sounds vespers! Plena gratia, ave Virgo—"

But it did not speak. Long hours, long weeks, the doctor mirabilis watched his creation, but iron lips were silent and the iron eyes dull, and no voice but the great man's own sounded in his monkish cell, nor was there ever an answer to all the questions that he asked—until one day when he sat surveying his work, composing a letter to Duns Scotus in distant Cologne—one day—

"Time is!" said the image, and smiled benignly.

The Friar looked up. "Time is, indeed," he echoed. "Time it is that you give utterance, and to some assertion less obvious than that time is. For of course time is, else there were nothing at all. Without time—"

"Time was!" rumbled the image, still smiling, but sternly at the statue of Draco.

"Indeed time was," said the Monk. "Time was, is, and will be, for time is that medium in which events occur. Matter exists in space, but events—"

The image smiled no longer. "Time is past!" it roared in tones deep as the cathedral bell outside, and burst into ten thousand pieces.

*   *   *   *   *

"There," said old Haskel van Manderpootz, shutting the book, "is my classical authority in this experiment. This story, overlaid as it is with mediaeval myth and legend, proves that Roger Bacon himself attempted the experiment—and failed." He shook a long finger at me. "Yet do not get the impression, Dixon, that Friar Bacon was not a great man. He was—extremely great, in fact; he lighted the torch that his namesake Francis Bacon took up four centuries later, and that now van Manderpootz rekindles."

I stared in silence.

"Indeed," resumed the Professor, "Roger Bacon might almost be called a thirteenth century van Manderpootz, or van Manderpootz a twenty-first century Roger Bacon. His *Opus Majus, Opus Minus*, and *Opus Tertium*—"

"What," I interrupted impatiently, "has all this to do with—that?" I indicated the clumsy metal robot standing in the corner of the laboratory.

"Don't interrupt!" snapped van Manderpootz. "I'll—"

At this point I fell out of my chair. The mass of metal had ejaculated something like "*A-a-gh-rasp*" and had lunged a single pace toward the window, arms upraised. "What the devil!" I sputtered as the thing dropped its arms and returned stolidly to its place.

"A car must have passed in the alley," said van Manderpootz indifferently. "Now as I was saying, Roger Bacon—"

I ceased to listen. When van Manderpootz is determined to finish a statement, interruptions are worse than futile. As an ex-student of his, I know. So I permitted my thoughts to drift to certain personal problems of my own, particularly Tips Alva, who was the most pressing problem of the moment. Yes, I mean Tips Alva the 'vision dancer, the little blonde imp who entertains on the Yerba Mate hour for that Brazilian company. Chorus girls, dancers, and television stars are a weakness of mine; maybe it indicates that there's a latent artistic soul in me. Maybe.

I'm Dixon Wells, you know, scion of the N. J. Wells Corporation, Engineers Extraordinary. I'm supposed to be an engineer myself; I say supposed, because in the seven years since my graduation, my father hasn't given me much opportunity to prove it. He has a strong sense of value of time, and I'm cursed with the unenviable quality of being late to anything and for everything. He even asserts that the occasional designs I submit are late Jacobean, but that isn't fair. They're Post-Romanesque.

Old N. J. also objects to my penchant for ladies of the stage and 'vision screen, and periodically threatens to cut my allowance, though that's supposed to be a salary. It's inconvenient to be so dependent, and sometimes I regret that unfortunate market crash of 2009 that wiped out my own money, although it did keep me from marrying Whimsy White, and van Manderpootz, through his subjunctivisor, succeeded in proving that that would have been a catastrophe. But it turned out nearly as much of a disaster anyway, as far as my feelings were concerned. It took me months to forget Joanna Caldwell and her silvery eyes. Just another instance when I was a little late.

Van Manderpootz himself is my old Physics Professor, head of the Department of Newer Physics at N. Y. U., and a genius, but a bit eccentric. Judge for yourself.

"And that's the thesis," he said suddenly, interrupting my thoughts.

"Eh? Oh, of course. But what's that grinning robot got to do with it?"

He purpled. "I've just told you!" he roared. "Idiot! Imbecile! To dream while van Manderpootz talks! Get out! Get out!"

I got. It was late anyway, so late that I overslept more than usual in the morning, and suffered more than the usual lecture on promptness from my father at the office.

*   *   *   *   *

Van Manderpootz had forgotten his anger by the next time I dropped in for an evening. The robot still stood in the corner near the window, and I lost no time asking its purpose.

"It's just a toy I had some of the students construct," he explained. "There's a screen of photoelectric cells behind the right eye, so connected that when a certain pattern is thrown on them, it activates the mechanism. The thing's plugged into the light-circuit, but it really ought to run on gasoline."

"Why?"

"Well, the pattern it's set for is the shape of an automobile. See here." He picked up a card from his desk, and cut in the outlines of a streamlined car like those of that year. "Since only one eye is used," he continued, "The thing can't tell the difference between a full-sized vehicle at a distance and this small outline nearby. It has no sense of perspective."

He held the bit of cardboard before the eye of the mechanism. Instantly came its roar of "*A-a-gh-rasp!*" and it leaped forward a single pace, arms upraised. Van Manderpootz withdrew the card, and again the thing relapsed stolidly into its place.

"What the devil!" I exclaimed. "What's it for?"

"Does van Manderpootz ever do work without reason back of it? I use it as a demonstration in my seminar."

"To demonstrate what?"

"The power of reason," said van Manderpootz solemnly.

"How? And why ought it to work on gasoline instead of electric power?"

"One question at a time, Dixon. You have missed the grandeur of van Manderpootz's concept. See here, this creature, imperfect as it is, represents the predatory machine. It is the mechanical parallel of the tiger, lurking in its jungle to leap on living prey. *This* monster's jungle is the city; its prey is the unwary machine that follows the trails called streets. Understand?"

"No."

"Well, picture this automaton, not as it is, but as van Manderpootz could make it if he wished. It lurks gigantic in the shadows of buildings; it creeps stealthily through dark alleys; it skulks on deserted streets, with its gasoline engine purring quietly. Then—an unsuspecting automobile flashes its image on the screen behind its eyes. It leaps. It seizes its prey, swinging it in steel arms to its steel jaws. Through the metal throat of its victim crash steel teeth; the blood of its prey—the gasoline, that is—is drained into its stomach, or its gas-tank. With renewed strength it flings away the husk and prowls on to seek other prey. It is the machine-carnivore, the tiger of mechanics."

I suppose I stared dumbly. It occurred to me suddenly that the brain of the great van Manderpootz was cracking. "What the—?" I gasped.

"That," he said blandly, "is but a concept. I have many another use for the toy. I can prove anything with it, anything I wish."

"You can? Then prove something."

"Name your proposition, Dixon."

I hesitated, nonplussed.

"Come!" he said impatiently. "Look here; I will prove that anarchy is the ideal government, or that Heaven and Hell are the same place, or that—"

"Prove that!" I said. "About Heaven and Hell."

"Easily. First we will endow my robot with intelligence. I add a mechanical memory by means of the old Cushman delayed valve; I add a mathematical sense with any of the calculating machines; I give it a voice and a vocabulary with the magnetic-impulse wire phonograph. Now the point I make is this: Granted an intelligent machine, does it not follow that every other machine constructed like it must have the identical qualities? Would not each robot given the same insides have exactly the same character?"

"No!" I snapped. "Human beings can't make two machines exactly alike. There'd be tiny differences; one would react quicker than others, or one would prefer Fox Airsplitters as prey, while another reacted most vigorously to Carnecars. In other words, they'd have—*individuality*!" I grinned in triumph.

"My point exactly," observed van Manderpootz. "You admit, then, that this individuality is the result of imperfect workmanship. If our means of manufacture were perfect, all robots would be identical, and this individuality would not exist. Is that true?"

"I—suppose so."

"Then I argue that our own individuality is due to our falling short of perfection. All of us—even van Manderpootz—are individuals only because we are not perfect. Were we perfect, each of us would be exactly like everyone else. True?"

"Uh—yes."

"But Heaven, by definition, is a place where all is perfect. Therefore, in Heaven everybody is exactly like everybody else, and *therefore*, everybody is thoroughly and completely bored! There is no torture like boredom, Dixon, and—Well, have I proved my point?"

I was floored. "But—about anarchy, then?" I stammered.

"Simple. Very simple for van Manderpootz. See here; with a perfect nation—that is, one whose individuals are all exactly alike, which I have just proved to constitute perfection—with a perfect nation, I repeat, laws and government are utterly superfluous. If everybody reacts to stimuli in the same way, laws are quite useless, obviously. If, for instance, a certain event occurred that might lead to a declaration of war, why, everybody in such a nation would vote for war at the same instant. Therefore government is unnecessary, and therefore anarchy is the ideal government, since it is the proper government for a perfect race." He paused. "I shall now prove that anarchy is *not* the ideal government—"

"Never mind!" I begged. "Who am I to argue with van Manderpootz? But is *that* the whole purpose of this dizzy robot? Just a basis for logic?" The mechanism replied with its usual rasp as it leaped toward some vagrant car beyond the window.

"Isn't that enough?" growled van Manderpootz. "However,"— his voice dropped—"I have even a greater destiny in mind. My boy, van Manderpootz has solved the riddle of the universe!" He paused impressively. "Well, why don't you say something?"

"Uh!" I gasped. "It's—uh—marvelous!"

"Not for van Manderpootz," he said modestly.

"But—what is it?"

"Eh—Oh!" He frowned. "Well, I'll tell you, Dixon. You won't understand, but I'll tell you." He coughed. "As far back as the early twentieth century," he resumed, "Einstein proved that energy is particular. Matter is also particular, and now van Manderpootz adds that space and time are discrete!" He glared at me.

"Energy and matter are particular," I murmured, "and space and time are discrete! How very moral of them!"

"Imbecile!" he blazed. "To pun on the words of van Manderpootz! You know very well that I mean particular and discrete in the physical sense. Matter is composed of particles, therefore it is particular. The particles of matter are called electrons, protons, and neutrons, and those of energy, quanta. I now add two others, the particles of space I call spations, those of time, chronons."

"And what in the devil," I asked, "are particles of space and time?"

"Just what I said!" snapped van Manderpootz. "Exactly as the particles of matter are the smallest pieces of matter that can exist, just as there is no such thing as a half of an electron, or for that matter, half a quantum, so the chronon is the smallest possible fragment of time, and the spation the smallest possible bit of space. Neither time nor space is continuous; each is composed of these infinitely tiny fragments."

"Well, how long is a chronon in time? How big is a spation in space?"

"Van Manderpootz has even measured that. A chronon is the length of time it takes one quantum of energy to push one electron from one electronic orbit to the next. There can obviously be no shorter interval of time, since an electron is the smallest unit of matter and the quantum the smallest unit of energy. And a spation is the exact volume of a proton. Since nothing smaller exists, that is obviously the smallest unit of space."

"Well, look here," I argued. "Then what's in between these particles of space and time? If time moves, as you say, in jerks of one chronon each, what's between the jerks?"

"Ah!" said the great van Manderpootz. "Now we come to the heart of the matter. In between the particles of space and time, must obviously be something that is neither space, time, matter, nor energy. A hundred years ago Shapley anticipated van Manderpootz in a vague way when he announced his cosmo-plasma, the great underlying matrix in which time and space and the universe are embedded. Now van Manderpootz announces the ultimate unit, the universal particle, the focus in which matter, energy, time, and space meet, the unit from which electrons, protons, neutrons, quanta, spations, and chronons are all constructed. The riddle of the universe is solved by what I have chosen to name the cosmon." His blue eyes bored into me.

"Magnificent!" I said feebly, knowing that some such word was expected. "But what good is it?"

"What good is it?" he roared. "It provides—or will provide, once I work out a few details—the means of turning energy into time, or space into matter, or time into space, or—" He sputtered into silence. "Fool!" he muttered. "To think that you studied under the tutelage of van Manderpootz. I blush; I actually blush!"

One couldn't have told it if he were blushing. His face was always rubicund enough. "Colossal!" I said hastily. "What a mind!"

That mollified him. "But that's not all," he proceeded. "Van Manderpootz never stops short of perfection. I now announce the unit particle of thought—the psychon!"

This was a little too much. I simply stared.

"Well may you be dumbfounded," said van Manderpootz. "I presume you are aware, by hearsay at least, of the existence of thought. The psychon, the unit of thought, is one electron plus one proton, which are bound so as to form one neutron, embedded in one cosmon, occupying a volume of one spation, driven by one quantum for a period of one chronon. Very obvious; very simple."

"Oh, very!" I echoed. "Even I can see that that equals one psychon."

He beamed. "Excellent! Excellent!"

"And what," I asked, "will you do with the psychons?"

"Ah," he rumbled. "Now we go even *past* the heart of the matter, and return to Isaak here." He jammed a thumb toward the robot. "Here I will create Roger Bacon's mechanical head. In the skull of this clumsy creature will rest such intelligence as not even van Manderpootz—I should say, as *only* van Manderpootz—can conceive. It remains merely to construct my idealizator."

"Your idealizator?"

"Of course. Have I not just proven that thoughts are as real as matter, energy, time, or space? Have I not just demonstrated that one can be transformed, through the cosmon, into any other? My idealizator is the means of transforming psychons to quanta, just as, for instance, a Crookes tube or X-ray tube transforms matter to electrons. I will make your thoughts visible! And not your thoughts as they are in that numb brain of yours, but in *ideal* form. Do you see? The psychons of your mind are the same as those from any other mind, just as all electrons are identical, whether from gold or iron. Yes! Your psychons"—his voice quavered—"are identical with those from the mind of—van Manderpootz!" He paused, shaken.

"Actually?" I gasped.

"Actually. Fewer in number, of course, but identical. Therefore, my idealizator shows your thought released from the impress of your personality. It shows it—ideal!"

Well, I was late to the office again.

*   *   *   *   *

A week later I thought of van Manderpootz. Tips was on tour somewhere, and I didn't dare take anyone else out because I'd tried it once before and she'd heard about it. So, with nothing to do, I finally dropped around to the professor's quarter, found him missing, and eventually located him in his laboratory at the Physics Building. He was puttering around the table that had once held that damned subjunctivisor of his, but now it supported an indescribable mess of tubes and tangled wires, and as its most striking feature, a circular plane mirror etched with a grating of delicately scratched lines.

"Good evening, Dixon," he rumbled.

I echoed his greeting. "What's that?" I asked.

"My idealizator. A rough model, much too clumsy to fit into Isaak's iron skull. I'm just finishing it to try it out." He turned glittering blue eyes on me. "How fortunate that you're here. It will save the world a terrible risk."

"A risk?"

"Yes. It is obvious that too long an exposure to the device will extract too many psychons, and leave the subject's mind in a sort of moronic condition. I was about to accept the risk, but I see now that it would be woefully unfair to the world to endanger the mind of van Manderpootz. But you are at hand, and will do very well."

"Oh, no I won't!"

"Come, come!" he said, frowning. "The danger is negligible. In fact, I doubt whether the device will be able to extract *any* psychons from *your* mind. At any rate, you will be perfectly safe for a period of at least half an hour. I, with a vastly more productive mind, could doubtless stand the strain indefinitely, but my responsibility to the world is too great to chance it until I have tested the machine on someone else. You should be proud of the honor."

"Well, I'm not!" But my protest was feeble, and after all, despite his overbearing mannerisms, I knew van Manderpootz liked me, and I was positive he would not have exposed me to any real danger. In the end I found myself seated before the table facing the etched mirror.

"Put your face against the barrel," said van Manderpootz, indicating a stove-pipe-like tube. "That's merely to cut off extraneous sights, so that you can see only the mirror. Go ahead, I tell you! It's no more than the barrel of a telescope or microscope."

I complied. "Now what?" I asked.

"What do you see?"

"My own face in the mirror."

"Of course. Now I start the reflector rotating." There was a faint whir, and the mirror was spinning smoothly, still with only a slightly blurred image of myself. "Listen, now," continued van Manderpootz. "Here is what you are to do. You will think of a generic noun. 'House,' for instance. If you think of house, you will see, not an individual house, but your ideal house, the house of all your dreams and desires. If you think of a horse, you will see what your mind conceives as the perfect horse, such a horse as dream and longing create. Do you understand? Have you chosen a topic?"

"Yes." After all, I was only twenty-eight; the noun I had chosen was—girl.

"Good," said the professor. "I turn on the current."

There was a blue radiance behind the mirror. My own face still stared back at me from the spinning surface, but something was forming behind it, building up, growing. I blinked; when I focused my eyes again, it was—*she* was—there.

Lord! I can't begin to describe her. I don't even know if I saw her clearly the first time. It was like looking into another world and seeing the embodiment of all longings, dreams, aspirations, and ideals. It was so poignant a sensation that it crossed the borderline into pain. It was—well, exquisite torture or agonized delight. It was at once unbearable and irresistible.

But I gazed. I had to. There was a haunting familiarity about the impossibly beautiful features. I had seen the face—somewhere—sometime. In dreams? No; I realized suddenly what was the source of that familiarity. This was no living woman, but a synthesis. Her nose was the tiny, impudent one of Whimsy White at her loveliest moment; her lips were the perfect bow of Tips Alva; her silvery eyes and dusky velvet hair were those of Joan Caldwell. But the aggregate, the sum total, the face in the mirror—that was none of these; it was a face impossibly, incredibly, outrageously beautiful.

Only her face and throat were visible, and the features were cool, expressionless, and still as a carving. I wandered suddenly if she could smile, and with the thought, she did. If she had been beautiful before, now her beauty flamed to such a pitch that it was—well, insolent; it was an affront to be so lovely; it was insulting. I felt a wild surge of anger that the image before me should flaunt such beauty, and yet be—*non-existent*! It was deception, cheating, fraud, a promise that could never be fulfilled.

Anger died in the depths of that fascination. I wondered what the rest of her was like, and instantly she moved gracefully back until her full figure was visible. I must be a prude at heart, for she wasn't wearing the usual cuirass-and-shorts of that year, but an iridescent four-paneled costume that all but concealed her dainty knees. But her form was slim and erect as a column of cigarette smoke in still air, and I knew that she could dance like a fragment of mist on water. And with that thought she did move, dropping in a low curtsy, and looking up with the faintest possible flush crimsoning the curve of her throat. Yes, I must be a prude at heart; despite Tips Alva and Whimsy White and the rest, my ideal was modest.

It was unbelievable that the mirror was simply giving back my thoughts. She seemed as real as myself, and—after all—I guess she was. As real as myself, no more, no less, because she was part of my own mind. And at this point I realized that van Manderpootz was shaking me and bellowing, "Your time's up. Come out of it! Your half-hour's up!"

He must have switched off the current. The image faded, and I took my face from the tube, dropping it on my arms.

"O-o-o-o-o-oh!" I groaned.

"How do you feel?" he snapped.

"Feel? All right—physically." I looked up.

Concern flickered in his blue eyes. "What's the cube root of 4913?" he crackled sharply.

I've always been quick at figures. "It's—uh—17," I returned dully. "Why the devil—?"

"You're all right mentally," he announced. "Now—why were you sitting there like a dummy for half an hour? My idealizator must have worked, as is only natural for a van Manderpootz creation, but what were you thinking of?"

"I thought—I thought of 'girl'," I groaned.

He snorted. "Hah! You would, you idiot! 'House' or 'horse' wasn't good enough; you had to pick something with emotional connotations. Well, you can start right in forgetting her, because she doesn't exist."

I couldn't give up hope, as easily as that. "But can't you—can't you—?" I didn't even know what I meant to ask.

"Van Manderpootz," he announced, "is a mathematician, not a magician. Do you expect me to materialize an ideal for you?" When I had no reply but a groan, he continued. "Now I think it safe enough to try the device myself. I shall take—let's see—the thought 'man.' I shall see what the superman looks like, since the ideal of van Manderpootz can be nothing less than superman." He seated himself. "Turn that switch," he said. "Now!"

I did. The tubes glowed into low blue light. I watched dully, disinterestedly; nothing held any attraction for me after that image of the ideal.

"Huh!" said van Manderpootz suddenly. "Turn it on, I say! I see nothing but my own reflection."

I stared, then burst into a hollow laugh. The mirror was spinning; the banks of tubes were glowing; the device was operating.

Van Manderpootz raised his face, a little redder than usual. I laughed half hysterically. "After all," he said huffily, "one might have a lower ideal of man than van Manderpootz. I see nothing nearly so humorous as your situation."

The laughter died. I went miserably home, spent half the remainder of the night in morose contemplation, smoked nearly two packs of cigarettes, and didn't get to the office at all the next day.

*   *   *   *   *

Tips Alva got back to town for a week-end broadcast, but I didn't even bother to see her, just phoned her and told her I was sick. I guess my face lent credibility to the story, for she was duly sympathetic, and her face in the phone screen was quite anxious. Even at that, I couldn't keep my eyes away from her lips because, except for a bit too lustrous make-up, they were the lips of the ideal. But they weren't enough; they just weren't enough.

Old N. J. began to worry again. I couldn't sleep late of mornings any more, and after missing that one day, I kept getting down earlier and earlier until one morning I was only ten minutes late. He called me in at once.

"Look here, Dixon," he said. "Have you been to a doctor recently?"

"I'm not sick," I said listlessly.

"Then for Heaven's sake, marry the girl! I don't care what chorus she kicks in, marry her and act like a human being again."

"I—can't."

"Oh. She's already married, eh?"

Well, I couldn't tell him she didn't exist. I couldn't say I was in love with a vision, a dream, an ideal. He thought I was a little crazy, anyway, so I just muttered "Yeah," and didn't argue when he said gruffly: "Then you'll get over it. Take a vacation. Take *two* vacations. You might as well for all the good you are around here."

I didn't leave New York; I lacked the energy. I just mooned around the city for a while, avoiding my friends, and dreaming of the impossible beauty of the face in the mirror. And by and by the longing to see that vision of perfection once more began to become overpowering. I don't suppose anyone except me can understand the lure of that memory; the face, you see, had been my ideal, my concept of perfection. One sees beautiful women here and there in the world; one falls in love, but always, no matter how great their beauty or how deep one's love, they fall short in some degree of the secret vision of the ideal. But not the mirrored face; she was my ideal, and therefore, whatever imperfections she might have had in the minds of others, in my eyes she had none. None, that is, save the terrible one of being only an ideal, and therefore unattainable—but that is a fault inherent in all perfection.

It was a matter of days before I yielded. Common sense told me it was futile, even foolhardy, to gaze again on the vision of perfect desirability. I fought against the hunger, but I fought hopelessly, and was not at all surprised to find myself one evening rapping on van Manderpootz's door in the University Club. He wasn't there; I'd been hoping he wouldn't be, since it gave me an excuse to seek him in his laboratory in the Physics Building, to which I would have dragged him anyway.

There I found him, writing some sort of notations on the table that held the idealizator. "Hello, Dixon," he said. "Did it ever occur to you that the ideal university cannot exist? Naturally not since it must be composed of perfect students and perfect educators, in which case the former could have nothing to learn and the latter, therefore, nothing to teach."

What interest had I in the perfect university and its inability to exist? My whole being was desolate over the non-existence of another ideal. "Professor," I said tensely, "may I use that—that thing of yours again? I want to—uh—see something."

My voice must have disclosed the situation, for van Manderpootz looked up sharply. "So!" he snapped. "So you disregarded my advice! Forget her, I said. Forget her because she doesn't exist."

"But—I can't! Once more, Professor—only once more!"

He shrugged, but his blue, metallic eyes were a little softer than usual. After all, for some inconceivable reason, he likes me. "Well, Dixon," he said, "you're of age and supposed to be of mature intelligence. I tell you that this is a very stupid request, and van Manderpootz always knows what he's talking about. If you want to stupefy yourself with the opium of impossible dreams, go ahead. This is the last chance you'll have, for tomorrow the idealizator of van Manderpootz goes into the Bacon head of Isaak there. I shall shift the oscillators so that the psychons, instead of becoming light quanta, emerge as an electron flow—a current which will actuate Isaak's vocal apparatus and come out as speech." He paused musingly. "Van Manderpootz will hear the voice of the ideal. Of course Isaak can return only what psychons he receives from the brain of the operator, but just as the image in the mirror, the thoughts will have lost their human impress, and the words will be those of an ideal." He perceived that I wasn't listening, I suppose. "Go ahead, imbecile!" he grunted.

I did. The glory that I hungered after flamed slowly into being, incredible in loveliness, and somehow, unbelievably, even more beautiful than on that other occasion. I know why now; long afterwards, van Manderpootz explained that the very fact that I had seen an ideal once before had altered my ideal, raised it to a higher level. With that face among my memories, my concept of perfection was different than it had been.

So I gazed and hungered. Readily and instantly the being in the mirror responded to my thoughts with smile and movement. When I thought of love, her eyes blazed with such tenderness that it seemed as if—I—I, Dixon Wells—were part of those pairs who had made the great romances of the world, Heloise and Abelard, Tristram and Isolde, Aucassin and Nicolette. It was like the thrust of a dagger to feel van Manderpootz shaking me, to hear his gruff voice calling, "Out of it! Out of it! Time's up."

I groaned and dropped my face on my hands. The Professor had been right, of course; this insane repetition had only intensified an unfulfillable longing, and had made a bad mess ten times as bad. Then I heard him muttering behind me. "Strange!" he murmured. "In fact, fantastic. Oedipus—oedipus of the magazine covers and billboards."

I looked dully around. He was standing behind me, squinting, apparently, into the spinning mirror beyond the end of the black tube. "Huh?" I grunted wearily.

"That face," he said. "Very queer. You must have seen her features on a hundred magazines, on a thousand billboards, on countless 'vision broadcasts. The oedipus complex in a curious form."

"Eh? Could *you* see her?"

"Of course!" he grunted. "Didn't I say a dozen times that the psychons are transmuted to perfectly ordinary quanta of visible light? If you could see her, why not I?"

"But—what about billboards and all?"

"That face," said the professor slowly. "It's somewhat idealized, of course, and certain details are wrong. Her eyes aren't that pallid silver-blue you imagined; they're green—sea-green, emerald colored."

"What the devil," I asked hoarsely, "are you talking about?"

"About the face in the mirror. It happens to be, Dixon, a close approximation of the features of de Lisle d'Agrion, the Dragon Fly!"

"You mean—she's real? She exists? She lives? She—"

"Wait a moment, Dixon. She's real enough, but in accordance with your habit, you're a little late. About twenty-five years too late, I should say. She must now be somewhere in the fifties— let's see—fifty-three, I think. But during your very early childhood, you must have seen her face pictured everywhere, de Lisle d'Agrion, the Dragon Fly."

I could only gulp. That blow was devastating.

"You see," continued van Manderpootz, "one's ideals are implanted very early. That's why you continually fall in love with girls who possess one or another feature that reminds you of her, her hair, her nose, her mouth, her eyes. Very simple, but rather curious."

"Curious!" I blazed. "Curious, you say! Everytime I look into one of your damned contraptions I find myself in love with a myth! A girl who's dead, or married, or unreal, or turned into an old woman! Curious, eh? Damned funny, isn't it?"

"Just a moment," said the professor placidly. "It happens, Dixon, that she has a daughter. What's more, Denise resembles her mother. And what's still more, she's arriving in New York next week to study American letters at the University here. She writes, you see."

That was too much for immediate comprehension. "How— how do you know?" I gasped.

It was one of the few times I have seen the colossal blandness of van Manderpootz ruffled. He reddened a trifle, and said slowly, "It also happens, Dixon, that many years ago in Amsterdam, Haskel van Manderpootz and de Lisle d'Agrion were—very friendly—more than friendly, I might say, but for the fact that two such powerful personalities as the Dragon Fly and van Manderpootz were always at odds." He frowned. "I was almost her second husband. She's had seven, I believe; Denise is the daughter of her third."

"Why—why is she coming here?"

"Because," he said with dignity, "van Manderpootz is here. I am still a friend of de Lisle's." He turned and bent over the complex device on the table. "Hand me that wrench," he ordered. "Tonight I dismantle this, and tomorrow start reconstructing it for Isaak's head."

*   *   *   *   *

But when, the following week, I rushed eagerly back to van Manderpootz's laboratory, the idealizator was still in place. The professor greeted me with a humorous twist to what was visible of his bearded mouth. "Yes, it's still here," he said, gesturing at the device. "I've decided to build an entirely new one for Isaak, and besides, this one has afforded me considerable amusement. Furthermore, in the words of Oscar Wilde, who am I to tamper with a work of genius. After all, the mechanism is the product of the great van Manderpootz."

He was deliberately tantalizing me. He knew that I hadn't come to hear him discourse on Isaak, or even on the incomparable van Manderpootz. Then he smiled and softened, and turned to the little inner office adjacent, the room where Isaak stood in metal austerity. "Denise!" he called, "come here."

I don't know exactly what I expected, but I do know that the breath left me as the girl entered. She wasn't exactly my image of the ideal, of course; she was perhaps the merest trifle slimmer, and her eyes—well, they must have been much like those of de Lisle d'Agrion, for they were the clearest emerald I've ever seen. They were impudently direct eyes, and I could imagine why van Manderpootz and the Dragon Fly might have been forever quarreling; that was easy to imagine, looking into the eyes of the Dragon Fly's daughter.

Nor was Denise, apparently, quite as femininely modest as my image of perfection. She wore the extremely unconcealing costume of the day, which covered, I suppose, about as much of her as one of the one-piece swimming suits of the middle years of the twentieth century. She gave an impression, not so much of fleeting grace as of litheness and supple strength, an air of independence, frankness, and—I say it again—impudence.

"Well!" she said coolly as van Manderpootz presented me. "So you're the scion of the N. J. Wells Corporation. Every now and then your escapades enliven the Paris Sunday supplements.

Wasn't it you who snared a million dollars in the market so you could ask Whimsy White—?"

I flushed. "That was greatly exaggerated," I said hastily, "and anyway I lost it before we—uh—before I—"

"Not before you made somewhat of a fool of yourself, I believe," she finished sweetly.

Well, that's the sort she was. If she hadn't been so infernally lovely, if she hadn't looked so much like the face in the mirror, I'd have flared up, said "Pleased to have met you," and never have seen her again. But I couldn't get angry, not when she had the dusky hair, the perfect lips, the saucy nose of the being who to me was ideal.

So I did see her again, and several times again. In fact, I suppose I occupied most of her time between the few literary courses she was taking, and little by little I began to see that in other respects besides the physical she was not so far from my ideal. Beneath her impudence was honesty, and frankness, and, despite herself, sweetness, so that even allowing for the head-start I'd had, I fell in love pretty hastily. And what's more, I knew she was beginning to reciprocate.

That was the situation when I called for her one noon and took her over to van Manderpootz's laboratory. We were to lunch with him at the University Club, but we found him occupied in directing some experiment in the big laboratory beyond his personal one, untangling some sort of mess that his staff had blundered into. So Denise and I wandered back into the smaller room, perfectly content to be alone together. I simply couldn't feel hungry in her presence; just talking to her was enough of a substitute for food.

"I'm going to be a good writer," she was saying musingly. "Some day, Dick, I'm going to be famous."

Well, everyone knows how correct that prediction was. I agreed with her instantly.

She smiled. "You're nice, Dick," she said. "Very nice."

"Very?"

"*Very!*" she said emphatically. Then her green eyes strayed over to the table that held the idealizator. "What crack-brained contraption of Uncle Haskel's is that?" she asked.

I explained, rather inaccurately, I'm afraid, but no ordinary engineer can follow the ramifications of a van Manderpootz conception. Nevertheless, Denise caught the gist of it and her eyes glowed emerald fire.

"It's fascinating!" she exclaimed. She rose and moved over to the table. "I'm going to try it."

"Not without the professor, you won't! It might be dangerous."

That was the wrong thing to say. The green eyes glowed brighter as she cast me a whimsical glance. "But I am," she said. "Dick, I'm going to—see my ideal man!" She laughed softly.

I was panicky. Suppose her ideal turned out tall and dark and powerful, instead of short and sandy-haired and a bit—well, chubby, as I am. "No!" I said vehemently. "I won't let you!"

She laughed again. I suppose she read my consternation, for she said softly, "Don't be silly, Dick." She sat down, placed her face against the opening of the barrel, and commanded. "Turn it on."

I couldn't refuse her. I set the mirror whirling, then switched on the bank of tubes. Then immediately I stepped behind her, squinting into what was visible of the flashing mirror, where a face was forming, slowly—vaguely.

I thrilled. Surely the hair of the image was sandy. I even fancied now that I could trace a resemblance to my own features. Perhaps Denise sensed something similar, for she suddenly withdrew her eyes from the tube and looked up with a faintly embarrassed flush, a thing most unusual for her.

"Ideals are dull!" she said. "I want a real thrill. Do you know what I'm going to see? I'm going to visualize ideal horror. That's what I'll do. I'm going to see absolute horror!"

"Oh, no you're not!" I gasped. "That's a terribly dangerous idea." Off in the other room I heard the voice of van Manderpootz, "Dixon!"

"Dangerous—bosh!" Denise retorted. "I'm a writer, Dick. All this means to me is material. It's just experience, and I want it."

Van Manderpootz again. "Dixon! Dixon! Come here." I said, "Listen, Denise. I'll be right back. Don't try anything until I'm here—please!"

I dashed into the big laboratory. Van Manderpootz was facing a cowed group of assistants, quite apparently in extreme awe of the great man.

"Hah, Dixon!" he rasped. "Tell these fools what an Emmerich valve is, and why it won't operate in a free electronic stream. Let 'em see that even an ordinary engineer knows that much."

Well, an ordinary engineer doesn't, but it happened that I did. Not that I'm particularly exceptional as an engineer, but I *did* happen to know that because a year or two before I'd done some work on the big tidal turbines up in Maine, where they have to use Emmerich valves to guard against electrical leakage from the tremendous potentials in their condensers. So I started explaining, and van Manderpootz kept interpolating sarcasms about his staff, and when I finally finished, I suppose I'd been in there about half an hour. And then—I remembered Denise!

I left van Manderpootz staring as I rushed back, and sure enough, there was the girl with her face pressed against the barrel, and her hands gripping the table edge. Her features were hidden, of course, but there was something about her strained position, her white knuckles—

"Denise!" I yelled. "Are you all right? *Denise!*"

She didn't move. I stuck my face in between the mirror and the end of the barrel and peered up the tube at her visage, and what I saw left me all but stunned. Have you ever seen stark, mad, infinite terror on a human face? That was what I saw in Denise's—inexpressible, unbearable horror, worse than the fear of death could ever be. Her green eyes were widened so that the whites showed around them; her perfect lips were contorted, her whole face strained into a mask of sheer terror.

I rushed for the switch, but in passing I caught a single glimpse of—of what showed in the mirror. Incredible! Obscene, terror-laden, horrifying things—there just aren't words for them. There are no words.

Denise didn't move as the tubes darkened. I raised her face from the barrel and when she glimpsed me she moved. She flung herself out of that chair and away, facing me with such mad terror that I halted.

"Denise!" I cried. "It's just Dick. Look, Denise!"

But as I moved toward her, she uttered a choking scream, her eyes dulled, her knees gave, and she fainted. Whatever she had seen, it must have been appalling to the uttermost, for Denise was not the sort to faint.

*   *   *   *   *

It was a week later that I sat facing van Manderpootz in his little inner office. The grey metal figure of Isaak was missing, and the table that had held the idealizator was empty.

"Yes," said van Manderpootz. "I've dismantled it. One of van Manderpootz's few mistakes was to leave it around where a pair of incompetents like you and Denise could get to it. It seems that I continually overestimate the intelligence of others. I suppose I tend to judge them by the brain of van Manderpootz."

I said nothing. I was thoroughly disheartened and depressed, and whatever the professor said about my lack of intelligence, I felt it justified.

"Hereafter," resumed van Manderpootz, "I shall credit nobody except myself with intelligence, and will doubtless be much more nearly correct." He waved a hand at Isaak's vacant corner. "Not even the Bacon head," he continued. "I've abandoned that project, because, when you come right down to it, what need has the world of a mechanical brain when it already has that of van Manderpootz?"

"Professor," I burst out suddenly, "why won't they let me see Denise? I've been at the hospital every day, and they let me into her room just once—just once, and that time she went right into a fit of hysterics. Why? Is she—?" I gulped.

"She's recovering nicely, Dixon."

"Then why can't I see her?"

"Well," said van Manderpootz placidly, "it's like this. You see, when you rushed into the laboratory there, you made the mistake of pushing your face in front of the barrel. She saw your features right in the midst of all those horrors she had called up. Do you see? From then on your face was associated in her mind with the whole hell's brew in the mirror. She can't even look at you without seeing all of it again."

"*Good—God!*" I gasped. "But she'll get over it, won't she? She'll forget that part of it?"

"The young psychiatrist who attends her—a bright chap, by the way, with a number of my own ideas—believes she'll be quite over it in a couple of months. But personally, Dixon, I don't think she'll ever welcome the sight of your face, though I myself have seen uglier visages somewhere or other."

I ignored that. "Lord!" I groaned. "What a mess!" I rose to depart, and then—then I knew what inspiration means!

"Listen!" I said, spinning back. "Listen, professor! Why can't you get her back here and let her visualize the ideally beautiful? And then I'll—I'll stick my face into that!" Enthusiasm grew. "It can't fail!" I cried. "At the worst, it'll cancel that other memory. It's marvelous!"

"But as usual," said van Manderpootz, "a little late."

"Late? Why? You can put up your idealizator again. You'd do that much, wouldn't you?"

"Van Manderpootz," he observed, "is the very soul of generosity. I'd do it gladly, but it's still a little late, Dixon. You see, she married the bright young psychiatrist this noon."

Well, I've a date with Tips Alva tonight, and I'm going to be late for it, just as late as I please. And then I'm going to do nothing but stare at her lips all evening.

THE POINT OF VIEW

ORIGINALLY PUBLISHED IN *WONDER STORIES*
JANUARY 1936

The Point of View

"I am too modest!" snapped the great Haskel van Manderpootz, pacing irritably about the limited area of his private laboratory, glaring at me the while. "That is the trouble. I undervalue my own achievements, and thereby permit petty imitators like Corveille to influence the committee and win the Morell prize."

"But," I said soothingly, "you've won the Morell physics award half a dozen times, professor. They can't very well give it to you every year."

"Why not, since it is plain that I deserve it?" bristled the professor. "Understand, Dixon, that I do not regret my modesty, even though it permits conceited fools like Corveille, who have infinitely less reason than I for conceit, to win awards that mean nothing save prizes for successful bragging. Bah! To grant an award for research along such obvious lines that I neglected to mention them, thinking that even a Morell judge would appreciate their obviousness! Research on the psychon, eh! Who discovered the psychon? Who but van Manderpootz?"

"Wasn't that what you got last year's award for?" I asked consolingly. "And after all, isn't this modesty, this lack of jealousy on your part, a symbol of greatness of character?"

"True—true!" said the great van Manderpootz, mollified. "Had such an affront been committed against a lesser man than myself, he would doubtless have entered a bitter complaint against the judges. But not I. Anyway, I know from experience that it wouldn't do any good. And besides, despite his greatness, van Manderpootz is as modest and shrinking as a violet." At this point he paused, and his broad red face tried to look violet-like.

I suppressed a smile. I knew the eccentric genius of old, from the days when I had been Dixon Wells, undergraduate student of engineering, and had taken a course in Newer Physics (that is, in Relativity) under the famous professor. For some unguessable reason, he had taken a fancy to me, and as a result, I had been involved in several of his experiments since graduation. There was the affair of the subjunctivisor, for instance, and also that of the idealizator; in the first of these episodes I had suffered the indignity of falling in love with a girl two weeks after she was apparently dead, and in the second, the equal or greater indignity of falling in love with a girl who didn't exist, never had existed, and never would exist—in other words, with an ideal. Perhaps I'm a little susceptible to feminine charms, or rather, perhaps I used to be, for since the disaster of the idealizator, I have grimly relegated such follies to the past, much to the disgust of various 'vision entertainers, singers, dancers, and the like.

So of late I had been spending my days very seriously, trying wholeheartedly to get to the office on time just once, so that I could refer to it next time my father accused me of never getting anywhere on time. I hadn't succeeded yet, but fortunately the N. J. Wells Corporation was wealthy enough to survive even without the full-time services of Dixon Wells, or should I say even *with* them? Anyway, I'm sure my father preferred to have me late in the morning after an evening with van Manderpootz than after one with Tips Alva or Whimsy White, or one of the numerous others of the ladies of the 'vision screen. Even in the twenty-first century, he retained a lot of old-fashioned ideas.

Van Manderpootz had ceased to remember that he was as modest and shrinking as a violet. "It has just occurred to me," he announced impressively, "that years have character much as humans have. This year, 2015, will be remembered in history as a very stupid year, in which the Morell prize was given to a nincompoop. Last year, on the other hand, was a very intelligent year, a jewel in the crown of civilization. Not only was the Morell prize given to van Manderpootz, but I announced my discrete field theory in that year, and the University unveiled Gogli's statue of me as well." He sighed. "Yes, a very intelligent year! What do you think?"

"It depends on how you look at it," I responded glumly. "I didn't enjoy it so much, what with Joanna Caldwell and Denise d'Agrion, and your infernal experiments. It's all in the point of view."

The professor snorted. "Infernal experiments, eh! Point of view! Of course it's all in the point of view. Even Einstein's simple little synthesis was enough to prove that. If the whole world could adopt an intelligent and admirable point of view—

that of van Manderpootz, for instance—all troubles would be over. If it were possible—" He paused, and an expression of amazed wonder spread over his ruddy face.

"What's the matter?" I asked.

"Matter? I am astonished! The astounding depths of genius awe me. I am overwhelmed with admiration at the incalculable mysteries of a great mind."

"I don't get the drift."

"Dixon," he said impressively, "you have been privileged to look upon an example of the workings of a genius. More than that, you have planted the seed from which perhaps shall grow the towering tree of thought. Incredible as it seems, you, Dixon Wells, have given van Manderpootz an idea! It is thus that genius seizes upon the small, the unimportant, the negligible, and turns it to its own grand purposes. I stand awe-struck!"

"But what—?"

"Wait," said van Manderpootz, still in rapt admiration of the majesty of his own mind. "When the tree bears fruit, you shall see it. Until then, be satisfied that you have played a part in its planting."

*   *   *   *   *

It was perhaps a month before I saw van Manderpootz again, but one bright spring evening his broad, rubicund face looked out of the phone-screen at me.

"It's ready," he announced impressively.

"What is?"

The professor looked pained at the thought that I could have forgotten. "The tree has borne fruit," he explained. "If you wish to drop over to my quarters, we'll proceed to the laboratory and try it out. I do not set a time, so that it will be utterly impossible for you to be late."

I ignored that last dig, but had a time been set, I would doubtless have been even later than usual, for it was with some misgivings that I induced myself to go at all. I still remembered the unpleasantness of my last two experiences with the inventions of van Manderpootz. However, at last we were seated in the small laboratory, while out in the larger one the professor's technical assistant, Carter, puttered over some device, and in the far corner his secretary, the plain and unattractive Miss Fitch, transcribed lecture notes, for van Manderpootz abhorred the thought that his golden utterances might be lost to posterity. On the table between the professor and myself lay a curious device, something that looked like a cross between a pair of nose-glasses and a miner's lamp.

"There it is," said van Manderpootz proudly. "There lies my attitudinizor, which may well become an epoch-making device."

"How? What does it do?"

"I will explain. The germ of the idea traces back to that remark of yours about everything depending on the point of view. A very obvious statement, of course, but genius seizes on the obvious and draws from it the obscure. Thus the thoughts of even the simplest mind can suggest to the man of genius his sublime conceptions, as is evident from the fact that I got this idea from you."

"What idea?"

"Be patient. There is much you must understand first. You must realize just how true is the statement that everything depends on the point of view. Einstein proved that motion, space, and time depend on the particular point of view of the observer, or as he expressed it, on the scale of reference used. I go farther than that, infinitely farther. I propound the theory that the observer *is* the point of view. I go even beyond that, I maintain that the world itself is merely the point of view!"

"Huh?"

"Look here," proceeded van Manderpootz. "It is obvious that the world I see is entirely different from the one in which you live. It is equally obvious that a strictly religious man occupies a different world than that of a materialist. The fortunate man lives in a happy world; the unfortunate man sees a world of misery. One man is happy with little, another is miserable with much. Each sees the world from his own point of view, which is the same as saying that each lives in his own world. Therefore there are as many worlds as there are points of view."

"But," I objected, "that theory is to disregard reality. Out of all the different points of view, there must be one that is right, and all the rest are wrong."

"One would think so," agreed the professor. "One would think that between the point of view of you, for instance, as contrasted with that of, say van Manderpootz, there would be small doubt as to which was correct. However, early in the twentieth century, Heisenberg enunciated his Principle of Uncertainty, which proved beyond argument that a completely accurate scientific picture of the world is quite impossible, that the law of cause and effect is merely a phase of the law of chance, that no infallible predictions can ever be made, and that what science used to call natural laws are really only descriptions of the way in which the human mind perceives nature. In other words, the character of the world depends entirely on the mind observing it, or, to return to my earlier statement, the point of view."

"But no one can ever really understand another person's point of view," I said. "It isn't fair to undermine the whole basis of science because you can't be sure that the color we both call red wouldn't look green to you if you could see it through my eyes."

"Ah!" said van Manderpootz triumphantly. "So we come now to my attitudinizor. Suppose that it were possible for me to see through your eyes, or you through mine. Do you see what a boon such an ability would be to humanity? Not only from the standpoint of science, but also because it would obviate all troubles due to misunderstandings. And even more." Shaking his finger, the professor recited oracularly, "'Oh, wad some pow'r the giftie gie us to see oursel's as ithers see us.' Van Manderpootz is that power, Dixon. Through my attitudinizor, one may at last adopt the viewpoint of another. The poet's plaint of more than two centuries ago is answered at last."

"How the devil do you see through somebody else's eyes?"

"Very simply. You will recall the idealizator. Now it is obvious that when I peered over your shoulder and perceived in the mirror your conception of the ideal woman, I was, to a certain extent, adopting your point of view. In that case the psychons given off by your mind were converted into quanta of visible light, which could be seen. In the case of my attitudinizor, the process is exactly reversed. One flashes the beam of this light on the subject whose point of view is desired; the visible light is reflected back with a certain accompaniment of psychons, which are here intensified to a degree which will permit them to be, so to speak, appreciated?"

"Psychons?"

"Have you already forgotten my discovery of the unit particle of thought? Must I explain again how the cosmons, chronons, spations, psychons, and all other particles are interchangeable? And that," he continued abstractedly, "leads to certain interesting speculations. Suppose I were to convert, say, a ton of material protons and electrons into spations—that is, convert matter into space. I calculate that a ton of matter will produce approximately a cubic mile of space. Now the question is, where would we put it, since all the space we have is already occupied by space? Or if I manufactured an hour or two of time? It is obvious that we have no time to fit in an extra couple of hours, since all our time is already accounted for. Doubtless it will take a certain amount of thought for even van Manderpootz to solve these problems, but at the moment I am curious to watch the workings of the attitudinizor. Suppose you put it on, Dixon."

"I? Haven't *you* tried it out yet?"

"Of course not. In the first place, what has van Manderpootz to gain by studying the viewpoints of other people? The object of the device is to permit people to study nobler viewpoints than their own. And in the second place, I have asked myself whether it is fair to the world for van Manderpootz to be the first to try out a new and possibly untrustworthy device, and I reply, 'No!'"

"But *I* should try it out, eh? Well, everytime I try out any of your inventions I find myself in some kind of trouble. I'd be a fool to go around looking for more difficulty, wouldn't I?"

"I assure you that *my* viewpoint will be much less apt to get you into trouble than your own," said van Manderpootz with dignity. "There will be no question of your becoming involved in some impossible love affair as long as you stick to that."

Nevertheless, despite the assurance of the great scientist, I was more than a little reluctant to don the device. Yet I was curious, as well; it seemed a fascinating prospect to be able to look at the world through other eyes, as fascinating as visiting a new world—which it was, according to the professor. So after a few moments of hesitation, I picked up the instrument, slipped it over my head so that the eyeglasses were in the proper position, and looked inquiringly at van Manderpootz.

"You must turn it on," he said, reaching over and clicking a switch on the frame. "Now flash the light to my face. That's the way; just center the circle of light on my face. And now what do you see?"

I didn't answer; what I saw was, for the moment, quite indescribable. I was completely dazed and bewildered, and it was only when some involuntary movement of my head at last flashed the light from the professor's face to the table top that a measure of sanity returned, which proves at least that tables do not possess any point of view.

"O-o-o-h!" I gasped.

Van Manderpootz beamed. "Of course you are overwhelmed. One could hardly expect to adopt the view of van Manderpootz without some difficulties of adjustment. A second time will be easier."

I reached up and switched off the light. "A second time will not only be easier, but also impossible," I said crossly. "I'm not going to experience another dizzy spell like that for anybody."

"But of course you will, Dixon. I am certain that the dizziness will be negligible on the second trial. Naturally the unexpected heights affected you, much as if you were to come without warning to the brink of a colossal precipice. But this time you will be prepared, and the effect will be much less."

Well, it was. After a few moments I was able to give my full attention to the phenomena of the attitudinizor, and queer phenomena they were, too. I scarcely know how to describe the sensation of looking at the world through the filter of another's mind. It is almost an indescribable experience, but so, in the ultimate analysis, is any other experience.

What I saw first was a kaleidoscopic array of colors and shapes, but the amazing, astounding, inconceivable thing about the scene was that there was no single color I could recognize! The eyes of van Manderpootz, or perhaps his brain, interpreted color in a fashion utterly alien to the way in which my own functioned, and the resultant spectrum was so bizarre that there is simply no way of describing any single tint in words. To say, as I did to the professor, that his conception of red looked to me like a shade between purple and green conveys absolutely no meaning, and the only way a third person could appreciate the meaning would be to examine my point of view through an attitudinizor *while* I was examining that of van Manderpootz.

Thus he could apprehend my conception of van Manderpootz's reaction to the color red.

And shapes! It took me several minutes to identify the weird, angular, twisted, distorted appearance in the center of the room as the plain laboratory table. The room itself, aside from its queer form, looked smaller, perhaps because van Manderpootz is somewhat larger than I.

But by far the strangest part of his point of view had nothing to do with the outlook upon the physical world, but with the more fundamental elements—with his *attitudes*. Most of his thoughts, on that first occasion, were beyond me, because I had not yet learned to interpret the personal symbolism in which he thought. But I did understand his attitudes. There was Carter, for instance, toiling away out in the large laboratory; I saw at once what a plodding, unintelligent drudge he seemed to van Manderpootz. And there was Miss Fitch; I confess that she had always seemed unattractive to me, but my impression of her was Venus herself beside that of the professor! She hardly seemed human to him and I am sure that he never thought of her as a woman, but merely as a piece of convenient but unimportant laboratory equipment.

At this point I caught a glimpse of myself through the eyes of van Manderpootz. Ouch! Perhaps I'm not a genius, but I'm dead certain that I'm not the grinning ape I appeared to be in his eyes. And perhaps I'm not exactly the handsomest man in the world either, but if I thought I looked like that—! And then, to cap the climax, I apprehended van Manderpootz's conception of himself!

"That's enough!" I yelled. "I won't stay around here just to be insulted. I'm through!"

I tore the attitudinizor from my head and tossed it to the table, feeling suddenly a little foolish at the sight of the grin on the face of the professor.

"That is hardly the spirit which has led science to its great achievements, Dixon," he observed amiably. "Suppose you describe the nature of the insults, and if possible, something about the workings of the attitudinizor as well. After all, that is what you were supposed to be observing."

I flushed, grumbled a little, and complied. Van Manderpootz listened with great interest to my description of the difference in our physical worlds, especially the variations in our perceptions of form and color.

"What a field for an artist!" he ejaculated at last. "Unfortunately, it is a field that must remain forever untapped, because even though an artist examined a thousand viewpoints and learned innumerable new colors, his pigments would continue to impress his audience with the same old colors each of them had always known." He sighed thoughtfully, and then proceeded. "However, the device is apparently quite safe to use. I shall therefore try it briefly, bringing to the investigation a calm, scientific mind which refuses to be troubled by the trifles that seem to bother you."

He donned the attitudinizor, and I must confess that he stood the shock of the first trial somewhat better than I did. After a surprised "Oof!" he settled down to a complacent analysis of my point of view, while I sat somewhat self-consciously under his calm appraisal. Calm, that is, for about three minutes.

Suddenly he leaped to his feet, tearing the device from a face whose normal ruddiness had deepened to a choleric angry color. "Get out!" he roared. "So *that's* the way van Manderpootz looks to you! Moron! Idiot! Imbecile! Get out!"

*   *   *   *   *

It was a week or ten days later that I happened to be passing the University on my way from somewhere to somewhere else, and I fell to wondering whether the professor had yet forgiven me. There was a light in the window of his laboratory over in the Physics Building, so I dropped in, making my way past the desk where Carter labored, and the corner where Miss Fitch sat in dull primness at her endless task of transcribing lecture notes.

Van Manderpootz greeted me cordially enough, but with a curious assumption of melancholy in his manner. "Ah, Dixon," he began, "I am glad to see you. Since our last meeting, I have learned much of the stupidity of the world, and it appears to me now that you are actually one of the more intelligent contemporary minds."

This from van Manderpootz! "Why—thank you," I said.

"It is true. For some days I have sat at the window overlooking the street there, and have observed the viewpoints of the passers-by. Would you believe"—his voice lowered—"would you believe that only seven and four-tenths percent are even aware of the *existence* of van Manderpootz? And doubtless many of the few that are, come from among the students in the neighborhood. I knew that the average level of intelligence was low, but it had not occurred to me that it was as low as that."

"After all," I said consolingly, "you must remember that the achievements of van Manderpootz are such as to attract the attention of the intelligent few rather than of the many."

"A very silly paradox!" he snapped. "On the basis of that theory, since the higher one goes in the scale of intelligence, the fewer individuals one finds, the greatest achievement of all is one that *nobody* has heard of. By that test you would be greater than van Manderpootz, an obvious *reductio ad absurdum*."

He glared his reproof that I should even have thought of the point, then something in the outer laboratory caught his ever-observant eye.

"Carter!" he roared. "Is that a synobasical interphasometer in the positronic flow? Fool! What sort of measurements do you expect to make when your measuring instrument itself is part of the experiment? Take it out and start over!"

He rushed away toward the unfortunate technician. I settled idly back in my chair and stared about the small laboratory, whose walls had seen so many marvels. The latest, the attitudinizor, lay carelessly on the table, dropped there by the professor after his analysis of the mass viewpoint of the pedestrians in the street below.

I picked up the device and fell to examining its construction. Of course this was utterly beyond me, for no ordinary engineer can hope to grasp the intricacies of a van Manderpootz concept. So, after a puzzled but admiring survey of its infinitely delicate wires and grids and lenses, I made the obvious move. I put it on.

My first thought was the street, but since the evening was well along, the walk below the window was deserted. Back in my chair again, I sat musing idly when a faint sound that was not the rumbling of the professor's voice attracted my attention. I identified it shortly as the buzzing of a heavy fly, butting its head stupidly against the pane of glass that separated the small laboratory from the large room beyond. I wondered casually what the viewpoint of a fly was like, and ended by flashing the light on the creature.

For some moments I saw nothing other than I had been seeing right along from my own personal point of view, because, as van Manderpootz explained later, the psychons from the miserable brain of a fly are too few to produce any but the vaguest of impressions. But gradually I became aware of a picture, a queer and indescribable scene.

Flies are color-blind. That was my first impression, for the world was a dull panorama of greys and whites and blacks. Flies are extremely nearsighted; when I had finally identified the scene as the interior of the familiar room, I discovered that it seemed enormous to the insect, whose vision did not extend more than six feet, though it did take in almost a complete sphere, so that the creature could see practically in all directions at once. But perhaps the most astonishing thing, though I did not think of it until later, was that the compound eye of the insect, did not convey to it the impression of a vast number of separate pictures, such as the eye produces when a microphotograph is taken through it. The fly sees one picture just as we do; in the same way as our brain rights the upside-down image cast on our retina, the fly's brain reduces the compound image to one. And beyond these impressions were a wild hodge-podge of smell-sensations, and a strange desire to burst through the invisible glass barrier into the brighter light beyond. But I had no time to analyze these sensations, for suddenly there was a flash of something infinitely clearer than the dim cerebrations of a fly.

For half a minute or longer I was unable to guess what that momentary flash had been. I knew that I had seen something incredibly lovely, that I had tapped a viewpoint that looked upon something whose very presence caused ecstasy, but whose viewpoint it was, or what that flicker of beauty had been, were questions beyond my ability to answer.

I slipped off the attitudinizor and sat staring perplexedly at the buzzing fly on the pane of glass. Out in the other room van Manderpootz continued his harangue to the repentant Carter, and off in a corner invisible from my position I could hear the rustle of papers as Miss Fitch transcribed endless notes. I puzzled vainly over the problem of what had happened, and then the solution dawned on me.

The fly must have buzzed between me and one of the occupants of the outer laboratory. I had been following its flight with the faintly visible beam of the attitudinizor's light, and that beam must have flickered momentarily on the head of one of the three beyond the glass. But which? Van Manderpootz himself? It must have been either the professor or Carter, since the secretary was quite beyond range of the light.

It seemed improbable that the cold and brilliant mind of van Manderpootz could be the agency of the sort of emotional ecstasy I had sensed. It must therefore, have been the head of the mild and inoffensive little Carter that the beam had tapped. With a feeling of curiosity I slipped the device back on my own head and sent the beam sweeping dimly into the larger room.

It did not at the time occur to me that such a procedure was quite as discreditable as eavesdropping, or even more dishonorable, if you come right down to it, because it meant the theft of far more personal information than one could ever convey by the spoken word. But all I considered at the moment was my own curiosity; I wanted to learn what sort of viewpoint could produce that strange, instantaneous flash of beauty. If the proceeding was unethical—well, Heaven knows I was punished for it.

So I turned the attitudinizor on Carter. At the moment, he was listening respectfully to van Manderpootz, and I sensed clearly his respect for the great man, a respect that had in it a distinct element of fear. I could hear Carter's impression of the booming voice of the professor, sounding somewhat like the modulated thunder of a god, which was not far from the little man's actual opinion of his master. I perceived Carter's opinion of himself, and his self-picture was an even more mouselike portrayal than my own impression of him. When, for an instant, he glanced my way, I sensed his impression of me, and while I'm sure that Dixon Wells is not the imbecile he appears to van Manderpootz, I'm equally sure that he's not the debonair man of the world he seemed to Carter. All in all, Carter's point of view seemed that of a timid, inoffensive, retiring, servile little man, and I wondered all the more what could have caused that vanished flash of beauty in a mind like his.

There was no trace of it now. His attention was completely taken up by the voice of van Manderpootz, who had passed from a personal appraisal of Carter's stupidity to a general lecture on the fallacies of the unified field theory as presented by his rivals Corveille and Shrimski. Carter was listening with an almost worshipful regard, and I could feel his surges of indignation against the villains who dared to disagree with the authority of van Manderpootz.

I sat there intent on the strange double vision of the attitudinizor, which was in some respects like a Horsten psychomat—that is, one is able to see both through his own eyes and through the eyes of his subject. Thus I could see van Manderpootz and Carter quite clearly, but at the same time I could see or sense what Carter saw and sensed. Thus I perceived suddenly through my own eyes that the professor had ceased talking to Carter, and had turned at the approach of somebody as yet invisible to me, while at the same time, through Carter's eyes, I saw that vision of ecstasy which had flashed for a moment in his mind. I saw—description is utterly impossible, but I saw a woman who, except possibly for the woman of the idealizator screen, was the most beautiful creature I had ever seen!

I say description is impossible. That is the literal truth, for her coloring, her expression, her figure, as seen through Carter's eyes, were completely unlike anything expressible by words. I was fascinated, I could do nothing but watch, and I felt a wild surge of jealousy as I caught the adoration in the attitude of the humble Carter. She was glorious, magnificent, indescribable. It was with an effort that I untangled myself from the web of fascination enough to catch Carter's thought of her name. "Lisa," he was thinking. "Lisa."

What she said to van Manderpootz was in tones too low for me to hear, and apparently too low for Carter's ears as well, else I should have heard her words through the attitudinizor. But both of us heard van Manderpootz's bellow in answer.

"I don't care how the dictionary pronounces the word!" he roared. "The way van Manderpootz pronounces a word is right!"

The glorious Lisa turned silently and vanished. For a few moments I watched her through Carter's eyes, but as she neared the laboratory door, he turned his attention again to van Manderpootz, and she was lost to my view.

And as I saw the professor close his dissertation and approach me, I slipped the attitudinizor from my head and forced myself to a measure of calm.

"Who is she?" I demanded. "I've got to meet her!"

He looked blankly at me. "Who's who?"

"Lisa! Who's Lisa?"

There was not a flicker in the cool blue eyes of van Manderpootz. "I don't know any Lisa," he said indifferently.

"But you were just talking to her! Right out there!"

Van Manderpootz stared curiously at me; then little by little a shrewd suspicion seemed to dawn in his broad, intelligent features. "Hah!" he said. "Have you, by any chance, been using the attitudinizor?"

I nodded, chill apprehension gripping me.

"And is it also true that you chose to investigate the viewpoint of Carter out there?" At my nod, he stepped to the door that joined the two rooms, and closed it. When he faced me again, it was with features working into lines of amusement that suddenly found utterance in booming laughter. "Haw!" he roared. "Do you know who beautiful Lisa is? She's Fitch!"

"Fitch? You're mad! She's glorious, and Fitch is plain and scrawny and ugly. Do you think I'm a fool?"

"You ask an embarrassing question," chuckled the professor. "Listen to me, Dixon. The woman you saw was my secretary, Miss Fitch, seen through the eyes of Carter. Don't you understand? The idiot Carter's in love with her!"

*   *   *   *   *

I suppose I walked the upper levels half the night, oblivious alike of the narrow strip of stars that showed between the towering walls of twenty-first century New York, and the intermittent roar of traffic from the freight levels. Certainly this was the worst predicament of all those into which the fiendish contraptions of the great van Manderpootz had thrust me.

In love with a point of view! In love with a woman who had no existence apart from the beglamoured eyes of Carter. It wasn't Lisa Fitch I loved; indeed, I rather hated her angular ugliness. What I had fallen in love with was the way she looked to Carter, for there is nothing in the world quite as beautiful as a lover's conception of his sweetheart.

This predicament was far worse than my former ones. When I had fallen in love with a girl already dead, I could console myself with the thought of what might have been. When I had fallen in love with my own ideal—well, at least she was *mine*, even if I couldn't have her. But to fall in love with another man's conception! The only way that conception could even continue to exist was for Carter to remain in love with Lisa Fitch, which rather effectually left me outside the picture altogether. She was absolutely unattainable to me, for Heaven knows I didn't want the real Lisa Fitch—"real" meaning, of course, the one who was real to me. I suppose in the end Carter's Lisa Fitch was as real as the skinny scarecrow my eyes saw.

She was unattainable—or was she? Suddenly an echo of a long-forgotten psychology course recurred to me. Attitudes are habits. Viewpoints are attitudes. Therefore viewpoints are habits. And habits can be learned!

There was the solution! All I had to do was to learn, or to acquire by practice, the viewpoint of Carter. What I had to do was literally to put myself in his place, to look at things in his way, to see his viewpoint. For once I learned to do that, I could see in Lisa Fitch the very things he saw, and the vision would become reality to me as well as to him.

I planned carefully. I did not care to face the sarcasm of the great van Manderpootz; therefore I would work in secret. I would visit his laboratory at such times as he had classes or lectures, and I would use the attitudinizor to study the viewpoint of Carter, and to, as it were, practice that viewpoint. Thus I would have the means at hand of testing my progress, for all I had to do was glance at Miss Fitch without the attitudinizor. As soon as I began to perceive in her what Carter saw, I would know that success was imminent.

Those next two weeks were a strange interval of time. I haunted the laboratory of van Manderpootz at odd hours, having learned from the University office what periods he devoted to his courses. When one day I found the attitudinizor missing, I prevailed on Carter to show me where it was kept, and he, influenced doubtless by my friendship for the man he practically worshipped, indicated the place without question. But later I suspect that he began to doubt his wisdom in this, for I know he thought it very strange for me to sit for long periods staring at him; I caught all sorts of puzzled questions in his mind, though as I have said, these were hard for me to decipher until I began to learn Carter's personal system of symbolism by which he thought. But at least one man was pleased—my father, who took my absences from the office and neglect of business as signs of good health and spirits, and congratulated me warmly on the improvement.

But the experiment was beginning to work, I found myself sympathizing with Carter's viewpoint, and little by little the mad world in which he lived was becoming as logical as my own. I learned to recognize colors through his eyes; I learned to understand form and shape; most fundamental of all, I learned his values, his attitudes, his tastes. And these last were a little inconvenient at times, for on the several occasions when I supplemented my daily calls with visits to van Manderpootz in the evening, I found some difficulty in separating my own respectful regard for the great man from Carter's unreasoning worship, with the result that I was on the verge of blurting out the whole thing to him several times. And perhaps it was a guilty conscience, but I kept thinking that the shrewd blue eyes of the professor rested on me with a curiously suspicious expression all evening.

The thing was approaching its culmination. Now and then, when I looked at the angular ugliness of Miss Fitch, I began to catch glimpses of the same miraculous beauty that Carter found in her—glimpses only, but harbingers of success. Each day I arrived at the laboratory with increasing eagerness, for each day brought me nearer to the achievement I sought. That is, my eagerness increased until one day I arrived to find neither Carter nor Miss Fitch present, but van Manderpootz, who should have been delivering a lecture on indeterminism, very much in evidence.

"Uh—hello," I said weakly.

"Umph!" he responded, glaring at me. "So Carter was right, I see. Dixon, the abysmal stupidity of the human race continually astounds me with new evidence of its astronomical depths, but I believe this escapade of yours plumbs the uttermost regions of imbecility."

"M-my escapade?"

"Do you think you can escape the piercing eye of van Manderpootz? As soon as Carter told me you had been here in my absence, my mind leaped nimbly to the truth. But Carter's information was not even necessary, for half an eye was enough to detect the change in your attitude on these last few evening visits. So you've been trying to adopt Carter's viewpoint, eh? No doubt with the idea of ultimately depriving him of the charming Miss Fitch!"

"W-why—"

"Listen to me, Dixon. We will disregard the ethics of the thing and look at it from a purely rational viewpoint, if a rational viewpoint is possible to anybody but van Manderpootz. Don't you realize that in order to attain Carter's attitude toward Fitch, you would have to adopt his *entire* viewpoint? Not," he added tersely, "that I think his point of view is greatly inferior to yours, but I happen to prefer the viewpoint of a donkey to that of a mouse. Your particular brand of stupidity is more agreeable to me than Carter's timid, weak, and subservient nature, and some day you will thank me for this. Was his impression of Fitch worth the sacrifice of your own personality?"

"I—I don't know."

"Well, whether it was or not, van Manderpootz has decided the matter in the wisest way. For it's too late now, Dixon. I have given them both a month's leave and sent them away—on a honeymoon. They left this morning."

THE STORIES OF

OF

HAMILTON

HAMMONDS

Parasite Planet

Originally Published in *Astounding Stories*
February 1935

Parasite Planet

Part I

Luckily for "Ham" Hammond it was mid-winter when the mudspout came. Mid-winter, that is, in the Venusian sense, which is nothing at all like the conception of the season generally entertained on Earth, except possibly, by dwellers in the hotter regions of the Amazon basin, or the Congo.

They, perhaps, might form a vague mental picture of winter on Venus by visualizing their hottest summer days, multiplying the heat, discomfort and unpleasant denizens of the jungle by ten or twelve.

On Venus, as is now well known, the seasons occur alternately in opposite hemispheres, as on the Earth, but with a very important difference. Here, when North America and Europe swelter in summer, it is winter in Australia and Cape Colony and Argentina. It is the northern and southern hemispheres which alternate their seasons.

But on Venus, very strangely, it is the eastern and western hemispheres, because the seasons of Venus depend, not on inclination to the plane of the ecliptic, but on libration. Venus does not rotate, but keeps the same face always toward the Sun, just as the Moon does toward the earth. One face is forever daylight, and the other forever night, and only along the twilight zone, a strip five hundred miles wide, is human habitation possible, a thin ring of territory circling the planet.

Toward the sunlit side it verges into the blasting heat of a desert where only a few Venusian creatures live, and on the night edge the strip ends abruptly in the colossal ice barrier produced by the condensation of the upper winds that sweep endlessly from the rising air of the hot hemisphere to cool and sink and rush back again from the cold one.

The chilling of warm air always produces rain, and at the edge of the darkness the rain freezes to form these great ramparts. What lies beyond, what fantastic forms of life may live in the starless darkness of the frozen face, or whether that region is as dead as the airless Moon—those are mysteries.

But the slow libration, a ponderous wabbling of the planet from side to side, does produce the effect of seasons. On the lands of the twilight zone, first in one hemisphere and then the other, the cloud-hidden Sun seems to rise gradually for fifteen days, then sink for the same period. It never ascends far, and only near the ice barrier does it seem to touch the horizon; for the libration is only seven degrees, but it is sufficient to produce noticeable fifteen-day seasons.

But such seasons! In the winter the temperature drops sometimes to a humid but bearable ninety, but, two weeks later, a hundred and forty is a cool day near the torrid edge of the zone. And always, winter and summer, the intermittent rains drip sullenly down to be absorbed by the spongy soil and given back again as sticky, unpleasant, unhealthy steam.

And that, the vast amount of moisture on Venus, was the greatest surprise of the first human visitors; the clouds had been seen, of course, but the spectroscope denied the presence of water, naturally, since it was analyzing light reflected from the upper cloud surfaces, fifty miles above the planet's face.

That abundance of water has strange consequences. There are no seas or oceans on Venus, if we except the probability of vast, silent, and eternally frozen oceans on the sunless side. On the hot hemisphere evaporation is too rapid, and the rivers that flow out of the ice mountains simply diminish and finally vanish, dried up.

A further consequence is the curiously unstable nature of the land of the twilight zone. Enormous subterranean rivers course invisibly through it, some boiling, some cold as the ice from which they flow. These are the cause of the mud eruptions that make human habitation in the Hotlands such a gamble; a perfectly solid and apparently safe area of soil may be changed suddenly into a boiling sea of mud in which buildings sink and vanish, together, frequently, with their occupants.

There is no way of predicting these catastrophes; only on the rare outcroppings of bed rock is a structure safe, and so all permanent human settlements cluster about the mountains.

*   *   *   *   *

Ham Hammond was a trader. He was one of those adventurous individuals who always appear on the frontiers and fringes of habitable regions. Most of these fall into two classes; they are either reckless daredevils pursuing danger, or outcasts, criminal or otherwise, pursuing either solitude or forgetfulness.

Ham Hammond was neither. He was pursuing no such abstractions, but the good, solid lure of wealth. He was, in fact, trading with the natives for the spore-pods of the Venusian plant xixtchil, from which terrestrial chemists would extract trihydroxyl-tertiary-tolunitrile-beta-anthraquinone, the xixtline or triple-T-B-A that was so effective in rejuvenation treatments.

Ham was young and sometimes wondered why rich old men—and women—would pay such tremendous prices for a few more years of virility, especially as the treatments didn't actually increase the span of life, but just produced a sort of temporary and synthetic youth.

Gray hair darkened, wrinkles filled out, bald heads grew fuzzy, and then, in a few years, the rejuvenated person was just as dead as he would have been, anyway. But as long as triple-T-B-A commanded a price about equal to its weight in radium, why, Ham was willing to take the gamble to obtain it.

He had never really expected the mudspout. Of course it was an ever-present danger, but when, staring idly through the window of his shack over the writhing and steaming Venusian plain, he had seen the sudden boiling pools erupting all around, it had come as a shocking surprise.

For a moment he was paralyzed; then he sprang into immediate and frantic action. He pulled on his enveloping suit of rubberlike transkin; he strapped the great bowls of mudshoes to his feet; he tied the precious bag of spore-pods to his shoulders, packed some food, and then burst into the open.

The ground was still semisolid, but even as he watched, the black soil boiled out around the metal walls of the shack, the cube tilted a trifle, and then sank deliberately from sight, and the mud sucked and gurgled as it closed gently above the spot.

Ham caught himself. One couldn't stand still in the midst of a mudspout, even with the bowl-like mudshoes as support. Once let the viscous stuff flow over the rim and the luckless victim was trapped; he couldn't raise his foot against the suction, and first slowly, then more quickly, he'd follow the shack.

So Ham started off over the boiling swamp, walking with the peculiar sliding motion he had learned by much practice, never raising the mudshoes above the surface, but sliding them along, careful that no mud topped the curving rim.

It was a tiresome motion, but absolutely necessary. He slid along as if on snowshoes, bearing west because that was the direction of the dark side, and if he had to walk to safety, he might as well do it in coolness. The area of swamp was unusually large; he covered at least a mile before he attained a slight rise in the ground, and the mudshoes clumped on solid, or nearly solid, soil.

He was bathed in perspiration; and his transkin suit was hot as a boiler room, but one grows accustomed to that on Venus. He'd have given half his supply of xixtchil pods for the opportunity to open the mask of the suit, to draw a breath of even the steamy and humid Venusian air, but that was impossible; impossible, at least, if he had any inclination to continue living.

One breath of unfiltered air anywhere near the warm edge of the twilight zone was quick and very painful death; Ham would have drawn in uncounted millions of the spores of those fierce Venusian molds, and they'd have sprouted in furry and nauseating masses in his nostrils, his mouth, his lungs, and eventually in his ears and eyes.

Breathing them wasn't even a necessary requirement; once he'd come upon a trader's body with the molds springing from his flesh. The poor fellow had somehow torn a rip in his transkin suit, and that was enough.

The situation made eating and drinking in the open a problem on Venus; one had to wait until a rain had precipitated the spores, when it was safe for half an hour or so. Even then the water must have been recently boiled and the food just removed from its can; otherwise, as had happened to Ham more than once, the food was apt to turn abruptly into a fuzzy mass of molds that grew about as fast as the minute hand moved on a clock. A disgusting sight! A disgusting planet!

*   *   *   *   *

That last reflection was induced by Ham's view of the quagmire that had engulfed his shack. The heavier vegetation had gone with it, but already avid and greedy life was emerging, wriggling mud grass and the bulbous fungi called "walking balls." And all around a million little slimy creatures slithered across the mud, eating each other rapaciously, being torn to bits, and each fragment re-forming to a complete creature.

A thousand different species, but all the same in one respect; each of them was all appetite. In common with most Venusian beings, they had a multiplicity of both legs and mouths; in fact some of them were little more than blobs of skin split into dozens of hungry mouths, and crawling on a hundred spidery legs.

All life on Venus is more or less parasitic. Even the plants that draw their nourishment directly from soil and air have also the ability to absorb and digest—and, often enough, to trap— animal food. So fierce is the competition on that humid strip of land between the fire and the ice that one who has never seen it must fail even to imagine it.

The animal kingdom wars incessantly on itself and the plant world; the vegetable kingdom retaliates, and frequently outdoes the other in the production of monstrous predatory horrors that one would even hesitate to call plant life. A terrible world!

In the few moments that Ham had paused to look back, ropy creepers had already entangled his legs; transkin was impervious, of course, but he had to cut the things away with his knife, and the black, nauseating juices that flowed out of them smeared on his suit and began instantly to grow furry as the molds sprouted. He shuddered.

"Hell of a place!" Ham growled, stooping to remove his mudshoes, which he slung carefully over his back.

He slogged away through the writhing vegetation, automatically dodging the awkward thrusts of the Jack Ketch trees as they cast their nooses hopefully toward his arms and head.

Now and again he passed one that dangled some trapped creature, usually unrecognizable because the molds had enveloped it in a fuzzy shroud, while the tree itself was placidly absorbing victim and molds alike.

"Horrible place!" Ham muttered, kicked a writhing mass of nameless little vermin from his path.

He mused; his shack had been situated rather nearer the hot edge of the twilight zone; it was a trifle over two hundred and fifty miles to the shadow line, though of course that varied with the libration. But one couldn't approach the line too closely, anyway, because of the fierce, almost inconceivable, storms that raged where the hot upper winds encountered the icy blasts of the night side, giving rise to the birth throes of the ice barrier.

So a hundred and fifty miles due west would be sufficient to bring coolness, to enter a region too temperate for the molds, where he could walk in comparative comfort. And then, not more than fifty miles north, lay the American settlement Erotia, named, obviously, after that troublesome mythical son of Venus, Cupid.

Intervening, of course, were the ranges of the Mountains of Eternity, not those mighty twenty-mile-high peaks whose summits are occasionally glimpsed by Earthly telescopes, and that forever sunder British Venus from the American possessions, but, even at the point he planned to cross, very respectable mountains indeed. He was on the British side now; not that any one cared. Traders came and went as they pleased.

Well, that meant about two hundred miles. No reason why he couldn't make it; he was armed with both automatic and flame-pistol, and water was no problem, if carefully boiled. Under pressure of necessity, one could even eat Venusian life—but it required hunger and thorough cooking and a sturdy stomach.

It wasn't the taste so much as the appearance, or so he'd been told. He grimaced; beyond doubt he'd be driven to find out for himself, since his canned food couldn't possibly last out the trip. Nothing to worry about, Ham kept telling himself. In fact, plenty to be glad about; the xixtchil pods in his pack represented as much wealth as he could have accumulated by ten years of toil back on Earth.

No danger—and yet, men had vanished on Venus, dozens of them. The molds had claimed them, or some fierce unearthly monster, or perhaps one of the many unknown living horrors, both plant and animal.

Ham trudged along, keeping always to the clearings about the Jack Ketch trees, since these vegetable omnivores kept other life beyond the reach of their greedy nooses. Elsewhere progress was impossible, for the Venusian jungle presented such a terrific tangle of writhing and struggling forms that one could move only by cutting the way, step by step, with infinite labor.

Even then there was the danger of Heaven only knew what fanged and venomous creatures whose teeth might pierce the protective membrane of transkin, and a crack in that meant death. Even the unpleasant Jack Ketch trees were preferable company, he reflected, as he slapped their questing lariats aside.

Six hours after Ham had started his involuntary journey, it rained. He seized the opportunity, found a place where a recent mudspout had cleared the heavier vegetation away, and prepared to eat. First, however, he scooped up some scummy water, filtered it through the screen attached for that purpose to his canteen, and set about sterilizing it.

Fire was difficult to manage, since dry fuel is rare indeed in the Hotlands of Venus, but Ham tossed a thermide tablet into the liquid, and the chemicals boiled the water instantly, escaping themselves as gases. If the water retained a slight ammoniacal taste—well, that was the least of his discomforts, he mused, as he covered it and set it by to cool.

He uncapped a can of beans, watched a moment to see that no stray molds had remained in the air to infect the food, then opened the visor of his suit and swallowed hastily. Thereafter he drank the blood-warm water and poured carefully what remained into the water pouch within his transkin, where he could suck it through a tube to his mouth without the deadly exposure to the molds.

Ten minutes after he had completed the meal, while he rested and longed for the impossible luxury of a cigarette, the fuzzy coat sprang suddenly to life on the remnants of food in the can.

* * * * *

Part II.

An hour later, weary and thoroughly soaked in perspiration, Ham found a Friendly tree, so named by the explorer Burlingame because it is one of the few organisms on Venus sluggish enough to permit one to rest in its branches. So Ham climbed it, found the most comfortable position available, and slept as best he could.

It was five hours by his wrist watch before he awoke, and the tendrils and little sucking cups of the Friendly tree were fastened all over his transkin. He tore them away very carefully, climbed down, and trudged westward.

It was after the second rain that he met the doughpot, as the creature is called in British and American Venus. In the French strip, it's the pot à colle, the "paste pot"; in the Dutch—well, the Dutch are not prudish, and they call the horror just what they think it warrants.

Actually, the doughpot is a nauseous creature. It's a mass of white, dough-like protoplasm, ranging in size from a single cell to perhaps twenty tons of mushy filth. It has no fixed form; in fact, it's merely a mass of de Proust cells—in effect, a disembodied, crawling, hungry cancer.

It has no organization and no intelligence, nor even any instinct save hunger. It moves in whatever direction food touches its surfaces; when it touches two edible substances, it quietly divides, with the larger portion invariably attacking the greater supply.

It's invulnerable to bullets; nothing less than the terrific blast of a flame-pistol will kill it, and then only if the blast destroys every individual cell. It travels over the ground absorbing everything, leaving bare black soil where the ubiquitous molds spring up at once—a noisome, nightmarish creature.

Ham sprang aside as the doughpot erupted suddenly from the jungle to his right. It couldn't absorb the transkin, of course, but to be caught in that pasty mess meant quick suffocation. He glared at it disgustedly and was sorely tempted to blast it with his flame-pistol as it slithered past at running speed. He would have, too, but the experienced Venusian frontiersman is very careful with the flame-pistol.

It has to be charged with a diamond, a cheap black one, of course, but still an item to consider. The crystal, when fired, gives up all its energy in one terrific blast that roars out like a lightning stroke for a hundred yards, incinerating everything in its path.

The thing rolled by with a sucking and gulping sound. Behind it opened the passage it had cleared; creepers, snake vines, Jack Ketch trees—everything had been swept away down to the humid earth itself, where already the molds were springing up on the slime of the doughpot's trail.

The alley led nearly in the direction Ham wanted to travel; he seized the opportunity and strode briskly along, with a wary eye, nevertheless, on the ominous walls of jungle. In ten hours or so the opening would be filled once more with unpleasant life, but for the present it offered a much quicker progress than dodging from one clearing to the next.

It was five miles up the trail, which was already beginning to sprout inconveniently, that he met the native galloping along on his four short legs, his pincerlike hands shearing a path for him. Ham stopped for a palaver.

"Murra," he said.

The language of the natives of the equatorial regions of the Hotlands is a queer one. It has, perhaps, two hundred words, but when a trader has learned those two hundred, his knowledge of the tongue is but little greater than the man who knows none at all.

The words are generalized, and each sound has anywhere from a dozen to a hundred meanings. Murra, for instance, is a word of greeting; it may mean something much like "hello," or "good morning." It also may convey a challenge—"on guard!" It means besides, "Let's be friends," and also, strangely, "Let's fight this out."

It has, moreover, certain noun senses; it means peace, it means war, it means courage, and, again, fear. A subtle language; it is only recently that studies of inflection have begun to reveal its nature to human philologists. Yet, after all, perhaps English, with its "to," "too," and "two," its "one," "won," "wan," "wen," "win," "when," and a dozen other similarities, might seem just as strange to Venusian ears, untrained in vowel distinctions.

Moreover, humans can't read the expressions of the broad, flat, three-eyed Venusian faces, which in the nature of things must convey a world of information among the natives themselves.

But this one accepted the intended sense. "Murra," he responded, pausing. "Usk?" That was, among other things, "Who are you?" or "Where did you come from?" or "Where are you bound?"

Ham chose the latter sense. He pointed off into the dim west, then raised his hand in an arc to indicate the mountains. "Erotia," he said. That had but one meaning, at least.

The native considered this in silence. At last he grunted and volunteered some information. He swept his cutting claw in a gesture west along the trail. "Curky," he said, and then, "Murra." The last was farewell; Ham pressed against the wriggling jungle wall to permit him to pass.

Curky meant, together with twenty other senses, trader. It was the word usually applied to humans, and Ham felt a pleasant anticipation in the prospect of human company. It had been six months since he had heard a human voice other than that on the tiny radio now sunk with his shack.

*   *   *   *   *

True enough, five miles along the doughpot's trail Ham emerged suddenly in an area where there had been a recent mudspout. The vegetation was only waist-high, and across the quarter-mile clearing he saw a structure, a trading hut. But far more pretentious than his own iron-walled cubicle; this one boasted three rooms, an unheard-of luxury in the Hotlands, where every ounce had to be laboriously transported by rocket from one of the settlements. That was expensive, almost prohibitive. Traders took a real gamble, and Ham knew he was lucky to have come out so profitably.

He strode over the still spongy ground. The windows were shaded against the eternal daylight, and the door—the door was locked. This was a violation of the frontier code. One always left doors unlocked; it might mean the salvation of some strayed trader, and not even the most dishonorable would steal from a hut left open for his safety.

Nor would the natives; no creature is as honest as a Venusian native, who never lies and never steals, though he might, after due warning, kill a trader for his trade goods. But only after a fair warning.

Ham stood puzzled. At last he kicked and tramped a clear space before the door, sat down against it, and fell to snapping away the numerous and loathsome little creatures that swarmed over his transkin. He waited.

It wasn't half an hour before he saw the trader plowing through the clearing—a short, slim fellow; the transkin shaded his face, but Ham could make out large, shadowed eyes. He stood up.

"Hello!" he said jovially. "Thought I'd drop in for a visit. My name's Hamilton Hammond—you guess the nickname!"

The newcomer stopped short, then spoke in a curiously soft and husky voice, with a decidedly English accent. "My guess would be 'Boiled Pork,' I fancy." The tones were cold, unfriendly. "Suppose you step aside and let me in. Good day!"

Ham felt anger and amazement. "The devil!" he snapped. "You're a hospitable sort, aren't you?"

"No. Not at all." The other paused at the door. "You're an American. What are you doing on British soil? Have you a passport?"

"Since when do you need a passport in the Hotlands?"

"Trading, aren't you?" the slim man said sharply. "In other words, poaching. You've no rights here. Get on."

Ham's jaw set stubbornly behind his mask. "Rights or none," he said, "I'm entitled to the consideration of the frontier code. I want a breath of air and a chance to wipe my face, and also a chance to eat. If you open that door I'm coming in after you."

An automatic flashed into view. "Do, and you'll feed the molds."

Ham, like all Venusian traders, was of necessity bold, resourceful, and what is called in the States "hard-boiled." He didn't flinch, but said in apparent yielding:

"All right; but listen, all I want is a chance to eat."

"Wait for a rain," said the other coolly and half turned to unlock the door.

As his eyes shifted, Ham kicked at the revolver; it went spinning against the wall and dropped into the weeds. His opponent snatched for the flame-pistol that still dangled on his hip; Ham caught his wrist in a mighty clutch.

Instantly the other ceased to struggle, while Ham felt a momentary surprise at the skinny feel of the wrist through its transkin covering.

"Look here!" he growled. "I want a chance to eat, and I'm going to get it. Unlock that door!"

He had both wrists now; the fellow seemed curiously delicate. After a moment he nodded, and Ham released one hand. The door opened, and he followed the other in.

*   *   *   *   *

Again, unheard-of magnificence. Solid chairs, a sturdy table, even books, carefully preserved, no doubt, by lycopodium against the ravenous molds that sometimes entered Hotland shacks in spite of screen filters and automatic spray. An automatic spray was going now to destroy any spores that might have entered with the opening door.

Ham sat down, keeping an eye on the other, whose flame-pistol he had permitted to remain in its holster. He was confident of his ability to outdraw the slim individual, and, besides, who'd risk firing a flame-pistol indoors? It would simply blow out one wall of the building.

So he set about opening his mask, removing food from his pack, wiping his steaming face, while his companion—or opponent—looked on silently. Ham watched the canned meat for a moment; no molds appeared, and he ate.

"Why the devil," he rasped, "don't you open your visor?" At the other's silence, he continued: "Afraid I'll see your face, eh? Well, I'm not interested; I'm no cop."

No reply.

He tried again. "What's your name?"

The cool voice sounded: "Burlingame. Pat Burlingame."

Ham laughed. "Patrick Burlingame is dead, my friend. I knew him." No answer. "And if you don't want to tell your name, at least you needn't insult the memory of a brave man and a great explorer."

"Thank you." The voice was sardonic. "He was my father."

"Another lie. He had no son. He had only a——" Ham paused abruptly; a feeling of consternation swept over him. "Open your visor!" he yelled.

He saw the lips of the other, dim through the transkin, twitch into a sarcastic smile.

"Why not?" said the soft voice, and the mask dropped.

Ham gulped; behind the covering were the delicately modeled features of a girl, with cool gray eyes in a face lovely despite the glistening perspiration on cheeks and forehead.

The man gulped again. After all, he was a gentleman despite his profession as one of the fierce, adventurous traders of Venus. He was university-educated—an engineer—and only the lure of quick wealth had brought him to the Hotlands.

"I—I'm sorry," he stammered.

"You brave American poachers!" she sneered. "Are all of you so valiant as to force yourselves on women?"

"But—how could I know? What are you doing in a place like this?"

"There's no reason for me to answer your questions, but"—she gestured toward the room beyond—"I'm classifying Hotland flora and fauna. I'm Patricia Burlingame, biologist."

He perceived now the jar-enclosed specimens of a laboratory in the next chamber. "But a girl alone in the Hotlands! It's—it's reckless!"

"I didn't expect to meet any American poachers," she retorted.

He flushed. "You needn't worry about me. I'm going." He raised his hands to his visor.

Instantly Patricia snatched an automatic from the table drawer. "You're going, indeed, Mr. Hamilton Hammond," she said coolly. "But you're leaving your xixtchil with me. It's crown property; you've stolen it from British territory, and I'm confiscating it."

He stared. "Look here!" he blazed suddenly. "I've risked all I have for that xixtchil. If I lose it I'm ruined—busted. I'm not giving it up!"

"But you are."

He dropped his mask and sat down. "Miss Burlingame," he said, "I don't think you've nerve enough to shoot me, but that's what you'll have to do to get it. Otherwise I'll sit here until you drop of exhaustion."

Her gray eyes bored silently into his blue ones. The gun held steadily on his heart, but spat no bullet. It was a deadlock.

At last the girl said, "You win, poacher." She slapped the gun into her empty holster. "Get out, then."

"Gladly!" he snapped.

He rose, fingered his visor, then dropped it again at a sudden startled scream from the girl. He whirled, suspecting a trick, but she was staring out of the window with wide, apprehensive eyes.

*   *   *   *   *

Ham saw the writhing of vegetation and then a vast whitish mass. A doughpot—a monstrous one, bearing steadily toward their shelter. He heard the gentle clunk of impact, and then the window was blotted out by the pasty mess, as the creature, not quite large enough to engulf the building, split into two masses that flowed around and merged on the other side. Another cry from Patricia. "Your mask, fool!" she rasped. "Close it!"

"Mask? Why?" Nevertheless, he obeyed automatically.

"Why? That's why! The digestive acids—look!" She pointed at the walls; indeed, thousands of tiny pinholes of light were appearing. The digestive acids of the monstrosity, powerful enough to attack whatever food chance brought, had corroded the metal; it was porous; the shack was ruined. He gasped as fuzzy molds shot instantly from the remains of his meal, and a red-and-green fur sprouted from the wood of chairs and table.

The two faced each other.

Ham chuckled. "Well," he said, "you're homeless, too. Mine went down in a mudspout."

"Yours would!" Patricia retorted acidly. "You Yankees couldn't think of finding shallow soil, I suppose. Bed rock is just six feet below here, and my place is on pilons."

"Well, you're a cool devil! Anyway, your place might as well be sunk. What are you going to do?"

"Do? Don't concern yourself. I'm quite able to manage."

"How?"

"It's no affair of yours, but I have a rocket call each month."

"You must be a millionaire, then," he commented. "The Royal Society," she said coldly, "is financing this expedition. The rocket is due——"

She paused; Ham thought she paled a little behind her mask.

"Due when?"

"Why—it just came two days ago. I'd forgotten."

"I see. And you think you'll just stick around for a month waiting for it. Is that it?"

Patricia stared at him defiantly.

"Do you know," he resumed, "what you'd be in a month? It's ten days to summer and look at your shack." He gestured at the walls, where brown and rusty patches were forming; at his motion a piece the size of a saucer tumbled in with a crackle. "In two days this thing will be a caved-in ruin. What'll you do during fifteen days of summer? What'll you do without shelter when the temperature reaches a hundred and fifty—a hundred and sixty? I'll tell you—you'll die." She said nothing.

"You'll be a fuzzy mass of molds before the rocket returns," Ham said. "And then a pile of clean bones that will go down with the first mudspout."

"Be still!" she blazed.

"Silence won't help. Now I'll tell you what you can do. You can take your pack and your mudshoes and walk along with me. We may make the Cool Country before summer—if you can walk as well as you talk."

"Go with a Yankee poacher? I fancy not!"

"And then," he continued imperturbably, "we can cross comfortably to Erotia, a good American town."

Patricia reached for her emergency pack, slung it over her shoulders. She retrieved a thick bundle of notes, written in aniline ink on transkin, brushed off a few vagrant molds, and slipped it into the pack. She picked up a pair of diminutive mudshoes and turned deliberately to the door.

"So you're coming?" he chuckled.

"I'm going," she retorted coldly, "to the good British town of Venoble. Alone!"

"Venoble!" he gasped. "That's two hundred miles south! And across the Greater Eternities, too!"

*   *   *   *   *

Part III.

Patricia walked silently out of the door and turned west toward the Cool Country. Ham hesitated a moment, then followed. He couldn't permit the girl to attempt that journey alone; since she ignored his presence, he simply trailed a few steps behind her, plodding grimly and angrily along.

For three hours or more they trudged through the endless daylight, dodging the thrusts of the Jack Ketch trees, but mostly following the still fairly open trail of the first doughpot.

Ham was amazed at the agile and lithe grace of the girl, who slipped along the way with the sure skill of a native. Then a memory came to him; she was a native, in a sense. He recalled now that Patrick Burlingame's daughter was the first human child born on Venus, in the colony of Venoble, founded by her father.

Ham remembered the newspaper articles when she had been sent to Earth to be educated, a child of eight; he had been thirteen then. He was twenty-seven now, which made Patricia Burlingame twenty-two.

Not a word passed between them until at last the girl swung about in exasperation.

"Go away," she blazed.

Ham halted. "I'm not bothering you."

"But I don't want a bodyguard. I'm a better Hotlander than you!"

He didn't argue the point. He kept silent, and after a moment she flashed:

"I hate you, Yankee! Lord, how I hate you!" She turned and trudged on.

An hour later the mudspout caught them. Without warning, watery muck boiled up around their feet, and the vegetation swayed wildly. Hastily, they strapped on their mudshoes, while the heavier plants sank with sullen gurgles around them. Again Ham marveled at the girl's skill; Patricia slipped away across the unstable surface with a speed he could not match, and he shuffled far behind.

Suddenly he saw her stop. That was dangerous in a mudspout; only an emergency could explain it. He hurried; a hundred feet away he perceived the reason. A strap had broken on her right shoe, and she stood helpless, balancing on her left foot, while the remaining bowl was sinking slowly. Even now black mud slopped over the edge.

She eyed him as he approached. He shuffled to her side; as she saw his intention, she spoke.

"You can't," she said.

Ham bent cautiously, slipping his arms about her knees and shoulders. Her mudshoes was already embedded, but he heaved mightily, driving the rims of his own dangerously close to the surface. With a great sucking gulp, she came free and lay very still in his arms, so as not to unbalance him as he slid again into careful motion over the treacherous surface. She was not heavy, but it was a hairbreadth chance, and the mud slipped and gurgled at the very edge of his shoe-bowls. Even though Venus has slightly less surface gravitation than Earth, a week or so gets one accustomed to it, and the twenty per cent advantage in weight seems to disappear.

A hundred yards brought firm footing. He sat her down and unstrapped her mudshoes.

"Thank you," she said coolly. "That was brave."

"You're welcome," he returned dryly. "I suppose this will end any idea of your traveling alone. Without both mudshoes, the next spout will be the last for you. Do we walk together now?"

Her voice chilled. "I can make a substitute shoe from tree skin."

"Not even a native could walk on tree skin."

"Then," she said, "I'll simply wait a day or two for the mud to dry and dig up my lost one."

He laughed and gestured at the acres of mud. "Dig where?" he countered. "You'll be here till summer if you try that."

She yielded. "You win again, Yankee. But only to the Cool Country; then you'll go north and I south."

*　　*　　*　　*　　*

They trudged on. Patricia was as tireless as Ham himself and was vastly more adept in Hotland lore. Though they spoke but little, he never ceased to wonder at the skill she had in picking the quickest route, and she seemed to sense the thrusts of the Jack Ketch trees without looking. But it was when they halted at last, after a rain had given opportunity for a hasty meal, that he had real cause to thank her.

"Sleep?" he suggested, and as she nodded: "There's a Friendly tree."

He moved toward it, the girl behind.

Suddenly she seized his arm. "It's a Pharisee!" she cried, jerking him back.

None too soon! The false Friendly tree had lashed down with a terrible stroke that missed his face by inches. It was no Friendly tree at all, but an imitator, luring prey within reach by its apparent harmlessness, then striking with knife-sharp spikes.

Ham gasped. "What is it? I never saw one of those before."

"A Pharisee! It just looks like a Friendly tree."

She took out her automatic and sent a bullet into the black, pulsing trunk. A dark stream gushed, and the ubiquitous molds sprang into life about the hole. The tree was doomed.

"Thanks," said Ham awkwardly. "I guess you saved my life."

"We're quits now." She gazed levelly at him. "Understand? We're even."

Later they found a true Friendly tree and slept. Awakening, they trudged on again, and slept again, and so on for three nightless days. No more mudspouts burst about them, but all the other horrors of the Hotlands were well in evidence. Doughpots crossed their path, snake vines hissed and struck, the Jack Ketch trees flung sinister nooses, and a million little crawling things writhed underfoot or dropped upon their suits.

Once they encountered a uniped, that queer, kangaroolike creature that leaps, crashing through the jungle on a single mighty leg, and trusts to its ten-foot beak to spear its prey.

When Ham missed his first shot, the girl brought it down in mid-leap to thresh into the avid clutches of the Jack Ketch trees and the merciless molds.

On another occasion, Patricia had both feet caught in a Jack Ketch noose that lay for some unknown cause on the ground. As she stepped within it, the tree jerked her suddenly, to dangle head down a dozen feet in the air, and she hung helplessly until Ham managed to cut her free. Beyond doubt, either would have died alone on any of several occasions; together they pulled through.

Yet neither relaxed the cool, unfriendly attitude that had become habitual. Ham never addressed the girl unless necessary, and she in the rare instances when they spoke, called him always by no other name than Yankee poacher. In spite of this, the man found himself sometimes remembering the piquant loveliness of her features, her brown hair and level gray eyes, as he had glimpsed them in the brief moments when rain made it safe to open their visors.

At last one day a wind stirred out of the west, bringing with it a breath of coolness that was like the air of heaven to them. It was the underwind, the wind that blew from the frozen half of the planet, that breathed cold from beyond the ice barrier. When Ham experimentally shaved the skin from a writhing weed, the molds sprang out more slowly and with encouraging sparseness; they were approaching the Cool Country.

They found a Friendly tree with lightened hearts; another day's trek might bring them to the uplands where one could walk unhooded, in safety from the molds, since these could not sprout in a temperature much below eighty.

Ham woke first. For a while he gazed silently across at the girl, smiling at the way the branches of the tree had encircled her like affectionate arms. They were merely hungry, of course, but it looked like tenderness. His smile turned a little sad as he realized that the Cool Country meant parting, unless he could discourage that insane determination of hers to cross the Greater Eternities.

He sighed, and reached for his pack slung on a branch between them, and suddenly a bellow of rage and astonishment broke from him.

His xixtchil pods! The transkin pouch was slit; they were gone.

Patricia woke startled at his cry. Then, behind her mask, he sensed an ironic, mocking smile.

"My xixtchil!" he roared. "Where is it?"

She pointed down. There among the lesser growths was a little mound of molds.

"There," she said coolly. "Down there, poacher."

"You——" He choked with rage.

"Yes. I slit the pouch while you slept. You'll smuggle no stolen wealth from British territory."

Ham was white, speechless. "You damned devil!" he bellowed at last. "That's every cent I had!"

"But stolen," she reminded him pleasantly, swinging her dainty feet.

Rage actually made him tremble. He glared at her; the light struck through the translucent transkin, outlining her body and slim rounded legs in shadow. "I ought to kill you!" he muttered tensely.

His hand twitched, and the girl laughed softly. With a groan of desperation, he slung his pack over his shoulders and dropped to the ground.

"I hope—I hope you die in the mountains," he said grimly, and stalked away toward the west.

A hundred yards distant he heard her voice.

"Yankee! Wait a moment!"

He neither paused nor glanced back, but strode on.

*   *   *   *   *

Half an hour later, glancing back from the crest of a rise, Ham perceived that she was following him. He turned and hurried on. The way was upward now, and his strength began to outweigh her speed and skill.

When next he glimpsed her, she was a plodding speck far behind, moving, he imagined, with a weary doggedness. He frowned back at her; it had occurred to him that a mudspout would find her completely helpless, lacking the vitally important mudshoes.

Then he realized that they were beyond the region of mudspouts, here in the foothills of the Mountains of Eternity, and anyway, he decided grimly, he didn't care.

For a while Ham paralleled a river, doubtless an unnamed tributary of the Phlegethon. So far there had been no necessity to cross watercourses, since naturally all streams on Venus flow from the ice barrier across the twilight zone to the hot side, and therefore, had coincided with their own direction.

But now, once he attained the tablelands and turned north, he would encounter rivers. They had to be crossed either on logs or, if opportunity offered and the stream was narrow, through the branches of Friendly trees. To set foot in the water was death; fierce fanged creatures haunted the streams.

He had one near catastrophe at the rim of the tableland. It was while he edged through a Jack Ketch clearing; suddenly there was a heave of white corruption, and tree and jungle wall disappeared in the mass of a gigantic doughpot.

He was cornered between the monster and an impenetrable tangle of vegetation, so he did the only thing left to do. He snatched his flame-pistol and sent a terrific, roaring blast into the horror, a blast that incinerated tons of pasty filth and left a few small fragments crawling and feeding on the debris.

The blast also, as it usually does, shattered the barrel of the weapon. He sighed as he set about the forty-minute job of replacing it—no true Hotlander ever delays that—for the blast had cost fifteen good American dollars, ten for the cheap diamond that had exploded, and five for the barrel. Nothing at all when he had had his xixtchil, but a real item now. He sighed again as he discovered that the remaining barrel was his last; he had been forced to economize on everything when he set out.

Ham came at last to the table-land. The fierce and predatory vegetation of the Hotlands grew scarce; he began to encounter true plants, with no power of movement, and the underwind blew cool in his face.

He was in a sort of high valley; to his right were the gray peaks of the Lesser Eternities, beyond which lay Erotia, and to his left, like a mighty, glittering rampart, lay the vast slopes of the Greater Range, whose peaks were lost in the clouds fifteen miles above.

He looked at the opening of the rugged Madman's Pass where it separated two colossal peaks; the pass itself was twenty-five thousand feet in height, but the mountains out-topped it by fifty thousand more. One man had crossed that jagged crack on foot—Patrick Burlingame—and that was the way his daughter meant to follow.

Ahead, visible as a curtain of shadow, lay the night edge of the twilight zone, and Ham could see the incessant lightnings that flashed forever in this region of endless storms. It was here that the ice barrier crossed the ranges of the Mountains of Eternity, and the cold underwind, thrust up by the mighty range, met the warm upper winds in a struggle that was one continuous storm, such a storm as only Venus could provide. The river Phlegethon had its source somewhere back in there.

Ham surveyed the wildly magnificent panorama. Tomorrow, or rather, after resting, he would turn north. Patricia would turn south, and, beyond doubt, would die somewhere on Madman's Pass. For a moment he had a queerly painful sensation, then he frowned bitterly.

Let her die, if she was fool enough to attempt the pass alone just because she was too proud to take a rocket from an

American settlement. She deserved it. He didn't care; he was still assuring himself of that as he prepared to sleep, not in a Friendly tree, but in one of the far more friendly specimens of true vegetation and in the luxury of an open visor.

The sound of his name awakened him. He gazed across the table-land to see Patricia just topping the divide, and he felt a moment's wonder at how she managed to trail him, a difficult feat indeed in a country where the living vegetation writhes instantly back across one's path. Then he recalled the blast of his flame-pistol; the flash and sound would carry for miles, and she must have heard or seen it.

Ham saw her glancing anxiously around.

"Ham!" she shouted again—not Yankee or poacher, but "Ham!"

He kept a sullen silence; again she called. He could see her bronzed and piquant features now; she had dropped her transkin hood. She called again; with a despondent little shrug, she turned south along the divide, and he watched her go in grim silence. When the forest hid her from view, he descended and turned slowly north.

Very slowly; his steps lagged; it was as if he tugged against some invisible elastic bond. He kept seeing her anxious face and hearing in memory the despondent call. She was going to her death, he believed, and, after all, despite what she had done to him, he didn't want that. She was too full of life, too confident, too young, and above all, too lovely to die.

True, she was an arrogant, vicious, self-centered devil, cool as crystal, and as unfriendly, but—she had gray eyes and brown hair, and she was courageous. And at last, with a groan of exasperation, he halted his lagging steps, turned, and rushed with almost eager speed into the south.

*   *   *   *   *

Trailing the girl was easy here for one trained in the Hotlands. The vegetation was slow to mend itself, here in the Cool Country, and now again he found imprints of her feet, or broken twigs to mark her path. He found the place where she had crossed the river through tree branches, and he found a place where she had paused to eat.

But he saw that she was gaining on him; her skill and speed outmatched his, and the trail grew steadily older. At last he stopped to rest; the table-land was beginning to curve upward toward the vast Mountains of Eternity, and on rising ground he knew he could overtake her. So he slept for a while in the luxurious comfort of no transkin at all, just the shorts and shirt that one wore beneath. That was safe here; the eternal underwind, blowing always toward the Hotlands, kept drifting mold spores away, and any brought in on the fur of animals died quickly at the first cool breeze. Nor would the true plants of the Cool Country attack his flesh.

He slept five hours. The next "day" of traveling brought another change in the country. The life of the foothills was sparse compared to the table-lands; the vegetation was no longer a jungle, but a forest, an unearthly forest, true, of treelike growths whose boles rose five hundred feet and then spread, not into foliage, but flowery appendages. Only an occasional Jack Ketch tree reminded him of the Hotlands.

Farther on, the forest diminished. Great rock outcroppings appeared, and vast red cliffs with no growths of any kind. Now and then he encountered swarms of the planet's only aerial creatures, the gray, mothlike dusters, large as hawks, but so fragile that a blow shattered them. They darted about, alighting at times to seize small squirming things, and tinkling in their curiously bell-like voices. And apparently almost above him, though really thirty miles distant, loomed the Mountains of Eternity, their peaks lost in the clouds that swirled fifteen miles overhead.

Here again it grew difficult to trail, since Patricia scrambled often over bare rock. But little by little the signs grew fresher; once again his greater strength began to tell. And then he glimpsed her, at the base of a colossal escarpment split by a narrow, tree-filled canyon.

She was peering first at the mighty precipice, then at the cleft, obviously wondering whether it offered a means of scaling the barrier, or whether it was necessary to circle the obstacle. Like himself, she had discarded her transkin and wore the usual shirt and shorts of the Cool Country, which, after all, is not very cool by terrestrial standards. She looked, he thought, like some lovely forest nymph of the ancient slopes of Pelion.

He hurried as she moved into the canyon. "Pat!" he shouted; it was the first time he had spoken her given name. A hundred feet within the passage he overtook her.

"You!" she gasped. She looked tired; she had been hurrying for hours, but a light of eagerness flashed in her eyes. "I thought you had—I tried to find you."

Ham's face held no responsive light. "Listen here, Pat Burlingame," he said coldly. "You don't deserve any consideration, but I can't see you walking into death. You're a stubborn devil but you're a woman. I'm taking you to Erotia."

The eagerness vanished. "Indeed, poacher? My father crossed here. I can, too."

"Your father crossed in midsummer, didn't he? And midsummer's to-day. You can't make Madman's Pass in less than five days, a hundred and twenty hours, and by then it will nearly winter, and this longitude will be close to the storm line. You're a fool."

She flushed. "The pass is high enough to be in the upper winds. It will be warm."

"Warm! Yes—warm with lightning." He paused; the faint rumble of thunder rolled through the canyon. "Listen to that. In five days that will be right over us." He gestured up at the utterly barren slopes. "Not even Venusian life can get a foothold up there—or do you think you've got brass enough to be a lightning rod? Maybe you're right."

Anger flamed. "Rather the lightning than you!" Patricia snapped, and then as suddenly softened. "I tried to call you back," she said irrelevantly.

"To laugh at me," he retorted bitterly.

"No. To tell you I was sorry, and that——"

"I don't want your apology."

"But I wanted to tell you that——"

"Never mind," he said curtly. "I'm not interested in your repentance. The harm's done." He frowned coldly down on her.

Patricia said meekly: "But I——"

A crashing and gurgling interrupted her, and she screamed as a gigantic doughpot burst into view, a colossus that filled the canyon from wall to wall to a six-foot height as it surged toward them. The horrors were rarer in the Cool Country, but larger, since the abundance of food in the Hotlands kept subdividing them. But this one was a giant, a behemoth, tons and tons of nauseous, ill-smelling corruption heaving up the narrow way. They were cut off.

Ham snatched his flame-pistol, but the girl seized his arm.

"No, no!" she cried. "Too close! It will spatter!"

*   *   *   *   *

Patricia was right. Unprotected by transkin, the touch of a fragment of that monstrosity was deadly, and, beyond that, the blast of a flame-pistol would shower bits of it upon them. He grasped her wrist and they fled up the canyon, striving for vantage way enough to risk a shot. And a dozen feet behind surged the doughpot, traveling blindly in the only direction it could—the way of food.

They gained. Then, abruptly, the canyon, which had been angling southwest, turned sharply south. The light of the eternally eastward Sun was hidden; they were in a pit of perpetual shadow, and the ground was bare and lifeless rock. And as it reached that point, the doughpot halted; lacking any organization, any will, it could not move when no food gave it direction. It was such a monster as only the life-swarming climate of Venus could harbor; it lived only by endless eating.

The two paused in the shadow.

"Now what?" muttered Ham.

A fair shot at the mass was impossible because of the angle; a blast would destroy only the portion it could reach.

Patricia leaped upward, catching a snaky shrub on the wall, so placed that it received a faint ray of light. She tossed it against the pulsing mass; the whole doughpot lunged forward a foot or two.

"Lure it in," she suggested.

They tried. It was impossible; vegetation was too sparse.

"What will happen to the thing?" asked Ham.

"I saw one stranded on the desert edge of the Hotlands," replied the girl. "It quivered around for a long time, and then the cells attacked each other. It ate itself." She shuddered. "It was—horrible!"

"How long?"

"Oh, forty to fifty hours."

"I won't wait that long," growled Ham. He fumbled in his pack, pulling out his transkin.

"What will you do?"

"Put this on and try to blast that mass out of here at close range." He fingered his flame-pistol. "This is my last barrel," he said gloomily, then more hopefully: "But we have yours."

"The chamber of mine cracked last time I used it, ten or twelve hours ago. But I have plenty of barrels."

"Good enough!" said Ham.

He crept cautiously toward the horrible, pulsating wall of white. He thrust his arm so as to cover the greatest angle, pulled the trigger, and the roar and blazing fire of the blast bellowed echoing through the canyon. Bits of the monster spattered around him, and the thickness of the remainder, lessened by the incineration of tons of filth, was now only three feet.

"The barrel held!" he called triumphantly. It saved much time in recharging.

Five minutes later the weapon crashed again. When the mass of the monstrosity stopped heaving, only a foot and a half of depth remained, but the barrel had been blown to atoms.

"We'll have to use yours," he said.

Patricia produced one, he took it, and then stared at it in dismay. The barrels of her Enfield-made weapon were far too small for his American pistol stock!

He groaned. "Of all the idiots!" he burst out.

"Idiots!" she flared. "Because you Yankees use trench mortars for your barrels?"

"I meant myself. I should have guessed this." He shrugged. "Well, we have our choice now of waiting here for the doughpot to eat himself, or trying to find some other way out of this trap. And my hunch is that this canyon's blind."

It was probable, Patricia admitted. The narrow cleft was the product of some vast, ancient upheaval that had split the mountain in halves. Since it was not the result of water erosion, it was likely enough that the cleft ended abruptly in an unscalable precipice, but it was possible, too, that somewhere those sheer walls might be surmountable.

"We've time to waste, anyway," she concluded. "We might as well try it. Besides—" She wrinkled her dainty nose distastefully at the doughpot's odor.

*   *   *   *   *

Still in his transkin, Ham followed her through the shadowy half dusk. The passage narrowed, then veered west again, but now so high and sheer were the walls that the Sun, slightly south of east, cast no light into it. It was a place of shades like the region of the storm line that divides the twilight zone from the dark hemisphere, not true night, nor yet honest day, but a dim middle state.

Ahead of him Patricia's bronzed limbs showed pale instead of tan, and when she spoke her voice went echoing queerly between the opposing cliffs. A weird place, this chasm, a dusky, unpleasant place.

"I don't like this," said Ham. "The pass is cutting closer and closer to the dark. Do you realize no one knows what's in the dark parts of the Mountains of Eternity?"

Patricia laughed; the sound was ghostly. "What danger could there be? Anyway, we still have our automatics."

"There's no way up here," Ham grumbled. "Let's turn back."

Patricia faced him. "Frightened, Yankee?" Her voice dropped. "The natives say these mountains are haunted," she went on mockingly. "My father told me he saw queer things in Madman's Pass. Do you know that if there is life on the night side, here is the one place it would impinge on the twilight zone? Here in the Mountains of Eternity?"

She was taunting him; she laughed again. And suddenly her laughter was repeated in a hideous cacophony that hooted out from the sides of the cliffs above them in a horrid medley.

She paled; it was Patricia who was frightened now. They stared apprehensively up at the rock walls where strange shadows flickered and shifted.

"What—what was it?" she whispered. And then: "Ham! Did you see that?"

Ham had seen it. A wild shape had flung itself across the strip of sky, leaping from cliff to cliff far above them. And again came a peal of hooting that sounded like laughter, while shadowy forms moved, flylike, on the sheer walls.

"Let's go back!" she gasped. "Quickly!"

As she turned, a small black object fell and broke with a sullen pop before them. Ham stared at it. A pod, a spore-sac, of some unknown variety. A lazy, dusky cloud drifted over it, and suddenly both of them were choking violently. Ham felt his head spinning in dizziness, and Patricia reeled against him.

"It's narcotic!" she gasped. "Back!"

But a dozen more plopped around them. The dusty spores whirled in dark eddies, and breathing was a torment. They were being drugged and suffocated at the same time.

Ham had a sudden inspiration. "Mask!" he choked, and pulled his transkin over his face.

The filter that kept out the molds of the Hotlands cleaned the air of these spores as well; his head cleared. But the girl's covering was somewhere in her pack; she was fumbling for it. Abruptly she sat down, swaying.

"My pack," she murmured. "Take it out with you. Your— your—" She broke into a fit of coughing.

He dragged her under a shallow overhang and ripped her transkin from the pack. "Put it on!" he snapped.

A score of pods were popping.

A figure flitted silently far up on the wall of rock. Ham watched its progress, then aimed his automatic and fired. There was a shrill, rasping scream, answered by a chorus of dissonant ululations, and something as large as a man whirled down to crash not ten feet from him.

The thing was hideous. Ham stared appalled at a creature not unlike a native, three-eyed, two-handed, four-legged, but the hands, though two-fingered like the Hotlanders', were not pincer-like, but white and clawed.

And the face! Not the broad, expressionless face of the others, but a slanting, malevolent, dusky visage with each eye double the size of the natives'. It wasn't dead; it glared hatred and seized a stone, flinging it at him with weak viciousness. Then it died.

Ham didn't know what it was, of course. Actually it was a triops noctivivans—the "three-eyed dweller in the dark," the strange, semi-intelligent being that is as yet the only known creature of the night side, and a member of that fierce remnant still occasionally found in the sunless parts of the Mountains of Eternity. It is perhaps the most vicious creature in the known planets, absolutely unapproachable, and delighting in slaughter.

At the crash of the shot, the shower of pods had ceased, and a chorus of laughing hoots ensued. Ham seized the respite to pull the girl's transkin over her face; she had collapsed with it only half on.

Then a sharp crack sounded, and a stone rebounded to strike his arm. Others pattered around him, whining past, swift as bullets. Black figures flickered in great leaps against the sky, and their fierce laughter sounded mockingly. He fired at one in mid-air; the cry of pain rasped again, but the creature did not fall.

Stones pelted him. They were all small ones, pebble-sized, but they were flung so fiercely that they hummed in passage, and they tore his flesh through his transkin. He turned Patricia on her face, but she moaned faintly as a missile struck her back. He shielded her with his own body.

*   *   *   *   *

The position was intolerable. He must risk a dash back, even though the doughpot blocked the opening. Perhaps, he thought, armored in transkin he could wade through the creature. He knew that was an insane idea; the gluey mass would roll him into itself to suffocate—but it had to be faced. He gathered the girl in his arms and rushed suddenly down the canyon.

Hoots and shrieks and a chorus of mocking laughter echoed around him. Stones struck him everywhere. One glanced from his head, sending him stumbling and staggering against the cliff. But he ran doggedly on; he knew now what drove him. It was the girl he carried; he had to save Patricia Burlingame.

Ham reached the bend. Far up on the west wall glowed cloudy sunlight, and his weird pursuers flung themselves to the dark side. They couldn't stand daylight, and that gave him some assistance; by creeping very close to the eastern wall he was partially shielded.

Ahead was the other bend, blocked by the doughpot. As he neared it, he turned suddenly sick. Three of the creatures were grouped against the mass of white, eating—actually eating!—the corruption. They whirled, hooting, as he came, he shot two of them, and as the third leaped for the wall, he dropped that one as well, and it fell with a dull gulping sound into the doughpot.

Again he sickened; the doughpot drew away from it, leaving the thing lying in a hollow like the hole of a giant doughnut. Not even that monstrosity would eat these creatures.[1]

[1 It was not known then that while the night-side life of Venus can eat and digest that of the day side, the reverse is not true. No day-side creature can absorb the dark life because of the presence of various metabolic alcohols, all poisonous.]

But the thing's leap had drawn Ham's attention to a twelve-inch ledge. It might be—yes, it was possible that he could traverse that rugged trail and so circle the doughpot. Nearly hopeless, no doubt, to attempt it under the volley of stones, but he must. There was no alternative.

He shifted the girl to free his right arm. He slipped a second clip in his automatic and then fired at random into the flitting shadows above. For a moment the hail of pebbles ceased, and with a convulsive, painful struggle, Ham dragged himself and Patricia to the ledge.

Stones cracked about him once more. Step by step he edged along the way, poised just over the doomed doughpot. Death below and death above! And little by little he rounded the bend; above him both walls glowed in sunlight, and they were safe.

At least, he was safe. The girl might be already dead, he thought frantically, as he slipped and slid through the slime of the doughpot's passage. Out on the daylit slope he tore the mask from her face and gazed on white, marble-cold features.

*   *   *   *   *

It was not death, however, but only drugged torpor. An hour later she was conscious, though weak and very badly frightened. Yet almost her first question was for her pack.

"It's here," Ham said. "What's so precious about that pack? Your notes?"

"My notes? Oh, no!" A faint flush covered her features. "It's— I kept trying to tell you—it's your xixtchil."

"What?"

"Yes. I—of course I didn't throw it to the molds. It's yours by rights, Ham. Lots of British traders go into the American Hotlands. I just slit the pouch and hid it here in my pack. The molds on the ground were only some twigs I threw there to—to make it look real."

"But—but—why?"

The flush deepened. "I wanted to punish you," Patricia whispered, "for being so—so cold and distant."

"I?" Ham was amazed. "It was you!"

"Perhaps it was, at first. You forced your way into my house, you know. But—after you carried me across the mudspout, Ham—it was different."

Ham gulped. Suddenly he pulled her into his arms. "I'm not going to quarrel about whose fault it was," he said. "But we'll settle one thing immediately. We're going to Erotia, and that's where we'll be married, in a good American church if they've put one up yet, or by a good American justice if they haven't. There's no more talk of Madman's Pass and crossing the Mountains of Eternity. Is that clear?"

She glanced at the vast, looming peaks and shuddered. "Quite clear!" she replied meekly.

THE LOTUS EATERS

ORIGINALLY PUBLISHED IN *ASTOUNDING STORIES*
APRIL 1935

THE LOTUS EATERS

"Whew!" whistled "Ham" Hammond, staring through the right forward observation port. "What a place for a honeymoon!"

"Then you shouldn't have married a biologist," remarked Mrs. Hammond over his shoulder, but he could see her gray eyes dancing in the glass of the port. "Nor an explorer's daughter," she added. For Pat Hammond, until her marriage to Ham a scant four weeks ago, had been Patricia Burlingame, daughter of the great Englishman who had won so much of the twilight zone of Venus for Britain, exactly as Crowly had done for the United States.

"I didn't," observed Ham, "marry a biologist. I married a girl who happened to be interested in biology; that's all. It's one of her few drawbacks."

He cut the blast to the underjets, and the rocket settled down gently on a cushion of flame toward the black landscape below. Slowly, carefully, he dropped the unwieldy mechanism until there was the faintest perceptible jar; then he killed the blast suddenly, the floor beneath them tilted slightly, and a strange silence fell like a blanket after the cessation of the roaring blast.

"We're here," he announced.

"So we are," agreed Pat. "Where's here?"

"It's a point exactly seventy-five miles east of the Barrier opposite Venoble, in the British Cool Country. To the north is, I suppose, the continuation of the Mountains of Eternity, and to the south is Heaven knows what. And this last applies to the east."

"Which is a good technical description of nowhere." Pat laughed. "Let's turn off the lights and look at nowhere."

She did, and in the darkness the ports showed as faintly luminous circles.

"I suggest," she proceeded, "that the Joint Expedition ascend to the dome for a less restricted view. We're here to investigate; let's do a little investigating."

"This joint of the expedition agrees," chuckled Ham.

He grinned in the darkness at the flippancy with which Pat approached the serious business of exploration. Here they were, the Joint Expedition of the Royal Society and the Smithsonian Institute for the Investigation of Conditions on the Dark Side of Venus, to use the full official title.

Of course Ham himself, while technically the American half of the project, was in reality a member only because Pat wouldn't consider anything else; but she was the one to whom the bearded society and institute members addressed their questions, their terms, and their instructions.

And this was no more than fair, for Pat, after all, was the leading authority on Hotland flora and fauna, and, moreover, the first human child born on Venus, while Ham was only an engineer lured originally to the Venusian frontier by a dream of quick wealth in xixtchil trading in the Hotlands.

It was there he had met Patricia Burlingame, and there, after an adventurous journey to the foothills of the Mountains of Eternity, that he had won her. They had been married in Erotia, ihe American seitlement, less than a month ago, and then had come the offer of the expedition to the dark side.

Ham had argued against it. He had wanted a good terrestrial honeymoon in New York or London, but there were difficulties. Primarily there was the astronomical one; Venus was past perigee, and it would be eight long months before its slow swing around the Sun brought it back to a point where a rocket could overtake the Earth. Eight months in primitive, frontier-built Erotia, or in equally primitive Venoble, if they chose the British settlement, with no amusement save hunting, no radio, no plays, even very few books. And if they must hunt, Pat argued, why not add the thrill and danger of the unknown?

No one knew what life, if any, lurked on the dark side of the planet; very few had even seen it, and those few from rockets speeding over vast mountain ranges or infinite frozen oceans. Here was a chance to explain the mystery, and explore it, expenses paid.

It took a multimillionaire to build and equip a private rocket, but the Royal Society and the Smithsonian Institute, spending government money, were above such considerations. There'd be danger, perhaps, and breathtaking thrills, but—they could be alone.

The last point had won Ham. So they had spent two busy weeks provisioning and equipping the rocket, had ridden high above the ice barrier that bounds the twilight zone, and dashed frantically through the storm line, where the cold Underwind from the sunless side meets the hot Upper Winds that sweep from the desert face of the planet.

For Venus, of course, has no rotation, and hence no alternate days and nights. One face is forever sunlit, and one forever dark, and only the planet's slow liberation gives the twilight zone a semblance of seasons. And this twilight zone, the only habitable part of the planet, merges through the Hotlands on one side to the blazing desert, and on the other side ends abruptly in ihe ice barrier where the Upper Winds yield their moisture to the chilling breaths of the Underwind.

So here they were, crowded into the tiny glass dome above the navigation panel, standing close together on the top rung of the ladder, and with just room in the dome for both their heads. Ham slipped his arm around the girl as they stared at the scene outside.

Away off to the west was the eternal dawn—or sunset, perhaps—where the light glistened on the ice barrier. Like vast columns, the Mountains of Eternity thrust themselves against the light, with their mighty peaks lost in the lower clouds twenty-five miles above. There, a little south, were the ramparts of the Lesser Eternities, bounding American Venus, and between the two ranges were the perpetual lightnings of the storm line.

But around them, illuminated dimly by the refraction of the sunlight, was a scene of dark and wild splendor. Everywhere was ice—hills of it, spires, plains, boulders, and cliffs of it, all glowing a pallid green in the trickle of light from beyond the barrier. A world without motion, frozen and sterile, save for the moaning of the Underwind outside, not hindered here as the barrier shielded it from the Cool Country.

"It's—glorious!" Pat murmured.

"Yes," he agreed, "but cold, lifeless, yet menacing. Pat, do you think there is life here?"

"I should judge so. If life can exist on such worlds as Titan and Iapetus, it should exist here. How cold is it?" She glanced at the thermometer outside the dome, its column and figures self-luminous. "Only thirty below zero, Fahrenheit. Life exists on Earth at that temperature."

"Exists, yes. But it couldn't have developed at a temperature below freezing. Life has to be lived in liquid water."

She laughed softly. "You're talking to a biologist, Ham. No; life couldn't have evolved at thirty below zero, but suppose it originated back in the twilight zone and migrated here? Or suppose it was pushed here by the terrific competition of the warmer regions? You know what conditions are in the Hotlands, with the molds and doughpots and Jack Ketch trees, and the millions of little parasitic things, all eating each other."

He considered this. "What sort of life should you expect?"

She chuckled. "Do you want a prediction? Very well. I'd guess, first of all, some sort of vegetation as a base, for animal life can't keep eating itself without some added fuel. It's like the story of the man with the cat farm, who raised rats to feed the cats, and then when he skinned the cats, he fed the bodies to the rats, and then fed more rats to the cats. It sounds good, but it won't work."

"So there ought to be vegetation. Then what?"

"Then? Heaven knows. Presumably the dark side life, if it exists, came originally from the weaker strains of twilight-zone life, but what it might have become—well, I can't guess. Of course, there's the triops noctivivans that I discovered in the Mountains of Eternity—"

"You discovered!" He grinned. "You were out as cold as ice when I carried you away from the nest of devils. You never even saw one!"

"I examined the dead one brovight into Venoble by the hunters," she returned imperturbably. "And don't forget that the society wanted to name it after me—the triops Patriciæ". Involuntarily a shudder shook her at the memory of those satanic creatures that had all but destroyed the two of them. "But I chose the other name—triops noctivivans, the three-eyed dweller in the dark."

"Romantic name for a devilish beast!"

"Yes; but what I was getting at is this—that it's probable that triops—or triopses—Say, what is the plural of triops?"

"Trioptes," he grunted. "Latin root."

"Well, it's probable that trioptes, then, are among the creatures to be found here on the night side, and that those fierce devils who attacked us in that shadowed canyon in the Mountains of Eternity are an outpost, creeping into the twilight zone through the dark and sunless passes in the mountains. They can't stand light; you saw that yourself."

"So what?"

Pat laughed at the Americanism. "So this: From their form and structure—six limbs, three eyes, and all—it's plain that the trioptes are related to ordinary native Hotlanders. Therefore I conclude that they're recent arrivals on the dark side; that they didn't evolve here, but were driven here quite lately, geologically speaking. Or geologically isn't quite the word, because geos means earth. Venusologically speaking, I should say."

"You shouldn't say. You're substituting a Latin root for a Greek one. What you mean is aphrodisiologically speaking."

She chuckled again. "What I mean, and should have said right away to avoid argument, is palæontologically speaking, which is better English. Anyway, I mean that trioptes haven't existed on the dark side for more than twenty to fifty thousand Earth years, or maybe less, because what do we know about the speed of evolution on Venus? Perhaps it's faster than on the Earth; maybe a triops could adapt itself to night life in five thousand."

"I've seen college students adapt themselves to night life in one semester!" He grinned.

She ignored this. "And therefore," she proceeded, "I argue that there must have been life here before triops arrived, since it must have found something to eat when it got here or it couldn't have survived. And since my examination showed that it's partly a carnivorous feeder, there must have been not only life here, but animal life. And that's as far as pure reason can carry the argument."

"So you can't guess what sort of animal life. Intelligent, perhaps?"

"I don't know. It might be. But in spite of the way you Yankees worship intelligence, biologically it's unimportant. It hasn't even much survival value."

"What? How can you say that, Pat? What except human intelligence has given man the supremacy of the Earth—and of Venus, too, for that matter?"

"But has man the supremacy of the Earth? Look here, Ham, here's what I mean about intelligence. A gorilla has a far better brain than a turtle, hasn't it? And yet which is the more successful—the gorilla, which is rare and confined only to a small region in Africa, or the turtle, which is common everywhere from the arctic to the antarctic? And as for man— well, if you had microscopic eyes, and could see every living thing on the Earth, you'd decide that man was just a rare specimen, and that the planet was really a nematode world— that is, a worm world—because the nematodes far outnumber all the other forms of life put together."

"But that isn't supremacy, Pat."

"I didn't say it was. I merely said that intelligence hasn't much survival value. If it has, why are the insects that have no intelligence, but just instinct, giving the human race such a battle? Men have better brains than corn borers, boll weevils, fruit flies, Japanese beetles, gypsy moths, and all the other pests, and yet they match our intelligence with just one weapon—their enormous fecundity. Do you realize that every time a child is born, until it's balanced by a death, it can be fed in only one way? And that way is by taking the food away from the child's own weight of insects."

"All that sounds reasonable enough, but what's it got to do with intelligence on the dark side of Venus?"

"I don't know," replied Pat, and her voice took on a queer tinge of nervousness. "I just mean—Look at it this way, Ham. A lizard is more intelligent than a fish, but not enough to give it any advantage. Then why did the lizard and its descendants keep on developing intelligence? Why—unless all life tends to become intelligent in time? And if that's true, then there may be intelligence even here—strange, alien, incomprehensible intelligence."

She shivered in the dark against him. "Never mind," she said in suddenly altered tones. "It's probably just fancy. The world out there is so weird, so unearthly—I'm tired, Ham. It's been a long day."

He followed her down into the body of the rocket. As the lights flicked on the strange landscape beyond the ports was blotted out, and he saw only Pat, very lovely in the scanty costume of the Cool Country.

"To-morrow, then," he said. "We've food for three weeks."

*   *   *   *   *

To-morrow, of course, meant only time and not daylight. They rose to the same darkness that had always blanketed the sunless half of Venus, with the same eternal sunset green on the horizon at the barrier. But Pat was in better humor, and went eagerly about the preparations for their first venture into the open. She brought out the parkas of inch-thick wool sheathed in rubber, and Ham, in his capacity as engineer, carefully inspected the hoods, each with its crown of powerful lamps.

These were primarily for vision, of course, but they had another purpose. It was known that the incredibly fierce trioptes could not face light, and thus, by using all four beams in the helmet, one could move, surrounded by a protective aura. But that did not prevent both of them from including in their equipment two blunt blue automatics and a pair of the terrifically destructive flame pistols. And Pat carried a bag at her belt, into which she proposed to drop specimens of any dark-side flora she encountered, and fauna, too, if it proved small and harmless enough.

They grinned at each other through their masks. "Makes you look fat," observed Ham maliciously, and enjoyed her sniff of annoyance.

She turned, threw open the door, and stamped into the open.

It was different from looking out through a port. Then the scene had some of the unreality and all of the immobility and silence of a picture, but now it was actually around them, and the cold breath and mournful voice of the Underwind proved definitely enough that the world was real. For a moment they stood in the circlet of light from the rocket ports, staring awe-struck at the horizon where the unbelievable peaks of the Greater Eternities towered black against the false sunset.

Nearer, for as far as vision reached through that sunless, moonless, starless region, was a desolate tumbled plain where peaks, minarets, spires, and ridges of ice and stone rose in indescribable and fantastic shapes, carved by the wild artistry of the Underwind.

Ham slipped a padded arm around Pat, and was surprised to feel her shiver. "Cold?" he asked, glancing at the dial thermometer on his wrist. "It's only thirty-six below."

"I'm not cold," replied Pat. "It's the scenery; that's all." She moved away. "I wonder what keeps the place as warm as it is. Without sunlight you'd think—"

"Then you'd be wrong," cut in Ham. "Any engineer knows that gases diffuse. The Upper Winds are going by just five or six miles over our heads, and they naturally carry a lot of heat from the desert beyond the twilight zone. There's some diffusion of the warm air into the cold, and then, besides, as the warm winds cool, they tend to sink. And what's more, the contour of the country has a lot to do with it."

He paused. "Say," he went on reflectively, "I shouldn't be surprised if we found sections near the Eternities where there was a down draft, where the Upper Winds slid right along the slope and gave certain places a fairly bearable climate."

He followed Pat as she poked around the boulders near the edge of the circle of light from the rocket.

"Ha!" she exclaimed. "There it is, Ham! There's our specimen of darkside plant life."

She bent over a gray bulbous mass, "Lichenous or fungoid," she continued. "No leaves, of course; leaves are only useful in sunlight. No chlorophyl for the same reason. A very primitive, very simple plant, and yet—in some ways—not simple at all. Look, Ham—a highly developed circulatory system!"

He leaned closer, and in the dim yellow light from the ports he saw the fine tracery of veins she indicated.

"That," she proceeded, "would indicate a sort of heart and—I wonder!" Abruptly she thrust her dial thermometer against the fleshy mass, held it there a moment, and then peered at it. "Yes! Look how the needle's moved, Ham. It's warm! A warm-blooded plant. And when you think of it, it's only natural, because that's the one sort of plant that could live in a region forever below freezing. Life must be lived in liquid water."

She tugged at the thing, and with a sullen plump it came free, and dark driblets of liquid welled out of the torn root.

"Ugh!" exclaimed Ham. "What a disgusting thing! 'And tore the bleeding mandragore,' eh? Only they were supposed to scream when you uprooted them."

He paused. A low, pulsing, wailing whimper came out of the quivering mass of pulp, and he turned a startled gaze on Pat. "Ugh!" he grunted again. "Disgusting!"

"Disgusting? Why, it's a beautiful organism! It's adapted perfectly to its environment."

"Well, I'm glad I'm an engineer," he growled, watching Pat as she opened the rocket's door and laid the thing on a square of rubber within. "Come on. Let's look around."

Pat closed the door and followed him away from the rocket. Instantly the night folded in around them like a black mist, and it was only by glancing back at the lighted ports that Pat could convince herself that they stood in a real world.

"Should we light our helmet lamps?" asked Ham. "We'd better, I suppose, or risk a fall."

Before either could move farther, a sound struck through the moaning of the Underwind, a wild, fierce, unearthly shrieking like laughter in hell, hoots and howls and mirthless chuckling noises.

"It's triops!" gasped Pat, forgetting plurals and grammar alike.

She was frightened; ordinarily she was as courageous as Ham, and rather more reckless and daring, but those uncanny shrieks brought back the moments of torment when they had been trapped in the canyon in the Mountains of Eternity. She was badly frightened and fumbled frantically and ineffectually at light switch and revolver.

Just as half a dozen stones hummed fast as bullets around them, and one crashed painfully on Ham's arm, he flicked on his lights. Four beams shot in a long cross on the glittering peaks, and the wild laughter rose in a crescendo of pain. He had a momentary glimpse of shadowy figures flinging themselves from pinnacle and ridge, flitting specterlike into the darkness, and then silence.

"O-o-oh!" murmured Pat. "I—was scared, Ham." She huddled against him, then continued more strongly: "But there's proof.

Triops noctivivans actually is a night-side creature, and those in the mountains are outposts or fragments that've wandered into the sunless chasms."

Far off sounded the hooting laughter. "I wonder," mused Ham, "if that noise of their's is in the nature of a language."

"Very probably. After all, the Hotland natives are intelligent, and these creatures are a related species. Besides, they throw stones, and they know the use of those smothering pods they showered on us in the canyon—which, by the way, must be the fruit of some night-side plant. The trioptes are doubtless intelligent in a fierce, blood-thirsty, barbaric fashion, but the beasts are so unapproachable that I doubt if human beings ever learn much of their minds or language."

Ham agreed emphatically, the more so as a viciously cast rock suddenly chipped glittering particles from an icy spire a dozen paces away. He twisted his head, sending the beams of his helmet lamps angling over the plain, and a single shrill cachinnation drifted out of the dark.

"Thank Heaven the lights keep 'em fairly out of range," he muttered. "These are pleasant little subjects of his majesty,[1] aren't they? God save the king if he had many more like 'em!"

[1 They were on British territory, being in the latitude of Venoble. The International Congress at Lisle had in 2020 apportioned the dark-side rights by giving to each nation owning Venusian possessions a wedge extending from the twilight zone to a point on the planet directly opposite the Sun in mid-autumn.]

But Pat was again engaged in her search for specimens. She had switched on her lamps now, and scrambled agilely in and out among the fantastic monuments of that bizarre plain. Ham followed her, watching as she wrenched up bleeding and whimpering vegetation. She found a dozen varieties, and one little wriggling cigar-shaped creature that she gazed at in perplexity, quite unable to determine whether it was plant, animal, or neither. And at last her specimen bag was completely filled, and they turned back over the plain toward the rocket, whose ports gleamed afar like a row of staring eyes.

But a shock awaited them as they opened the door to enter. Both of them started back at the gust of warm, stuffy, putrid, and unbreathable air that gushed into their faces with an odor of carrion.

"What——" gasped Ham, and then laughed. "Your mandragore!" He chuckled. "Look at it!"

The plant she had placed within was a mass of decayed corruption. In the warmth of the interior it had decomposed rapidly and completely and was now but a semiliquid heap on the rubber mat. She pulled it through the entrance and flung mat and all away.

They clambered into an interior still reeking, and Ham set a ventilator spinning. The air that came in was cold, of course, but pure with the breath of the Underwind, sterile and dustless from its sweep across five thousand miles of frozen oceans and mountains. He swung the door closed, set a heater going, and dropped his visor to grin at Pat.

"So that's your beautiful organism!" he chuckled.

"It was. It was a beautiful organism, Ham. You can't blame it because we exposed it to temperatures it was never supposed to encounter." She sighed and slung her specimen pouch to the table. "I'll have to prepare these at once, I suppose, since they don't keep."

Ham grunted and set about the preparation of a meal, working with the expert touch of a true Hotlander. He glanced at Pat as she bent over her specimens, injecting the bichloride solution.

"Do you suppose," he asked, "that the triops is the highest form of life on the dark side?"

"Beyond doubt," replied Pat. "If any higher form existed, it would long ago have exterminated those fierce devils."

But she was utterly wrong.

*   *   *   *   *

Within the span of four days they had exhausted the possibilities of the tumbled plain around the rocket. Pat had accumulated a variegated group of specimens, and Ham had taken an endless series of observations on temperature, on magnetic variations, on the direction and velocity of the Underwind.

So they moved their base, and the rocket flared into flight southward, toward the region where, presumably, the vast and mysterious Mountains of Eternity towered across the ice barrier into the dusky world of the night side. They flew slowly, throttling the reaction motors to a bare fifty miles an hour, for they were flying through night, depending on the beam of the forward light to warn against looming peaks.

Twice they halted, and each time a day or two sufficed to indicate that the region was similar to that of their first base. The same veined and bulbous plants, the same eternal Underwind, the same laughter from blood-thirsty trioptic throats.

But on the third occasion, there was a difference. They came to rest on a wild and bleak plateau among the foothills of the Greater Eternities. Far away to the westward, half the horizon still glowed green with the false sunset, but the whole span south of the due-west point was black, hidden from view by the vast ramparts of the range that soared twenty-five miles above them into the black heavens. The mountains were invisible, of course, in that region of endless night, but the two in the rocket felt the colossal nearness of those incredible peaks.

And there was another way in which the mighty presence of the Mountains of Eternity affected them. The region was warm—not warm by the standards of the twilight zone, but much warmer than the plain below. Their thermometers showed zero on one side of the rocket, five above on the other. The vast peaks, ascending into the level of the Upper Winds, set up eddies and stray currents that brought warm air down to temper the cold breath of the Underwind.

Ham stared gloomily over the plateau visible in the lights. "I don't like it," he grunted. "I never did like these mountains, not since you made a fool of yourself by trying to cross 'em back in the Cool Country."

"A fool!" echoed Pat. "Who named these mountains? Who crossed them? Who discovered them? My father, that's who!"

"And so you thought you inherited 'em," he retorted, "and that all you had to do was to whistle and they'd lie down and play dead, and Madman's Pass would turn into a park walk. With the result that you'd now be a heap of clean-picked bones in a canyon if I hadn't been around to carry you out of it."

"Oh, you're just a timid Yankee!" she snapped. "I'm going outside to have a look." She pulled on her parka and stepped to the door, and there paused. "Aren't you—aren't you coming, too?" she asked hesitantly.

He grinned. "Sure! I just wanted to hear you ask." He slipped into his own outdoor garb and followed.

There was a difference here. Outwardly the plateau presented the same bleak wilderness of ice and stone that they had found on the plain below. There were wind-eroded pinnacles of the utmost fantasy of form, and the wild landscape that glittered in the beams from their helmet lamps was the same bizarre terrain that they had first encountered.

But the cold was less bitter here; strangely, increasing altitude on this curious planet brought warmth instead of cold, as on the Earth, because it raised one closer to the region of the Upper Winds, and here in the Mountains of Eternity the Underwind howled less persistently, broken into gusts by the mighty peaks.

And the vegetation was less sparse. Everywhere were the veined and bulbous masses, and Ham had to tread carefully lest he repeat the unpleasant experience of stepping on one and hearing its moaning whimper of pain. Pat had no such scruples, insisting that the whimper was but a tropism; that the specimens she pulled up and dissected felt no more pain than an apple that was eaten; and that, anyway, it was a biologist's business to be a biologist.

Somewhere off among the peaks shrilled the mocking laughter of a triops, and in the shifting shadows at the extremities of their beams, Ham imagined more than once that he saw the forms of these demons of the dark. If there they were, however, the light kept them at a safe distance, for no stones hummed past.

Yet it was a queer sensation to walk thus in the center of a moving circle of light; he felt continually as if just beyond the boundary of visibility lurked Heaven only knew what weird and incredible creatures, though reason argued that such monsters couldn't have remained undetected.

Ahead of them their beams glistened on an icy rampart, a bank or cliff that stretched right and left across their course.

Pat gestured suddenly toward it. "Look there!" she exclaimed, holding her light steady. "Caves in the ice—burrows, rather. See?"

He saw—little black openings as large, perhaps, as a manhole cover, a whole row of them at the base of the ice rampart. Something black skittered laughing up the glassy slope and away—a triops. Were these the dens of the beasts? He squinted sharply.

"Something's there!" he muttered to Pat. "Look! Half the openings have something in front of them—or are those just rocks to block the entrance?"

Cautiously, revolvers in hand, they advanced. There was no more motion, but in the growing intensity of the beams, the objects were less and less rocklike, and at last they could make out the veinings and fleshy bulbousness of life.

At least the creatures were a new variety. Now Ham could distinguish a row of eyelike spots, and now a multiplicity of legs beneath them. The things were like inverted bushel baskets, about the size and contour, veined, flabby, and featureless save for a complete circle of eye spots. And now he could even see the semitransparent lids that closed, apparently, to shield the eyes from the pain of their lights.

They were barely a dozen feet from one of the creatures. Pat, after a moment of hesitation, moved directly before the motionless mystery.

"Well!" she said. "Here's a new one, Ham. Hello, old fella!"

An instant later both of them were frozen in utter consternation, completely overwhelmed by bewilderment, amazement, and confusion. Issuing, it seemed, from a membrane at the top of the creature, came a clicking, high-pitched voice.

"Hello, fella!" it said.

There was an appalled silence. Ham held his revolver, but had there been need, he couldn't have used it, nor even remembered it. He was paralyzed; stricken dumb.

But Pat found her voice. "It—isn't real," she said faintly. "It's a tropism. The thing just echoed whatever sounds strike it. Doesn't it, Ham? Doesn't it?"

"I—I—of course!" He was staring at the lidded eyes. "It must be. Listen!" He leaned forward and yelled, "Hello!" directly at the creature. "It'll answer."

It did. "It isn't a tropism," it clicked in shrill but perfect English.

"That's no echo!" gasped Pat. She backed away. "I'm scared," she whimpered, pulling at Ham's arm. "Come away—quick!"

He thrust her behind him. "I'm just a timid Yankee," he grunted, "but I'm going to cross-question this living phonograph until I find out what—or who makes it tick."

"No! No, Ham! I'm scared!"

"It doesn't look dangerous," he observed.

"It isn't dangerous," remarked the thing on the ice.

Ham gulped, and Pat gave a horrified little moan.

"Who—who are you?" he faltered.

There was no answer. The lidded eyes stared steadily at him.

"What are you?" he tried again.

Again no reply.

"How do you know English?" he ventured.

The clicking voice sounded: "I isn't know English."

"Then—uh—then why do you speak English?"

"You speak English," explained the mystery, logically enough.

"I don't mean why. I mean how?"

But Pat had overcome a part of her terrified astonishment, and her quick mind perceived a clue. "Ham," she whispered tensely, "it uses the words we use. It gets the meaning from us!"

"I gets the meaning from you," confirmed the thing ungrammatically.

Light dawned on Ham. "Lord!" he gasped. "Then it's up to us to give it a vocabulary."

"You speak, I speak," suggested the creature.

"Sure! See, Pat? We can say just anything." He paused. "Let's see—" "When in the course of human events it—"

"Shut up!" snapped Pat. "Yankee! You're on crown territory now. 'To be or not to be; that is the question just—'"

Ham grinned and was silent. When she had exhausted her memory, he took up the task: "Once upon a time there were three bears—"

And so it went. Suddenly the situation struck him as fantastically ridiculous—there was Pat carefully relating the story of Little Red Riding Hood to a humorless monstrosity of the night-side of Venus! The girl cast him a perplexed glance as he roared into a gale of laughter.

"Tell him the one about the traveling man and the farmer's daughter!" he said, choking. "See if you can get a smile from him!"

She joined his laughter. "But it's really a serious matter," she concluded. "Imagine it, Ham! Intelligent life on the dark side! Or are you intelligent?" she asked suddenly of the thing on the ice.

"I am intelligent," it assured her. "I'm intelligently intelligent."

"At least you're a marvelous linguist," said the girl.

"Did you ever hear of learning English in half an hour, Ham? Think of that!" Apparently her fear of the creature had vanished.

"Well; let's make use of it," suggested Ham. "What's your name, friend?" There was no reply.

"Of course," put in Pat. "He can't tell us his name until we give it to him in English, and we can't do that because—Oh, well, let's call him Oscar, then. That'll serve."

"Good enough. Oscar, what are you, anyway?"

"Human, I'm a man."

"Eh? I'll be damned if you are!"

"Those are the words you've given me. To me I am a man to you."

"Wait a moment. 'To me I am—' I see, Pat. He means that the only words we have for what he considers himself are words like man and human. Well, what are your people, then?"

"People."

"I mean your race. What race do you belong to?"

"Human."

"Ow!" groaned Ham. "You try, Pat."

"Oscar," said the girl, "you say you're human. Are you a mammal?"

"To me man is a mammal to you."

"Oh, good heavens!" She tried again. "Oscar, how does your race reproduce?"

"I have not the words."

"Are you born?"

The queer face, or faceless body, of the creature changed slightly. Heavier lids dropped over the semi-transparent ones that shielded its many eyes; it was almost as if the thing frowned in concentration.

"We are not born," he clicked.

"Then—seeds, spores, parthenogenesis? Or fissure?"

"Spores," shrilled the mystery, "and fissure."

"But—"

She paused, nonplussed. In the momentary silence came the mocking hoot of a triops far to their left, and both turned involuntarily, stared, and recoiled aghast. At the very extremity of their beam one of the laughing demons had seized and was bearing away what was beyond doubt one of the creatures of the caves. And to add to the horror, all the rest squatted in utter indifference before their burrows.

"Oscar!" Pat screamed. "They got one of you!"

She broke off suddenly at the crack of Ham's revolver, but it was a futile shot.

"O-oh!" she gasped. "The devils! They got one!" There was no comment at all from the creature before them. "Oscar," she cried, "don't you care? They murdered one of you! Don't you understand?"

"Yes."

"But—doesn't it affect you at all?" The creatures had come, somehow, to hold a sort of human sympathy in Pat's mind. They could talk; they were more than beasts. "Don't you care at all?"

"No."

"But what are those devils to you? What do they do that you let them murder you?"

"They eat us," said Oscar placidly.

"Oh!" gasped Pat in horror. "But—but why don't—"

She broke off; the creature was backing slowly and methodically into its burrow.

"Wait!" she cried. "They can't come here! Our lights—"

The clicking voice drifted out: "It is cold. I go because of the cold."

There was silence.

It was colder. The gusty Underwind moaned more steadily now, and glancing along the ridge, Pat saw that every one of the cave creatures was slipping like Oscar into his burrow. She turned a helpless gaze on Ham.

"Did I—dream this?" she whispered.

"Then both of us dreamed it, Pat." He took her arm and drew her back toward the rocket, whose round ports glowed an invitation through the dusk.

But once in the warm interior, with her clumsy outer garments removed, Pat drew her dainty legs under her, lighted a cigarette, and fell to more rational consideration of the mystery.

"There's something we don't understand about this, Ham. Did you sense anything queer about Oscar's mind?"

"It's a devilishly quick one!"

"Yes; he's intelligent enough. Intelligence of the human level, or even"—she hesitated—"above the human. But it isn't a human mind. It's different, somehow—alien, strange. I can't quite express what I felt, but did you notice Oscar never asked a question? Not one!"

"Why—he didn't, did he? That's queer!"

"It's darn queer. Any human intelligence, meeting another thinking form of life, would ask plenty of questions. We did." She blew a thoughtful puff of smoke. "And that isn't all. That—that indifference of his when the triops attacked his fellow—was that human, or even earthly? I've seen a hunting spider snatch one fly from a swarm of them without disturbing the rest, but could that happen to intelligent creatures? It couldn't; not even to brains as undeveloped as those in a herd of deer, or a flock of sparrows. Kill one and you frighten all."

"That's true, Pat. They're damn queer ducks, these fellow citizens of Oscar's. Queer animals."

"Animals? Don't tell me you didn't notice, Ham!"

"Notice what?"

"Oscar's no animal. He's a plant—a warm-blooded, mobile vegetable! All the time we were talking to him he was rooting around below him with his—well, his root. And those things that looked like legs—they were pods. He didn't walk on them; he dragged himself on his root. And what's more he—"

"What's more?"

"What's more, Ham, those pods were the same sort as the ones that the triops threw at us in the canyon of the Mountains of Eternity, the ones that choked and smothered us so—"

"The ones that laid you out so cold, you mean."

"Anyway, I had wits enough to notice them!" she retorted, flushing. "But there's part of the mystery, Ham. Oscar's mind is a vegetable mind!" She paused, puffing her cigarette as he packed his pipe.

"Do you suppose," she asked suddenly, "that the presence of Oscar and his crew represents a menace to human occupancy of Venus? I know they're dark-side creatures, but what if mines are discovered here? What if there turns out to be a field for commercial exploitation? Humans can't live indefinitely away from sunlight, I know, but there might be a need for temporary colonies here, and what then?"

"Well, what then?" rejoined Ham.

"Yes; what then? Is there room on the same planet for two intelligent races? Won't there be a conflict of interests sooner or later?"

"What of it?" he grunted. "Those things are primitive, Pat. They live in caves, without culture, without weapons. They're no danger to man."

"But they're magnificently intelligent. How do you know that these we've seen aren't just a barbaric tribe and that somewhere on the vastness of the dark side there isn't a vegetable civilization? You know civilization isn't the personal prerogative of mankind, because look at the mighty decadent culture on Mars and the dead remnants on Titan. Man has simply happened to have the strangest brand of it, at least so far."

"That's true enough, Pat," he agreed. "But if Oscar's fellows aren't any more pugnacious than they were toward that murderous triops, then they aren't much of a menace."

She shuddered. "I can't understand that at all. I wonder if—" She paused, frowning.

"If what?"

"I—don't know. I had an idea—a rather horrible idea." She looked up suddenly. "Ham, to-morrow I'm going to find out exactly how intelligent Oscar really is. Exactly how intelligent— if I can."

*   *   *   *   *

There were certain difficulties, however. When Ham and Pat approached the ice ridge, plodding across the fantastic terrain, they found themselves in utter perplexity as to which of the row of caves was the one before which they had stood in conversation with Oscar. In the glittering reflections from their lamps each opening appeared exactly like every other, and the creatures at their mouths stared at them with lidded eyes in which there was no readable expression.

"Well," said Pat in puzzlement, "we'll just have to try. You there, are you Oscar?"

The clicking voice sounded: "Yes."

"I don't believe it," objected Ham. "He was over more to the right. Hey! Are you Oscar?"

Another voice clicked: "Yes."

"You can't both be Oscar!"

Pat's choice responded: "We are all Oscar."

"Oh, never mind," cut in Pat, forestalling Ham's protests. "Apparently what one knows they all know, so it doesn't make any difference which we choose. Oscar, you said yesterday you were intelligent. Are you more intelligent than I am?"

"Yes. Much more intelligent."

"Hah!" snickered Ham. "Take that, Pat!"

She sniffed. "Well, that puts him miles above you, Yankee! Oscar, do you ever lie?"

Opaque lids dropped over translucent ones. "Lie," repeated the shrill voice. "Lie. No. There is no need."

"Well, do you—" She broke off suddenly at the sound of a dull pop. "What's that? Oh! Look, Ham, one of his pods burst!" She drew back,

A sharply pungent odor assailed them, reminiscent of that dangerous hour in the canyon, but not strong enough this time to set Ham choking or send the girl reeling into unconsciousness. Sharp, acrid, and yet not entirely unpleasant.

"What's that for, Oscar?"

"It is so we—" The voice cut short.

"Reproduce?" suggested Pat.

"Yes. Reproduce. The wind carries our spores to each other. We live where the wind is not steady."

"But yesterday you said fissure was your method."

"Yes. The spores lodge against our bodies and there is a—" Again the voice died.

"A fertilization?" suggested the girl.

"No."

"Well, a—I know! An irritation!"

"Yes."

"That causes a tumorous growth?"

"Yes. When the growth is complete, we split."

"Ugh!" snorted Ham. "A tumor!"

"Shut up!" snapped the girl. "That's all a baby is—a normal tumor."

"A normal—Well, I'm glad I'm not a biologist! Or a woman!"

"So'm I," said Pat demurely. "Oscar, how much do you know?"

"Everything."

"Do you know where my people come from?"

"From beyond the light."

"Yes; but before that?"

"No."

"We come from another planet," said the girl impressively. At Oscar's silence she said:-"Do you know what a planet is?"

"Yes."

"But did you know before I said the word?"

"Yes. Long before."

"But how? Do you know what machinery is? Do you know what weapons are? Do you know how to make them?"

"Yes."

"Then—why don't you?"

"There is no need."

"No need!" she gasped. "With light—even with fire—you could keep the triopses—trioptes, I mean—away. You could keep them from eating you!"

"There is no need."

She turned helplessly to Ham.

"The thing's lying," he suggested.

"I—don't think so," she murmured. "It's something else—something we don't understand. Oscar, how do you know all those things?"

"Intelligence."

At the next cave another pod popped sullenly.

"But how? Tell me how you discover facts."

"From any fact," clicked the creature on the ice, "intelligence can build a picture of the—" There was silence.

"Universe?" she suggested.

"Yes. The universe. I start with one fact and I reason from it. I build a picture of the universe. I start with another fact. I reason from it. I find that the universe I picture is the same as the first. I know that the picture is true."

Both listeners stared in awe at the creature. "Say!" gulped Ham. "If that's true we could find out anything from Oscar! Oscar, can you tell us secrets that we don't know?"

"No."

"Why not?"

"You must first have the words to give me. I cannot tell you that for which you have no words."

"It's true!" whispered Pat. "But, Oscar, I have the words time and space and energy and matter and law and cause. Tell me the ultimate law of the universe?"

"It is the law of—" Silence.

"Conservation of energy or matter? Gravitation?"

"No."

"Of—of God?"

"No."

"Of—life?"

"No. Life is of no importance."

"Of—what? I can't think of another word."

"There's a chance," said Ham tensely, "that there is no word!"

"Yes," clicked Oscar. "It is the law of chance. Those other words are different sides of the law of chance."

"Good Heaven!" breathed Pat. "Oscar, do you know what I mean by stars, suns, constellations, planets, nebulae, and atoms, protons, and electrons?"

"Yes."

"But—how? Have you ever seen the stars that are above these eternal clouds? Or the Sun there beyond the barrier?"

"No. Reason is enough, because there is only one possible way in which the universe could exist. Only what is possible is real; what is not real is also not possible."

"That—that seems to mean something," murmured Pat. "I don't see exactly what. But Oscar, why—why don't you use your knowledge to protect yourselves from your enemies?"

"There is no need. There is no need to do anything. In a hundred years we shall be—" Silence.

"Safe?"

"Yes—no."

"What?" A horrible thought struck her. "Do you mean—extinct?"

"Yes."

"But—oh, Oscar! Don't you want to live? Don't your people want to survive?"

"Want," shrilled Oscar. "Want—want—want. That word means nothing."

"It means—it means desire, need."

"Desire means nothing. Need—need. No. My people do not need to survive."

"Oh," said Pat faintly. "Then why do you reproduce?"

As if in answer, a bursting pod sent its pungent dust over them. "Because we must," clicked Oscar. "When the spores strike us, we must."

"I—see," murmured Pat slowly. "Ham, I think I've got it. I think I understand. Let's get back to the ship."

Without farewell she turned away and he followed her thoughtfully. A strange listlessness oppressed him.

They had one slight mishap. A stone flung by some stray trioptes sheltered behind the ridge shattered the left lamp in Pat's helmet. It seemed hardly to disturb the girl; she glanced briefly aside and plodded on. But all the way back, in the gloom to their left now illumined only by his own lamp, hoots and shrieks and mocking laughter pursued them.

Within the rocket Pat swung her specimen bag wearily to the table and sat down without removing her heavy outer garment. Nor did Ham; despite the oppressive warmth of it, he, too, dropped listlessly to a seat on the bunk.

"I'm tired," said the girl, "but not too tired to realize what that mystery out there means."

"Then let's hear it."

"Ham," she said, "what's the big difference between plant and animal life?"

"Why—plants derive their sustenance directly from soil and air. Animals need plants or other animals as food."

"That isn't entirely true, Ham. Some plants are parasitic, and prey on other life. Think of the Hotlands, or think, even, of some terrestrial plants—the fungi, the pitcher plant, the Dionaea that trap flies."

"Well, animals move, then, and plants don't."

"That's not true, either. Look at microbes; they're plants, but they swim about in search of food."

"Then what is the difference?"

"Sometimes it's hard to say," she murmured, "but I think I see it now. It's this: Animals have desire and plants necessity. Do you understand?"

"Not a damn bit."

"Listen, Then. A plant—even a moving one—acts the way it does because it must, because it's made so. An animal acts because it wants to, or because it's made so that it wants to."

"What's the difference?"

"There is a difference. An animal has will, a plant hasn't. Do you see now? Oscar has all the magnificent intelligence of a god, but he hasn't the will of a worm. He has reactions, but no desire. When the wind is warm he comes out and feeds; when it's cold he crawls back into the cave melted by his body heat, but that isn't will, it's just a reaction. He has no desires!"

Ham stared, roused out of his lassitude. "I'll be damned if it isn't true!" he cried. "That's why he—or they—never ask questions. It takes desire or will to ask a question! And that's why they have no civilization and never will have!"

"That and other reasons," said Pat. "Think of this: Oscar has no sex, and in spite of your Yankee pride, sex has been a big factor in building civilization. It's the basis of the family, and among Oscar's people there is no such thing as parent and child. He splits; each half of him is an adult, probably with all the knowledge and memory of the original.

"There's no need for love, no place for it, in fact, and therefore no call to fight for mate and family, and no reason to make life easier than it already is, and no cause to apply his intelligence to develop art or science or—or anything!" She paused. "And did you ever hear of the Malthusian law, Ham?"

"Not that I remember."

"Well, the law of Malthus says that population presses on the food supply. Increase the food and the population increases in proportion. Man evolved under that law; for a century or so it's been suspended, but our race grew to be human under it."

"Suspended! It sounds sort of like repealing the law of gravitation or amending the law of inverse squares."

"No, no," she said. "It was suspended by the development of machinery in the nineteenth and twentieth centuries, which shot the food supply so far ahead, that population hasn't caught up. But it will and the Malthusian law will rule again."

"And what's that got to do with Oscar?"

"This, Ham: He never evolved under that law. Other factors kept his numbers below the limit of the food supply, and so his species developed free of the need to struggle for food. He's so perfectly adapted to his environment that he needs nothing more. To him a civilization would be superfluous!"

"But—then what of the triops?"

"Yes, the triops. You see, Ham, just as I argued days ago, the triops is a newcomer, pushed over from the twilight zone. When those devils arrived, Oscar's people were already evolved, and they couldn't change to meet the new conditions, or couldn't change quickly enough. So—they're doomed.

"As Oscar says, they'll be extinct soon—and—and they don't even care." She shuddered. "All they do, all they can do, is sit before their caves and think. Probably they think godlike thoughts, but they can't summon even a mouse-like will. That's what a vegetable intelligence is; that's what it has to be!"

"I think—I think you're right," he muttered. "In a way it's horrible, isn't it?"

"Yes." Despite her heavy garments she shivered. "Yes; it's horrible. Those vast, magnificent minds and no way for them to work. It's like a powerful gasoline motor with its drive shaft broken, and no matter how well it runs it can't turn the wheels. Ham, do you know what I'm going to name them? The Lotophagi Veneris—the Lotus Eaters! Content to sit and dream away existence while lesser minds—ours and the trioptes'—battle for their planet."

"It's a good name, Pat." As she rose he asked in surprise: "Your specimens? Aren't you going to prepare them?"

"Oh, to-morrow." She flung herself, parka and all, on her bunk.

"But they'll spoil! And your helmet light—I ought to fix it."

"To-morrow," she repeated wearily, and his own languor kept him from further argument.

When the nauseous odor of decay awakened him some hours later Pat was asleep, still garbed in the heavy suit. He flung bag and specimens from the door, and then slipped the parka from her body. She hardly stirred as he tucked her gently into her bunk.

*   *   *   *   *

Pat never missed the specimen bag at all, and, somehow, the next day, if one could call that endless night a day, found them trudging over the bleak plateau with the girl's helmet lamp still unrepaired. Again at their left, the wildly mocking laughter of the night dwellers followed them, drifting eerily down on the Underwind, and twice far-flung stones chipped glittering ice from neighboring spires. They plodded listlessly and silently, as if in a sort of fascination, but their minds seemed strangely clear.

Pat addressed the first Lotus Eater they saw. "We're back, Oscar," she said with a faint rebirth of her usual flippancy. "How'd you spend the night?"

"I thought," clicked the thing.

"What'd you think about?"

"I thought about—" The voice ceased.

A pod popped, and the curiously pleasant pungent odor was in their nostrils.

"About—us?"

"No."

"About—the world?"

"No."

"About—What's the use?" she ended wearily. "We could keep that up forever, and perhaps never hit on the right question."

"If there is a right question," added Ham. "How do you know there are words to fit it? How do you even know that it's the kind of thought our minds are capable of conceiving? There must be thoughts that are beyond our grasp."

Off to their left a pod burst with a dull pop. Ham saw the dust move like a shadow across their beams as the Underwind caught it, and he saw Pat draw a deep draft of the pungent air as it whirled around her. Queer how pleasant the smell was, especially since it was the same stuff which in higher concentration had nearly cost their lives. He felt vaguely worried as that thought struck him, but could assign no reason for worry.

He realized suddenly that both of them were standing in complete silence before the Lotus Eater. They had come to ask questions, hadn't they?

"Oscar," he said, "what's the meaning of life?"

"No meaning. There is no meaning."

"Then why fight for it so?"

"We do not fight for it. Life is unimportant."

"And when you're gone, the world goes on just the same? Is that it?" "When we are gone it will make no difference to any except the trioptes who eat us."

"Who eat you," echoed Ham.

There was something about that thought that did penetrate the fog of indifference that blanketed his mind. He peered at Pat, who stood passively and silently beside him, and in the glow of her helmet lamp he could see her clear gray eyes behind her goggles, staring straight ahead in what was apparently abstraction or deep thought. And beyond the ridge sounded suddenly the yells and wild laughter of the dwellers in the dark.

"Pat," he said.

There was no answer.

"Pat!" he repeated, raising a listless hand to her arm. "We have to go back." To his right a pod popped. "We have to go back," he repeated.

A sudden shower of stones came glancing over the ridge. One struck his helmet, and his forward lamp burst with a dull explosion. Another struck his arm with a stinging pain, though it seemed surprisingly unimportant.

"We have to go back," he reiterated doggedly.

Pat spoke at last without moving. "What's the use?" she asked dully.

He frowned over that. What was the use? To go back to the twilight zone? A picture of Erotia rose in his mind, and then a vision of that honeymoon they had planned on the Earth, and then a whole series of terrestrial scenes—New York, a tree-girt campus, the sunny farm of his boyhood. But they all seemed very far away and unreal.

A violent blow that stung his shoulder recalled him, and he saw a stone bound from Pat's helmet. Only two of her lamps glowed now, the rear and the right, and he realized vaguely that on his own helmet shone only the rear and the left. Shadowy figures were skittering and gibbering along the crest of the ridge now left dark by the breaking of their lights, and stones were whizzing and spattering around them.

He made a supreme effort and seized her arm. "We've got to go back!" he muttered.

"Why? Why should we?"

"Because we'll be killed if we stay."

"Yes. I know that, but—"

He ceased to listen and jerked savagely at Pat's arm. She spun around and staggered after him as he turned doggedly toward the rocket.

Shrill hoots sounded as their rear lamps swept the ridge, and as he dragged the girl with infinite slowness, the shrieks spread out to the right and left. He knew what that meant; the demons were circling them to get in front of them where their shattered forward lamps cast no protecting light.

Pat followed listlessly, making no effort of her own. It was simply the drag of his arm that impelled her, and it was becoming an intolerable effort to move even himself. And there directly before him, flitting shadows that howled and hooted, were the devils that sought their lives.

Ham twisted his head so that his right lamp swept the area. Shrieks sounded as they found shelter in the shadows of peaks and ridges, but Ham, walking with his head sidewise, tripped and tumbled.

Pat wouldn't rise when he tugged at her. "There's no need of it," she murmured, but made no resistance when he lifted her.

An idea stirred vaguely; he bundled her into his arms so that her right lamp shot its beam forward, and so he staggered at last to the circle of light about the rocket, opened the door, and dumped her on the floor within.

He had one final impression. He saw the laughing shadows that were the trioptes skipping and skittering across the darkness toward the ridge where Oscar and his people waited in placid acceptance of their destiny.

The rocket was roaring along at two hundred thousand feet, because numberless observations and photographs from space had shown that not even the vast peaks of the Mountains of

Eternity project forty miles above the planet's surface. Below them the clouds glistened white before and black behind, for they were just entering the twilight zone. At that height one could even see the mighty curvature of the planet.

"Half cue ball, half eight ball," said Ham, staring down. "Hereafter we stick to the cue-ball half."

"It was the spores," proceeded Pat, ignoring him. "We knew they were narcotic before, but we couldn't be expected to guess that they'd carry a drug as subtle as that—to steal away your will and undermine your strength. Oscar's people are the Lotus Eaters and the Lotus, all in one. But I'm—somehow—I'm sorry for them. Those colossal, magnificent, useless minds of theirs!" What snapped you out of it?"

"Oh, it was a remark of Oscar's, something about his being only a square meal for a triops."

"Well?"

"Well, did you know we've used up all our food? That remark reminded me that I hadn't eaten for two days!"

The Planet Of Doubt

Originally Published in *Astounding Stories*
October 1935

THE PLANET OF DOUBT

Hamilton Hammond started nervously as the voice of Cullen, the expedition's chemist, sounded from his station aft. "I see something!" he called.

Ham bent over the floor port, staring into the eternal green-gray fog that blankets Uranus. He glanced hastily at the dial of the electric plumb; fifty-five feet, it said with an air of positiveness, but that was a lie, for it had registered that same figure for a hundred and sixty miles of creeping descent. The fog itself reflected the beam.

The barometer showed 86.2 cm. That too was an unreliable guide, but better than the plumb, for the intrepid Young, four decades earlier in 2060, had noted an atmospheric pressure of 86 in his romantic dash from Titan to the cloudy planet's southern pole. But the Gaea was dropping now at the opposite pole, forty-five thousand miles from Young's landing, and no one knew what vast hollows or peaks might render his figures utterly useless.

"I see nothing," Ham muttered.

"Nor I," said Patricia Hammond, his wife—or more officially, biologist of the Smithsonian's Gaea expedition. "Or—yes! Something moved!" She peered closer. "Up! Up!" she screamed. "Put up!"

Harbord was a good astrogator. He asked no questions, nor even took his glance from his controls. He simply slapped the throttle; the underjets roared in crescendo, and the upward thrust pressed all of them hard against the floor.

Barely in time. A vast gray wave of water rushed smoothly below the port, so close that its crest was carved by the blast, and spray clouded the glass.

"Whew!" whistled Ham. "That was close. Too close. If we'd touched that it would have cracked our jets for sure. They're white-hot."

"Ocean!" said Patricia disgustedly. "Young reported land."

"Yeah, forty-five thousand miles away. For all we know this sea is broader than the whole surface of the Earth."

She considered this, frowning. "Do you suppose," she asked, "that this fog goes right down to the surface everywhere?"

"Young says so."

"But on Venus the clouds form only at the junction of the upper winds and the underwind."

"Yes, but Venus is closer to the Sun. The heat here is evenly distributed, because the Sun accounts for practically none of it. Most of the surface heat seeps through from within, as it does on Saturn and Jupiter, only since Uranus is smaller, it's also cooler. It's cool enough to have a solid crust instead of being molten like the larger planets, but it's considerably colder than the Venusian twilight zone."

"But," she objected, "Titan is as cold as a dozen Nova Zemblas, yet it's one perpetual hurricane."

He grinned. "Trying to trip me? It isn't absolute temperature that causes wind—it's differences in temperature between one place and another. Titan has one side warmed by Saturn, but here the warmth is even or practically even, all around the planet, since it comes from within."

He glanced suddenly at Harbord. "What are we waiting for?" he asked.

"For you," grunted the astrogator. "You're in command now. I command until we sight the surface, and we've just done that."

"By golly, that's right!" exclaimed Ham in a satisfied voice. On his last expedition, that to the night side of Venus, he had been technically under Patricia's orders, and the reversal pleased him. "And now," he said severely, "if the biologist will kindly step aside—"

Patricia sniffed. "So you can pilot us, I suppose. I'll bet you haven't a single idea."

"But I have." He turned to Harbord. "Southeast," he ordered, and the afterjets added their voices to the roar of the others. "Put up to thirty thousand meters," he continued, "we might run into mountains."

The Gaea, named for the ancient goddess of Earth, who was wife to the god Uranus, plunged through the infinity of mist away from the planet's pole. In one respect that pole is unique among the Sun's family, for Uranus revolves, not like Jupiter or

Saturn or Mars or the Earth, in the manner of a spinning top, but more with the motion of a rolling ball. Its poles are in the plane of its orbit, so that at one point its southern pole faces the Sun, while forty-two years later, halfway around the vast orbit, the opposite pole is Sunward.

Four decades earlier Young had touched at the southern pole; it would be another forty years before that pole again saw noon.

"The trouble with women," grumbled Harbord, "is that they ask too many questions."

Patricia spun on him. "Schopenhauer!" she hissed. "You ought to be grateful that Patrick Burlingame's daughter is lending her aid to a Yankee expedition!"

"Yeah? Why Schopenhauer?"

"He was a woman-hater, wasn't he? Like you!"

"Then he was a greater philosopher than I thought," grunted Harbord.

"Anyway," she retorted acidly, "a couple of million dollars is a lot of money to pay for a square mile of foggy desert. You won't hog this planet the way you tried to hog Venus."

She was referring, of course, to the Council of Berne's decision of 2059, that the simple fact of an explorer's landing on a planet did not give his nation possession of the entire planet, but only of the portion actually explored. On fog-wrapped Uranus that portion would be small indeed.

"Never mind," put in Ham. "No other nation will argue if America claims the whole fog-ball, because no other nation has a base near enough to get here."

That was true. By virtue of its possession of Saturn's only habitable moon, Titan, the United States was the only nation that could send an exploratory rocket to Uranus. A direct flight from the Earth is out of the question, since the nearest approach to the two planets is 1,700,000,000 miles. The flight is made in two jumps; first to Titan, then to Uranus.

But this condition limits the frequency of the visits enormously, for though Saturn and Earth are in conjunction at intervals of a little over a year, Uranus and Saturn are in conjunction only once in about forty years. Only at these times is it possible to reach the vast, mysterious, fog-shrouded planet.

So inconceivably remote is Uranus that the distance to its neighbor, Saturn, is actually greater than the total distance from Saturn to Jupiter, from Jupiter to the asteroids, from these to Mars, and from Mars to the Earth. It is a wild, alien, mystery-cloaked planet with only icy Neptune and Pluto between it and the interstellar void.

Patricia whirled on Ham. "You!" she snapped. "Southeast, eh! Why southeast? Just a guess, isn't it? Truthfully, isn't it?"

"Nope," he grinned. "I have my reasons. I'm trying to save whatever time I can, because our stay here is limited if we don't want to be marooned for forty years until the next conjunction."

"But why southeast?"

"I'll tell you. Did you ever look at a globe of the Earth, Pat? Then maybe you've noticed that all continents, all large islands, and all important peninsulas are narrowed to points toward the south. In other words, the northern hemisphere is more favorable for land formation, and as a matter of fact, by far the greater part of the Earth's land is north of the equator.

"The Arctic Ocean is nearly surrounded by a ring of land, but the Antarctic's wide open. And that same thing is true of Mars, assuming that the dark, swampy plains are old ocean beds, and also true of the frozen oceans on the night side of Venus.

"So I assume that if all planets had a common origin, and all of them solidified under the same conditions, Uranus must have the same sort of land distribution. What Young found was the land that corresponds to our Antarctica; what I'm looking for is the land that ought to surround this north polar sea."

"Ought to, but maybe doesn't," retorted Pat. "Anyway why southeast instead of due south?"

"Because that direction describes a spiral and lessens the chance of our striking some strait or channel between lands. With a visibility of about fifty feet, it wouldn't take a very wide channel to make us think we were over ocean.

"Even your English Thames would look like the Pacific in this sort of fog, if we happened to come down more than half a hundred feet from either bank."

"And I suppose your American Mississippi would look like Noah's flood," said the girl, and fell to gazing at the gray waste of fog that swirled endlessly past the ports.

Somewhat less than an hour later the Gaea was again descending gingerly and hesitatingly. At 85 cm. of air pressure Ham had the rocket slowed almost to a complete stop, and thereafter it dropped on the cushioning blast of the underjets at a speed of inches per minute.

When the barometer read 85.8 cm., Cullen's voice sounded from the stern, where the port was less obscured by the jets them-selves. "Something below!" he called.

There was something. The fog seemed definitely darker, and features or markings of some sort were visible. As the ship settled slowly, Ham watched intently, and at last snapped out the order to land. The Gaea dropped, with a faint jar, to a resting place on a bare, gray graveled plain domed with a hemisphere of mist that shut off vision as definitely as a wall.

There was something wild and alien about the limited scene before them. As the blast died, all of them stared silently into the leaden-hued vapors and Cullen came wordlessly in to join them. In the sudden silence that followed the cutting of the blast, the utter strangeness of the world outside was thrust upon them.

Venus, where Pat had been born, was a queer enough world with its narrow habitable twilight zone, its life-teeming Hotlands, and its mysterious dark side, but it was twin sister to the Earth.

Mars, the desert planet with its great decadent civilization, was yet stranger, but not utterly alien. Out on the moons of Jupiter were outlandish creatures of bizarre little worlds, and on cold Titan, that circled Saturn, were fantastic beings born to that wild and frigid satellite.

But Uranus was a major planet, no more than half-brother to the little inner worlds, and less than cousin to the tiny satellites. It was mysterious, unrelated, alien; no one had ever set foot on a major planet save the daring Young and his men forty years before.

He had explored, out of all the millions of square miles of surface, just one square kilometer forty-five thousand miles away from where they stood. All the rest was mystery, and the thought was enough to subdue even the irrepressible Patricia.

But not for long. "Well," she observed finally, "it looks just like London to me. Same sort of weather we had last time we were there. I think I'll step outside and look for Piccadilly."

"You won't go out yet," snapped Ham. "I want an atmospheric test first."

"For what? Young and his men breathed this air. I suppose you're going to say that that was forty-five thousand miles away, but even a biologist knows that the law of diffusion of gases would keep a planet from having one sort of air at one pole and another at the opposite. If the air was safe there, it is here."

"Yeah?" asked Ham. "Diffusion's all right, but did it ever occur to you that this fog-ball gets most of its heat from inside? That means high volcanic activity, and it might mean an eruption of poisonous gases somewhere near here. I'm having Cullen make a test."

Patricia subsided, watching the silent and efficient Cullen as he drew a sample of Uranian air into an ampule. After a moment she flexed her knees and asked, "Why is the gravitation so weak here? Uranus is fifty-four times as large as the Earth and fifteen times as massive, yet I don't feel any heavier here than at home." Home to Pat, of course, was the little frontier town of Venoble, in the Venusian Cool Country.

"That's the answer," said Ham. "Fifty-four times the size of the Earth or Venus, but only fifteen times as heavy. That means its density is much smaller—to be exact .27. Figures out to about nine-tenths the surface gravitation of the Earth, but it feels to me almost equal. We'll check a kilogram weight on the spring balance after a while and get an accurate figure on its mass.

"Safe to breathe?"

"Perfectly. Argon's an inert gas, and a substance can't possibly be poisonous unless it can react chemically in the body."

Pat sniffed. "See? It was safe all the time. I'm going outside."

"You'll wait for me," he growled. "Every time I've indulged that reckless disposition of yours you've got into trouble." He checked the thermometer beyond the port, nine degrees centigrade—the temperature of late autumn back home. "There's the cause of this perpetual fog," he observed. "The surface is always warmer than the air."

Pat was already pulling a jacket over her shoulders. Ham followed suit, and fell to twisting the handle of the air lock.

There was a subdued hissing as the slightly denser Uranian air forced its way in, and he turned to speak to Harbord, who was lighting a pipe with great satisfaction—an indulgence strictly forbidden in space, but harmless now that an air supply was assured.

"Keep an eye on us, will you?" Ham said. "Watch us through the port, just in case something happens and we need help."

"We?" grunted Harbord. "Your wife's out of sight already."

With a muttered imprecation, Ham spun around. It was true. The outer door of the air lock was open, and a lazy wisp of fog drifted in, scarcely moving in the utterly stagnant Uranian air.

"The crazy little— Here! Give me that!" He seized a belt with twin holsters, holding a standard automatic as well as a terribly destructive flame pistol. He whipped it around him, seized another bundle, and plunged into the eternal mists of Uranus.

It was exactly as if he stood under an inverted bowl of dull silver. A weird, greenish, half twilight filtered down, but his whole world consisted of the metal ship at his back and a fifty-foot semicircle before him. And Pat—Pat was nowhere visible.

He shouted her name. "Pat!" The sound muffled by the cold dampness of the fog sounded queerly soft to his ears. He bellowed again at the top of his voice, and then swore violently from sheer relief as a thin, hushed reply drifted back out of the grayness.

In a moment she appeared, swinging a zigzag, ropy, greenish-gray organism.

"Look!" she called triumphantly. "Here's the first specimen of Uranian plant life. Loosely organized, reproduces by partition, and—what the devil is the matter?"

"Matter! Don't you know you might have been lost? How did you expect to get back here?"

"Compass," she retorted coolly.

"How do you know it works? We may be right on the magnetic pole, if Uranus has one."

She glanced at her wrist. "Come to think of it, it doesn't work. The needle's swinging free."

"Yes, and you went out unarmed besides. Of all the fool tricks!"

"Young reported no animal life, didn't he? And—wait a minute. I know what you're going to say. `Forty-five thousand miles away!' "

He glared. "Hereafter," he growled, "you're under orders. You don't go out except in company, and roped together." He drew a length of heavy silken cord from his pocket, and snapped one end to her belt, and the other to his own.

"Oh, don't be so timid! I feel like a puppy on a leash."

"I have to be timid," he responded grimly, "when I'm dealing with a reckless, improvident, careless imp like you."

He disregarded her sniff of disapproval, and set about unwrapping the bundle he had brought. He produced an American flag, and proceeded to dig a depression in the gravel, planted the staff in it and said formally, "I take possession of this land in the name of the United States of America."

"All fifty feet of it?" murmured Patricia, but softly, for, after all, despite her flippant manner, she was loyal to the country of her husband. She fell silent, and the two of them stared at the flag.

It was a strange echo from a pleasant little planet nearly two billion miles away; it meant people and friends and civilization— things remote and almost unreal as they stood here on the soil of this vast, lonely, mysterious planet.

Ham roused from his thoughts. "So!" he said. "Now we'll have a look around."

Young had indicated the technique of exploration on this world where the explorer faced difficulties all but insurmountable.

Ham snapped the end of a fine steel wire to a catch beside the air lock. On a spool at his waist was a thousand foot length of it, to serve as an infallible guide back through the obscurity— the only practical means in a region where sound was muffled and even radio waves were shielded almost as completely as by a grounded metal dome. The wire played the part not only of guide but of messenger, since a tug on it rang a bell within the rocket.

Ham waved at Harbord, visibly puffing his pipe behind the port, and they set out. To the limit of their permitted time, Uranus would have to be explored in thousand-foot circles, moving the rocket each time the details of the area were recorded. A colossal task. It was likely, he remarked to Pat, that the vast planet would never be completely explored, especially with the forty-year interval that must pass between visits.

"And especially," she amended, "if they send timorous little better-be-safe-than-sorry explorers like you."

"At least," he retorted, "I expect to return to tell what I've explored even if it's only a myriare, like Young's achievement."

"But don't you see," she rejoined impatiently, "that wherever we go, just beyond our vision there may be something marvelous? We take little thousand-foot samples of the country, and each time we might be just missing something that may be the whole significance of this planet. What we're doing is like marking off a few hundred-foot circles on the Earth; how much chance is there of finding part of a city, or a house, or even a human being in our circle?"

"Perfectly true, Pat, but what can we do about it?"

"We could at least sacrifice a few precautions and cover a little more territory."

"But we won't. I happen to care about your safety."

"Oh!" she said irritably, turning away. "You're—" Her words were muffled as she ranged out to the full length of the silken cord that bound her to him. She was completely invisible, but occasional jerks and tugs as they tried to move at cross-purposes were evidence enough that they were still joined.

Ham walked slowly forward, examining the pebbled, lifeless terrain where now and then a pool of condensed moisture showed dull, and very occasionally, he came upon one of the zigzag weeds like the one Pat had dropped near the rocket. Apparently rain was unknown on windless Uranus, and the surface moisture followed an endless cycle of condensation in the cool air and evaporation on the warm ground.

Ham came to a spot where boiling mud seemed to be welling up from below, and steamy plumes whirled up to lose themselves in the fog—evidence of the vast internal heat that warmed the planet. He stood staring at it, and suddenly a violent jerk on the cord nearly toppled him backward.

He spun around. Patricia materialized abruptly out of the fog, one hand clutching a ropy plant. She dropped it as she saw him, and suddenly she was clinging frantically to him.

"Ham!" she gasped. "Let's go back! I'm scared!"

"Scared? Of what?" He knew her character; she was valiant to the point of recklessness against any danger she could understand, but let there be a hint of mystery in an occurrence, and her active imagination painted horrors beyond her ability to face.

"I don't know!" she panted. "I—I saw things!"

"Where?"

"In the fog! Everywhere!"

Ham disengaged his arms and dropped his hands to the butts of the weapons in his belt. "What sort of things?" he asked. "Horrible things! Nightmarish things!"

He shook her gently. "Who's timid now?" he asked, but kindly. The query had the effect he sought; she gripped herself and calmed.

"I'm not frightened!" she snapped. "I was startled. I saw—" She paled again.

"Saw what?"

"I don't know. Shapes in the mist. Great moving things with faces. Gargoyles—devils—nightmares!" She shuddered, then calmed once more.

"I was bending over a little pool out there, examining a biopod, and everything was quiet—sort of deadly quiet. And then a shadow passed in the pool—a reflection of something over me—and I looked up and saw nothing. But then I began to hear rustles and murmurs and noises like muffled voices and I began to see the fog shapes—horrible shapes—all around me. And I screamed, and then realized you couldn't hear a scream, so I jerked the rope. And then I guess I just closed my eyes and rushed through them to you." She shivered against him.

"All around you?" he asked sharply. "Do you mean between you and me?"

She nodded. "Everywhere."

Ham laughed shortly. "You've had a day dream, Pat. The rope isn't long enough for anything to pass between us without coming so close to one of us that he could see it clearly, and I saw nothing—absolutely nothing."

"Well, I saw something," she insisted, "and it wasn't imaginary. Do you think I'm just a nervous child afraid of strange places? Why I was born on an alien planet!" At his indulgent grin she flared in indignation. "All right! Let's both of us stand here perfectly quiet; perhaps they'll come back again; then we'll see what you think of them."

He nodded agreement, and they stood silently under the translucent dome of mist. There was nothing, nothing but a deep and endless grayness, and an infinite silence, but a silence not like any Ham had ever experienced in his life. For on Venus — even in the sultriest part of the Hotlands—there is always the rustle of teeming life, and the eternal moaning of the underwind, while on the Earth no day nor night is ever quite silent.

There is always somewhere the sighing of leaves or the rustle of grass or the murmur of water or the voices of insects, or even in the driest desert, the whisper of sand as it warms or cools. But not here; here was such utter stillness that the girl's breathing beside him was an actual relief; it was a silence utter enough to hear.

He did hear it—or was it simply his own blood pulsing in his ears? A formless throbbing, an infinitely faint rustling, a vague whispering. He frowned in the concentration of listening, and Patricia quivered against him.

"There!" she hissed. "There!"

He peered into the gray dimness. Nothing at all—or was there something? A shadow—but what here could cause a shadow, here in this sunless region of fog? A condensation of mist, that was all. But it moved; mist can't move without the thrust of wind, and here there was no wind.

He strained his eyes in an effort to pierce the obscurity. He saw—or he imagined it—a vast, looming figure, or a dozen figures. They were all around; one passed silently overhead, and numberless others weaved and swayed just beyond the range of vision. There were murmurings and susurrations, sounds like breathing and whispering, patters and rustles. The fog shapes were weirdly unstable, looming from little patches of darkness into towering shadows, dissipating and forming like figures of smoke.

"Good Lord!" gasped Ham. "What can—"

He tried to focus his gaze on one individual in the shadowy throng. It was difficult; they all seemed to shift, to merge, advance, recede, or simply materialize and fade out. But one surprising phenomenon suddenly caught his attention, and for a moment stunned him into rigidity. He saw faces!

Not exactly human faces. They were more such appearances as Patricia had described—the faces of gargoyles or devils, leering, grimacing, grinning in lunatic mirth or seeming to weep in mockery of sorrow. One couldn't see them clearly enough for anything but fleeting impressions—so vague and instantaneous that they had the qualities of an illusion or dream.

They must be illusions, he thought confusedly, if only because their conformation, though not human, imitated the human. It was beyond the bounds of reason to suppose that Uranus harbored a race of humans, or even humanlike beings.

Beside him Patricia whimpered, "Let's go back, Ham. Please let's go back."

"Listen," he said, "those things are illusory, at least in part."

"How do you know?"

"Because they're anthropomorphic. There can't be any creatures here with nearly human faces. Our own minds are adding details that don't exist, just as every time you see a cloud or a crack on the ceiling you try to make a face out of it. All we're seeing is denser spots in the mist."

"I wish I thought you were sure of that," she quavered.

He wasn't at all sure, but he reaffirmed it. "Of course I am. I'll tell you an easy way to prove it, too. We'll turn the infra-red camera on them, and that'll bring out enough detail to judge by."

"I'd be afraid to look at the plates," said the girl, shivering as she peered apprehensively at the vague horrors in the fog. "Suppose—suppose they do show those faces. What will you say then?"

"I'll say that it's a queer and unexpected coincidence that Uranian life—if they are forms of life—has developed along somewhat the same lines as terrestrial—at least in outward form."

"And you'll be wrong," she murmured. "A thing like this is beyond coincidence." She trembled against him. "Do you know what I think? Ham, do you suppose it's possible that science has gone all wrong, and that Uranus is Hell? And that those are the damned?"

He laughed, but even his laugh sounded hollow, muffled by the smothering fog. "That's the maddest idea that even your wild imagination has ever produced, Pat. I tell you they're—"

A scream from the girl interrupted him. They had been standing huddled together, staring at divergent angles into the dome of mist, and he spun around now to gaze in the direction she faced.

For a moment his vision was blinded by the shift, and he blinked frantically in an effort to focus his eyes. Then he saw what had startled her. It was a vast, dusky shadow that seemed to originate somewhere near the surface, but was springing upward and curving over them as if it actually climbed a veritable dome of mist, like a dim river of darkness flowing upward.

Despite his derision of Patricia's fear-born imaginings, his nerves were taut. It was a purely automatic gesture that brought his weapon to his hand, and it was pure impulse that sent a bullet flaming into the mist. There was a curiously muffled report from the shot—a single full echo—and then utter silence.

Utter silence. The rustles and murmurings were gone—and so were the fog-shapes. Blinking into the mist, they saw only the sullen grayness of the eternal cloud itself, and they heard no sound but their own tense breathing and the faint after-ring of their eardrums from the concussion.

"They're gone!" the girl gasped.

"Sure. Just what I said. Illusions!"

"Illusions don't run away from gunshots," retorted Patricia, her courage revived instantly with the vanishing of the fog shapes. "They're real. I'm not nearly as afraid of real things as of—well, of things I can't understand."

"Do you understand these?" he rejoined. "And as for illusions not running away from gunshots, I say they might. Suppose these appearances were due to a sort of self-hypnosis, or even merely to the eye strain of staring through this fog. Don't you think a shot would startle us out of the proper mental state, so that we'd no longer see them?"

"Maybe," she said doubtfully. "Anyway, I'm not scared any more. Whatever they are, I guess they're harmless."

She turned her attention to the puddle of mud before them, in which a few curious feathery growths swayed to the bubbling of the surface. "Cryptogamoid," she said, stooping over them. "Probably the only sort of plant that can exist on Uranus, since there's no sign of bees, or other pollen carriers."

Ham grunted, peering into the dismal gray mist. Suddenly both of them were startled into sudden alertness by the sound of the bell on the drum that held the guide wire. One ring; a warning from the Gaea!

Pat sprang erect. Ham tugged the wire in instant reply, and muttered, "We'd better go back. Harbord and Cullen must have seen something. It's probably the same sort of things we saw, but we'd better go back."

They began to retrace their steps, the thousand feet of wire humming softly as it wound back on the spring drum at Ham's waist. Other than that and the crunch of their steps on the gravel, there was silence, and the fog was merely a featureless dome of faintly greenish grayness. They had progressed perhaps two hundred yards when it changed.

Patricia saw the fog shapes first. "They're back!" she hissed in his ear, with no sound of fear in her voice now.

He saw them too. Now they were no longer surrounding the two of them, but were rushing past from the direction of the Gaea in two parallel streams, or perhaps dividing into two streams just beyond the point of visibility. He and Pat were moving down an alley walled by a continuous double line of rushing shadows.

They huddled closer to each other and bored on through the fog. They were no more than a hundred and fifty feet from the rocket now. And then, with a suddenness that brought them to a sharp halt, something more solid than fog, more solid than fog shapes, loomed darkly straight before them.

It—whatever it was—was approaching. It was visible now as a dark circle at the level of the ground, perhaps six feet in diameter, upright and broadside on. It was moving as fast as a man walks, and it materialized rapidly into a distinct solidity.

Ham and Pat stared fascinated. The thing was featureless— just a dull black circle and a tubular body that stretched off into the fog. Or not quite featureless. Now they could perceive an organ that projected from the center of the circle—a loose, quivering member like a large pancake on a finger-thick stem, whose edges quivered and cupped toward them, as if to catch sounds or scent. The creature was blind.

Yet it possessed some sense that could register distant objects. Thirty feet from them the stalked disc cupped deeply in their direction, the creature swerved slightly, and rushed silently toward the pair!

Ham was ready. His automatic roared its muffled blast, and roared again. The attacker seemed to telescope in upon itself and rolled aside, and behind it appeared a creature identical in all respects—the same featureless black circle, the same quivering disc. But a high, piercing whine of pain slipped like a sharp knife through the fog.

This was a danger Patricia could understand. There was no fear about her now; she had faced too many outlandish creatures on the Hotlands frontiers of Venus, or in the mysterious wilds of the Mountains of Eternity.

She snatched her companion's flame pistol from its holster and stood with the weapon ready to vomit its single blast of destruction. She knew that it represented a last resort, not to be used until other means had failed, so she simply held it, and tugged on the wire to the Gaea. Three pulls, and then again three, would summon aid from Cullen and Harbord.

The second creature—or was it another segment of the same animal?—came charging forward. Ham sent two more bullets into the blank, faceless front of it, and again that keening note of pain sounded. The monster swerved and collapsed, and another black circle was rushing toward them. His shot failed to drop this one, but the creature veered.

Suddenly the thing was roaring past them, black and huge as a railroad train. It was a segmented being; it was composed of dozens of eight-foot links, like a train of miniature cars, three pairs of legs to a section.

But it ran like a single creature, with ripples of motion flowing back along its countless legs in exactly the way a centipede runs. Ham had a flashing glimpse of the manner in which the segments were joined by finger-thick ropes of flesh.

He sent three bullets into the middle of a passing section. It was a bad mistake; the segment spouted black liquid and rolled out of line, but the one behind it suddenly turned its stalked member toward the two defenders and came rushing at them. And off in the fog the first section was circling back. They had two to face now instead of one.

Ham had three cartridges left in the clip. He grimly fired one shot full at the quivering disc of flesh that cupped toward him, saw the monster collapse, and sent another bullet into the segment that followed. The thing—or things—seemed to extend indefinitely into the fog.

Beside him he heard the roar of the flame pistol. Pat had waited until the other monster was nearly upon her, so that her single blast might do as much damage as possible.

Ham stole time for a momentary glance at the result; the terrific discharge had simply incinerated a dozen segments, and one solitary survivor was crawling away into the fog.

"Good girl!" he muttered and sent his last bullet into the on-rushing monstrosity. It dropped, and behind it, driving inexorably on, came the follower. He flung his empty weapon at the fleshy disc, saw it bound off the black skin, and waited, thrusting Pat behind him.

There was a great, roaring light. A flame pistol! Dim in the fog were the figures of Harbord and Cullen, tracing their way along the wire, and before him were writhing segments of the blasted monster.

What remained of the creature had had enough punishment, apparently, for it veered to the left and went thundering away into the mist, now no more than ten segments long. And all around the group, just beyond visibility, the fog shapes gestured and grimaced and gibbered, and then they too vanished.

Not a word was spoken as the four traced the wire to the door of the Gaea. Once within, Patricia let out a low whistle of relief as she pulled off her dripping jacket. "Well," she breathed. "That was a thrill."

"A thrill!" snorted Ham. "Say, you can have this whole soggy planet for all of me. And I've a mind to limit you to the ship, too. This is no place for a thoughtless imp like you; you draw trouble the way honey draws flies."

"As if I had anything to do with it!" she retorted. "All right; order me to stay aboard if you think it'll do any good."

He grunted and turned to Harbord. "Thanks," he said.

"That was close until you two showed up. And by the way, what was the warning for? The fog shapes?"

"Do you mean that Mardi Gras parade that's been going by?" asked Harbord. "Or was it a spiritualist convention? No; we weren't sure they were real. It was for the thing you did get tangled up with; it came humping by here in your direction."

"It or they?" corrected Ham.

"Did you see more'n one of them?"

"I made more than one of them. I cut it in half, and both halves went for us. Pat took care of one with the flame pistol, but all my bullets seemed to do was to knock off pieces." He frowned. "Do you understand the thing, Pat?"

"Better than you do," she retorted sharply. His threat to restrain her to the ship still rankled. "This would be a fine expedition without a biologist, wouldn't it?"

"That's the reason I'm being careful about von," he grinned. "I'm afraid I would be without a biologist. But what's your idea concerning that series of detachable worms out there?"

"Just that. It's a multiple animal. Did you ever hear of Henri Fabre?"

"Not that I remember."

"Well, he was a great French naturalist of about two centuries ago. Among other things, he studied some interesting little insects called processionary caterpillars, who spin themselves a cozy nest of silk and march out of it every night to feed."

"Well?"

"Just listen a moment," said the girl. "They march out single file, every caterpillar touching its head to the tail of the one preceding it. They're blind, you see; so each one trusts the one ahead. The first one's the leader; he picks the route, leads them to the proper tree, and there the column breaks up for feeding. And at sunrise, they form again into little columns, which join again into the big procession, and back they go to their nest."

"I still don't see—"

"You will. Now, whichever caterpillar is in front is the leader. If you take a stick and break the column at any point, the one behind the gap becomes the leader for his followers, and leads them back to the cobweb nest just as efficiently as the original leader. And if you segregate any one caterpillar, he finds his own way, being leader and column in one."

"I begin to see," muttered Ham.

"Yes. That think or those things—are something like the processionary caterpillars. They're blind; in fact, eyes would have much less value on Uranus than on the Earth, and perhaps no Uranian creatures developed eyes—unless the fog shapes possess them. But I think these creatures are a long way ahead of processionaries, because the caterpillars establish their contact along a thread of silk, but these fellows, apparently, do it through actual nerve ganglia."

"Eh?" queried Ham.

"Of course. Didn't you notice how they were joined? That flat organ in front—each one had it slapped like a sucking disc against the one before him—was always placed in identically the same position. And when you shot one out of the middle of the file, I saw the pulpy lump it had covered on the one it followed. And besides—" She paused.

"Besides what?"

"Well, didn't it strike you as strange that the whole line cooperated so well? Their legs moved in a sort of rhythm, like the legs of a single creature, like the legs of a myriapod—a centipede.

"I don't think habit or training or discipline could ever account for the way that file of creatures acted, rushing and stop-ping and veering and circling, all in perfect unison. The whole line must have been under the direct neutral control of the leader—hearing and smelling what he heard and smelled, even, perhaps, responding to his desires, hating with him and finally fearing with him!"

"Damned if I don't think you're right!" exclaimed Ham. "The whole bunch of them acted like one animal!"

"Until you carelessly created two by breaking the line," corrected the girl. "You see—"

"I made another leader!" finished Ham excitedly. "The one behind the break in the file became a second leader, able to act independently." He frowned. "Say, do you suppose those things accumulate their intelligence when they join? Does each one add his reasoning power—if any—to the dominating brain of the leader?"

"I doubt it," said the girl. "If that were true, they would be able to build up a colossal intellect just by adding more sections. No matter how stupid each individual might be, they'd only have to click together enough of them to create a godlike intelligence.

"If anything like that existed here, or ever had existed, they wouldn't be rushing around weaponless and savage. There'd be some sort of civilization, wouldn't there? But," she added, "they might pool their experience. The leader might have all the individual memories at his disposal, which wouldn't add a darn thing to his reasoning powers."

"Sounds plausible," agreed Ham. "Now as to the fog shapes. Have you figured out anything about them?"

She shuddered. "Not much," she confessed. "I think there's a relationship between them and these others, though."

"Why?"

"Because they came streaming by us just before the attack. They might simply have been running away from the multiple creature, but in that case they ought to have scattered. They didn't; they came rushing by in two distinct streams, and not only that, but all during the fight they were flickering and shimmering in the background. Didn't you notice that?"

"My attention was occupied," replied Ham dryly. "But what about it?"

"Well, did you ever hear of the indicator albirostris—the honey-guide?"

"It sounds vaguely familiar."

"It's an African bird of the cuckoo family, and it guides human beings to the wild bee colonies. Then the man gets the honey and the bird gets the grubs." She paused. "I think," she concluded, "that the fog shapes played honey-guide to the others. I think they led the creatures to us either because your shot angered them, or because they wanted the leavings after the others were through with us, or because they're just plain destructive. Anyway, that's my guess."

"If they're real," added Ham. "We'll have to turn the infra-red camera on the next group or herd or swarm or flock, or what-ever you call their gatherings. I still think they're mostly illusory."

She shuddered. "I hope you're right," she murmured.

"Bah!" said Harbord suddenly. "Women don't belong in places like this. Too timid."

"Yeah?" retorted Ham, now fully prepared to defend Patricia. "She was cool enough to notice details during that fracas out there."

"But afraid of shadows!" grumbled Harbord.

However, they weren't shadows. Some hours later Cullen reported that the fog around the Gaea was full of shifting, skittering shapes, and he trundled the long-wave camera from port to port.

Handicapped by the argon-laden air with its absorption spectrum that filtered out long rays, the infra-red plates were nevertheless more sensitive than the human eye, though perhaps less responsive to detail. But a photographic plate is not amenable to suggestion; it never colors what it sees by the tint of past experience; it records coldly and unemotionally the exact pattern of the light rays that strike it.

When Cullen was ready to develop his plates, Patricia was still asleep, tired out by the hectic first day on the planet, but Ham came out drowsily to watch the results.

These might have been less than she feared, but they were more than Ham expected. He squinted through a negative toward the light, then took a sheaf of prints from Cullen, frowning down at them.

"Humph!" he muttered. The prints showed something, beyond doubt, but something not much more definite than the unaided eye had seen. Indubitably the fog shapes were real, but it was equally certain that they weren't anthropomorphic.

The demoniac faces, the leering visages, the sardonic countenances, were decidedly absent to the eye of the camera; to that extent the beings they had seen were illusions, whose features had been superimposed by their own minds on the shadows in the fog. But only to that extent, for behind the illusion lay something unmistakably real. Yet what physical forms could achieve that flickering and shifting and change of shape and size that they had observed?

"Don't let Pat see these unless she asks to," he said thoughtfully. "And I think I'll confine her to the ship for the present. Judging from the couple of acres we've seen so far, this place isn't the friendliest sort of locality."

But he figured without the girl on both counts. When, fifteen hours later, he moved the rocket a mile south and prepared for another circuit in the fog, she met his order with a storm of protest.

"What's this expedition for?" she demanded. "The most important thing on a planet is the life it supports, and that's a biologist's business, isn't it?"

She turned indignant eyes on Ham. "Why do you think the Institute chose me for this job? Just to sit idly in the rocket while a couple of incompetents look around—a chemist and an engineer who don't know an epiphyte from a hemipteron?"

"Well, we could bring in specimens," muttered Ham miserably.

That brought a renewed storm. "Listen to me!" she snapped. "If you want the truth, I'm not here because of you. You're here because of me! They could have found a hundred engineers and chemists and astrogators, but how many good extraterrestrial biologists? Darn few!"

Ham had no ready reply, for it was quite true. Despite her youth, Patricia, born on Venus and educated in Paris, was admittedly preeminent in her field. Nor, in all fairness to the backers of the expedition, could he handicap her in her work. After all, not even the government-financed Smithsonian could afford to spend somewhat over two million dollars without getting fair return for its money.

Sending a rocket out into the depths where Uranus plowed its lonely orbit was a project so expensive that in simple justice the expedition had to do its utmost, especially since forty long years would elapse before there would be another opportunity to visit the doubtful planet. So he sighed and yielded.

"That shows a faint glimmering of intelligence," said Patricia. "Do you think I'm afraid of some animated links of sausages? I won't make the mistake of cutting them in the middle. And as for those funny-faced shadows, you said yourself that they were illusions, and—by the way, where are the pictures you were going to take of them? Did they show anything?"

Cullen hesitated, then at Ham's resigned nod, he passed her the sheaf of prints. At the first glance she frowned suddenly.

"They're real!" she said, and then bent over them with so intent an expression that Ham wondered what she could read from so vague and shadowy a record. He saw, or fancied he saw, a queer gleam of satisfaction in her eyes, and felt a sensation of relief that at least she wasn't upset by the discovery.

"What d'you make of them?" he asked curiously. She smiled and made no answer.

Apparently Ham's fears concerning Patricia were ill-founded on all counts. The days passed uneventfully; Cullen analyzed and filed his samples, and took innumerable tests of the greenish Uranian atmosphere; Ham checked and rechecked his standard weights, and in spare moments examined the reaction motor on which the Gaea and their lives depended; and Patricia collected and classified her specimens without the least untoward incident.

Harbord, of course, had nothing to do until the rocket plunged once more into the vastness of space, so he served as cook and general utility man—an easy enough task consisting largely of opening cans and disposing of the debris.

Four times the Gaea soared aloft, picked her way through the eternal mists to a new station, and settled down while Ham and Patricia explored another thousand-foot circle. And somewhere in the grayness above, forever invisible, Saturn swung into conjunction, passed the slower-moving Uranus, and began to recede. Time was growing short; every hour meant additional distance to cover on the return.

On the fifth shift of position, Harbord announced the limit of their stay. "Not more than fifty hours more," he warned, "unless you have an inclination to spend the next forty years here."

"Well, it's not much worse than London," observed Ham, pulling on his outdoor clothing. "Come on, Pat. This'll be our last look at the pleasant Uranian landscape."

She followed him into the gray open, waiting while he clicked his guide wire to the rocket, and the silken rope to her belt. "I'd like to get one more look at our chain-gang friends," she complained. "I have an idea, and I'd like to investigate it."

"And I hope you don't," he grunted. "One look was plenty for me."

The Gaea disappeared in the eternal mist. Around them the fog shapes flickered and grimaced as they had done ever since that first appearance, but neither of them paid any attention now. Familiarity had removed any trace of fear.

This was a region of small stony hillocks, and Patricia ranged back and forth at the full length of the rope, culling, examining, discarding, or preserving the rare Uranian flora. Most of the time she was beyond sight or sound, but the cord that joined them gave evidence of her safety.

Ham tugged impatiently. "Like leading a puppy past a row of trees," he growled as she appeared. "Wire's end!" he called. "We'll circle back."

"But there's something beyond!" she cried. By virtue of the rope she could range an additional fifty feet into the obscurity. "There's something growing just out of reach there—something new! I want to see it."

"Hell, you can't. It's out of reach and that's that. We can lengthen the wire a little and come back for it."

"Oh, it's just a few feet." She turned away. "I'll release the rope, take a look, and come back."

"You won't!" he roared. "Pat! Come here!"

He tugged mightily on the rope. A faint exclamation of disgust drifted out of the dimness, and then, suddenly, the rope came free in his hands. She had freed herself!

"Pat!" he bellowed. "Come back! Come back, I say!"

A smothered reply sounded, all but inaudible. Then there was utter silence. He shouted again. The all-enveloping fog muffled his voice in his own ears. He waited a moment, then repeated his call. Nothing; no sound but the rustle of the fog shapes.

He was in a desperate quandary. After another pause he fired his revolver into the air, all ten shots at brief intervals. He waited, then fired another clip without response from the passive, leaden-hued fog. He swore bitterly at the girl's foolhardiness, at his own helplessness, and at the grimacing fog shapes.

He had to do something. Go back to the Gaea and set Harbord and Cullen searching. That wasted precious time; every moment Patricia might be wandering blindly away. He muttered a phrase that might have been either an imprecation or a prayer, pulled a pencil and a piece of paper from his pocket, and scrawled a message: "Pat lost. Bring additional spool and attach to wire. Circle for me. Will try to stay within two-thousand-foot radius."

He clipped the paper to the wire's end, weighted it with a stone, and then tugged three times to summon the two from the Gaea. Then he deliberately released himself and plunged unguided into the fog.

He never knew how far or how long he walked. The fog shapes gibbered and mocked him, the condensation gathered on his face and dripped from his nose and chin, the fog pressed in about him. He shouted, he fired his automatic, he whistled, hoping that the shriller sounds might carry, he zigzagged back and forth across his route. Surely, he thought, Pat had sense enough not to wander. Surely a girl trained in the Hotlands of Venus knew that the proper procedure when lost was to remain still, lest one stray still farther from safety.

Ham himself was utterly lost now. He had no faintest conception of where the Gaea lay, nor in what direction was the guiding wire. Now and again he thought he spied the silver filament of safety, but each time it was only the glint of water or the dull sparkle of stone. He moved under on inverted bowl of fog that blocked off vision on every hand.

In the end it was the very weakness of the lost that saved him. After hours of hopeless plunging through the mist, he tripped—actually tripped—over the wire. He had circled.

Cullen and Harbord loomed suddenly beside him, joined by a silken rope. He gasped. "Have you—have you—"

"No," said Harbord gloomily, his lined visage looking bleak and worn. "But we will. We will."

"Say," said Cullen, "why don't you go aboard and rest up? You look about done in, and we can carry on for you." "No," said Ham grimly.

Harbord was unexpectedly gentle. "Don't worry," he said. "She's a sensible sort. She'll stay put until we find her. She can't have wandered a full thousand feet beyond the wire's end."

"Unless," responded Ham miserably, "she was driven—or carried."

"We'll find her," repeated Harbord.

But ten hours later, after they had completely circled the Gaea at a dozen different distances, it became obvious that Patricia was not within the circumference described by their two-thousand-foot wire. Fifty times during the intolerable circuit

Ham had fought against the impulse to free himself of the wire, to probe just a little farther into the tantalizing fog.

She might be sitting despondently just beyond sight and earshot, or she might be lying injured within an easy stone's throw of the circle, and they'd never know it. Yet to release himself from the one guide that marked their base was little better than suicide and somewhat more than sheer insanity.

When they reached the stake that Cullen had driven to mark their starting point, Ham paused. "Back to the ship," he ordered grimly. "We'll move her four thousand feet in this direction and circle again. Pat can't have wandered a mile from the point I lost her."

"We'll find her," reiterated Harbord.

But they didn't find her. After a futile, exhausting search, Ham ordered the Gaea to a point at which their wirebound circle was tangent to the two circles already explored, and grimly began again.

Thirty-one hours had passed since the girl had disappeared, and the three were nearing exhaustion. It was Cullen who yielded first, and groped his way wearily back to the ship. When the other two returned to move to a new base, they found him sleeping fully clothed beside a half-drained cup of coffee.

The hours dropped slowly into eternity. Saturn was pulling steadily ahead of the misty planet, bound placidly for their next meeting forty years in the future. Harbord said not a word concerning the passing of time; it was Ham who broached the subject.

"Look here," he said as the Gaea slanted down to a new position. "Time's short. I don't want you two marooned here, and if we don't find Pat in this area, I want you and Cullen to leave. Do you understand?"

"I understand English," said Harbord, "but not that sort."

"There's no reason for you two to stay. I'm staying. I'll take our portion of food and all the arms and ammunition, and I'll stay."

"Bah!" growled Harbord. "What's forty years?" He had turned sixty.

"I'm ordering you to leave," said Ham quietly.

"You don't command once we're clear of the surface," grunted the other. "We're staying. We'll find her."

But it began to seem utterly hopeless. Cullen awoke and joined them as they emerged into the infinite fog, and they took their places at six hundred and sixty foot intervals along the wire. Ham took the outermost position and they began their endless plodding through the mists.

He was close to the breaking point. For forty hours he had neither slept nor eaten, save for a hurried gulp of coffee and a bite of chocolate when they moved the Gaea. The fog shapes were beginning to take the weirdest conformations in his tired eyes, and they seemed to loom ever closer, and to grin more malevolently.

So it was that he had to blink and squint and peer very closely when, a quarter way around the circuit, he saw something a little denser than the fog shapes in the gloom.

He jerked the wire once to halt Harbord and Cullen, and stared fixedly. There was a sound, too—a faint, steady thrumming quite different from the eerie rustles of the fog shapes. He started sharply as he heard still another sound, indescribable, muffled, but certainly a physical sound. He jerked the wire three times; that would summon his companions.

They came, and he pointed out the dusky mass. "We can reach it," he suggested, "if we tie a couple of our ropes together. Two should be plenty."

They moved cautiously into the mist. Something—something was stirring there. They crept quietly on, fifty feet, sixty. And suddenly Ham realized that he saw a chain of the multiple creatures—a vast chain, apparently, for it was still passing before them. In utter despondency he stopped, staring hopelessly ahead; then, very slowly, he turned back toward the wire.

A sound—a sharp sound—froze him. It sounded like a cough!

He whirled back. Regardless of the dangerous file close before him, he shouted. "Pat! Pat!"

The sublimity of relief! A thin little voice quavered beyond the line. "Ham! Oh, Ham!"

"Are—you—are you safe?"

"Y-yes."

He was at the very side of the passing file. Beyond, pale as the mist itself, was Patricia, no more than ten feet away.

"Thank God!" he muttered. "Pat, when this chain passes, run straight here. Don't move a single step aside—not a single step!"

"Passes?" she quavered. "Oh, it won't pass! It isn't a file. It's a circle!"

"A circle!" Comprehension dawned. "A circle! Then how—how can we get you out? We can't break it or—" He paused. Now the queer parade was leaderless, helpless, but once it were broken at any point, it would turn into a fierce and bloodthirsty thing—and it might attack the girl. "Lord!" he gasped.

Harbord and Cullen were beside him. "Here!" he snapped. He seized the remaining rope. "I'm going across. Stand close."

He crawled to the shoulders of the two. From that height it might be possible to leap the creatures. It had to be possible.

He made it, though it left Cullen and Harbord groaning from the thrust of his hundred and eighty pounds, Uranus weight. He spent only a moment holding Patricia to him; the menace of those circling monsters was too imminent.

He flung an end of the rope to the two beyond the circle. "Can you swing across if we hold it high enough, Pat?" The girl seemed on the verge of exhaustion.

"Of course," she murmured.

He helped her lock elbows and knees around the rope. Slowly, painfully, she inched her way in the manner of a South American tree sloth. Ham had one terrible instant of fear as she wavered directly over the file, but she made it, dropping weakly into Harbord's arms beyond.

Then she cried out, "Ham! How can you get across?"

"Vault 'em!" he flashed.

He spent no time in reflection. He gathered all the strength remaining in his body, drew back for a short run, and actually cleared the six-foot barrier of deadliness, his knuckles just touching a black, blubbery back.

Patricia struggled to her feet, clinging to him. He held her a moment, then said huskily, "Lord! If we hadn't found you—"

"But you did!" she whispered. Suddenly she began to laugh hysterically, the sound broken by choking coughs. "Only what kept you? I expected you sooner!" She stared wildly at the circling file. "I short-circuited them!" she cried. "I—short-circuited —their brains!"

She collapsed against him. Without a word he lifted her and followed Harbord and Cullen back along the wire to the Gaea.

Behind him, revolving endlessly, was the circle of doomed creatures.

Uranus was a banded green globe behind the flare of the afterjets, and Saturn a brilliant blue star to the left of a tiny, very fierce sun. Patricia, her cough already improved in the conditioned air of the Gaea, lay passively in a pivot chair and smiled at Ham.

"You see," she said, "after I cast off the rope—Wait! Don't lecture me again about that!—I stepped just the merest few paces into the fog, and then, after all, the plants I had seen turned out to be the same old zigzag ones I named Cryptogami Urani, so I started back and you were gone."

"Gone! I hadn't moved."

"You were gone," she repeated imperturbably. "I walked a short distance and then shouted, but the shouts just sort of muffled out. And then I heard a couple of shots in another direction, and started that way—and suddenly the chain gang came plunging out of the fog!"

"What'd you do?"

"What could I do? They were too close for me to draw my gun, so I ran. They're fast, but so am I, and I kept ahead until I began to lose breath. Then I discovered that by sharp dodging I could keep away—they don't turn very quickly—and I managed for a few minutes, although that blinding fog kept me in danger of tripping. And then I had an inspiration!"

"You needed one!" he muttered.

She ignored him. "Do you remember when I mentioned Fabre and his studies of the pine processionary caterpillars? Well, one of his experiments was to lead the procession around the edge of a big garden vase and close the circle! He did away with the leader, and do you know what happened?"

"I can guess."

"You're right. Lacking leadership, the circle just kept revolving for hours, days, I don't know how long, until at last some caterpillar dropped from exhaustion, and a new leader was created by the gap. And suddenly that experiment occurred to me, and I set about duplicating it. I dodged back toward the rear end of my procession, with the front end following me!"

"I see!" muttered Ham.

"Yes. I intended to close the circle and dodge outside, but something went wrong. I caught up with the rear all right, but I was just about worn out and I stumbled or something, and the next thing I remember was lying on the ground with the feet of the things pounding by my face. And I was inside the circle!"

"You probably fainted from exhaustion."

"I never faint," said Patricia with dignity.

"You did when I got you out."

"That," she retorted, "was simply a case of going to sleep after about forty hours of staying awake without food. Fainting, or syncope, is quite different, being due to an undersupply of blood to the brain—"

"All right," cut in Ham. "If fainting needs a brain, obviously you couldn't faint. Go on."

"Well," she resumed placidly, "there I was. I could have shot a break in the circle, of course, but that would have brought an attack, and besides, I hadn't the least idea where the Gaea was. So I sat there, and I sat a week or ten days or a month—"

"Forty hours."

"And the fog shapes kept rustling over the file of sausage creatures, and they kept flickering and rustling and whispering until I thought I'd go mad. It was terrible—even knowing what they were, it was terrible!"

"Knowing what— Do you know what they are?"

"I figured out one good guess. In fact, I had a suspicion as soon as I saw Cullen's infra-red photographs."

"Then what the devil are they?"

"Well, you see I had a good chance to examine the chain things at close range, and they're not perfect creatures."

"I'll say they're not!"

"I mean they're not fully developed. In fact, they're larvae. And I think the fog shapes are what they grow up to be. That's why the fog shapes led the things to us. Don't you see? The chain creatures are their children. It's like caterpillar and moth!"

"Well, that's possible, of course, but what about the weird faces of the fog shapes, and their ability to change size?"

"They don't change size. See here—the light on that part of Uranus comes from directly overhead, doesn't it? Well, any shadows are thrown straight down, then; that's obvious. So what we saw—all that flickering, shifting crew of gargoyles—were just the shadows of floating things, flying things, projected on the fog. That's why the fog shapes grew and shrank and changed shape; they were just shadows following some winged creature that moved up and down and around. Do you see?"

"It sounds plausible. We'll report it that way, and in eighty years, when the north pole part of Uranus gets around to the Sunlight again, somebody can run up and check the theory. Maybe Harbord'll pilot them. Eh, Harbord? Think you'd be willing to visit the place again in eighty years?"

"Not with a woman aboard," grunted the astrogator.

THE
PLANETARY
STORIES

FLIGHT ON TITAN

ORIGINALLY PUBLISHED IN *ASTOUNDING STORIES*
JANUARY 1935

FLIGHT ON TITAN

The gale roared incessantly like all the tormented souls since creation's dawn, driving the two sliding and tumbling into the momentary shelter of a ridge of ice. A cloud of glittering ice needles swept by, rainbow-hued in the brilliant night, and the chill of eighty below zero bit through the sponge rubber of their suits.

The girl placed her visor close against the man's helmet and said steadily: "This is the end, isn't it, Tim? Because I'm glad I came with you, then. I'm glad it's both of us together."

The man groaned despairingly, and the blast tore the sound away. He turned aside, thinking regretfully of the past.

The year 2142, as most people recall, was a disastrous one in the financial world. It was the year of the collapse of the Planetary Trading Corporation and the year that ushered in the resultant depression.

Most of us remember the hysterical two years of speculation that preceded the crash. These followed the final development of the Hocken Rocket in 2030, the annexation of the arid and useless Moon by Russia, and the discovery by the international expeditions of a dead civilization on Mars and a primitive one on Venus. It was the Venus report that led to the formation of the P.T.C. and the debacle that followed.

No one knows now who was to blame. All the members of those intrepid expeditions have suffered under the cloud; two of them were murdered in Paris only a little more than a year ago, presumably by vengeful investors in Planetary. Gold will do such things to men; they will take mad risks with what they have, pursuing a vision of what they hope to have, and, when the crashcomes, turn on any scapegoat that's luckless enough to be handy.

At any rate, regardless of responsibility, the rumor started that gold was as common on Venus as iron on Earth—and then the damage was done. No one stopped to reflect that the planet's density is less than the Earth's, and that gold, or any heavy metal, should be even rarer there, if not utterly absent, as on the Moon.

The rumors spread like an epidemic, and stories circulated that the expedition members had returned wealthy. All one had to do, it seemed, was to trade beads and jack-knives to the obliging Venusian natives for golden cups, golden axes, golden ornaments.

The shares of the quickly organized Planetary Trading Corporation skyrocketed from a par of fifty to a peak of thirteen hundred. Vast paper fortunes were made; the civilized world went into a frenzy of speculative fervor; prices of everything shot up-ward in anticipation of a flood of new gold—food, rent, clothing, machinery.

We all remember the outcome. Planetary's first two trading expeditions looked long and arduously for the gold. They found the natives; they found them eager enough for beads and jack-knives, but they found them quite destitute of gold. They brought back neat little carvings and a quantity of silver, scientifically valuable records, and a handful of pearlike stones from Venusian seas—but no gold. Nothing to pay dividends to the avid stock-holders; nothing to support the rumor-puffed structure of prices, which crashed as quickly as the shares of Planetary, once the truth was out.

The collapse affected investors and noninvestors alike, and among them, Timothy Vick and his Canadian wife Diane. The spring of 2142 found them staring at each other in their New York apartment, all but penniless, and in the very depths of despair. Jobs were vanishing, and Tim's training as a salesman of 'vision sets was utterly useless in a world where nobody could afford to buy them. So they sat and stared hopelessly, and said very little.

Tim at last broke the gloomy silence. "Di," he said, "what'll we do when it's all gone?"

"Our money? Tim, something will come before then. It has to!"

"But if it doesn't?" At her silence, he continued: "I'm not going to sit and wait. I'm going to do something."

"What, Tim? What is there to do?"

"I know!" His voice dropped. "Di, do you remember that queer gem the government expedition brought back from Titan? The one Mrs. Advent paid half a million dollars for, just so she could wear it to the opera?"

"I remember the story, Tim. I never heard of Titan."

"One of Saturn's moons. United States possession; there's a confirmatory settlement on it. It's habitable."

"Oh!" she said, puzzled. "But—what about it?"

"Just this: Last year half a dozen traders went up there after more. One of 'em returned to-day with five of the things; I saw it on the news broadcast. He's rich, Di. Those things are almost priceless."

Diane began to see. "Tim!" she said huskily.

"Yes. That's the idea. I'm going to leave you all I can, except what money I must have, and go up there for a year. I've read up on Titan; I know what to take." He paused. "It's coming near Perigee now. There'll be a rocket leaving for Nivia—that's the settlement—in a week."

"Tim!" murmured Diane again. "Titan—oh, I did hear of it! That's—that's the cold one, isn't it?"

"Cold as Dante's hell," replied Tim. He saw her lips form a word of protest and his blue eyes went narrow and stubborn.

She changed her unspoken word. "I'm going with you," she said. Her brown eyes narrowed to meet his.

Diane had won. That was over now—the long hours of argument, the final submission, the months of insufferably stuffy air abroad the rocket, the laborious struggle to erect the tiny hemispherical metal-walled shack that served as living quarters. The rocket had dropped them, cargo and all, at a point determined after a long conference back on Earth with Simonds, the returned trader.

He had been an agreeable sort, but rather discouraging; his description of the Titan climate had sounded rather like a word picture of an Eskimo hell. He hadn't exaggerated, either; Tim realized that now and cursed the weakness that had made him yield to Diane's insistence.

Well, there they were. He was smoking his one permitted daily cigarette, and Diane was reading aloud from a history of the world, taken because it had some thousand pages and would last a long time. Outside was the unbelievable Titanian night with its usual hundred-mile gale screaming against the curved walls, and the glitter of ice mountains showing green under the glare of Saturn with its rings visible edgewise from the satellite since it revolved in the same plane.

Beyond the Mountains of the Damned—so named by Young, the discoverer—a hundred miles away, lay Nivia, the City of Snow. But they might as well have been on a planet of Van Maanen's star so far as human contacts went; surely no one could survive a cross-country journey here through nights that were generally eighty below zero, or even days that sometimes attained the balmy warmth of just above freezing. No; they were marooned here until the rocket returned next year.

Tim shivered as the grinding roar of a shifting mountain sounded above the scream of the wind. That was common enough here; they were always shifting under the enormous tidal pull of the giant Saturn and the thrust of that incredible wind. But it was disquieting, none the less; it was an ever-present danger to their little dwelling.

"Br-r-r!" He shuddered. "Listen to that!"

Diane looked up. "Not used to it yet, after three months?"

"And never will be!" he returned. "What a place!"

She smiled. "I know what'll cheer you," she said, rising. From a tin box she poured a cascade of fire. "Look, Tim! Six of them. Six flame-orchids!"

He gazed at the glowing eggs of light. Like the flush of life itself, rainbow rings rolled in a hundred tints beneath their surfaces. Diane passed her hand above them, and they responded to its warmth with a flame of changing colors that swept the entire keyboard of the spectrum, reds merging into blues, violets, greens, and yellows, then orange and scarlet of blood.

"They're beautiful!" Tim whispered, staring fascinated. "No wonder rich women bleed themselves dry for them. Diane, we'll save one out—the prettiest—for you."

She laughed. "There are things I'd rather have, Tim."

A pounding sounded above the windy bellowing. They knew what it meant; Tim rose and peered through the reenforced window into the brilliant night, and, after a moment of blinking, made out the four-foot-long body of a native sprawled before his door, his curved claws hooked into the ice. On Titan, of course, no creature stood erect against those perpetual howling blasts, no creature, that is, save man, a recent arrival from a gentler world.

Tim opened the door, slipping it wider notch by notch on its retaining chain, since muscular power would have been inadequate to hold it. The wind bellowed gleefully in, sweeping the hanging utensils on the walls into a clanging chorus, spinning a loose garment into a mad dance, chilling the air to bitterness.

The native slithered through like a walrus, his streamlined body seallike and glistening with its two-inch protective layer of blubbery flesh. As Tim cranked the door shut, the creature raised the filmy underlids from its eyes, and they showed large, luminous, and doglike.

This was a Titanian native, not much more intelligent than a St. Bernard dog, perhaps, but peacable and inoffensive, beautifully adapted to its forbidding environment, and the highest form of life yet known on Titan.

He reached into the pouch opening on his rubbery back. "Uh!" he said, displaying a white ovoid. As the comparatively warm air of the room struck it, the flame-orchid began to glow in exquisite colors.

Diane took it; against her palms the tints changed more quickly, deepened gloriously. It was a small one, no larger than a robin's egg, but perfect except where it had been attached to some frigid rock.

"Oh!" she exclaimed. "What a beauty, Tim!"

He grinned. "That's no way to bargain."

He pulled out the black case that contained their trade goods, opening it to display the little mirrors, knives, beads, matches, and nondescript trinkets.

The coal-black eyes of the native glittered avidly; he glanced from one article to the next in an agony of longing indecision. He touched them with his clawed, three-fingered hands; he cooed huskily. His eyes wandered over the room.

"Huss!" he said abruptly, pointing. Diane burst into a sudden laugh. He was indicating an old and battered eight-day clock,quite useless to the pair since it lacked the adjustment to permit them to keep other than Earth time. The ticking must have attracted him.

"Oh, no!" She chuckled. "It's no good to you. Here!" She indicated a box of trinkets.

"Ugha! Huss!" The native was insistent.

"Here, then!"

She passed him the clock; he held it close to his skin-shielded ears and listened. He cooed.

Impulsively, Diane picked a pocketknife from the box.

"Here," she said, "I won't cheat you. Take this, too."

The native gurgled. He pried open the glittering blade with his hooked claws, closed it and slipped it carefully into his back pouch, stuffing the clock after it. The pouch stood out like a miniature hump as he turned and scuttled toward the door.

"Uh!" he said.

Tim led him out, watching through the window as he slipped across the slope, his blunt nose pointed into the wind as he moved sideways.

Tim faced Diane. "Extravagance!" He grinned.

"Oh, a fifty-cent knife for this!" She fondled the gem.

"Fifty cents back home," he reminded her. "Just remember what we paid for freight, and you'll see what I mean. Why, look at Nivia; they mine gold there, pure, virgin gold right out of the rocks, and by the time the cost of shipping it back to Earth is deducted, and the insurance, it barely pays—just barely."

"Gold?"

"Yes. That's simple to understand. You know how little freight a rocket can carry when it has to be fueled and provisioned for a flight from the Earth to Titan, or vice versa. A mere jaunt of seven hundred and eighty million miles and plenty of chance for trouble on the way. I think the insurance on gold is thirty per cent of the value."

"Tim, shall we have to insure these? How shall we ever manage?"

"We won't. We won't insure these because we'll be going with 'em."

"But if they're lost?"

"If they're lost, Diane, insurance wouldn't help us, because, then, we'll be lost, too."

Three more months dragged by. Their little hoard of flame-orchids reached fifteen, then eighteen. They realized, of course, that the gem wouldn't command the fabuolus price of that first one, but half that price, even a tenth of it, meant wealth, meant leisure and luxury. It was worth the year of sacrifice.

Titan swung endlessly about its primary. Nine-hour days succeeded nine-hour nights of unbelievable ferocity. The eternal wind howled and bit and tore, and the shifting ice mountains heaved and roared under Saturn's tidal drag.

Sometimes, during the day, the pair ventured into the open, fought the boisterous winds, clung precariously to frigid slopes. Once Diane was swept bodily away, saving herself miraculously on the verge of one of the deep and mysterious crevasses that bounded their mountain slope, and thereafter they were very cautious.

Once they dared to penetrate the grove of rubbery and elastic whiplash trees that grew in the shelter of the nearest cliff. The things lashed out at them with resounding strokes, not violent enough to fell them, but stinging sharply even through the inch-thick layer of sponge rubber that insulated their bodies from the cold.

And every seven and a half days the wind died to a strange and oddly silent calm, was still for half an hour or so, and then roared with renewed ferocity from the opposite direction. Thus it marked Titan's revolution.

At almost equal intervals, every eight days, the native appeared with the clock. The creature seemed unable to master the intricate problem of winding it and always presented it mournfully, brightening at once as Diane set it ticking again.

There was one impending event that worried Tim at times. Twice in its thirty-year period Saturn eclipses the Sun, and for four Titanian days, seventy-two hours, Titan is in utter darkness. The giant planet was nearing that point now and would reach it long before the rocket ship, speeding from the Earth at perigee, was due.

Human occupation dated back only six years; no one knew what four days of darkness might do to the little world of Titan.

The absolute zero of space? Probably not, because of the dense and xenon-rich atmosphere, but what storms, what titanic upheavals of ice, might accompany that night of eclipse? Glowing Saturn itself supplied a little heat, of course, about a third as much as the distant Sun.

Well, worry was futile. Tim glanced at Diane, mending a rip in the furry face-mask of her outdoor garment, and suggested a stroll. "A stroll in the sunlight," he phrased it sardonically. It was August back on Earth.

Diane agreed. She always agreed, cheerfully and readily. Without her this project would have been utterly unbearable, and he wondered amazedly how Simonds had stood it, how those others scattered around Titan's single little continent were standing it. He sighed, slipped into this thick garment, and opened the door into the roaring hell outside.

That was the time they came near disaster. They crawled, crept, and struggled their way into the lee of an ice hummock, and stood there panting and gasping for a moment's rest. Tim raised his head to peer over the crest and saw through his visor's protecting goggles something unique in his experience on Titan. He frowned at it through the dense refractive air of the planet; it was hard to judge distances when the atmosphere made everything quiver like heat waves.

"Look, Di!" he exclaimed. "A bird!"

It did look like one, sailing on the wind toward them, wings outspread. It grew larger; it was as large as a pterodactyl, bearing down on them with the force of that hundred-mile wind behind it. Tim could make out a fierce, three-foot beak.

Diane screamed. The thing was headed for them; it was diving now at airplane speed. It was the girl who seized and flung a jagged piece of ice; the thing veered higher, swept like a cloud above them, and was gone. It could not fly upwind.

They looked it up in Young's book at the shack. That intrepid explorer had seen and named the creature; it was a knife-kite, the same sort of beast that had accounted for the death of one of his men. It wasn't a bird; it didn't really fly; it just sailed like a kite before the terrific blasts of Titan, and touched ground only during the weekly calm or when it had succeeded in stabbing some prey.

But life was scarce indeed on the icy little world. Except for the occasional natives, who came and went mysteriously as spirits, and that single knife-kite, and the whiplash trees near the cliff, they saw nothing living. Of course the crystal bubbles of the ice-ants marked the glacial surface of the hills, but these creatures never emerged, laboring incessantly beneath their little domes that grew like mushrooms as they melted within and received fresh deposits of ice crystals without. A lonely world, a wild, bizarre, forbidding, and unearthly little planet.

It never actually snowed on Titan. The chill air could absorb too little water vapor for condensation as snow, but there was a substitute. During the days, when the temperature often passed the melting point, shallow pools formed on the frozen oceans, augmented sometimes by mighty eruptions of frigid brine from below. The ferocious winds swept these pools into a spindrift that froze and went rushing as clouds of icy needles around the planet.

Often during the darkness Diane had watched from the window as one of these clouds loomed glittering in the cold-green Saturn-light, sweeping by with a scream and slithering of ice crystals on the walls, and seeming to her mind like a tall, sheeted ghost. At such times, despite the atom-generated warmth of the tiny dwelling, she was apt to shiver and draw her garment closer about her, though she was careful that Tim never observed it.

So time passed in the trading shack, slowly and dismally. The weather, of course, was uniformly, unvaryingly terrible, such weather as only Titan, nearly nine hundred million miles from the moderating Sun, can present. The little world, with its orbital period of fifteen days and twenty-three hours, has no perceptible seasons; only the recurrent shifting of the winds from east to west marks its swing about gigantic Saturn.

The season is always winter—fierce, bitter, unimaginable winter, to which the earthly storms of desolate Antarctica are as April on the Riviera. And little by little, Saturn edged closer to the Sun, until one day the western streak of its rings knifed a dark gash across the reddish disk. The eclipse was at hand.

That night saw the catastrophe. Tim was dozing on the bunk; Diane was dreaming idly of green fields and warm sunlight. Outside roared a gale more than usually vociferous, and a steady parade of ice ghosts streamed past the windows. Low and ominous came the roar of shifting glacial mountains; Saturn and the Sun, now nearly in a direct line, heaved at the planet with a redoubled tidal pull. And then suddenly came the clang of warning; a bell rang ominously.

Diane knew what it meant. Months before, Tim had driven a row of posts into the ice, extending toward the cliff that sheltered the whiplash grove. He had foreseen the danger; he had rigged up an alarm. The bell meant that the cliff had shifted, had rolled upon the first of the stakes. Danger!

Tim was springing frantically from the bunk. "Dress for outside!" he snapped. "Quickly!"

He seized her heavy sponge-rubber parka and tossed it to her.

He dragged on his own, cranked the door open to the pandemonium without, and a fierce and bitter blast swept in, upsetting a chair, spinning loose articles around the room.

"Close the emergency pack!" he yelled above the tumult.

"I'll take a look."

Diane suppressed her upsurging fear as he vanished. She strapped the pack tightly, then poured the precious eighteen flame-orchids into a little leather pouch, and suspended this about her throat. She forced calmness upon herself; perhaps the ice cliff had stopped, or perhaps only the wind itself had snapped the warning post. She righted the chair and sat with her visor open despite the knife-sharp blasts from the door.

Tim was coming. She saw his gloved hand as he seized the doorframe, then his fur-masked face, eyes grim behind the non-frosting goggles.

"Outside!" he yelled, seizing the pack.

She rose and scrambled after him into the howling inferno just as the second bell clanged.

Barely in time! As the tornado sent her sprawling and clutching, she had a sharply etched glimpse of a mighty pinnacle of glittering ice looming high above the shack; there was a rumble and a roar deeper than the winds, and the shack was gone. One iron wall, caught by the gale, swept like a giant bat above her, and she heard it go clanging and clattering along the slope to the cast.

Dazed and horribly frightened, she clawed her way after Tim into the shelter of a ridge, watching him while he wrestled the pack that struggled in the blast like something living. She was calm when at last he got it strapped to his shoulders.

"This is the end, isn't it, Tim?" she said, putting her visor close against his helmet, "Because I'm glad I came with you, then. I'm glad it's both of us together."

Tim groaned despairingly, and the blast tore the sound away. He turned suddenly, slipping his arms around her figure. "I'm sorry, Di," he said huskily.

He wanted to kiss her—an impossibility, of course, in a Titanian night. It would have been a kiss of death; they would have died with lips frozen together. He put away the thought that maybe that might be a pleasanter way, since death was inevitable now, anyway. Better, he decided, to die fighting. He pulled her down into the lee of the ridge and sat thinking.

They couldn't stay here; that was obvious. The rocket wasn't due for three months, and long before then they'd be frozen corpses, rolling away before the hurricane or buried in some crevasse. They couldn't build a habitable shelter without tools, and if they could, their atomic stove was somewhere under the shifting cliff. They couldn't attempt the journey to Nivia, a hundred miles away across the Mountains of the Damned—or could they? That was the only possible alternative.

"Di," Tim said tensely, "we're going to Nivia. Don't be startled. Listen. The wind's just shifted. It's behind us; we have almost eight Earth days before it changes. If we can make it—twelve, thirteen miles a day— if we can make it, we'll be safe. If we don't make it before the wind shifts—" He paused. "Well, it's no worse than dying here."

Diane was silent. Tim frowned thoughtfully behind his goggles. It was a possibility. Pack, parka, and all, he weighed less than Earth weight; not as much less as one would think, of course. Titan, although no larger than Mercury, is a dense little world, and, besides, weight depends not only on a planet's density, but also on distance from its center. But the wind might not hinder them so much, since they were traveling with it, not against it. Its terrible thrust, fiercer than even an equal Earth wind because the air contained thirty per cent of the heavy gas xenon, would be dangerous enough, but—Anyway, they had no choice.

"Come on. Di," Tim said, rising. They had to keep moving now; they could rest later, after sunrise, when the danger of afrozen sleep was less.

Another terrible thought struck Tim—there would be only three more sunrises. Then for four Titanian days, the little satellite would be in the mighty shadow of Saturn, and during that long eclipse, Heaven alone knew what terrific forces might attack the harrassed pair crawling painfully toward Nivia, the City of Snow.

But that had to be faced, too. There was no alternative. Tim lifted Diane to her feet, and they crept cautiously out of the shelter of the ridge, bowing as the cruel wind caught them and bruised them, even through their thick suits, by flying ice fragments.

It was a dark night for Titan; Saturn was on the other side of the little world, along with the Sun it was soon to eclipse, but the stars shone brilliant and twinkling through the shallow, but very dense and refractive, atmosphere. The Earth, which had so often lent a green spark of cheer to the lonely couple, was not among them; from the position of Titan, it was always near the Sun and showed only just before sunrise or just after sunset. Its absence now seemed a desolate omen.

They came to a long, smooth, wind-swept slope. They made the error of trying to cross it erect, trusting to their cleated shoes for secure footing. It was misjudgment; the wind thrust them suddenly into a run, pressed them faster and faster until it was impossible to stop, and they were staggering through the darkness toward unknown terrain ahead.

Tim flung himself recklessly against Diane; they fell in a heap and went sliding and rolling, to crash at last against a low wall of ice a hundred feet beyond.

They struggled up, and Diane moaned inaudibly from the pain of a bruised knee. They crept cautiously on; they circled a bottomless crevasse from the depths of which came strange roarings and shriekings; they slipped miserably past a glittering cliff that shook and shifted above them. And when at last the vast hulk of Saturn rose over the wild land before them, and the tiny reddish Sun followed like a ruby hung on a pendant, they were near exhaustion.

Tim supported Diane to a crevice facing the Sun. For many minutes they were silent, content to rest, and then he took a bar of chocolate from the pack and they ate, slipping the squares hastily through visors opened for each bite.

But under the combined radiance of Saturn and the Sun, the temperature rose rapidly more than a hundred degrees; when Tim glanced at his wrist thermometer it was already nearly thirty-eight, and pools of water were forming in the wind-sheltered spots. He scooped some up with a rubber cup, and they drank. Water at least was no problem.

Food might be, however, if they lived long enough to consume that in the pack. Humans couldn't eat Titanian life because of its arsenical metabolism; they had to exist on food laboriously transported from the Earth, or, as did the Nivian settlers, on Titanian creatures from whose substance the arsenic had first been chemically removed. The Nivians ate the ice-ants, the whiplash trees, and occasionally, it was sometimes whispered, the Titanian natives.

Diane had fallen asleep, lying huddled in a pool of icy water that flowed off into the open and then was whirled into sparkling spray by the wind. He shook her gently; they couldn't afford to lose time now, not with the shadow of the eclipse looming ominously so few hours away. But it tore his heart to see her eyes crinkle in a weary smile as she rose; he damned himself again for ever bringing her to this.

So they plodded on, battered and trampled by the fierce and ruthless gale. He had no idea how far they had traveled during the night; from the crest of a high ridge he looked back, but the shifting hills of ice made localities hard to recognize, and he could not be sure that the grim escarpment far behind was actually the cliff that had crushed their shack.

He let Diane rest again from noon until sunset, nearly five hours. She regained much of the strength spent in the struggle of the night, but when the dropping sun set his wrist thermometer tumbling far toward the hundred-below-zero mark, it seemed to her as if she had not rested at all. Yet they survived another night of inferno, and the gray of dawn found them still staggering and stumbling before the incredible ferocity of that eternal wind.

During the morning a native appeared. They recognized him; in his clawed hands was the battered case of the eight-day clock. He sidled up to them, head toward the wind, and held out hisshort arms to display the mechanism; he whined plaintively and obviously thought himself cheated.

Tim felt an unreasoning hope at the sight of him, but it vanished immediately. The creature simply couldn't understand their predicament; Titan was the only world he knew, and he couldn't conceive of beings not adapted to its fierce environment. So the man stood silently as Diane wound the clock and responded dully to her smile as she returned it.

"This time, old fellow," she said to the native, "it's ticking away our lives. If we're not in Nivia by the time it stops again— She patted the blunt head; the creature cooed and sidled away.

They rested and slept again during the afternoon, but it was a weary pair that faced the inferno of night. Diane was nearing exhaustion, not from lack of nourishment, but simply from the incessant battering she had received from the wind, and the terrific struggle that every step required. Tim was stronger, but his body ached, and the cold, striking somehow through the inch-thick parka had left him with a painfully frostbitten shoulder.

By two hours after sunset, he perceived hopelessly that Diane was not going to survive the night. She was struggling bravely, but she was unequal to the effort. She was weakening; the pitiless wind kept lashing her to her knees, and each time she rose more slowly, leaned more heavily on Tim's supporting arm. AU too quickly came the moment he had foreseen with despairing heart, when she did not rise at all.

He crouched beside her; tears misted his goggles as he distinguished her words above the screaming of the blast.

"You go on, Tim," she murmured. She gestured toward the bag on her throat. "Take the flame-orchids and leave me."

Tim made no answer, but cradled her tired body in his arms, shielding her as best he could from the furious winds. He thought desperately. To remain here was quick death; at least he might carry Diane to some more sheltered spot, where they could sink more slowly into the fatal sleep of cold. To leave her was unthinkable; she knew that, too, but it had been a brave offer to make.

She clung weakly to him as he lifted her; he staggered a dozen steps before the wind toppled him, and the last struggle brought him to the lee of a low hillock. He dropped behind it and gathered the girl into his arms to wait for the cold to do its work.

He stared hopelessly ahead. The wild splendor of a Titanian night was before him, with the icy stars glittering on cold and glassy peaks. Just beyond their hillock stretched the smooth surface of a wind-swept glacier, and here and there were the crystalline bubbles of the ice-ants.

The ice-ants! Lucky little creatures! He remembered Young's description of them in the book at the shack. Within those domes it was warm; the temperature was above forty. He stared at them, fragile and yet resisting that colossal wind. He knew why; it was their ovoid shape, the same principle that enables an egg to resist the greatest pressure on its two ends. No one can break an egg by squeezing it endways.

Suddenly he started. A hope! He murmured a word to Diane, lifted her, and staggered out on the mirror-surface of the ice. There! There was a dome large enough—fully six feet across. He circled to the lee side and kicked a hole in the glittering roundness.

Diane crawled weakly through. He followed, crouching beside her in the dusk. Would it work? He gave a long cry of relief as he perceived the scurrying three-inch figures of the ice-ants, saw them patching the dome with crystal fragments.

Steam misted his nonfrosting goggles. He drew Diane against him and then opened his visor. Warm air! It was like balm after the bitter air without; it was musty, perhaps—but warm! He opened Diane's; she was sleeping in exhaustion and never stirred as he uncovered her pale, drawn features.

His eyes grew accustomed to the gloomy starlight that filtered through the dome. He could see the ice-ants, little three-legged ruddy balls that ran about with a galloping motion. They weren't ants at all, of course, nor even insects in the terrestrial sense; Young had named them ants because they lived in antlike colonies.

Tim saw the two holes that pierced the saucerlike floor; through one, he knew, warm air came up from the mysterious hive below, and the other drained away the melting water of the dome. That dome would grow until it burst, but the ants didn't care; they'd sense the bursting point and have a new dome already started above the holes.

For a time he watched them; they paid no attention at all to the intruders, whose rubber suits offered nothing edible. They were semicivilized little creatures; he observed them curiously as they scraped a gray mold from the ice, loaded it on tiny sledges that he recognized as leaves of the whiplash tree, and tugged the load to one of the holes, dumping it in, presumably, to a handling crew below. And after a while he fell asleep, and precious time trickled away.

Hours later something awakened him to daylight. He sat up; he had been lying with his head pillowed on his arm to keep his face from the water, and he rubbed the half-paralyzed limb ruefully as he stared about. Diane was still sleeping, but her face was more peaceful, more rested. He smiled gently down on her, and suddenly a flicker of motion caught his eye and, at the same time, a flash of brilliance.

The first was only an ice-ant scurrying across the rubber of her parka. The flash was—he started violently—it was a flame-orchid rolling sluggishly in the stream of water to the vent, and there went another! The ants had cut and carried away for food the little leather bag, exposed on Diane's breast by the opening of her visor.

He snatched the rolling gem of flame from the trickling water and searched desperately for the others. No use. Of their eighteen precious ovoids, he had retrieved exactly one—the small but perfect one for which they had traded the clock. He gazed in utter despondency at the flaming little egg for which they had risked—and probably lost—everything.

Diane stirred, sat up. She saw at once the consternation in his face. "Tim!" she cried. "What's wrong now?"

He told her. "It's my fault," he concluded grimly. "I opened your suit. I should have foreseen this." He slipped the lone gem into his left gauntlet, where it nestled against his palm.

"It's nothing, Tim," said Diane softly. "What use would all eighteen be to us, or a hundred? We might as well die with one as with all of them."

He did not answer directly. He said: "Even one will be enough if we get back. Perhaps eighteen would have glutted the market; perhaps we'll get almost as much for one as we would have for all."

That was a lie, of course; other traders would be increasing the supply, but it served to distract her mind.

Tim noticed then that the ice-ants were busy around the two vents at the center; they were building an inner dome. The crystal egg above them, now eight feet through, was about to crack.

He saw it coming, and they closed their visors. There was a jagged streak of light on the west, and suddenly, with a glistening of fragments, the walls collapsed and went spinning away over the icy floor, and the wind howled down upon them, nearly flattening them to the glacier! It began to thrust them over the ice.

They slid and crawled their way to the jagged crags beyond. Diane was strong again; her young body recovered quickly. In a momentary shelter, he noticed something queer about the light and glanced up to see gigantic Saturn almost half obscuring the Sun. He remembered then. This was the last day; for seventy-two hours there would be night.

And night fell far too quickly. Sunset came with the red disk three quarters obscured, and the bitter cold swept out of the west with a horde of ice ghosts, whose sharp needles clogged the filters of their masks and forced them to shake them out time after time.

The temperature had never been higher than forty below all day, and the night air, coming after that cold day, dropped rapidly to a hundred below, and even the warming filters could not prevent that frigid air from burning in their lungs like searing flame.

Tim sought desperately for an ice-ant bubble. Those large enough were rare, and when at last he found one, it was already too large, and the ice-ants didn't trouble to repair the hole he kicked, but set at once to build a new dome. In half an hour the thing collapsed, and they were driven on.

Somehow, they survived the night, and dawn of the fourth day found them staggering all but helpless into the lee of a cliff. They stared hopelessly at that strange, sunless, Saturn-lighted dawn that brought so little warmth.

An hour after the rising of the eclipsed Sun, Tim glanced at his wrist thermometer to find the temperature risen only to seventy below. They ate some chocolate, but each bite was a burning pain for the moment that their visors were open, and the chocolate itself was numbing cold.

When numbness and drowsiness began to attack his limbs, Tim forced Diane to rise, and they struggled on. Day was no better than night now, except for the cold Saturn light. The wind battered them more fiercely than ever; it was scarcely mid-afternoon, when Diane, with a faintly audible moan, collapsed to her knees and could not rise.

Tim stared frantically about for an ice bubble. At last, far over to the right, he saw a small one, three feet through, perhaps, but big enough for Diane. He could not carry her; he took her shoulders and dragged her painfully to it. She managed to creep wearily in and he warned her to sleep with her visor closed, lest the ants attack her face. A quarter of a mile downwind he found one for himself.

It was the collapse of the bubble that wakened him. It was night again, a horrible, shrieking, howling, blasting night when the temperature on his thermometer showed a hundred and forty below. Stark fear gripped him. If Diane's shelter had fallen! He fought his way madly against the wind to the spot and shouted in relief. The dome had grown, but still stood; he kicked his way in to find Diane trembling and pallid; she had feared him lost or dead. It was almost dawn before the shelter collapsed.

Strangely, that day was easier. It was bitterly cold, but they had reached the foothills of the Mountains of the Damned, and ice-covered crags offered shelter from the winds. Diane's strength held better; they made the best progress they had yet achieved.

But that meant little now, for there before them, white and glittering and cold, loomed the range of mountains, and Tim despaired when he looked at them. Just beyond, perhaps twenty-five miles away, lay Nivia and safety, but how were they ever to cross those needle peaks?

Diane was still on her feet at nightfall. Tim left her standing in the shelter of a bank of ice and set out to find an ant bubble. But this time he failed. He found only a few tiny six-inch domes; there was nothing that offered refuge from a night that promised to be fiercer than any he had seen. He returned at last in despair.

"We'll have to move farther," he told her.

Her grave, weary eyes frightened him.

"No matter," she said quietly. "We'll never cross the Mountains of the Damned, Tim. But I love you."

They moved on. The night dropped quickly to a hundred and forty below, and their limbs turned numb and slow to respond. Ice ghosts whirred past them; cliffs quaked and rumbled. In half an hour they were both nearing exhaustion, and no crystal shelter appeared.

In the lee of a ridge Diane paused, swaying against him, "No use, Tim," she murmured. "I'd rather die here than fight longer. I can't." She let herself sink to the ice, and that action saved their lives.

Tim bent over her, and as he did a black shadow and glistening beak cleaved the air where his head had been. A knife-kite! Its screech of anger drifted faintly back as it whirled away on that hundred-mile wind.

"You see," said the girl, "it's hopeless."

Tim gazed dully around, and it was then that he saw the funnel. Young had mentioned these curious caves in the ice, and sometimes in the rocks, of the Mountains of the Damned. Opening always north or south, he had thought them the homes of the natives, so placed and shaped to prevent their filling with ice needles. But the traders had learned that the natives have no homes.

"We're going in there!" Tim cried.

He helped Diane to her feet and they crept into the opening. The funnellike passage narrowed, then widened suddenly into a chamber, where steam condensed instantly on their goggles. That meant warmth; they opened their visors, and Tim pulled out his electric torch.

"Look!" gasped Diane. In the curious chamber, walled half by ice and half by rock of the mountain, lay what was unmistakably a fallen, carved column.

"Good Heaven!" Tim was startled momentarily from his worries. "This iceberg harbored a native culture once! I'd never have given those primitive devils credit for it."

"Perhaps the natives weren't responsible," said the girl. "Perhaps there was once some higher creature on Titan, hundreds of thousands of years ago, when Saturn was hot enough to warm it. Or perhaps there still is."

Her guess was disastrously right. A voice said, "Uzza, uzza, uzza," and they turned to stare at the creature emerging from ahole in the rock wall. A face—no, not a face, but a proboscis like the head end of a giant earthworm, that kept thrusting itself to a point, then contracting to a horrible, red, ringed disk.

At the point was the hollow fang or sucking tooth, and above it on a quivering stalk, the ice-green, hypnotic eye of a Titanian threadworm, the first ever to be faced by man. They gazed in horrified fascination as the tubular body slid into the chamber, its ropelike form diminishing at the end to the thickness of a hair.

"Uzza, uzza, uzza," it said, and strangely, their minds translated the sounds. The thing was saying "Sleep, sleep, sleep," over and over.

Tim snatched for his revolver—or intended to. The snatch turned into a gentle, almost imperceptible movement, and then died to immobility. He was held utterly helpless under the glare of the worm's eye.

"Uzza, uzza, uzza,"thrummed the thing in a soothing, slumberous buzz. "Uzza, uzza, uzza." The sound drummed sleepily in his ears. He was sleepy anyway, worn to exhaustion by the hell without. "Uzza, uzza, uzza." Why not sleep?

It was the quick-witted Diane who saved them. Her voice snapped him to wakefulness. "We are sleeping," she said. "We're both asleep. This is the way we sleep. Don't you see? We're both fast asleep."

The thing said "Uzza, uzza," and paused as if perplexed. "I tell you we're sleeping!" insisted Diane.

"Uzza!" buzzed the worm.

It was silent, stretching its terrible face toward Diane. Suddenly Tim's arm snapped in sharp continuation of his interrupted movement, the gun burned cold through his glove, and then spat blue flame.

A shriek answered. The worm, coiled like a spring, shot its bloody face toward the girl. Unthinking, Tim leaped upon it; his legs tangled in its ropy length and he crashed on his hands against the rocky wall. But the worm was fragile; it was dead and in several pieces when he rose.

"Oh!" gasped Diane, her face white. "How—how horrible! Let's get away—quickly!" she swayed and sat weakly on the floor. "It's death outside," said Tim grimly.

He gathered the ropy worm in his hands, stuffed it back into the hole whence it had emerged. Then, very cautiously, he flashed his beam into the opening, peered through. He drew back quickly.

"Ugh!" he said, shuddering.

"What, Tim? What's there?"

"A—a brood of 'em." He raised the broken end of the column in his arms; the shaft fitted the hole. "At least that will fall if another comes," he muttered. "We'll be warned. Di, we've got to rest here a while. Neither of us could last an hour out there."

She smiled wanly. "What's the difference, Tim? I'd rather die in clean cold than by—by those things." But in five minutes she was sleeping.

As soon as she slept, Tim slipped the glove from his left hand and stared gloomily at their lone flame-orchid. He had felt it shatter when he struck the wall, and there it lay, colorless, broken, worthless. They had nothing left now, nothing but life, and probably little more of that.

He cast the pieces to the rock-dusty floor and then seized a fragment of stone and viciously pounded the jewel into dull powder and tiny splinters. It vented his feelings.

Despite his determination, he must have dozed. He woke with a start, glanced fearfully at the plugged hole, and then noticed that dim green light filtered through the ice wall. Dawn. At least, as much dawn as they'd get during the eclipse. They'd have to leave at once, for to-day they must cross the peaks. They must, for to-night would see the shifting of the wind, and when that occurred, hope would vanish.

He woke Diane, who sat up so wearily that his eyes felt tears of pity. She made no comment when he suggested leaving, but there was no hope in her obedience. He rose to creep through the funnel, to be there to help her when the wind struck her.

"Tim!" she shrieked. "Tim! What's that?

He spun around. She was pointing at the floor where he had slept and where now flashed a thousand changing colors like rain-bow fire. Flame-orchids! Each splinter he had cracked from the ruined one was now a fiery gem; each tiny grain was sprouting from the rock dust of the floor.

Some were as large as the original, some were tiny flames no bigger than peas, but all glowed perfect and priceless. Fifty of them—a hundred, if one counted the tiny ones.

They gathered them. Tim told her of their origin, and carefully wrapped a few grains of the rock dust in tinfoil from their chocolate.

"Have it analyzed," he explained. "Perhaps we can raise 'em back on Earth."

"If we ever—" began Diane, and then was silent. Let Tim find what pleasure he could in the discovery.

She followed him through the passage into the howling inferno of Titanian eclipse weather.

That day gave both of them all the experience of souls condemned to hell. They struggled hour after hour up the ice-coated slopes of the Mountains of the Damned. The air thinned and turned so cold that the hundred and fifty below which was the minimum on Tim's thermometer dial was insufficient and the needle rested full against the stop.

The wind kept flinging them flat against the slopes, and a dozen times the very mountains heaved beneath them. And this was day; what, he wondered fearfully, would night be like, here among the peaks of the Mountains of the Damned?

Diane drove herself to the limit, and even beyond. This was their last chance; at least they must surmount the crest before the wind shifted. Again and again she fell, but each time she rose and clambered on. And for a time, just before evening, it seemed that they might make it.

A mile from the summit the wind died to that weird, unnatural calm that marked, if you care to call it so, the half-hour Titanian summer season. They burst into a final effort; they rushed up the rugged slope until their blood pounded in their ears. And a thousand feet short of the summit, while they clung helplessly to a steep icy incline, they heard far off the rising whine that meant failure.

Tim paused; effort was useless now. He cast one final glance over the wild magnificence of the Titanian landscape, then leaned close to Diane.

"Good-by, ever valiant," he murmured. "I think you loved me more than I deserved."

Then, with a bellow of triumph, the wind howled down from the peaks, sending them sliding along the crag into darkness.

It was night when Tim recovered. He was stiff, numb, battered, but living. Diane was close beside him; they had been caught in a cupped hollow full of ice crystals.

He bent over the girl. In that roaring wind he couldn't tell if she lived; at least her body was limp, not yet frozen or set in the rigor of death. He did the only thing possible to him; he clutched her wrist and started clawing his way against that impossible gale, dragging her behind him.

A quarter mile away showed the summit. He ascended a dozen feet; the wind hurled him back. He gained fifty feet; the wind smashed him back into the hollow. Yet, somehow, dazed, all but unconscious, he managed to drag, push, roll Diane's body along with him.

He never knew how long it took, but he made it. While the wind bellowed in colossal anger, somehow, by some miracle of doggedness, he thrust Diane across the ridge of the summit, dragged himself after, and gazed without comprehension on the valley beyond, where glowed the lights of Nivia, the City of Snow.

For a while he could only cling there, then some ghost of reason returned. Diane, loyal, courageous Diane, was here dying, perhaps dead. Doggedly, persistently, he pushed and rolled her down the slope against a wind that sometimes lifted her into mid-air and flung her back against his face. For a long time he remembered nothing at all, and then suddenly he was pounding on a metal door, and it was opening.

Tim couldn't sleep yet. He had to find out about Diane, so he followed the government man back through the sunken passage to the building that served Nivia as hospital. The flame-orchids were checked, safe; theft was impossible in Nivia, with only fifty inhabitants and no way for the thief to escape.

The doctor was bending over Diane; he had stripped off her parka and was flexing her arms, then her bared legs.

"Nothing broken," he said to Tim. "Just shock, exposure, exhaustion, half a dozen frostbites, and a terrific mauling from the wind. Oh, yes—and a minor concussion. And a hundred bruises, more or less."

"Is that all?" breathed Tim. "Are you sure that's all?"

"Isn't that enough?" snapped the doctor.

"But she'll—live?"

"She'll tell you so herself in half an hour." His tone changed to admiration. "I don't see how you did it! This'll be a legend, I tell you. And I hear you're rich, too," he added enviously. "Well, I've a feeling you deserve it."

The Red Peri

Originally Published in *Astounding Stories*
November 1935

THE RED PERI

Part I

The Dutch rocket Aardkin—out of Middleburg, passengers and freight—dropped gingerly toward the mist and cloud-girt Earth some twelve thousand miles below, underjets cushioning the fall. This last leg of the journey from Venus was the ticklish part of the trip; for the great cigar-shaped rockets, beautifully swift in space, were anything but maneuverable in a strong gravitational field; and Captain Peter Ten Eyck had no particular desire to descend in either central Europe or mid-Atlantic, to the resultant disgust of the home office. He wanted to hit Middleburg in Zeeland.

Off to the right appeared a very curious shape, visible no more than a quarter of a mile away through the bridge room port. "Donder!" said Captain Ten Eyck feelingly.

At the same moment the annunciator beside him remarked, "Cut your jets!"

"Aasvogel!" rejoined the captain. "Vaarken!" His other epithets were somewhat too expressive for permanent record.

The apparition against the black sky was swiftly drifting closer. It was distinguishable now as a glittering, metal rocket, but in no way like the tapering, cylindrical Aardkin, nor like any other rocket—save one.

It was a tubular triangle, from each corner of which rose a strong girder to meet an apex above. In effect, its sides and girders outlined a skeleton tetrahedron, and from the apex of the girders, the blue atomic blast flared down to spread fanlike into the space below. As it approached, the strange vessel was dwarfed by the giant freighter; it was no more than a hundred feet on a side, not an eighth the length of the Aardkin.

Again the annunciator uttered its metallic tones. It was responding, apparently, to a beam from the stranger. "Cut your jets!" it repeated. "Cut your jets, or we'll top you!"

Captain Ten Eyck ended his mutterings in a heavy sigh. He had no wish to have his vessel exposed to the withering blast of the pirate. He grumbled an order into the box beside him, and the roar of the jets ceased. Whatever maneuverability the lumbering freighter possessed was gone now; there was no longer any chance of ramming the agile attacker.

With the cessation of the jets came also complete weightlessness, since they were in a free fall; but a twelve-thousand-mile fall takes considerable time to become serious. Ten Eyck sighed again, ordered the floor magnets on, and waited phlegmatically for further directions. After all, he reflected, his cargo was insured, and Boyd's Marine could afford the indemnity. Besides, Boyd's was an English concern, and he had no mind to risk a good Netherlands ship and—if he did say it himself—a good Netherlands captain to save an English insurance company from loss.

The door to the bridge room opened. Hawkins, the first officer, clattered in. "What's here?" he shrilled. "The jets are off—" He caught sight of the glistening shape beyond the port. "The Red Peri! The blasted pirate!"

Captain Ten Eyck said nothing, but his pale blue eyes stared moodily at the painted figure plainly visible on the attacker's hull—the figure of a crimson, winged imp. He needed no sign to identify the pirate; the queer construction of the vessel was proof enough, for there wasn't another such ship in the sky.

The voice sounded again. "Open your air lock." Ten Eyck gave the order and stalked grimly out to receive the boarding party. He heard the thud of the extending gangway as it struck, and the faint grind as the magnet bit to the freighter's hull. There came a brisk pounding on the inner door of the lock. The captain gave the order to open, his voice curiously equable. He was thinking again of the insurance company.

Most of the Aardkin's score of passengers were crowded along the passage. The cutting of the jets, and perhaps the sound of Hawkins' voice from the beam room as he called hopefully for assistance, had apprised all of them of the events, and the glittering triangle of the Red Peri indicated their nature.

The lock swung inward, opening upon the steel-ribbed, rubber-sheathed tunnel of the gangway. Figures in space suits, worn either for disguise or simply as precaution against the possible need of cutting their way in, filed through the circular door-way, automatics and gas guns menacingly visible.

There were no words spoken; a dozen buccaneers clanked methodically away toward the aft hold, and one, a slighter figure, stood grimly guarding the lock. In five minutes they were filing back, dragging whatever loot they had found, with the queer movement of inertia without weight—much as if they floated the objects through water.

Ten Eyck saw the cases of xixtchil pods, valuable as so many diamonds, disappear into the lock; and the seventeen crated ingots of Venusian silver followed. He swore under his breath as he recognized the casket of emeralds from the mines in the Dutch Alps of Venus, and wondered blasphemously how they had managed to crack the Aardkin's safe with neither torch nor explosive.

Glancing into the purser's office, he saw a queer, jagged hole in the big steel box, that looked more as if it had rusted or simply broken away than as if it had been cut. Then the freebooters were silently passing back to their vessel, having neither addressed nor molested officers, crew, or passengers.

Except, perhaps, for one: among the group of watchers was young Frank Keene, American radiologist and physicist returning from the solar-analysis station of Patrick's Peak in the Mountains of Eternity. He had edged close to the air lock, and now, as the departing marauders passed through, he suddenly leaned forward with narrowed eyes, and peered boldly into the cloudy visor of the guard.

"Hah!" he said. "A redhead, eh?"

The guard said nothing, but raised a steel-guantleted hand. The metal thumb and forefinger bit viciously into Kcene's sun-tanned nose, and he was thrust violently back into the crowd, with two spots of blood welling from the abused organ.

Keen grunted in pain. "O.K., fellow," he said stolidly. "I'll see you again some day."

The guard spoke at last in a voice that clinked out metallically from the helmet's diaphragm. "When you do, there'd better be two of you." Then this figure followed the rest; the outer lock clanged shut; the magnets released the gangway's grip; and the Red Peri, agile as a swallow and swift as a comet at perihelion, flared into the black void.

Beside Keene sounded the voice of Captain Ten Eyck. "What a ship! Mynheer Keene, is that not a ship—that Red Peri?"

He was still exclaiming over it at intervals during the laborious task of laying a new landing course; and when, an hour later, a blunt little League rocket appeared in answer to Hawkin's call, he informed its officers flatly that the pirate was hopelessly beyond reach. "Even if your fat beeste of a boat could match its acceleration, which it couldn't."

*   *   *   *   *

A year later Frank Keene had almost completely forgotten the Red Peri and the red-headed pirate, though occasionally, during the interval, mention of the famous marauder had brought his experience to mind. After all, when a freebooter has scoured the skyways for nearly fifteen years without capture, he becomes something of a legend, a figure of heroic proportions. Papers and broadcasts give daily references to him, and he is blamed for, or perhaps credited with, many a feat performed by some less-celebrated desperado.

The lair of the Red Peri remained a mystery, though League ships scoured asteroids, the far side of the desolate Moon, and even the diminutive satellites of Mars. The swift pirate, striking invariably as his victim inched gingerly through some planet's gravitational field, came and went untouched.

But Frank Keene had little time at the moment for consideration of the famous freebooter. He and his companion, fifty-five year old Solomon Nestor of the Smithsonian, were out where few men had ever been, and in a predicament that was perhaps unique. They were dropping their rocket Limbo toward the rugged, black disc of Pluto, two billion miles from home, and they were not happy about it.

"I tell you," growled Keene, "we've got to land. Do you think I'm settling on this chunk of coal from choice? We've got to make repairs. We can't navigate with one stern jet gone, unless you have a notion to fly in circles."

Old Solomon was a marvel on hard radiations, stellar chemistry, and astro-physics, but hardly an engineer. He said plaintively, "I don't see why we can't zigzag."

"Bah! I told you why. Didn't I spend five hours figuring out the time it'd take to reach the nearest inhabited place? That's Titan near Saturn, just one billion—one billion, I said—miles from here. And at the speed we could make zigzagging, because we couldn't keep a constant acceleration, it would take us just exactly four years and three months. We've got food enough for three months, but what would we live on during the four years? Atomic energy?"

"But what can we do on Pluto?" queried old Nestor. "And why didn't we carry a spare jet?"

"Jets aren't supposed to melt off," muttered Keene disgustedly. "As for what we can do, maybe we can find a virgin deposit of some refractory metal—platinum or iridium or tungsten, or any other with a high melting point—and build up a jet long enough to keep the blast from melting our stern away. Because that's what it'll do if we try running it this way."

"There's tungsten here," observed the older man hopefully, gazing down at the black expanse. "Hervey reported it, and so did Caspari. But there isn't any atmosphere, or rather, what there is, is liquid or solid, except about half a centimeter's pressure of helium. Pluto has a diameter of about ten thousand miles, a surface gravity of about 1.2, and an albedo—"

"Not interested," grunted Keene, and then, relenting, "Listen, Solomon, I'm sorry. I guess I'm taking it out on you because we had a defective jet. But it's a hell of a mess all the same, and somebody's going to suffer for it when we get back. With all the money the institute has, you'd think they'd be able to afford respectable equipment." He glared down through the floor port. "There she comes!"

With a rasp and a jar, the Limbo came to rest. Outside, a mixed column of dust and smoke billowed around the glasses, rose and then settled as quickly as a burst of sand, in the near vacuum that surrounded the ship.

Keene cut the blast. "Come on," he said, turning to a space suit swaying on its hook. "No use wasting time. We'll take a look around." He clambered into the heavy garment, noting irritably its greater weight on the surface of the black planet. The Plutonian gravitation added thirty-six pounds to his Terrestrial hundred and eighty.

"No gun?" asked Nestor.

"Gun? For what? This planet's dead as the brain of whoever tested that jet. How can there be organic life in no air and ten degrees absolute?" He pulled open the inner door of the air lock. "Well," he said, his voice sharply metallic through his helmet's diaphragm, "here goes the Smithsonian Expedition for the Determination of the Intensity of Cosmic Radiation in Extra-planetary Space. We determined it all right; now the only problem of the expedition is to get home with our statistics." He flung open the outer door and stepped out on the black surface of Pluto.

So far as Keene knew, he was the fourth man and Nestor the fifth to set foot on the black planet. Atsuki, of course, was the first, if one credits his figures and photographs, the intrepid Hervey the second, and Caspari the third. Here on this lonely outpost of the solar system, high noon was hardly brighter than full moonlight on Earth, and the queer, black surface that gives Pluto its low albedo made it seem still darker.

But Keene could distinguish the outlines of fantastic mountains beyond the hollow where the Limbo rested, and innumerable mysterious crags and hillocks, unweathered by wind or water, loomed closer. Directly to his right lay a patch of glistening, snow-like white; but he knew it wasn't snow, but frozen air. One dared not step in such a drift; for the cold would bite through his insulated space suit, since frozen air was a far better conductor of heat than the rocky ground.

Overhead glittered all the stars of the galaxy, as changeless as though he stood on a pleasant green planet two billion miles sunward, for what was two billion miles to the infinite remoteness of the stars? The landscape was bleak, black, desolate and cold. This was Pluto, the planet that circled at the very edge of the System.

The two started heavily toward a ridge where something glowed faintly, something that might he virgin metal. Strangely, their own footsteps were audible, for the substance of their space suits conducted the sound; but all else was a vast and ominous silence. They did not speak, for their suits, designed only for emergency repairs in space, had no radio; and to communicate it was necessary to touch hand or arm to one's companion; over such a material bridge, sound traveled easily enough.

At the ridge Keene paused, glowering down at a vein of bright, starlighted fragments. He placed a hand against Nestor's shoulder, "Pyritic," he grunted. "We'll have to look farther."

He turned right, treading heavily under nearly sixty pounds more than his Earth weight. Surely, he mused, old Solomon Nester wouldn't be capable of an extended search in such circumstances. He frowned; Caspari had reported great quantities of heavy metals here, and they shouldn't need such a lengthy search. He stopped sharply; a stone came sliding past him on the rocky surface. A signal.

Off in the dusk Nestor was gesturing. Keene turned and hurried back, clambering along the uneven terrain with such haste that his breath shortened and his visor began to cloud. He clapped his hand on the old man's arm. "What is it?" he asked. "Metal?"

"Metal? Oh, no." Nestor's voice was triumphant. "What did you say about no organic life on Pluto, eh? Well, what about inorganic life? Look there!"

Keene looked. Out of a narrow chasm or cleft in the ridge something moved. For a moment Keene thought he saw a brook flowing, but a brook—liquid water—was an impossibility on Pluto. He squinted sharply. Crystals! Masses of crystals, gray-white in the dusk, crawling in a slow parade.

"I'll be damned!" he said. "Caspari didn't say anything about this."

"Don't forget," said Nestor, "that Pluto has thirty-six per cent more surface than the whole Earth. Not a ten-thousandth part of it has been explored—probably never will be, because it's such a task to get a rocket here. If Atsuki—"

"I know. I know," interrupted Keene impatiently. "But these things aren't tungsten or platinum. Let's move on." But he still stared at the crawling, faintly radiant mass. In the silence he heard infinitely faint rustlings, cracklings, and susurrations, transmitted through the ground to his feet, and thence to his helmet. "What makes them move?" he asked. "Are they alive?"

"Alive? I don't know. Crystals are as close as inorganic matter comes to life. They feed; they grow."

"But they don't live!"

Old Solomon Nestor was in his element now. "Well," he proceeded in professorial tones, "what is the criterion of life? Is it movement? No; for wind, water, and fire move, while many living forms do not. Is it growth? No; for fire grows, and so do crystals. Is it reproduction? Again no; for again fire and crystals reproduce themselves, if their proper food supply is present. Then just what differentiates dead matter from living?"

"That's what I'm asking you!" snapped Keene.

"And I'm telling you. There's just one, or perhaps two criteria. First, living things show irritation. And second, and more important, they show adaptation."

"Eh?"

"Listen," continued Nestor. "Fire moves, grows, feeds, and reproduces, doesn't it? But it doesn't run away from water. It doesn't betray the irritation life shows in the presence of a poison, though water's poison to it. Any living thing that encounters poison makes an attempt to throw it off; it develops antibodies or fever, or it ejects the poisonous matter. Sometimes it dies, of course, but it tries to survive. Fire doesn't.

"As for adaptation, does fire ever make a voluntary attempt to reach its food? Does it deliberately flee from its enemies? Even the lowest form of life known does that; even the miserable amoeba makes positive gestures of adaptation to its environment."

Keene stared more closely at the sluggish crystalline stream, which was now impinging on the black plain at his feet. He bent over it, and suddenly perceived a fact that had hitherto escaped him.

"Look here," he said, touching old Solomon's arm. "These things are organisms. They're not loose crystals, but masses of them."

It was true. The rustling crystals moved in glittering chunks from thumbnail size to aggregations as large as dogs. They crackled and rustled along, apparently moving by a slow shifting of the lower crystals, much as a snake moves on its scaly belly, but far stiffer and slower. Abruptly Keene sent his metal boot crashing into one. It shattered with a blue flash of released static electricity, and the pieces passively resumed their progress.

"They certainly don't show irritation," he remarked.

"But look!" shrilled Nestor. "They do show adaptation. There's one feeding!"

He pulled Keene a few feet down the ridge. There was a small bluish deposit of something that looked like frozen clay, a product, perhaps, of the infinitely remote past when Pluto's own heat had maintained liquid water and gaseous air to grind its rocks to powder. A crystalline mass had paused at the edge, and before their gaze it was growing, gray-white crystals springing out of it as frost spreads over a winter-chilled windowpane.

"It's an aluminum-eater!" shrieked Nestor. "The crystals are alums; it's eating the clay!"

Keene was far less excited than old Solomon, perhaps because he was considerably more practical.

"Well," he said decisively, "we can't waste any more time here. We need refractory metal, and we need it bad. You try along the ridge, and I'll cross over."

He broke off suddenly, staring appalled at the foot with which he had shattered the moving crystals. On its surface glittered a spreading mass of tiny, sparkling points!

A break in the surface of his space suit meant death, for the oxygen generator could certainly never maintain its pressure against any appreciable leakage. He bent over, scraping desperately at the aluminum feeders, and then realized that the infection would spread—had spread to his gauntlets. While Nestor babbled futilely and inaudibly behind his visor, Keene rubbed his hands in the gritty, pyritic soil on which he stood.

That seemed to work. The rough substance scoured away the growing crystals, and with frantic vigor he rasped a handful along his shoe. If only no hole, no tiniest pin prick had opened! He scoured furiously, and at last the metal surface showed scratched and pitted, but free of the growths.

He stood up unsteadily, and placed his hand against the gesturing Nestor's side.

"Keep away from them!" he gasped. "They eat—"

Keene never finished his sentence. Something hard jarred against the back of his armor. A metallic voice clicked, "Stand still—both of you!"

Part II

"What the devil!" gulped Keene. He twisted his head within his immovable helmet, peering through the rear visor glasses.

Five—no, six figures in blue metal space suits were ranged behind him; they must have approached in the inaudibility of a vacuum while he had been scouring his suit free of the crystals. For a moment he had an eerie sensation of wonder, fearful that he faced some grotesque denizens of the mysterious black planet, but a glance revealed that the forms were human. So were the faces dim in the dusk behind the visors; so had been the voice he had heard.

Keene hesitated. "Listen," he said. "We're not interfering with you. All we want is some tungsten in order to fix our—"

"Move!" snapped the voice, whose tones traveled through the weapon hard against Keene's back. "And remember that I'm two thirds inclined to kill you anyway. Now move!"

Keene moved. There was little else he could do, considering the appearance of the threatening automatics in the hands of their captors. He tramped heavily along, feeling the thrust of the muzzle against his back, and beside him Solomon Nestor trudged with pace already showing the drag of weariness. The old man touched his arm.

"What's this about?" he quavered.

"How do I know?" snorted Keene.

"Shut up!" admonished the voice behind him.

They walked past the looming shape of the Limbo—five hundred feet past it, a thousand. Directly ahead was the other rim of the cup-shaped depression in which they had landed, high, black cliffs in fantastic shapes. Suddenly Keene started; what had seemed but a smaller cliff showed now as a skeleton, tetrahedral frame of metal, three webbed shafts rising to a point from a tubular triangle below.

"The Red Peri!" he gasped. "The Red Peri!"

"Yeah. Why the surprise?" queried the sardonic voice. "You found what you were looking for, didn't you?"

Keene said nothing. The appearance of the pirate ship had amazed him. No one had ever dreamed that the swift marauder could operate from a base as infinitely remote as the black planet. How could even the agile vessel scour the traffic lanes of the minor planets from dusky Pluto, two billion miles out in the empty cosmos?

To his knowledge only two ships—three, if Atsuki hadn't lied—had ever reached those vast depths before their own

Limbo, and he knew what endless travail and painful labor each of those journeys had cost. In his mind echoed Captain Ten Eyck's words of a year and a half before. "What a ship!" he muttered. "Lord, what a ship!"

There was an opening in the cliff wall as they rounded the bulk of the Red Peri. Yellow light streamed out, and he glimpsed an ordinary fluorolux bulb in the roof of the cavern. He was shoved forward into the opening, and suddenly his visor was clouded with moisture. That meant air and warmth, though he had seen no air lock, nor heard one operate. He suppressed the impulse to brush a metal-sheathed hand across the glass, knowing that he couldn't wipe the condensation away in that fashion.

The voice again, still queerly sardonic, yet somehow soft. "You can open your helmets. There's air."

Keene did so. He stared at the figures surrounding himself and Nestor, some still helmeted, others already removing the uncomfortable space suits. Before him stood a figure shorter than the rest, and he recalled the red-haired pirate on the Aardkin. The short one was twisting the cumbersome helmet.

It came off. Keene gulped again at the face revealed, for it was that of a woman. A woman? A girl, rather, for she seemed no more than seventeen. But Keene's gasp was not entirely surprise; mostly, it was sheer admiration.

Her hair was red, true enough, if one could call red a lovely and subtle shade between copper and mahogany. Her eyes were bright green, and her skin was the silken, soft, and pale skin of one whose flesh is but seldom exposed to the sunlight, yet gently tanned by the violet-rich rays of the fluorolux.

She let the cumbrous metal suit clank away from her, and stepped out in the quite civilized garb of shirt, shorts, and dainty, laced buskins, such as one had to wear in a space suit. Her figure—well, Keene was only twenty-six, but even old Nestor's pallid eyes were fixed on her as she turned toward them. She was slim, curved, firm; despite her slimness, there was a litheness and sturdiness to her limbs, the result, perhaps, of a lifetime under the supernormal gravitation of Pluto.

"Take off your suits," she ordered coldly, and as they complied, "Marco, lock these up with the rest."

A tall, dark individual gathered up the clanking garments.

"Yes, commander," he said, taking a key she held out and moving away into the cavern.

"Commander, eh?" said Keene. "So you're the Red Peri!"

Her green eyes flickered over him. She surveyed his own figure, which was still hard and brown and powerful from his swimming days at the university. "You," she said impassively. "I've seen you before."

"You have a good memory," he grunted. "I was on the Aardkin."

She gave him a momentary smile of amused remembrance.

"Yes. Did your nose scar?" She glanced at the organ. "I'm afraid not."

People—two or three of them—came hurrying up the long corridor of the cave to stand staring curiously at Keene and Nestor. Two were men; the third was a pale, pretty, flaxen-haired girl. The Red Peri glanced briefly at them and seated herself on a boulder against the rocky wall.

"Cigarette, Elza," she said, and took one from the pale girl.

The scent of tobacco tantalized Keene, for such indulgences were impossible in the precious air of a space ship. It had been four months since he had smoked, in the frigid little town of Nivia, the city of snow on Titan.

"May I have one?" he asked.

The green eyes turned an icy glance on him. "No," said the Red Peri briefly.

"Well, I'll be— Why not?" He was angered.

"I don't think you'll live long enough to finish it," responded the girl coolly, "and our supply is limited here."

"Yeah, limited to what you find on looted freighters!" he snapped.

"Yes," she agreed. She blew a tormenting plume of smoke toward him. "I'll tell you what I'll do. I'll trade you a cigarette for the information as to how you managed to trace us here."

"Trace you?" he echoed, puzzled.

"That's what I said. It's a generous offer, too, because I'm quite capable of torturing the knowledge out of you."

Staring into her lovely, glittering green eyes, Keene was not disposed to doubt her capability. He said mildly, "But we didn't trace you here."

"I suppose," she retorted, "that you came to Pluto looking for a good business corner. Or perhaps on a little camping trip. Is that your story?"

He flushed under her cool insolence. "We came here by accident," he growled. "One of our afterjets melted off, and if you don't believe it, go look at it."

"Jets don't melt unless they're planned to," said the Red Peri coldly. "And what were you doing in the neighborhood of Pluto anyway? And I suppose that out of all the millions of square miles of surface, you just accidentally picked this valley as a landing place. Well, it won't do you any good to lie, because you're going to die regardless, but you might die a little less painfully if you tell the truth."

"It just happens that I'm telling the truth!" he blazed. "Whether you believe it or not, we landed in this valley by pure chance. We're the Smithsonian's expedition to study cosmic rays in outer space, and you can verify that by our clearance papers from Nivia."

"A good disguise for the secret service," she sneered. "You could get any sort of government papers you want, couldn't you?"

"Disguise! Listen, if we were hunting the Red Peri, do you think we'd come armed with cameras, interferometers, electroscopes, polariscopes, and fly-wing bolometers? Search our ship; you'll find one gun in it—one measly automatic. I'll tell you where it is. It's in the upper right-hand drawer of the navigation table. And we landed here because Pluto was the nearest solid place to where we burned off our jet—and that's the truth!"

The Red Peri's glance was faintly speculative. "I don't see," she said thoughtfully, "that it makes much difference. If you're telling the truth, it simply means that you're a very unlucky expedition, because I certainly can't let you go, and I haven't any particular desire to keep you here. In other words, it still looks very much as if you were destined to die." She paused. "What are your names?"

"This is Smithsonian's Professor Solomon Nestor," he said, "and I'm Frank Keene, radiation engineer."

Her green eyes shifted to the old man. "I've heard of Solomon Nestor," she observed slowly. "I really shouldn't like to kill him, but I don't see exactly what other course is open." She flashed her gaze back to Keene. "Do you?" she asked coolly.

"You could take our words not to give out any information," he grunted.

She laughed. "The Red Peri trusts very little to promises," she retorted. "Anyway, would you give your word to that?"

For a full half minute he stared into her mocking eyes. "I wouldn't," he said at last. "When I entered the Smithsonian's service I took their usual oath to uphold the law in the far places. Maybe many of their explorers consider that oath just so many words; I know some of them have found wealth at the expense of the institute. But I keep my oaths."

The Red Peri laughed again. "No matter," she said indifferently. "I wouldn't trust my safety to any one's word. But the question of your disposal still remains." She smiled with a taint hint of malice. "Would you prefer to die instantly, or do you think you can stand the torture of suspense while I check your story and think it over? Because frankly, I think it will he necessary to kill you anyway. I see no alternative."

"We'll wait," said Keene stolidly.

"Very well." She flipped away the stub of her cigarette, crossed her dainty legs, and said, "Another, Elza."

Keene looked sharply at the yellow-haired girl as she held a light to the cigarette. There was something dimly inimical in her manner, as if she were struggling to suppress a hatred, a hidden enmity. She withdrew the flame with an abrupt, irritable gesture.

"That's all," said the green-eyed leader. "I'll lock you up somewhere until I'm ready."

"Wait a minute," said Keene. "Now will you answer a few of my questions?"

She shrugged. "Perhaps."

"Are you the only Red Peri?"

"The one and only," she smiled. "Why?"

`Because you must have been born like Lao-tse at the age of eighty, then. These raids have been going on for fifteen years,and you're not a day over seventeen. Or did you start your career of piracy at the age of two?

"I'm nineteen," she said coolly.

"Oh. You began at four, I suppose."

"Never mind. Any further questions?"

"Yes. Who designed your ship, the Red Peri?"

"A very clever designer," she said, and then murmured softly, "a very clever one."

"He must have been!" snapped Keene angrily.

"He was. Have you anything else to ask?"

"You haven't answered one question so far," he growled. "But here's another. What do you think will happen when the Limbo doesn't arrive in Nivia when due? Don't you know that the next government rocket will be out to look for us? And don't you realize that they'll look for us first on Pluto? Your base here is bound to be discovered, and if you murder us it'll go just that much harder with you."

The Red Peri laughed. "That isn't even a good bluff," she said. "Titan isn't a quarter of the way between the Earth and Pluto, and it's getting farther from us every day. The next conjunction of Saturn and Pluto is fifty years in the future, and about the only time your clumsy rockets can make the jump is at conjunction. You ought to know that.

"And what's more, by the time you're missed, there won't be a thing to do but give you up as lost, and you'll not be the first Smithsonian expedition to be lost. And finally, if they did send out a searching party, how would they expect to find you? By blind reckoning?"

"By radio!" grunted Keene.

"Oh. And have you a radio on the Limbo?" she asked gently.

He groaned and subsided. Of course there was no radio on the little expeditionary rocket; all its precious space was occupied by fuel, food, and necessary equipment, and besides, what possible use could a radio be to explorers out in the lonely vastness of extraplanetary space? The nearest settlement, Nivia on Titan, was hundreds of millions of miles beyond range of the most powerful beam yet developed.

The Red Peri knew as well as he how utterly hopeless was the expectation of any search for himself and Nestor. They'd simply be given up, called martyrs to science, regretted by the few experimenters who were interested in their results, and then forgotten,

"Any more questions?" asked the flaming-haired one mockingly.

Keene shrugged, but suddenly and unexpectedly old Solomon Nestor spoke. "That entrance," he squeaked irrelevantly, pointing to the arch of the cave. "How do you keep the air here from rushing out?"

Keene whirled and stared in amazement. It was true; the cave was open to the frigid, airless outdoors; he could see the dusky Plutonian twilight through an unglassed, unblocked archway.

"At least that question is sensible," said the Red Peri. "We do it with a field."

"A field!" echoed Keene. "What sort—"

"You've asked enough questions," she cut in tartly. "I answer no more." She turned. "Elza, take these two into any unoccupied room with a metal door. If they're hungry, send them food. That's all."

She rose without a glance at the prisoners. Keene's eyes followed the exquisitely graceful figure as she trod as lightly as if she walked an Earthly corridor, followed by the five men who remained. Her radiant hair glowed far down the length of the passage until she turned aside and vanished.

He and Nestor followed the flaxen-haired Elza, and behind them, grimly silent, came the two men who had first appeared with her. She led them past a number of niches, side aisles, and several obviously artificial chambers. The cavern seemed to stretch indefinitely into the depths of the Plutonian mountain, and was undubitably a natural cave, though here and there the floor or walls showed signs of human workmanship. At last the girl indicated a chamber to the right, and they entered a small room, furnished comfortably enough with an aluminum chair, a table, and two couches. These last were covered with deep and gloriously beautiful brocades, beyond doubt plunder from some freighter's cargo.

"This is yours," said Elza, and turned toward the door. She paused. "Are you hungry?" she asked.

"No," said Keene. He saw the two men standing in the corridor, and lowered his voice. "But will you talk to us a while, Elza? Alone?"

"Why?"

"I'd like to ask you something."

"What is it?"

He dropped his voice to a whisper. "You hate the Red Peri, don't you, Eliza? As much as we do?"

She turned abruptly to the door. "Father," she said evenly, "will you and Basil bring something to eat? I'll stay here; you can bolt the door on us."

There was a murmur without.

"Hush!" she said. "You heard. These two are gentlemen." The door closed and she faced them. "Well?"

"Can we be heard here?" asked Keene, glancing around the rock-walled chamber.

"Of course not. The Peri has no need to spy on her followers. She's clever enough to read men's feelings in their glances and the tone of their voices."

"Then she must know you hate her, Elza."

"I haven't said that I hate her."

"But you do. Does she know it?"

"I hope not."

"But you just said that she could read—"

"I said men," cut in the flaxen-haired girl.

Keene chuckled. "Why do you hate her, Elza?"

Her blue eyes hardened. "I will not say."

"Well, it doesn't matter, I suppose." He shrugged. "Elza, is there any chance of our escaping? Would you help us to—say, to steal the Red Peri? Our own ship's useless."

"They've gone to repair it. As for the Red Peri, I don't think you could operate it. It doesn't control like your rocket. I don't know how to run it."

"I could make a good try at it," said Keene grimly. "It would have to be the Red Peri anyway. They could run the Limbo down in three hours and blast it." A thought struck him. "Unless we could cripple the Red Peri first."

"I don't see how you could," said Elza. "She has the key to it hidden somewhere. And how could you even reach it? The space suits are locked up, too. You can't even step beyond the entrance."

That brought a new thought. "How do they seal the air at the entrance, Elza?"

"I don't understand how."

Solomon Nestor spoke. "I know that. She said they used a field. She meant—"

"Never mind now," said Keene. "Elza, are there any others here that might—well, side with us against the Peri?"

"No men. All of them worship her and"—her face darkened — "half of them love her."

"For which you can hardly blame them," muttered Keene. "She's about as lovely a female devil as you'd find this side of hell. Still, one would think she'd have some enemies, if only because of her cruel nature."

"She isn't cruel," said Elza reluctantly. "She's ruthless and arrogant and proud, but she isn't cruel—not exactly. I don't think she really enjoys torture."

"Well, her green eyes look cruel enough. Say, Elza, that dark fellow she called Marco. What of him?"

The girl flushed. "He's Marco Grandi. Why do you ask me about him?"

"Because he looks like a sly, calculating, shrewd customer, and there's a big reward for the Peri. I thought we might work on him."

Elza's flush darkened to anger. "He's—he's wonderful!" she blazed. "And if you think money would tempt him—or any of us—you're wrong. Each of us has a dozen times the amount of the reward."

Keene saw his error. "I'm sorry," he said hastily. "After all, I just caught a glimpse of him." He paused. "Does he, by any chance, love the Red Peri?"

She winced. "He's no different in that way than the rest."

"I see. But you—perhaps—wish that he were different—in that way?"

Elza brushed a white hand across her face. "All right," she said sullenly. "I love him. I admit it. That's why I hate her. He's dazzled; he thinks she'll learn to care for him; he can't see how utterly heartless and indifferent she is. That's why I'll do whatever I can to hurt her, but nothing to endanger him. If I help you, you must swear to protect him. If you escape, you must swear to that."

"I'll swear to it, but—can you help us?"

"I don't know. I'll try. I don't think she really wants to kill you, or she'd have blasted you there in the corridor. It isn't her way to hesitate and temporize and think things over. But you are a problem to her."

"That's good news," said Keene. "Say, how many residents are there in this pirate's paradise?"

"A hundred and five, including the children."

"A hundred and—Lord! This must be a pretty well established colony. How old is it?"

"Sixteen years. Her father built it, and it's almost self-supporting. There are gardens off in the side passages." She frowned. "I've lived here since I was four. I'm twenty now."

"And have you never seen the Earth?" Keene saw a chance now to offer more tangible inducement for aid. "Elza, you've missed the most glorious planet in the system—green fields and white snow, great cities and rolling, blue oceans, life, people, gaiety—"

"I went to school there for five years, at Gratia," she interposed coolly. "Don't you suppose we all visit there? Only of late the Peri has refused to let me go. I—I suppose she suspects."

"If we escape," said Keene softly, "you'll be free to live there forever. There will be life and happiness for you, Elza, once this pirate queen is taken and her band destroyed."

"Destroyed?" Her face paled again. "Not Marco. Not my father and my brother Basil. You promise me that. Promise it!"

"I'll promise. All I want is to bring the Red Peri to justice. I don't care about the rest, but"—he rubbed his nose—"I've a little score to settle with her. Just the Red Peri herself."

A knock sounded. "Elza!" came a voice.

"Yes, father. Unlock the door and I'll take the tray." She turned.

"But you'll help?" whispered Keene. "With the Red Peri gone, you and Marco—do you understand, Elza? Will you help—just against her?"

"To my last breath!" she whispered.

Part III

Keene woke with a sense of unaccustomed luxury, and for a moment was at a loss to account for it. Then he realized that it was the sweetness of the air, strange to his nostrils after so many months of an atmosphere that, despite the hard-working rectifiers of the Limbo, was anything but sweet. He wondered casually where the Red Peri secured her colony's supply of oxygen.

The Red Peri! He sat up sharply at the memory of the fantastically lovely pirate princess, for despite the reassurance of the girl Elza, he mistrusted the intentions behind the Peri's mocking green eyes. He rose, fumbled for the light switch, and glanced at his wrist watch. Though night and day were one in the cavern, he perceived that Pluto's ten-hour night was past, and that whatever daylight the black planet enjoyed was trickling over it.

Old Nestor still slept. Keene pulled a hanging aside and found water in a tiny pool; he bathed and pulled on the shirt, shorts, and shoes that were the only clothing he possessed. He ran his hand over his sandy, one-day beard, but his razor was inaccessably remote on the Limbo. Then he turned to see old Solomon's pale-blue eyes blinking at him.

"Morning," he grunted. "Glad to see we weren't murdered in our sleep by our pleasant hostess."

Solomon Nestor nodded. "I haven't slept so well since we left Nivia," he quavered. "Fresh air is a blessing."

"Yes. Wonder where she gets it."

"Mines it, I don't doubt," said Nestor. "There are millions of tons of it frozen out on the surface."

"That's true."

"And," continued the old man, "did you notice anything queer about it?"

"No, except that it smells good and fresh."

"I did. When that yellow-haired girl—Elza—lighted the Peri's cigarettes, did you notice the cast of the flame? Purple, distinctly purple."

"So what?"

"Why, it means neon. Nitrogen is scarce here; Hervey and Caspari both said that, and so they use neon as their filler. No one can breathe pure oxygen, and neon is a good substitute for nitrogen, nearly the same density, and absolutely inert and non-poisonous. That's important to remember. It may help us."

"Help us?'"

The old man waggled his head. "You'll see."

"Say," asked Keene suddenly, "what is the explanation of the cave entrance? We walked right through it—vacuum on one side, air on the other. She said they did it with a field—remember?"

"I remember. She meant an electrostatic field. You know that like charges repel, and the molecules of air, battering against the field, acquire the same charge. They're repelled; they can't cross the field. It's like the electric wind from a static discharge, but here the wind that tries to blow in just balances the wind that tries to go out. Result, no wind either way."

"But we walked through it. Motion through a field produces a current. I didn't feel any."

"Of course not. You didn't walk through at a mile per second like a gas molecule, did you? Whatever current your motion produced was instantly grounded through your body and space suit, which are conductors. Air at normal pressure is a very poor conductor, so it retains its charge. Gases do retain static charges, as witness ball lightning."

"I see," muttered Keene. "Clever. Better than an air lock as far as convenience goes, though heat must radiate away through the field. But if they use atomic heat, they can afford a little waste."

"There'd be less loss there," said Nestor, "than to the rock walls. Heat could radiate, true enough, but it couldn't escape by conduction. A vacuum is the best heat insulator there is; look at our thermos containers on the Limbo. Radiation at temperatures below red heat is a very slow process. And remember that, too."

"I will," grunted Keene, "but right now I'm remembering that we have had no breakfast. Do you suppose her method of execution is slow starvation?" He strode over to the door and pounded vigorously on it. "Hey! Hey, out there!"

There was no response. Irritably, he seized the knob and rattled it, and almost fell backward as the door swung smoothly open. It was unbarred!

"I'll be hanged!" he exploded. He peered into the deserted corridor. "Do you suppose this is Elza's doing—"

"If it is, it's not much help," said old Solomon.

"No. All the same, I'm going to take a look around. Come on; perhaps we can find some space suits."

"You'd need the key to the Red Peri, too, or at least the key to the Limbo, if they've locked it. I think"—old Nestor's brow wrinkled—"I'll sit right here and figure out something I've been thinking of. Even old heads sometimes get ideas."

"Suit yourself," grunted Keene, with very little faith in the potential ideas of the impractical old scientist. He strode boldly into the passageway.

There was no one visible. He turned left and proceeded toward the entrance of the cavern. Ahead of him a figure came suddenly out of an aisle—a feminine figure. He recognized the girl Elza, carrying a bright aluminum spade, and called her name softly.

She turned. "Hello," she said briefly, as he fell into step beside her.

"Been burying some pirate treasure, Elza?"

"No. Just some seeds in the garden."

"Did you unlock our door?" he asked.

"I? Yes. The Peri ordered it unlocked."

"Ordered it! Why?"

"Why not? Can you escape from here?" She gestured at a massive metal door as they passed. "Behind that is her room, and behind another within it are the space suits and the keys to both ships. You're as much a prisoner as ever."

"I know, but isn't she afraid—well, of violence? We could kill her."

"She isn't afraid of anything," said Elza. "Anyway, what good would killing her do? It would be simply committing suicide."

"That's true," said Keene. They were approaching the entrance with its invisible electrostatic seal; now they stood staring out over the dismal, black, airless, Plutonian valley, where a thousand feet away was the dark cylinder of the Limbo. Suddenly a flare of light appeared beside it, flashed a moment, then vanished.

"What's that?" he asked sharply.

"Father's out there welding your jet. She thinks she may have a use for your ship."

"For what?"

"I don't know. It has exactly the lines of a League guard rocket. Perhaps she plans to use it as a decoy."

"And perhaps," said a cool voice behind them, "as a flying mausoleum with you two among the occupants."

They whirled. The Red Peri was approaching with her steps muffled by the soft buskins on her feet; besides her stalked Marco Grandi. Keene did not fail to note Elza's flush as she met the gaze of the dark man, but he felt a surge of anger at himself as he realized that his own face was reddening under the green eyes and mocking smile of the red-haired girl. He spat angrily, "You're a pleasant player when you hold all the cards!"

She said only, "Have you eaten breakfast?"

"No!"

"Well, perhaps that explains your ill temper. Elza, go order a tray for two sent to my room, and one to Professor Nestor. And you, Marco—suppose you leave me."

"Here with him?"

She laughed and tapped an automatic at her belt. "I can take care of myself. Do you doubt it? You can go, Marco."

He muttered, "Yes, commander," and backed reluctantly away. The Red Peri turned her glorious, taunting eyes on Keene, smiled again, and said, "I've checked over your ship. Your story's straight enough."

"Well? What about us, then?'

"Oh, I haven't decided. You may have to die; it's more than likely that you will, but with no malice on my part. Purely as a matter of convenience, you understand."

He grunted. "Why'd you have our door unlocked?"

"Why not? I'm sure you can't escape. Look here." She took the bright aluminum spade Elza had placed against the wall, and thrust it half through the field into the airless outdoors beyond. He stared at it; except for a slight change in color as its crystals rearranged under the slow radiation of its heat, it seemed unaltered. When the knuckles of her dainty hand began to whiten with the cold of the metal, she tossed the implement on the floor at her feet.

Now it changed. Instantly white frost formed on the part that had been exposed; glittering crystals grew an inch thick, fuzzy covering, and began to spread along the handle. They sprang out as swift as the second hand on a watch, an inch—two inches deep.

The Peri laughed. "Would you like to stroll outside?" she gibed. "It's not cold—just ten above zero. Above absolute zero, I mean. Cold enough to liquefy and freeze all gases but hydrogen and helium. How long do you think it would take to freeze that hot blood and hotter head of yours?"

"Bah!" he said. "What's to keep me now from overpowering you, dragging you into some room, and using you as hostage to bargain for our safety?"

"If you could," she retorted coolly. "Even then it would be a poor idea; if you killed me your own death would follow very soon and very painfully; if you didn't, I'd never be bound to any promises you wrung from the others. Your wisest course is to leave things as they are until I decide what to do with you. And incidentally," she added, with a narrowing of her green eyes, "don't pin your faith on Elza."

"On—Elza?" He was startled. "What do you mean?"

"Oh, I know she hates me. She's in love with Marco, or fancies so. I amuse myself by tormenting her, and I suspect that she'd go to some lengths for revenge, but she's quite as helpless as you. As a matter of fact, I'm doing her a good turn, for Marco is not particularly honorable. So I save her and insure his loyalty to me, all with one stroke."

"You—devil!" Keene gasped. "If there's one thing I'd like above all else, it's to drag you to justice. Ever since that day on the Aardkin—"

"When I pinched your nose?" she queried sweetly. "Here, then." With a rapid snap of her hand she twisted the same member with painful violence, laughed into his exasperated face, and turned away. "Come on," she ordered. "Here's breakfast"

"I'll be damned if I'll eat with you!" he snarled.

She shrugged. "As you like. This is all the breakfast you'll get, I promise you."

After all, breakfast was breakfast—he growled and followed her to the massive metal door; as it swung open he forgot a part of his anger in sheer amazement at the luxury of her chamber.

She had, apparently, culled the prize plunder of a score of raids to furnish this room. There were deep, silken rugs on the floor, rich tapestries, paintings from the salon of some luxurious Venusian liner, delicately worked aluminum furniture, even a carved mirror whose utter perfection must have originated in the incomparable lost art of Mars.

The man who bore the breakfast tray placed it silently on a table and withdrew. Here was another surprise. Eggs! And fresh ones, too, judging by the smell.

"Oh, we have a few chickens," said the Red Peri, reading his glance. "Enough to supply me, at least. Feeding them is rather a problem, you see."

Keene remembered his anger in time to reply with an irritable "humph!" For a moment he wondered why the exquisite presence of the Peri should affect him so violently, for he realized that much of his irritation was directed at himself. But of one thing he was certain, and that was that his most ardent desire was to humble the arrogant, self-sufficient, proud, and mocking pirate princess, to see her pay the assigned penalty for her crimes.

Then he frowned. Was he anxious to sec her punished? What he really wanted was simply to sec her arrogance and insolence humbled, to see her—well, frightened, or pleading with him, as a sort of recompense for the contemptuous way in which she treated him.

She spoke. "You're a silent table partner," she observed, and yet I'm rather glad you two blundered in. I was getting frightfully tired and bored; I was considering paying a little visit to civilization."

"I suppose you realize," he growled, "that if we ever get back to Earth, your little visits are over. I'd be very glad to furnish a full description of the Red Peri."

"And do you think I'm the only red-head alive?"

"You're probably the most beautiful, and you know it."

She laughed contemptuously. "Keene, if you think you can play the sophisticated giver of compliments to my innocence, think again. I've been around. I've spend enough time in London, Paris and New York to know the social game. In fact, I have a carefully built-up identity there; my terrestrial friends think I live on Venus. So don't try what they call a fish net on me."

Her words gave him an idea. "Fish net?" he echoed with a deliberate air of sadness. "No. It's just that I have the misfortune to be about half in love with you, while the other half is pure hatred." Suddenly he wondered how much of a lie that really was.

She laughed again. "I half believe you."

"Which half?"

"Never mind. But," she added derisively, "whichever half it is, remember that it takes a better man than you to win the Red Peri's love."

"I didn't say I wanted it!" he snapped. "All you are to me is a vicious law breaker, and all I want is the chance to see you taken."

"Which you'll never have," she returned coolly. She leaned back in her chair and slipped a cigarette from a box. "Smoke?" she asked.

It was in the nature of a peace offering. He accepted both the truce and the cigarette, and puffed with thorough enjoyment.

"Keene," said the Peri, "would you like to see our establishment?"

He nodded. If the girl were proffering friendship, or at least tolerance, he was in no position to refuse it while she held the upper hand. But he would not accept it under false colors.

"Listen," he said, "there are lots of things I like about you. You've plenty of courage, and you've the devil's own beauty. But get this. If I see any chance of escape or any chance to capture you, I'm taking it. Is that plain?"

She nodded. "Keene, if you ever outwit the Red Peri, you're welcome to your winnings. But you never will."

She rose, and he followed her into the stone-walled corridor, glancing briefly at the mysterious archway with its invisible electrostatic seal.

"If your power ever failed," he said, "what would happen to your air here?"

"It won't fail. It's generated directly from disintegration. No moving parts at all. But if it should"—she gestured to the cavern roof—"there's an emergency air door. It will close instantly if there's any appreciable outward current. There's plenty of power to retain our atmosphere; we only keep a pressure of eleven to twelve pounds."

"About the same as the altitude of Denver," he muttered as he followed her. "Prepared for anything, aren't you?"

Ile was really impressed by the neat little gardens in the side aisles, raised on Plutonian soil carefully selected for the proper elements. "But nitrogen is a troublesome job," she explained. "There's little of it to be had, and what there is is all mixed with frozen argon. We fractionate it, and then form ammonia, and so finally get it into usable form."

"I know the process," he said.

They penetrated deeper into the series of caverns that pierced the black Plutonian mountain. The fluorolux lights were fewer now, and there were long stretches of dim side passages with no lights at all.

"They're sealed off," said the Peri. "We're approaching the seal of the main cavern now. Do you see where it narrows ahead there? That's an electrostatic seal, but the side passages are blocked with concrete to keep out the crystal crawlers."

"The crystal crawlers!" echoed Keene. He had almost forgotten those curious creatures of the Plutonian valley. "Why don't they come through the electrostatic seal?"

"They do, but they seldom get far. You'll see why."

"What are the things?" he asked. "Are they alive? No one — Atsuki or Hervey or Caspari—ever reported them."

"I think they originated in these caverns. This whole region is honey-combed, and those in the valley are just strays. Explorers wouldn't be apt to encounter them."

"But are they alive?" he persisted.

"No-o-o," said the Red Peri slowly. "Not exactly alive. They're—well—on the borderline. They're chemical-crystalline growths, and their movement is purely mechanical. There are half a dozen varieties—aluminum feeders and iron and silicon and sulphur feeders, and others." She smiled impishly. "I have a use for at least one sort. Do you remember, or did you notice, the safe of the Aardkin? An iron feeder comes in very handy at times."

He grunted; somehow it pained him to hear the girl refer to her piratical activities. Before he could make any other reply they came suddenly into a large natural cavern beyond which showed the narrow opening which the Peri had indicated as the place of the electrostatic seal. A single light shed a dim radiance from far above, and in the faint luminosity he perceived a narrow, deep gash, a gorge or pit, that crossed the chamber from wall to wall and even split the walls in dark tunnels to right and left.

"Here is our crawler trap," said the girl. She indicated a curious span across the chasm, a single heavy girder of metal that bridged the twenty-foot gap in four sharp zigzags. A precariously narrow bridge; the girder was no more than twelve inches in width.

"Copper!" he said.

"Yes. Apparently there are no such things as copper feeders to destroy our bridge. Do you see how the trap works? The crystal crawlers have no eyes nor sense of touch; they just crawl. The chances are infinitely against any of them moving at the proper angles to cross the gap. They go crashing down and crawl away below; although one blundered across once.

"Most of them aren't dangerous except to whatever they feed on." She gestured. "Beyond the seal is our air supply. There's a regular frozen subterranean sea of neon, argon, and oxygen, and we can draw on it almost forever. Don't you want to cross over and look at it?"

Keene stepped to the brink of the chasm and peered down. It was deep; the light from above trickled away into a mysterious darkness where only a few faint sparkles responded—crystals, doubtless, for a slow flicker of movement showed. He scowled at the precarious slenderness of the copper zigzag, and then, cautiously, he abandoned dignity, dropped to his knees, and crept slowly across on all fours.

It was only when he reached the far side and stood erect that he became conscious of the Peri's contemptuous sniff of laughter, and turned to see her walk casually and steadily across the angling span, balancing as easily as if she trod a wide roadway. He flushed a slow red; the girl had nerves of steel, true enough, but he realized she had done this as a deliberate taunt.

She strode to the narrow opening, where he now perceived the ring of copper points whence issued the electrostatic field, and above, on the roof, a suspended emergency lock like that at the outer arch.

"There," she said, pointing. "You can see it."

He squinted into the darkness. A dozen feet away, the passage seemed to widen again, but into such a vast hollow that tire light from behind him failed utterly to show its bounds. But dimly and faintly as a sea of ectoplasm, he made out a shimmering, illimitable expanse of white, a vast subterranean drift of Pluto's fossil air.

"There goes the pipe to it," said the Peri. "We can get all we need by the simple process of heat, but now and then we have to lengthen the pipe. That's why this end of our colony is sealed by electrostatic. Oh! O-o-oh!"

She broke off in a startled scream. Keene whirled; the cave floor between the two of them and the bridge was covered with a rustling, irregular parade of blackish crystals!

"What's the matter!" he gasped. "We can kick them aside." He moved as if to do so.

"No!" cried the Peri. She seized his arm, dragging him back. "They're carbon feeders! Don't you understand? They're carbon feeders! Your body has carbon. They're—Look out!"

Part IV

Keene started back, realizing that a gray-black, flat-crystalled, dully shining lump was almost at his feet. He stared at the crawling masses; they had come, apparently, from beyond a jutting wall of rock to his right. The floor was speckled everywhere with them, and now and again one slipped with a faint tinkle over the edge of the central pit. But there were hundreds more; one couldn't wait here until the floor had cleared. He skipped aside; another had silently approached almost to his feet.

He acted. Suddenly he seized the Peri, raised her bodily in his arms, and dashed in an angling, irregular course for the bridge. The girl squirmed and said, "Put me—" Then she lay very still as he picked his way as delicately as a dancer, sidestepping, skip-ping, twisting, to the copper span—and over it. Half running, he took the four sharp angles, and at last, breathless, he set the Peri on the rock on the far side.

She looked coolly up at him. "Well!" she said calmly. "Why did you do that?"

"That's pretty thanks for it!" he snapped.

"Don't you think I could have done as well?" she retorted. "I asked you why you did it."

"Because—" He paused. Why had he done it? He suddenly realized that he had no desire to see the exquisite Peri die. To see her humbled, yes. Even to see her punished—but not to see her die. "It was pure impulse," he finished grimly. "If I had thought a second or two, I'd have left you to die."

"Liar!" she said, but smiled. "Well, I thank you for your intentions, though I could have done quite as well alone. But you're very strong, and—Frank!" Her voice rose. "Your foot! Your shoe! Quickly!"

He blinked down. Scarcely visible on the leather, a grayish-black coating of crystals was spreading, and almost immediately came a prickling pain in his toe. With a growling oath he kicked violently. The skin buskin went sailing in an arc over the pit, to fall squarely among the crawlers. Instantly it was a fuzzy mass of needlelike crystals.

The Peri was on her knees. "Your toe!" she wailed. Swift as a serpent she planted her own dainty foot firmly upon the arch of his. From somewhere she snatched a tiny, jeweled penknife, its blade flashing sharp as a razor. Still resting her full weight on his foot, she cut.

Despite his bellow of pain and surprise, she sliced away half his toenail and a goodly strip of skin beneath, kicked the bloody strip into the pit, examined her own pink toes for a moment, and faced Keene. For the first time in their acquaintance she seemed shaken; her wild, green eyes were wide with concern.

But it passed instantly. "Fool!" she snapped. "Fool!"

He was staring aghast at his bleeding toe. "Good Lord!" he muttered. "That was a narrow escape. Well—I'm not so sparing in my thanks as you. I say thanks for it."

"Bah! Do you think I want carbon feeders on this side of the pit? That's why I did it!"

"You could have pushed me into the pit, then," he retorted.

"And I wish I had!" she snapped. She turned abruptly, and padded, barefooted, up the cavern toward the colony.

Keene shifted his remaining buskin to his injured foot and limped after. He was in a turmoil of emotions. There was something splendid about this pirate princess, something more than the simple fact of her exquisite and fantastic beauty. He swore angrily to himself for even admitting it, but limped hastily until he caught her.

"What's your name?" he asked abruptly.

"If you need a name to address me," she said coldly, "let it be commander."

"The only person I'll call commander is one I'm willing to serve, and that'll never be the Red Peri."

She glanced sidewise at him. "What's a name, anyway?" she asked in altered tones. "See here. You're Frank Keene, but you're neither keen enough to outwit me nor frank enough to admit you love me."

"Love you!" he snorted. "Love you! Why—" He broke off suddenly. "Even if it were true," he went on, "do you think I'd have anything to do with a pirate, a murderess? However I felt, I'd still exert every effort to bring you to justice. How many deaths have you caused? How much suffering?"

"I don't know," she said. "But murder? I never killed anybody except in sheer self-defense."

"So you say. What about the atrocities on the Hermes?"

She looked up at him. "Frank," she said softly, "I had nothing to do with the Hermes. Don't you realize that people blame everything on the Red Peri? Every captain who suffers from some sneaking little freebooter blames me for it. Why, I'd need a hundred ships to commit all the crimes they've pinned on me."

"But you're a pirate, nevertheless."

"Yes, but I have my reasons. I have, Frank. And—Oh, why should I justify myself to you, anyway? I don't care what you think of me."

"All the same," he growled, "I'll tell you what I think. I think your parents should have given you a series of good spankings. You're nothing but a spoiled, reckless, dangerous child."

"My parents," she echoed.

"Yes. Do you think they'd be proud of you now?"

"I hope," she said slowly, "that one of them would be." She paused at the door of her chamber, unlocking it. "Come in here," she ordered sharply.

He followed her into the lavish interior. She disappeared into an adjacent room, returning in a moment with a bottle and a strip of gauze. "Here," she said. "Dress your toe."

"It's nothing. It needs no dressing."

"Dress it!" she snapped. "I want no cases of infection here."

"I might"—he observed as he took the bottle—"die of the infection and thus save you a murder."

Her green eyes seemed to soften. "Remember this, Frank," she said in a low voice. "I could have let you die back there at the edge of the pit. I could have, but I didn't."

He had no answer. For a moment he gazed thoughtfully at the exquisite delicacy of her face, and then, irrelevantly, he asked again, "What is your name?"

She smiled. "Peri," she said.

"Really? Peri what? That's a strange name."

"Yes. It's the Persian word for imp or elf."

"I know. I've worked in Iraq. But it means more than just that; it's the name given to the child of a disobedient angel, waiting to be admitted into paradise."

Her features grew suddenly wistful. "Yes," she murmured. "Waiting to be admitted into paradise."

"But Peri what?" he repeated.

She hesitated. "If I told you," she said slowly, "you might understand. I think I will tell you, Frank. Did you ever hear of Perry Maclane?"

He frowned. "Perry Maclane," he muttered. "I—think so. Wait a minute. Do you mean Red Perry Maclane, the inventor who had the famous legal battle with Interplanetary? But that was years ago, years and years. I was a child of seven or eight; you must scarcely have been born."

"I was just born. Perry Maclane was my father."

"Red Perry your father? And—the ship! I see—Red Peri, named after him."

"Named by him, after me. He built it. He built it purposely to be a pirate craft. and you can't blame him!"

"Can't blame him! Why not?"

"Listen to me, Frank." Her glorious eyes were intense and serious. "Perry Maclane was robbed by Interplanetary and their associates. Do you know how dangerous space travel used to be, twenty-five or thirty years ago? Even fifty years after the first colonies were founded on Venus, it was a gamble with death to travel there.

"Trade was all but impossible; because the rocket blasts kept failing, and ships kept crashing in trying to land, or even plunged into the Sun. And then the thermoid expansion chamber was developed; the blasts became steady, safe, usable. Trade was possible, and Interplanetary became an enormous, wealthy corporation. But do you know who invented the expansion chamber? Do you?"

"Why—"

"Perry Maclane did! He invented it and patented it. But Interplanetary wouldn't let a little thing like honor stand in their way. They copied the patent; they claimed one of their engineers had developed the chamber first; they fought the case through every court, and at last they fought Perry Maclane out of money, and won. It took four years to do it: and in the last year I was born and my mother died; and Perry Maclane was ruined.

"But he didn't give up. He worked at anything he could find—he, the greatest rocket engineer in the world! He dug sewers and planned drainage systems; he did any sort of work, but mean-while, all the time, he was carrying the idea of revenge.

"Evenings he worked on the plans of such a ship as no one had dreamed of, a rocket with inherent stability, one that could flash through gravitational fields as easily as through interplanetary space, instead of teetering down on its jets, wabbling and compensating and inching lower. And when he had it—I was three then—he found those who supplied money to build it.

"He wasn't the only man Interplanetary had ruined; others hated the corporation, too. So he built the Red Peri, and began raiding corporation ships. He had no trouble manning his ship; he could have had a thousand men; but he picked and chose among the best for his crew.

"At first he worked out of the Australian desert as a base, but that became dangerous. He thought of the Moon, and of an asteroid; but at last, because he had a ship to which planetary distances meant nothing, he came here to build his colony. Save for the years I spent at school, I've lived here ever since."

"But what of Red Perry Maclane?" asked Keene.

"He was killed three years ago. Do you remember when Interplanetary's Captain Thorsen of the Lucrece shot one of the pirates? That was my father; he died and was buried as he wanted to be—in space. It was I who killed Thorsen, with my own hand as he shot at me."

He stared at her. Those were certainly tears in the glorious, emerald eyes. "Peri," he said softly, "but what will be the end of it? Are you going on all your life pursuing revenge for your father? You're not really hurting Interplanetary, you know; they carry insurance. But you are slowing down the development of the planets. It's come to a point where people are actually afraid to travel."

"Good!" she flashed. "Then it's less trade and fewer fares to swell the coffers of Interplanetary."

"But—good heavens, Peri! With a design like that of your ship you could make millions legitimately!"

"Oh, of course!" she retorted sarcastically. "Just as my father did from the thermoid expansion chamber."

There was no answer to that. He shook his head sadly. "Then do you intend to live out your life as a pirate until you're finally captured, or until you die out here on this miserable black planet?"

"I do not. I intend to carry out the plans of Red Perry Maclane. He wasn't fighting out of blind passion, you know. He built up his organization, here and on Earth, for a single purpose. Little by little, the plunder we take from Interplanetary goes back to Earth, to be turned into cash and securities, in banks in New York, London, Berlin, Paris, Tokyo. When I have enough—and a hundred million dollars will be enough—do you know what I'll do?"

"I don't, Peri." His eyes were glued to her tense, lovely face.

"Then listen!" she said fiercely. "I'll open a line competing with Interplanetary. I'll build ships like the Red Peri, and I'll drive their corporation to ruin! I'll have them groveling and begging, but this time I'll have money enough so they can't fight with crooked lawyers and bribed judges. I'll annihilate them!"

For a long time he stared at her strange loveliness, her wild, green eyes and flaming hair. "Oh, Peri!" he said at last, in tones of sadness. "Don't you see how insane such a plan is? Don't you know that once you produce the design of this ship, you'll be known as the pirate? No one else knows of it."

"I don't care!" she blazed. "The law can't touch anyone with a hundred million dollars. My father learned that from Interplanetary." And at his continued silence, she snapped,

"Your advice would be to take it lying down, I suppose. I prefer to fight."

"But you don't have to declare war on the whole Earth on account of an injury done your father."

"War on the Earth? I haven't. But"—her green eyes glowed fiercely—"if I ever should, I could give them such a war as they never dreamed of!"

"What do you mean, Peri?"

"I'll tell you! Suppose I were to take one of those carbon feeders, like the ones that nipped your toe. Suppose I took just one tiny Crystal and dropped it in the jungles of Africa or in Middle Europe or in the wheat belt of America. All life has carbon in it. What would happen to the pretty, green Earth, Frank? What would happen to the crooked lawyers and the bribed judges, and all the rest, honest and dishonest, right up to the heads of Interplanetary itself?"

"My Lord!" he said.

"Can't you see the crystal crawlers rustling their way along?" she cried. "Wheat fields, houses, horses, humans!"

"Listen!" he said huskily. "Do you know what I ought to do? I know what my duty is. It's to kill you, right now and here, while I've got you alone. Otherwise that mad and reckless spirit of yours may some day drive you to do just that. I ought to strangle you now, but—by heavens—I can't!"

All the passion drained suddenly from her face, leaving it alluringly wistful. "I'm glad you said those last two words, Frank," she murmured. "Look." She raised her arms; he saw her hand resting firmly on the butt of her revolver. "Would it please you," she asked softly, "if I promised you never to think again of that particular revenge?"

"You know it would!"

"Then I promise. And now, tell me if you still blame me for being—the Red Peri. Do you?"

"I don't know. I think—perhaps—you are justified for feeling as you do, but, Peri, it's madness."

"What would you want me to do?"

"Why—the sane course, the honorable course, would be to make restitution, to return everything you've stolen; and then to give yourself up, to expiate the wrongs you've done, and so be free to live without the need of burying yourself out here at the edge of nothingness. I don't say you could do all of that, but at least you could return what you've taken and live as you were meant to live—honorably and happily."

"Honorably and happily!" she echoed bitterly. "Yes, except for the realization that I had failed my father."

"Your father was wrong, Peri."

She blazed in sudden anger. "Oh, you're too smug and self-righteous to live. I was going to offer you your freedom; I thought you'd understand and protect me, but now do you think I dare trust you to return to Earth? Now you'll stay as my prisoner!"

"Some day," he said evenly, "I'll drag you back to justice, Peri, and after you're free you'll thank me for it."

"Get out!" she cried. "You're stupid! I hate stupidity!"

He looked quietly at her angry, exquisite face, rose, and stalked out of the door. For a moment he stood irresolute in the corridor; then he strode toward the room he shared with Solomon Nestor, ignoring the glances of a number of residents as he went. And as he opened the door, the first person he saw was the girl Elza, in close conversation with the old man.

They looked up as he entered, and the flaxen-haired girl drew away, staring at him with a curious expression in her blue eyes.

"Oh, bosh!" said the old man. "Elza, you're simply letting your imagination make you nervous. Listen, Frank—this girl came running here to tell me that you've been spending hours in the Red Peri's company, and that you were probably falling under her magic charms; and now Elza's afraid you're going to betray her to the Peri. Ridiculous, isn't it?"

"Utterly!" snapped Keene, wondering how much of it was ridiculous. He felt himself reddening, and repeated hastily, "Utterly ridiculous!"

"You see?" said old Nestor triumphantly. "All right, Elza, let's get on with this. You say you're sure you can't smuggle space suits to us?"

"I'm sure I can't. They're kept locked up by the Red Peri, and I can't get to them."

"But your father and brother wear them when they go to either ship, don't they?"

"Yes, but I wouldn't dare ask them. They'd tell the Peri. I know that."

"Well," said old Solomon thoughtfully, "if we can't get space suits, we'll have to do without. But you can get the key to one of the ships, can't you?"

"Not to the Red Peri," said Elza. "To your ship, perhaps, because my father has that while he's working on it. I could steal it away from him, I think. He just keeps it in a desk."

"What good would the Limbo do us?" grunted Keene. "They could run us down with the other. They could blast us to bits."

"They could, but they won't," retorted the old man. "You leave this to old Solomon. Now Elza when will your father have the jet repaired?"

"I think he's finishing it now.

"And could you smuggle the key to us to-night?"

"I think so. I'll try. To-night or tomorrow."

"Good!" said Solomon Nestor. "You run along now, Elza. You'll have your revenge on the Red Peri—if you're a good girl." The yellow-haired girl vanished. Old Nestor turned quizzical eyes on Keene and said mockingly, "Ridiculous, eh! Utterly ridiculous!"

"What?"

"That you should be impressed by the Red Peri. How could so unattractive a being effect the redoubtable Frank Keene? Very ridiculous!"

"Oh, shut up!" growled Keene. "I admit she's beautiful, and I admit that what she told me has changed my opinion of her. All the same, I think she's arrogant and overhearing. I'm just as anxious as ever to see her take a fall, and if I can trip her, that's fine. But I don't see how the key to the Limbo helps."

"You will. Tell me what the Peri said to you."

Keene recounted the story of "Red" Perry Maclane. Despite himself, he told it with a tinge of sympathy, and when, after concluding it, he described the events at the copper bridge, he was uncomfortable aware of old Nestor's steady gaze. He finished his tale and stared defiantly back.

"Well!" said the old man. "I suppose you realize that she risked her life for you—or at least the chance of having to cut off a finger or two. What if she'd touched the carbon feeders on your toe?"

"I—I hadn't thought of it."

"And now that you do think of it, are you still so bitterly determined to humble her?"

Keene considered. "Yes!" he snapped. "I am. I don't want to hurt her, but I do want to get back at her for the way she's insulted, browbeaten, and mocked me. I want to see her take a fall."

"Even though it means capture for her?"

Keene groaned. "Listen, Solomon. Right now I'm so puzzled that I'm not sure. But I do know that I want to see the Red Peri paid back for the way she's acted toward me."

"All right. I think you're in love with her, Frank, though it's none of my business."

"Damn' right it isn't!"

"But," proceeded Nestor, "just how badly do you want to do this?"

"With all my heart!"

"Would you risk your life and hers to do it?"

"My life," said Keene grimly, "but not hers."

"Good enough. Now the first thing to do is talk you out of a few superstitions."

"I haven't any."

"You have, but you don't know it. Listen, now." The old man bent closer and began to talk in a low, earnest voice. At his first words Keene paled and started; then he sat very still and very intent. After five minutes of listening, he drew a deep breath, expanding his mighty chest to the full.

"I used to plunge at the university," he said exultantly. "I could hold my breath for four minutes. I can still do three and a half!"

"That's plenty," said Nestor.

"Yes, if it works. If it works!"

"If I were you," said the old man, "I'd find out—now!"

For a full minute Keene stared at him. Suddenly he nodded, turned swiftly away, and darted out into the corridor. In five minutes he was back again, but sadly changed, for his lips were swollen, his eyes red, and his breath a rasping gurgle. But he was smiling.

"It works!" he gasped triumphantly. "It's unadulterated hell —but it works!"

Part V

Elza did not appear that night, although Keene tossed and twisted wakefully for miserable hours. In the darkness the thing he had to do appeared grotesque, fantastic, impossible; and this despite the fact that he had already tested the truth of old Solomon Nestor's reasoning. His toe ached and his lips and eyes burned, but more painful than all else was the idea of inflicting harm on the courageous and proud Red Peri.

When, well toward the end of the ten-hour Plutonian night, he finally fell into troubled slumber, it was but for a brief while, and he rose sullen and morose to pace the floor of the chamber.

The fluorolux light awakened old Nestor. For a few moments he watched the pacing Keene, and then asked, "Did Elza come?"

"No, and I hope she doesn't," snarled Keene. "I hope she couldn't get the key—and if she does get it, I'm not going through with this!"

"It's your business," said Nestor indifferently. "It doesn't mean anything to me, because I'd never live through it, not at my age. I have to stay here anyway, and I don't mind, because Elza said they'd moved my instruments into the cave; and I can work here almost as well as farther out in space. But if you love the girl so intently, why don't you act like a human being and tell her so?"

"Love her!" yelled Keene. "Just because I feel like a dirty dog at the thought of this, doesn't mean I love her! She's a girl, isn't she?"

"And a very beautiful one."

"Bah! She's a girl, and I hate to fight women!"

"Well, don't then," suggested old Solomon.

"Yet I want like the very devil to get back at her."

"Then do."

"And yet, in a way I can't blame her."

"Then don't."

Keene resuming his pacing. In another minute he stopped, faced the old man, and said defiantly, "Solomon, I can't do it. I know she's a pirate and a menace to trade and civilization, but I can't do it."

Before the other could reply, a knock sounded on the door. Keene whirled. "I hope," he muttered, "that it's breakfast—just breakfast."

It was. Elza brought it in silently, placed it on the table, and retired; and Keene felt a vast surge of relief. She hadn't managed to get the key! He was almost ready to sing until he picked up his cup of coffee and there it was—the familiar key to the outer door of the Limbo's air lock.

He met old Nestor's amused, blue eyes with a cold glare, and it was hardly softened by the other's murmur: "After all, Frank, you don't have to use it."

"I know I don't!" he snarled. "I have a fine choice, haven't I? I can stay here the rest of my life, if our hostess doesn't take a notion to kill me, or I can escape by following your scatterbrained plan of doing a thing I hate. I can't escape alone, for they'd simply run me down with their pirate ship."

"Or you could turn pirate," suggested Solomon Nestor.

"Gr-r-r!" said Keene amiably.

He was unaccustomed to this sort of agonized indecision. He had never encountered a situation that pulled so many ways at once; for in all his experience right had been right and wrong had been wrong—yet now he was not at all sure but that the laws of relativity operated in the moral field as well as in the physical. Certainly the Red Peri was not entirely in the wrong, yet equally certainly she was a pirate, a menace to progress, an antisocial being, and therefore a criminal. If she would only give up this mad purpose of hers; if she would make restitution; if she— He swore bitterly and strode out of the door, scarcely realizing that the Limbo's key was in his pocket.

He turned at random toward the outer arch of the cave. Figures in space suits were passing in and out through the electrostatic seal, and he noticed that the outgoing men were laden with cases, boxes, cans, and bundles. He stood at the very edge of the seal and stared out into the dim, nightlike morning of the black planet. Beside him a row of metal-clad figures clanked outward, their footsteps dropping to sudden silence the instant they trod into the airless outdoors. He watched them carry their burdens to the Red Peri, where an air lock swung open to admit them. They were loading the ship.

Keene stared disinterestedly, without comprehension. Then, abruptly, the meaning dawned on him. He stiffened, peered closely through narrowed eyes, and spun to accost a metal-sheathed figure that approached, Marco Grandi, for he could see the dark, aquiline features behind the visor.

"What's this?" Keene snapped. "You're cargoing the Peri. For what?"

Grandi made no answer, and Keene planted himself squarely in the other's way. "For what?" he blazed.

The metallic voice of the diaphragm clicked. "Stand aside. We're busy."

"I'll keep you busy!" he roared. "I'll—I'll—"

"You'll what?" queried the cool tones of the Peri.

Keene whirled. The girl stood at his side, clad in an all-enveloping, clinging robe of bright green that echoed the infinitely more brilliant emerald of her eyes.

"They're stocking the Red Peri!" he shouted.

"I know it."

"Why? For what purpose?"

"For purposes of business."

"Business! You mean for purposes of piracy!"

"Piracy," she said coldly, "is my business."

"It was your business, you mean!" With a great effort he controlled himself and faced the mocking green eyes. "Peri," he said more calmly, "I want to talk to you."

"It isn't mutual."

"I want to talk to you," he repeated stubbornly, "alone." He glanced at the hostile eyes of Marco Grandi.

The Peri shrugged. "Go on out, Marco," she ordered, and then to Keene, "Well? What is it?"

"Listen," he said. "I want you to quit this business. I want you to be fair to yourself. You're capable of infinitely greater things than piracy."

"I know it. When I'm ready, I'll achieve those greater things."

"Oh, revenge!" he snapped. "Suppose you succeed. Do you think you'll be any happier?"

"And if I'm not," she countered, "what is it to you?"

He drew a deep breath. "It's a lot to me," he said soberly, "because you see, Peri, I happen to love you."

Her green eyes did not change. "What you call love," she said contemptuously, "isn't my conception. If you loved me you'd take me exactly as I am."

"I was brought up to believe in honesty, Peri."

"And I," she retorted, "was brought up to believe in honor. Red Perry Maclane's honor needs avenging, and there's none but his daughter to see to it."

Keene pounded his fist impatiently against the wall. "Peri," he said at last, "do you love me?"

She made no immediate reply. From somewhere in her heavy silken gown she produced a cigarette, lighted it, and blew a gray plume of smoke toward the seal. "No," she said.

"Why did you risk your life for me back there at the pit? What if you had touched the carbon feeders?"

She glanced out into the cold, black valley. "I may have thought I loved you then," she murmured, eyes still averted. "That was before I knew how little you could understand my feelings. We're just—not the same sort."

"I think we are," said Keene. "We've simply learned different moral codes, but—Peri—my code's the right one. Even you can see that."

"It's not for me. What my father wanted is the thing I want and the thing I'm going to do."

He groaned and abandoned that line of attack. "What do you expect to do with Solomon Nestor and me?"

She made a helpless little gesture. "What can I do? I have to leave you here." She turned her green eyes back to him. "Frank, if you'd promise to keep this place and my identity a secret, I think I'd be willing to release you."

"I can't promise that."

Her voice hardened. "Then here you stay."

"So you've given up the idea of killing us?"

"Oh," she said indifferently, "I'm always indulgent to those who claim to be in love with me."

Her attitude angered him. "You're pretty confident, aren't you? If you leave us here while you're off pirating, you know damn well we'll be doing our best to overcome you."

"And I know damn well that you'll never outwit me," she retorted.

Keene's hand suddenly encountered the Limbo's key in his pocket. "I won't, eh?" he muttered. "See here, Peri. Are you determined once and for all to stick to this scheme of yours?"

"Once and for all, I am."

"And it makes no difference that I tell you I love you?" She turned abruptly and faced the grim outdoors, staring over the dead, cold, black Plutonian landscape. "It makes no difference, Frank."

"And nothing I can say will make a difference?"

She gestured impatiently, still staring far away. "Oh, what's the use of arguing? No, Frank."

He looked silently at her, seeing her, seeing her glorious hair flaming against the cold background of black mountains. He peered thoughtfully down the deserted corridor, and then at the Red Peri. The valley was lifeless; the men were within the vessel and the air lock was closed. Dim across the plain was the dull bulk of the Limbo, whose key was clutched in his hand.

"Well," he muttered sadly, "you've asked for it, Peri."

She did not turn. "For what, Frank?"

"For this!" he cried, and with a sudden lunge he sent her and himself staggering, unarmored, into the airless Plutonian plain, and into a temperature of ten degrees above absolute zero!

Part VI

Instantly he was in hell. The breath rushed out of his lungs in a faint expansion mist that dissipated at once, the blood pounded in his aching ear drums, his eyes seemed to bulge, and a thin stream of blood squirted darkly from his nose. His whole body felt terribly, painfully bloated as he passed from a pressure of twelve pounds per square inch to one of nearly zero. He fought his agony grimly; he had to hold consciousness as long as he could. But old Nestor had been right; he was living.

He had a momentary impression of the Peri's green gown billowing up from her glorious body like a balloon, to settle back instantly as the bound air escaped. Then she whirled, eyes wide, mouth open and straining for air that simply was not there, hands clutching frantically at her gasping throat. She was in full command of her own agile mind, and she sprang convulsively for the archway and the seal. Grimly he thrust her back.

She was trying to scream. Her breast rose and fell in futile, soundless, panting gasps; moisture formed on her forehead and vanished instantly. Swift as a deer she darted again for the archway; and again he controlled his agony to smash her back.

For once in her life the Peri knew sheer panic. No longer had she the coordination of mind and muscle that might yet have encompassed escape. Fierce pain and utter fright had robbed her of it; and for a few seconds she could only thrust aimlessly against Keene's braced body, her hands fluttering frantically, her legs pushing convulsively, her lovely, pain-racked, wild, green eyes but inches from his own.

He had a double task now; he had to hold her back from the entrance and at the same time keep any part of her twisting body save her shod feet from contact with the searing cold of the rocky ground. He clutched her violently against him. Suddenly her struggles grew weaker, her hands went vainly to her tortured throat, her hands closed, and she collapsed.

They were almost at the air lock of the Red Peri. He saw it fly open, he glimpsed Marco Grandi's appalled face behind his visor, but he had no fraction of a second to lose. He swung the Peri across his shoulder and set off on a staggering run for the Limbo, more than nine hundred feet away across a vacuum and a cold only less than those of space itself. Grandi could never catch him; no one could run in a space suit.

The Pen was not light; on Earth she might have weighed a hundred and fifteen pounds, but here it was more like a hundred and forty. His own weight was greater too, but he felt none of that; the excruciating torment that racked his body erased all lesser tortures.

He crashed unseeing through a parade of aluminum feeders, and blood spurted wildly from a tiny scratch on his ankle, and then—then he was fumbling at the Limbo's lock.

The door flew open from its inner pressure; he bundled himself and the Peri within, pulled it to, and collapsed as the hissing of the automatic valve sent a heavenly stream of air against his face. He had crossed a thousand feet of vacuum and still lived!

The air pressure reached normal. He fought to his knees, opened the inner door, and dragged the girl through it. She lay with her magnificent hair streaming on the steel floor; blood trickled from her nose—but she breathed.

Keene had work to do. He thrust wide the feed to the under-jets, and the ship roared, rising shakily as he peered through the floor port at Marco Grandi plodding desperately across the plain. He let the Limbo rise aimlessly; later he could set a course.

He dragged the limp Peri to a chair. About her slim waist he twisted the iron chain from the aft ventilator, and locked it with the padlock of Nestor's empty bolometer case. The other end he locked carefully to a hand hold on the wall, and only then, laboring and gasping, did he turn his attention to the medicine kit.

He poured a half tumbler of whiskey and forced a good portion of it between the Peri's lips. Still pain-tortured, it was yet agony to him to see the lines of anguish on her unconscious face, and to hear the choking of her breath. She coughed weakly from the liquor, and moved convulsively as he sprang back to the controls and set the Limbo nosing Sunward. That was close enough for the present; later he could lay a course for Titan.

The Peri stirred. Her uncomprehending green eyes looked vaguely toward him, and then about the chamber. She spoke, "Frank! Frank! Where am I?"

"On the Limbo."

"On the—" She glanced down; her hand had encountered the chain about her waist. "Oh!" she murmured, and stared at it a full half minute. When she looked up again her eyes were quite clear and conscious. "You—you've got me, Frank, haven't you?"

"Right where I want you," he said grimly. Strangely, there was no satisfaction in it. He had wanted to see her humbled, but now it was pure pain.

"Why—aren't we dead, Frank?" she asked slowly. "We were—in the airless valley, weren't we? How is it that we still live?"

"I'll tell you, Peri. It was old Solomon's idea. Everybody's been believing a lot of superstitions about space, but he figured out the truth. It isn't the vacuum that's dangerous, and it isn't the cold; it's the lack of air. We couldn't freeze, because a vacuum is the best insulator there is; we aren't like that aluminum spade of yours, because our bodies actually produced heat faster than we radiate it away. In fact, it really felt warm to me—as far as I could be conscious of any feeling in that hell.

"And as for all the gruesome stories of lungs collapsing and all that, every high school physics student sees the experiment of the mouse under the bell jar. An air pump exhausts the jar to the highest vacuum it can attain, the mouse loses consciousness—just as you did, Peri—but when the air returns, it recovers.

"Its lungs don't collapse because there's no outer pressure to crush them, and its body doesn't burst because the tissues are strong enough to maintain that much internal pressure. And if a mouse can stand it, why not a human being? And I knew I could stand lack of air longer than you."

"It seems you could," she admitted ruefully. "But still, Frank, that terrible drop in pressure! I see that we didn't explode from it, though it felt as though we should; but I still don't see why."

"I tell you because our tissues are too tough. Look here, Peri. The pressure at sea level on Earth is 14.7 pounds per square inch. The pressure on top of Mount Everest is four pounds per square inch. That's about six miles above sea level.

"A hundred and fifty years ago, way back in 1930, open airplanes flew over Mount Everest. The pilots didn't suffer much from lack of pressure; just as long as they had oxygen to breathe, they could live. Yet from sea level to 29,000 feet altitude is a drop of eleven pounds per square inch—almost exactly the drop from the pressure in your cave to the pressure outside.

"The human body can stand that much of a drop; all it really does is cause altitude sickness. As a matter of fact, a pearl diver going down in four of five fathoms of water meets a greater variation than that. Plenty of South Sea skin divers work in that depth, utterly unprotected. What might have happened to us is the bends, but your own air system thoughtfully prevented that danger."

"M-my own air system?"

"Yes, Peri. The bends are the result of decreasing pressure, which ordinarily causes the blood to give up its dissolved nitrogen as bubbles. It's the bubbles that cause the disease. But your air doesn't contain nitrogen; it's made of oxygen and neon, and neon doesn't dissolve! So—no dissolved gases, no bubbles, and no bends."

"But—it's fantastic! It's impossible!"

"We did it. What do you think of that?"

"Why"—her voice was meek—"I think you're very courageous, Frank. You're the only man ever to see the Red Peri frightened, and you've seen that—twice."

"Twice? When was the other time?"

"When—when I saw the carbon feeders on your foot."

"Peri!" he groaned. "This whole thing has hurt me enough, but now if you mean—"

"Of course I mean it," she said, looking steadily at him. "I love you, Frank."

"If I dared believe you, Peri—you know I love you, don't you?"

A faint trace of her old mockery glistened green in her eyes.

"Oh, of course," she said. "I could tell it because you've been so kind to me."

Her sarcasm tortured him. "I had to do it. I have to bring you over to my side of the fence, Peri—the honest side."

"And you think you can?"

"I can try."

"Really?" she taunted. "Frank, don't you know my ship will be alongside in a matter of minutes? You can't outrun the Red Peri in this tub. You have me helpless now, but I won't be so for long."

"Indeed? Well, tub or not, the Limbo's solid. They don't dare blast the ship with you aboard, and if they try to tie up and cut their way in"—he turned narrowed eyes on her—"I'll ram the Peri! As I said, this ship is solid, far more solid than your triangular speedster. I'll smash it!"

The faint color that had returned to the Peri's face drained out of it. After a moment she said in very low tones, "What are you going to do with me, Frank?"

"Peri, I'm going to take you back to trial. After you've expiated your crimes—and with your beauty in an American court the sentence will be light—I'm going to marry you."

"Marry? Yes, I'd marry you, Frank, but don't you realize piracy is tried under maritime law? The penalty is—death!"

"Not for such a woman as you. Three years—no more."

"But I'm wanted in every country on Earth, Frank. They'll extradite me. What if I'm tried for murder in an English court?"

"Murder?" he echoed blankly. "I—I hadn't thought of that. My Lord, Peri! What can we do?"

"What we do is in your hands," she said dully. He saw tears in her green eyes.

"I—don't know. I swore a solemn oath to uphold the law, I—can't break an oath. Peri," he cried fiercely, "I have money. I'll fight through every court in the country to prevent your extradition. You'll return all you've taken. They'll be lenient; they have to be!"

"Perhaps," she said tonelessly, "Well, I don't care. You've won, Frank. I love you for it."

Impulsively he dropped the controls, strode over to the chained girl, and kissed her. He had to make it brief, for his own eyes were suddenly misty. At the controls again, he swore bitterly to himself, for he realized now that he could never risk bringing the Red Peri to trial. He thought somberly of his broken oath; that meant nothing if keeping it endangered the girl he loved.

He formed a plan. At Nivia on Titan there'd be an inspection of the ship. He'd hide the Peri—in a cool jet, perhaps—and tell his story without mention of her capture. He'd disclose the location of the pirate base and let the government rockets rescue old Solomon and destroy the colony. And then he—

Then? Well, he'd land the Limbo in Iraq. He had friends there who'd keep the Peri safe. He'd fly home and resign his damned official position, and so he free to marry pirate or murderess or any one he chose—and no one would ever know that the lovely Mrs. Keene had once been the dreaded Red Peri.

For the present he'd let the girl believe he was taking her backto punishment; at least that might frighten her into a respectable life. He smiled, and looked up to find the luminous green eyes fixed steadily and unhappily on his face.

Before he could speak the buzzer of the static field sounded the signal that warned of meteors. But meteors were rare indeed out here beyond the orbit of Jupiter. He stared back at the vast black disc of Pluto, and true enough, there was a little flare of light against the blackness that could mean only a rocket blast. Second by second the flame approached, and the Red Peri rushed toward him as if his own blast were silent.

The pirate ship paralleled his course. Suddenly the annunciator above him spoke; they had trained an inductive beam on it. "Cut your jets!" came the words in a cold metallic voice that was still recognizable as Marco Grandi's.

He had no means of reply, so he bored grimly on. The Red Peri slipped close beside him. "Cut your jets," came the order, "or we'll blast you!"

Keene thought suddenly of the communication system from the pilot room to the stern. If he spoke into that, and if their tubes were sensitive enough, it was possible that their receiver might pick up the induced current. He switched it on full.

"Red Peri!" he called. "Can you hear me? Can you hear me?"

Reply was immediate. "We hear you. Cut your jets!"

"I won't," said Keene. "If you come a single yard closer I'll ram you. The Peri's aboard, and if you blast this ship you'll kill her as well as me."

There was a silence. "How do we know she's alive?" asked Grandi's voice.

"Watch the forward port," said Keene. He unlocked the chain at the hand hold. The girl made no resistance as he led her to the port, following as meekly as a puppy on a leash.

"I'll have to make this look serious," he said. "I'm sorry, Peri." He twisted his hand roughly in her glorious hair and thrust her close against the port. After a moment he released her, led her back to her chair, and relocked the chain.

"Red Peri," he called, "move away or I'll ram you. Keep a quarter mile distance."

There was no reply, but the pirate ship slanted silently away. Like a child's model it hung in the void, tenaciously paralleling his course. But he knew it was helpless; Grandi dared not risk the Peri's safety.

Nearly an hour passed before the Peri spoke. "I don't understand you, Frank," she said miserably. "When your life was in danger I risked mine to save you, but you risk your life to destroy me. Is that what you mean by love?"

"I risked mine, not to destroy you, but to save you," he muttered. "Peri, I couldn't bear the thought of your living such a life as you have been living. I want you to be happy."

"Happy," she echoed mournfully. "If this is your idea of happiness—" She left the sentence unfinished.

Hour after hour the pirate clung grimly beside them. After a long time Keene slept, trusting to the buzzer to rouse him if

Grandi should attempt to cut through. The last thing he saw was the luminescent eyes of the Peri, and they were the first thing he saw on awakening. She sat as if she had not moved.

Another day passed. Pluto was a pallid, tiny disk far behind them, Neptune and Uranus were beyond the Sun; but Saturn gleamed brightly. All day the Peri was mournfully silent, and when he kissed her before sleeping, she clung to him almost as if in panic. He remembered that later, for when he awoke she was —gone.

Gone! The chain was missing, and only a square of paper—a star chart—lay on her chair. She wasn't on the Limbo, and the Red Peri no longer hung silent on the left. He seized the note in a frantic clutch. He read.

Frank—dearest Frank—this is farewell. I love you; and the proof of it is that I could have escaped before this while you slept; but I wanted to stay. I was all but willing to suffer before the law if it meant having you—but I can't. Not even three years, because I'd die without freedom.

I had an iron feeder in my pocket, for I always carry them on raids, as you remember from the Aardkin. It's eating the chain now, but it won't attack chrome steel; your floors and walls are safe.

Frank, if you had weakened, if you had promised me safety, I think I should have stayed, but—perhaps-then I should have loved you less than I do now.

Good-by

The note was unsigned. She had taken a red chart pencil and drawn a creditable picture of a tiny, winged elf—a Red Peri.

Keene knew what she had done. There were no space suits on the Limbo, for he and Solomon had worn them to the pirate cave. She had signaled her ship, opened the air lock, and braved once more the vacuum of space to fling herself across.

When he had finally exhausted his vocabulary of expletives and blasphemies, when he had at last called himself all the varieties of fool he knew, Keene realized what he had to do. He couldn't find her on Pluto, since the Peri would certainly move her base elsewhere for fear he'd direct a government rocket there. But what he could do, what he had to do, was to get a job on an Interplanetary freighter, and then wait. Sooner or later— sooner or later, he repeated grimly—he'd meet the Red Peri again.

THE MAD MOON

ORIGINALLY PUBLISHED IN *ASTOUNDING STORIES*
DECEMBER 1935

THE MAD MOON

"Idiots!" howled Grant Calthorpe. "Fools—nitwits—imbeciles!" He sought wildly for some more expressive terms, failed and vented his exasperation in a vicious kick at the pile of rubbish on the ground.

Too vicious a kick, in fact; he had again forgotten the one-third normal gravitation of Io, and his whole body followed his kick in a long, twelve-foot arc.

As he struck the ground the four loonies giggled. Their great, idiotic heads, looking like nothing so much as the comic faces painted on Sunday balloons for children, swayed in unison on their five-foot necks, as thin as Grant's wrist.

"Get out!" he blazed, scrambling erect. "Beat it, skiddoo, scram! No chocolate. No candy. Not until you learn that I want ferva leaves, and not any junk you happen to grab. Clear out!"

The loonies—Lunae Jovis Magnicapites, or literally, Bigheads of Jupiter's Moon—backed away, giggling plaintively. Beyond doubt, they considered Grant fully as idiotic as he considered them, and were quite unable to understand the reasons for his anger. But they certainly realized that no candy was to be forthcoming, and their giggles took on a note of keen disappointment.

So keen, indeed, that the leader, after twisting his ridiculous blue face in an imbecilic grin at Grant, voiced a last wild giggle and dashed his head against a glittering stone-bark tree. His companions casually picked up his body and moved off, with his head dragging behind them on its neck like a prisoner's ball on a chain.

Grant brushed his hand across his forehead and turned wearily toward his stone-bark log shack. A pair of tiny, glittering red eyes caught his attention, and a slinker—Mus Sapiens—skipped his six-inch form across the threshold, bearing under his tiny, skinny arm what looked very much like Grant's clinical thermometer.

Grant yelled angrily at the creature, seized a stone, and flung it vainly. At the edge of the brush, the slinker turned its ratlike, semihuman face toward him, squeaked its thin gibberish, shook a microscopic fist in manlike wrath, and vanished, its batlike cowl of skin fluttering like a cloak. It looked, indeed, very much like a black rat wearing a cape.

It had been a mistake, Grant knew, to throw the stone at it. Now the tiny fiends would never permit him any peace, and their diminutive size and pseudo-human intelligence made them infernally troublesome as enemies. Yet, neither that reflection nor the loony's suicide troubled him particularly; he had witnessed instances like the latter too often, and besides, his head felt as if he were in for another siege of white fever.

He entered the shack, closed the door, and stared down at his pet parcat. "Oliver," he growled, "you're a fine one. Why the devil don't you watch out for slinkers? What are you here for?"

The parcat rose on its single, powerful hind leg, clawing at his knees with its two forelegs. "The red jack on the black queen," it observed placidly. "Ten loonies make one half-wit."

Grant placed both statements easily. The first was, of course, an echo of his preceding evening's solitaire game, and the second of yesterday's session with the loonies. He grunted abstractedly and rubbed his aching head. White fever again, beyond doubt.

He swallowed two ferverin tablets, and sank listlessly to the edge of his bunk, wondering whether this attack of blancha would culminate in delirium.

He cursed himself for a fool for ever taking this job on Jupiter's third habitable moon, Io. The tiny world was a planet of madness, good for nothing except the production of ferva leaves, out of which Earthly chemists made as many potent alkaloids as they once made from opium.

Invaluable to medical science, of course, but what difference did that make to him? What difference, even, did the munificent salary make, if he got back to Earth a raving maniac after a year in the equatorial regions of Io? He swore bitterly that when the plane from Junopolis landed next month for his ferva, he'd go back to the polar city with it, even though his contract with

Neilan Drug called for a full year, and he'd get no pay if he broke it. What good was money to a lunatic?

The whole little planet was mad—loonies, parcats, slinkers and Grant Calthorpe—all crazy. At least, anybody who ever ventured outside either of the two polar cities, Junopolis on the north and Herapolis on the south, was crazy. One could live there in safety from white fever, but anywhere below the twentieth parallel it was worse than the Cambodian jungles on Earth.

He amused himself by dreaming of Earth. Just two years ago he had been happy there, known as a wealthy, popular sportsman. He had been just that too; before he was twenty-one he had hunted knife-kite and threadworm on Titan, and triops and uniped on Venus.

That had been before the gold crisis of 2110 had wiped out his fortune. And—well, if he had to work, it had seemed logical to use his interplanetary experience as a means of livelihood. He had really been enthusiastic at the chance to associate himself with Neilan Drug.

He had never been on Io before. This wild little world was no sportsman's paradise, with its idiotic loonies and wicked, intelligent, tiny slinkers. There wasn't anything worth hunting on the feverish little moon, bathed in warmth by the giant Jupiter only a quarter million miles away.

If he had happened to visit it, he told himself ruefully, he'd never have taken the job; he had visualized Io as something like Titan, cold but clean.

Instead it was as hot as the Venus Hotlands because of its glowing primary, and subject to half a dozen different forms of steamy daylight—sun day, Jovian day, Jovian and sun day, Europa light, and occasionally actual and dismal night. And most of these came in the course of Io's forty-two-hour revolution, too—a mad succession of changing lights. He hated the dizzy days, the jungle, and Idiots' Hills stretching behind his shack.

It was Jovian and solar day at the present moment, and that was the worst of all, because the distant sun added its modicum of heat to that of Jupiter. And to complete Grant's discomfort now was the prospect of a white fever attack. He swore as his head gave an additional twinge, and then swallowed another ferverin tablet. His supply of these was diminishing, he noticed; he'd have to remember to ask for some when the plane called— no, he was going back with it.

Oliver rubbed against his leg. "Idiots, fools, nitwits, imbeciles," remarked the parcat affectionately. "Why did I have to go to that damn dance?"

"Huh?" said Grant. He couldn't remember having said anything about a dance. It must, he decided, have been said during his last fever madness.

Oliver creaked like the door, then giggled like a loony. "It'll be all right," he assured Grant. "Father is bound to come soon."

"Father!" echoed the man. His father had died fifteen years before. "Where'd you get that from, Oliver?"

"It must be the fever," observed Oliver placidly. "You're a nice kitty, but I wish you had sense enough to know what you're saying. And I wish father would come." He finished with a supressed gurgle that might have been a sob.

Grant stared dizzily at him. He hadn't said any of those things; he was positive. The parcat must have heard them from somebody else— Somebody else? Where within five hundred miles was there anybody else?

"Oliver!" he bellowed. "Where'd you hear that? Where'd you hear it?"

The parcat backed away, startled. "Father is idiots, fools, nitwits, imbeciles," he said anxiously. "The red jack on the nice kitty."

"Come here!" roared Grant. "Whose father? Where have you— Come here, you imp!"

He lunged at the creature. Oliver flexed his single hind leg and flung himself frantically to the cowl of the wood stove. "It must be the fever!" he squalled. "No chocolate!"

He leaped like a three-legged flash for the flue opening. There came a sound of claws grating on metal, and then he had scrambled through.

Grant followed him. His head ached from the effort, and with the still sane part of his mind he knew that the whole episode was doubtless white fever delirium, but he plowed on.

His progress was a nightmare. Loonies kept bobbing their long necks above the tall bleeding-grass, their idiotic giggles and imbecilic faces adding to the general atmosphere of madness.

Wisps of fetid, fever-bearing vapors spouted up at every step on the spongy soil. Somewhere to his right a slinker squeaked and gibbered; he knew that a tiny slinker village was over in that direction, for once he had glimpsed the neat little buildings, constructed of small, perfectly fitted stones like a miniature medieval town, complete to towers and battlements. It was said that there were even slinker wars.

His head buzzed and whirled from the combined effects of ferverin and fever. It was an attack of blancha, right enough, and he realized that he was an imbecile, a loony, to wander thus away from his shack. He should be lying on his bunk; the fever was not serious, but more than one man had died on Io, in the delirium, with its attendant hallucinations.

He was delirious now. He knew it as soon as he saw Oliver, for Oliver was placidly regarding an attractive young lady in perfect evening dress of the style of the second decade of the twenty-second century. Very obviously that was a hallucination, since girls had no business in the Ionian tropics, and if by some wild chance one should appear there, she would certainly not choose formal garb.

The hallucination had fever, apparently, for her face was pale with the whiteness that gave blancha its name. Her gray eyes regarded him without surprise as he wound his way through the bleeding-grass to her.

"Good afternoon, evening, or morning," he remarked, giving a puzzled glance at Jupiter, which was rising, and the sun, which was setting. "Or perhaps merely good day, Miss Lee Neilan."

She gazed seriously at him. "Do you know," she said, "you're the first one of the illusions that I haven't recognized? All my friends have been around, but you're the first stranger. Or are you a stranger? You know my name—but you ought to, of course, being my own hallucination."

"We won't argue about which of us is the hallucination," he suggested. "Let's do it this way. The one of us that disappears first is the illusion. Bet you five dollars you do."

"How could I collect?" she said. "I can't very well collect from my own dream."

"That is a problem." He frowned. "My problem, of course, not yours. I know I'm real."

"How do you know my name?" she demanded.

"Ah!" he said. "From intensive reading of the society sections of the newspapers brought by my supply plane. As a matter of fact, I have one of your pictures cut out and pasted next to my bunk. That probably accounts for my seeing you now. I'd like to really meet you some time."

"What a gallant remark for an apparition!" she exclaimed. "And who are you supposed to be?"

"Why, I'm Grant Calthorpe. In fact, I work for your father, trading with the loonies for ferva."

"Grant Calthorpe," she echoed. She narrowed her fever-dulled eyes as if to bring him into better focus. "Why, you are!"

Her voice wavered for a moment, and she brushed her hand across her pale brow. "Why should you pop out of my memories? It's strange. Three or four years ago, when I was a romantic schoolgirl and you the famous sportsman, I was madly in love with you. I had a whole book filled with your pictures—Grant Calthorpe dressed in parka for hunting threadworms on Titan— Grant Calthorpe beside the giant uniped he killed near the Mountains of Eternity. You're-you're really the pleasantest hallucination I've had so far. Delirium would be—fun"—she pressed her hand to her brow again—"if one's head—didn't ache so!"

"Gee!" thought Grant, "I wish that were true, that about the book. This is what psychology calls a wish-fulfillment dream." A drop of warm rain plopped on his neck. "Got to get to bed," he said aloud. "Rain's bad for blancha. Hope to see you next time I'm feverish."

"Thank you," said Lee Neilan with dignity. "It's quite mutual."

He nodded, sending a twinge through his head. "Here, Oliver," he said to the drowsing parcat. "Come on."

"That isn't Oliver," said Lee. "It's Polly. It's kept me company for two days, and I've named it Polly."

"Wrong gender," muttered Grant. "Anyway, it's my parcat, Oliver. Aren't you Oliver?"

"Hope to see you," said Oliver sleepily.

"It's Polly. Aren't you, Polly?"

"Bet you five dollars," said the parcat. He rose, stretched and loped off into the underbrush. "It must be the fever," he observed as he vanished.

"It must be," agreed Grant. He turned away. "Good-by, Miss—or I might as well call you Lee, since you're not real. Good-by, Lee."

"Good-by, Grant. But don't go that way. There's a slinker village over in the grass."

"No. It's over there."

"It's there," she insisted. "I've been watching them build it. But they can't hurt you anyway, can they? Not even a slinker could hurt an apparition. Good-by, Grant." She closed her eyes wearily.

It was raining harder now. Grant pushed his way through the bleeding-grass, whose red sap collected in bloody drops on his boots. He had to get back to his shack quickly, before the white fever and its attendant delirium set him wandering utterly astray. He needed ferverin.

Suddenly he stopped short. Directly before him the grass had been cleared away, and in the little clearing were the shoulder-high towers and battlements of a slinker village—a new one, for half-finished houses stood among the others, and hooded six-inch forms toiled over the stones.

There was an outcry of squeaks and gibberish. He backed away, but a dozen tiny darts whizzed about him. One stuck like a toothpick in his boot, but none, luckily, scratched his skin, for they were undoubtedly poisoned. He moved more quickly, but all around in the thick, fleshy grasses were rustlings, squeakings, and incomprehensible imprecations.

He circled away. Loonies kept popping their balloon heads over the vegetation, and now and again one giggled in pain as a slinker bit or stabbed it. Grant cut toward a group of the creatures, hoping to distract the tiny fiends in the grass, and a tall, purple-faced loony curved its long neck above him, giggling and gesturing with its skinny fingers at a bundle under its arm.

He ignored the thing, and veered toward his shack. He seemed to have eluded the slinkers, so he trudged doggedly on, for he needed a ferverin tablet badly. Yet, suddenly he came to a frowning halt, turned, and began to retrace his steps.

"It can't be so," he muttered. "But she told me the truth about the slinker village. I didn't know it was there. Yet how could a hallucination tell me something I didn't know?"

Lee Neilan was sitting on the stone-bark log exactly as he had left her with Oliver again at her side. Her eyes were closed, and two slinkers were cutting at the long skirt of her gown with tiny, glittering knives.

Grant knew that they were always attracted by Terrestrial textiles; apparently they were unable to duplicate the fascinating sheen of satin, though the fiends were infernally clever with their tiny hands. As he approached, they tore a strip from thigh to ankle, but the girl made no move. Grant shouted, and the vicious little creatures mouthed unutterable curses at him, as they skittered away with their silken plunder.

Lee Neilan opened her eyes. "You again," she murmured vaguely. "A moment ago it was father. Now it's you." Her pallor had increased; the white fever was running its course in her body.

"Your father! Then that's where Oliver heard—Listen, Lee. I found the slinker village. I didn't know it was there, but I found it just as you said. Do you see what that means? We're both real!"

"Real?" she said dully. "There's a purple loony grinning over your shoulder. Make him go away. He makes me feel—sick."

He glanced around; true enough, the purple-faced loony was behind him. "Look here," he said, seizing her arm. The feel of her smooth skin was added proof. "You're coming to the shack for ferverin." He pulled her to her feet. "Don't you understand? I'm real!"

"No, you're not," she said dazedly.

"Listen, Lee. I don't know how in the devil you got here or why, but I know Io hasn't driven me that crazy yet. You're real and I'm real." He shook her violently. "I'm real!" he shouted.

Faint comprehension showed in her dazed eyes. "Real?" she whispered. "Real! Oh, Lord! Then take—me out of this mad place!" She swayed, made a stubborn effort to control herself, then pitched forward against him.

Of course on Io her weight was negligible, less than a third Earth normal. He swung her into his arms and set off toward the shack, keeping well away from both slinker settlements. Around him bobbed excited loonies, and now and again the purple-faced one, or another exactly like him, giggled and pointed and gestured.

The rain had increased, and warm rivulets flowed down his neck, and to add to the madness, he blundered near a copse of stinging palms, and their barbed lashes stung painfully through his shirt. Those stings were virulent too, if one failed to disinfect them; indeed, it was largely the stinging palms that kept traders from gathering their own ferva instead of depending on the loonies.

Behind the low rain clouds, the sun had set and it was ruddy Jupiter daylight, which lent a false flush to the cheeks of the unconscious Lee Neilan, making her still features very lovely.

Perhaps he kept his eyes too steadily on her face, for suddenly Grant was among slinkers again; they were squeaking and sputtering, and the purple loony leaped in pain as teeth and darts pricked his legs. But, of course, loonies were immune to the poison.

The tiny devils were around his feet now. He swore in a low voice and kicked vigorously, sending a ratlike form spinning fifty feet in the air. He had both automatic and flame pistol at his hip, but he could not use them for several reasons.

First, using an automatic against the tiny hordes was much like firing into a swarm of mosquitoes; if the bullet killed one or two or a dozen, it made no appreciable impression on the remaining thousands. And as for the flame pistol, that was like using a Big Bertha to swat a fly. Its vast belch of fire would certainly incinerate all the slinkers in its immediate path, along with grass, trees, and loonies, but that again would make but little impress on the surviving hordes, and it meant laboriously recharging the pistol with another black diamond and another barrel.

He had gas bulbs in the shack, but they were not available at the moment, and besides, he had no spare mask, and no chemist has yet succeeded in devising a gas that would kill slinkers without being also deadly to humans. And, finally, he couldn't use any weapon whatsoever right now, because he dared not drop Lee Neilan to free his hands.

Ahead was the clearing around the shack. The space was full of slinkers, but the shack itself was supposed to be slinkerproof, at least for reasonable lengths of time, since stone-bark logs were very resistant to their tiny tools.

But Grant perceived that a group of the diminutive devils were around the door, and suddenly he realized their intent. They had looped a cord of some sort over the knob, and were engaged now in twisting it!

Grant yelled and broke into a run. While he was yet half a hundred feet distant, the door swung inward and the rabble of slinkers flowed into the shack.

He dashed through the entrance. Within was turmoil. Little hooded shapes were cutting at the blankets on his bunk, his extra clothing, the sacks he hoped to fill with ferva leaves, and were pulling at the cooking utensils, or at any and all loose objects.

He bellowed and kicked at the swarm. A wild chorus of squeaks and gibberish arose as the creatures skipped and dodged about him. The fiends were intelligent enough to realize that he could do nothing with his arms occupied by Lee Neilan. They skittered out of the way of his kicks, and while he threatened a group at the stove, another rabble tore at his blankets.

In desperation he charged the bunk. He swept the girl's body across it to clear it, dropped her on it, and seized a grass broom he had made to facilitate his housekeeping. With wide strokes of its handle he attacked the slinkers, and the squeals were checkered by cries and whimpers of pain.

A few broke for the door, dragging whatever loot they had. He spun around in time to see half a dozen swarming around Lee Neilan, tearing at her clothing, at the wrist watch on her arm, at the satin evening pumps on her small feet. He roared a curse at them and battered them away, hoping that none had pricked her skin with virulent dagger or poisonous tooth.

He began to win the skirmish. More of the creatures drew their black capes close about them and scurried over the threshold with their plunder. At last, with a burst of squeaks, the remainder, laden and empty-handed alike, broke and ran for safety, leaving a dozen furry, impish bodies slain or wounded.

Grant swept these after the others with his erstwhile weapon, closed the door in the face of a loony that bobbed in the opening, latched it against any repetition of the slinker's trick, and stared in dismay about the plundered dwelling.

Cans had been rolled or dragged away. Every loose object had been pawed by the slinkers' foul little hands, and Grant's clothes hung in ruins on their hooks against the wall. But the tiny robbers had not succeeded in opening the cabinet nor the table drawer, and there was food left.

Six months of Ionian life had left him philosophical; he swore heartily, shrugged resignedly, and pulled his bottle of ferverin from the cabinet.

His own spell of fever had vanished as suddenly and completely as blancha always does when treated, but the girl, lacking ferverin, was paper-white and still. Grant glanced at the bottle; eight tablets remained.

"Well, I can always chew ferva leaves," he muttered. That was less effective than the alkaloid itself, but it would serve, and Lee Neilan needed the tablets. He dissolved two of them in a glass of water, and lifted her head.

She was not too inert to swallow, and he poured the solution between her pale lips, then arranged her as comfortably as he could. Her dress was a tattered silken ruin, and he covered her with a blanket that was no less a ruin. Then he disinfected his palm stings, pulled two chairs together, and sprawled across them to sleep.

He started up at the sound of claws on the roof, but it was only Oliver, gingerly testing the flue to see if it were hot. In a moment the parcat scrambled through, stretched himself, and remarked, "I'm real and you're real."

"Imagine that!" grunted Grant sleepily.

*   *   *   *   *

When he awoke it was Jupiter and Europa light, which meant he had slept about seven hours, since the brilliant little third moon was just rising. He rose and gazed at Lee Neilan, who was sleeping soundly with a tinge of color in her face that was not entirely due to the ruddy daylight. The blancha was passing.

He dissolved two more tablets in water, then shook the girl's shoulder. Instantly her gray eyes opened, quite clear now, and she looked up at him without surprise.

"Hello, Grant," she murmured. "So it's you again. Fever isn't so bad, after all."

"Maybe I ought to let you stay feverish," he grinned. "You say such nice things. Wake up and drink this, Lee."

She became suddenly aware of the shack's interior. "Why—Where is this? It looks—real!"

"It is. Drink this ferverin."

She obeyed, then lay back and stared at him perplexedly. "Real?" she said. "And you're real?"

"I think I am."

A rush of tears clouded her eyes. "Then—I'm out of that place? That horrible place?"

"You certainly are." He saw signs of her relief becoming hysteria, and hastened to distract her. "Would you mind telling me how you happened to be there—and dressed for a party too?"

She controlled herself. "I was dressed for a party. A party. A party in Herapolis. But I was in Junopolis, you see."

"I don't see. In the first place, what are you doing on Io, anyway? Every time I ever heard of you, it was in connection with New York or Paris society."

She smiled. "Then it wasn't all delirium, was it? You did say that you had one of my pictures—Oh, that one!" She frowned at the print on the wall. "Next time a news photographer wants to snap my picture, I'll remember not to grin like—like a loony. But as to how I happen to be on Io, I came with father, who's looking over the possibilities of raising ferva on plantations instead of having to depend on traders and loonies. We've been here three months, and I've been terribly bored. I thought Io would be exciting, but it wasn't—until recently."

"But what about that dance? How'd you manage to get here, a thousand miles from Junopolis?"

"Well," she said slowly, "it was terribly tiresome in Junopolis. No shows, no sport, nothing but an occasional dance. I got restless. When there were dances in Herapolis, I formed the habit of flying over there. It's only four or five hours in a fast plane, you know. And last week—or whatever it was—I'd planned on flying down, and Harvey—that's father's secretary—was to take me. But at the last minute father needed him and forbade my flying alone."

Grant felt a strong dislike for Harvey. "Well?" he asked.

"So I flew alone," she finished demurely.

"And cracked up, eh?"

"I can fly as well as anybody," she retorted. "It was just that I followed a different route, and suddenly there were mountains ahead."

He nodded. "The Idiots' Hills," he said. "My supply plane detours five hundred miles to avoid them. They're not high, but they stick right out above the atmosphere of this crazy planet. The air here is dense but shallow."

"I know that. I knew I couldn't fly above them, but I thought I could hurdle them. Work up full speed, you know, and then throw the plane upward. I had a closed plane, and gravitation is so weak here. And besides, I've seen it done several times, especially with a rocket-driven craft. The jets help to support the plane even after the wings are useless for lack of air."

"What a damn fool stunt!" exclaimed Grant. "Sure it can be done, but you have to be an expert to pull out of it when you hit the air on the other side. You hit fast, and there isn't much falling room."

"So I found out," said Lee ruefully. "I almost pulled out, but not quite, and I hit in the middle of some stinging palms. I guess the crash dazed them, because I managed to get out before they started lashing around. But I couldn't reach my plane again, and it was—I only remember two days of it—but it was horrible!"

"It must have been," he said gently.

"I knew that if I didn't eat or drink, I had a chance of avoiding white fever. The not eating wasn't so bad, but the not drinking—well, I finally gave up and drank out of a brook. I didn't care what happened if I could have a few moments that weren't thirst-tortured. And after that it's all confused and vague."

"You should have chewed ferva leaves."

"I didn't know that. I wouldn't have even known what they looked like, and besides, I kept expecting father to appear. He must be having a search made by now."

"He probably is," rejoined Grant ironically. "Has it occurred to you that there are thirteen million square miles of surface on little Io? And that for all he knows, you might have crashed on any square mile of it? When you're flying from north pole to south pole, there isn't any shortest route. You can cross any point on the planet."

Her gray eyes started wide. "But I—"

"Furthermore," said Grant, "this is probably the last place a searching party would look. They wouldn't think anyone but a loony would try to hurdle Idiots' Hills, in which thesis I quite agree. So it looks very much, Lee Neilan, as if you're marooned here until my supply plane gets here next month!"

"But father will be crazy! He'll think I'm dead!"

"He thinks that now, no doubt."

"But we can't—" She broke off, staring around the tiny shack's single room. After a moment she sighed resignedly, smiled, and said softly, "Well, it might have been worse, Grant. I'll try to earn my keep."

"Good. How do you feel, Lee?"

"Quite normal. I'll start right to work." She flung off the tattered blanket, sat up, and dropped her feet to the floor. "I'll fix dinn—Good night! My dress!" She snatched the blanket about her again.

He grinned. "We had a little run-in with the stinkers after you had passed out. They did for my spare wardrobe too."

"It's ruined!" she wailed.

"Would needle and thread help? They left that, at least, because it was in the table drawer."

"Why, I couldn't make a good swimming suit out of this!" she retorted. "Let me try one of yours."

By dint of cutting, patching, and mending, she at last managed to piece one of Grant's suits to respectable proportions. She looked very lovely in shirt and trousers, but he was troubled to note that a sudden pallor had overtaken her.

It was the riblancha, the second spell of fever that usually followed a severe or prolonged attack. His face was serious as he cupped two of his last four ferverin tablets in his hand.

"Take these," he ordered. "And we've got to get some ferva leaves somewhere. The plane took my supply away last week, and I've had bad luck with my loonies ever since. They haven't brought me anything but weeds and rubbish."

Lee puckered her lips at the bitterness of the drug, then closed her eyes against its momentary dizziness and nausea. "Where can you find ferva?" she asked.

He shook his head perplexedly, glancing out at the setting mass of Jupiter, with its bands glowing creamy and brown, and the Red Spot boiling near the western edge. Close above it was the brilliant little disk of Europa. He frowned suddenly, glanced at his watch and then at the almanac on the inside of the cabinet door.

"It'll be Europa light in fifteen minutes," he muttered, "and true night in twenty-five—the first true night in half a month. I wonder—"

He gazed thoughtfully at Lee's face. He knew where ferva grew. One dared not penetrate the jungle itself, where stinging palms and arrow vines and the deadly worms called toothers made such a venture sheer suicide for any creatures but loonies and slinkers. But he knew where ferva grew—

In Io's rare true night even the clearing might be dangerous. Not merely from slinkers, either; he knew well enough that in the darkness creatures crept out of the jungle who otherwise remained in the eternal shadows of its depths—toothers, bullet-head frogs, and doubtless many unknown slimy, venomous, mysterious beings never seen by man. One heard stories in Herapolis and—

But he had to get ferva, and he knew where it grew. Not even a loony would try to gather it there, but in the little gardens or farms around the tiny slinker towns, there was ferva growing.

He switched on a light in the gathering dusk. "I'm going outside a moment," he told Lee Neilan. "If the blancha starts coming back, take the other two tablets. Wouldn't hurt you to take 'em anyway. The slinkers got away with my thermometer, but if you get dizzy again, you take 'em."

"Grant! Where—"

"I'll be back," he called, closing the door behind him.

A loony, purple in the bluish Europa light, bobbed up with a long giggle. He waved the creature aside and set off on a cautious approach to the neighborhood of the slinker village— the old one, for the other could hardly have had time to cultivate its surrounding ground. He crept warily through the bleeding-grass, but he knew his stealth was pure optimism. He was in exactly the position of a hundred-foot giant trying to approach a human city in secrecy—a difficult matter even in the utter darkness of night.

He reached the edge of the slinker clearing. Behind him, Europa, moving as fast as the second hand on his watch, plummeted toward the horizon. He paused in momentary surprise at the sight of the exquisite little town, a hundred feet away across the tiny square fields, with lights flickering in its hand-wide windows. He had not known that slinker culture included the use of lights, but there they were, tiny candles or perhaps diminutive oil lamps.

He blinked in the darkness. The second of the ten-foot fields looked like—it was—ferva. He stooped low, crept out, and reached his hand for the fleshy, white leaves. And at that moment came a shrill giggle and the crackle of grass behind him. The loony! The idiotic purple loony!

Squeaking shrieks sounded. He snatched a double handful of ferva, rose, and dashed toward the lighted window of his shack. He had no wish to face poisoned barbs or disease-bearing teeth, and the slinkers were certainly aroused. Their gibbering sounded in chorus; the ground looked black with them.

He reached the shack, burst in, slammed and latched the door. "Got it!" he grinned. "Let 'em rave outside now."

They were raving. Their gibberish sounded like the creaking of worn machinery. Even Oliver opened his drowsy eyes to listen. "It must be the fever," observed the parcat placidly.

Lee was certainly no paler; the riblancha was passing safely. "Ugh!" she said, listening to the tumult without. "I've always hated rats, but slinkers are worse. All the shrewdness and viciousness of rats plus the intelligence of devils."

"Well," said Grant thoughtfully, "I don't see what they can do. They've had it in for me anyway."

"It sounds as if they're going off," said the girl, listening. "The noise is fading."

Grant peered out of the window. "They're still around. They've just passed from swearing to planning, and I wish I knew what. Some day, if this crazy little planet ever becomes worth human occupation, there's going to be a showdown between humans and slinkers."

"Well? They're not civilized enough to be really a serious obstacle, and they're so small, besides."

"But they learn," he said. "They learn so quickly, and they breed like flies. Suppose they pick up the use of gas, or suppose they develop little rifles for their poisonous darts. That's possible, because they work in metals right now, and they know fire. That would put them practically on a par with man as far as offense goes, for what good are our giant cannons and rocket planes against six-inch slinkers? And to be just on even terms would be fatal; one slinker for one man would be a hell of a trade."

Lee yawned. "Well, it's not our problem. I'm hungry, Grant."

"Good. That's a sign the blancha's through with you. We'll eat and then sleep a while, for there's five hours of darkness."

"But the slinkers?"

"I don't see what they can do. They couldn't cut through stone-bark walls in five hours, and anyway, Oliver would warn us if one managed to slip in somewhere."

It was light when Grant awoke, and he stretched his cramped limbs painfully across his two chairs. Something had wakened him, but he didn't know just what. Oliver was pacing nervously beside him, and now looked anxiously up at him.

"I've had bad luck with my loonies," announced the parcat plaintively. "You're a nice kitty."

"So are you," said Grant. Something had wakened him, but what?

Then he knew, for it came again—the merest trembling of the stone-bark floor. He frowned in puzzlement. Earthquakes? Not on Io, for the tiny sphere had lost its internal heat untold ages ago. Then what?

Comprehension dawned suddenly. He sprang to his feet with so wild a yell that Oliver scrambled sideways with an infernal babble. The startled parcat leaped to the stove and vanished up the flue. His squall drifted faintly back.

"It must be the fever!"

Lee had started to a sitting position on the bunk, her gray eyes blinking sleepily.

"Outside!" he roared, pulling her to her feet. "Get out! Quickly!"

"Wh-what—why—"

"Get out!" He thrust her through the door, then spun to seize his belt and weapons, the bag of ferva leaves, a package of chocolate. The floor trembled again, and he burst out of the door with a frantic leap to the side of the dazed girl.

"They've undermined it!" he choked. "The devils undermined the—"

He had no time to say more. A corner of the shack suddenly subsided; the stone-bark logs grated, and the whole structure collapsed like a child's house of blocks. The crash died into silence, and there was no motion save a lazy wisp of vapor, a few black, ratlike forms scurrying toward the grass, and a purple loony bobbing beyond the ruins.

"The dirty devils!" he swore bitterly. "The damn little black rats! The—"

A dart whistled so close that it grazed his ear and then twitched a lock of Lee's tousled brown hair. A chorus of squeaking sounded in the bleeding-grass.

"Come on!" he cried. "They're out to exterminate us this time. No—this way. Toward the hills. There's less jungle this way."

They could outrun the tiny slinkers easily enough. In a few moments they had lost the sound of squeaking voices, and they stopped to gaze ruefully back on the fallen dwelling.

"Now," he said miserably, "we're both where you were to start with."

"Oh, no." Lee looked up at him. "We're together now, Grant. I'm not afraid."

"We'll manage," he said with a show of assurance. "We'll put up a temporary shack somehow. We'll——"

A dart struck his boot with a sharp blup. The slinkers had caught up to them.

Again they ran toward Idiots' Hills. When at last they stopped, they could look down a long slope and far over the Ionian jungles. There was the ruined shack, and there, neatly checkered, the fields and towers of the nearer slinker town. But they had scarcely caught their breath when gibbering and squeaking came out of the brush.

They were being driven into Idiots' Hills, a region as unknown to man as the icy wastes of Pluto. It was as if the tiny fiends behind them had determined that this time their enemy, the giant trampler and despoiler of their fields, should be pursued to extinction.

Weapons were useless. Grant could not even glimpse their pursuers, slipping like hooded rats through the vegetation. A bullet, even if chance sped it through a slinker's body, was futile, and his flame pistol, though its lightning stroke should incinerate tons of brush and bleeding-grass, could no more than cut a narrow path through the horde of tormentors. The only weapons that might have availed, the gas bulbs, were lost in the ruins of the shack.

Grant and Lee were forced upward. They had risen a thousand feet above the plain, and the air was thinning. There was no jungle here, but only great stretches of bleeding-grass, across which a few loonies were visible, bobbing their heads on their long necks.

"Toward—the peaks!" gasped Grant, now painfully short of breath. "Perhaps we can stand rarer air than they."

Lee was beyond answer. She panted doggedly along beside him as they plodded now over patches of bare rock. Before them were two low peaks, like the pillars of a gate. Glancing back, Grant caught a glimpse of tiny black forms on a clear area, and in sheer anger he fired a shot. A single slinker leaped convulsively, its cape flapping, but the rest flowed on. There must have been thousands of them.

The peaks were closer, no more than a few hundred yards away. They were sheer, smooth, unscalable.

"Between them," muttered Grant.

The passage that separated them was bare and narrow. The twin peaks had been one in ages past; some forgotten volcanic convulsion had split them, leaving this slender canyon between.

He slipped an arm about Lee, whose breath, from effort and altitude, was a series of rasping gasps. A bright dart tinkled on the rocks as they reached the opening, but looking back, Grant could see only a purple loony plodding upward, and a few more to his right. They raced down a straight fifty-foot passage that debouched suddenly into a sizable valley—and there, thunderstruck for a moment, they paused.

A city lay there. For a brief instant Grant thought they had burst upon a vast slinker metropolis, but the merest glance showed otherwise. This was no city of medieval blocks, but a poem in marble, classical in beauty, and of human or near-human proportions. White columns, glorious arches, pure curving domes, an architectural loveliness that might have been born on the Acropolis. It took a second look to discern that the city was dead, deserted, in ruins.

Even in her exhaustion, Lee felt its beauty. "How—how exquisite!" she panted. "One could almost forgive them—for being—slinkers!"

"They won't forgive us for being human," he muttered. "We'll have to make a stand somewhere. We'd better pick a building."

But before they could move more than a few feet from the canyon mouth, a wild disturbance halted them. Grant whirled, and for a moment found himself actually paralyzed by amazement. The narrow canyon was filled with a gibbering horde of slinkers, like a nauseous, heaving black carpet. But they came no further than the valley end, for grinning, giggling, and bobbing, blocking the opening with tramping three-toed feet, were four loonies!

It was a battle. The slinkers were biting and stabbing at the miserable defenders, whose shrill keenings of pain were less giggles than shrieks. But with a determination and purpose utterly foreign to loonies, their clawed feet tramped methodically up and down, up and down.

Grant exploded, "I'll be damned!" Then an idea struck him. "Lee! They're packed in the canyon, the whole devil's brood of 'em!"

He rushed toward the opening. He thrust his flame pistol between the skinny legs of a loony, aimed it straight along the canyon, and fired.

Inferno burst. The tiny diamond, giving up all its energy in one terrific blast, shot a jagged stream of fire that filled the canyon from wall to wall and vomited out beyond to cut a fan of fire through the bleeding-grass of the slope.

Idiots' Hills reverberated to the roar, and when the rain of debris settled, there was nothing in the canyon save a few bits of flesh and the head of an unfortunate loony, still bouncing and rolling.

Three of the loonies survived. A purple-faced one was pulling his arm, grinning and giggling in imbecile glee. He waved the thing aside and returned to the girl.

"Thank goodness!" he said. "We're out of that, anyway."

"I wasn't afraid, Grant. Not with you."

He smiled. "Perhaps we can find a place here," he suggested. "The fever ought to be less troublesome at this altitude. But— say, this must have been the capital city of the whole slinker race in ancient times. I can scarcely imagine those fiends creating an architecture as beautiful as this—or as large. Why, these buildings are as colossal in proportion to slinker size as the skyscrapers of New York to us!"

"But so beautiful," said Lee softly, sweeping her eyes over the glory of the ruins. "One might almost forgive—Grant! Look at those!"

He followed the gesture. On the inner side of the canyon's portals were gigantic carvings. But the thing that set him staring in amazement was the subject of the portrayal. There, towering far up the cliff sides, were the figures, not of slinkers, but of—loonies! Exquisitely carved, smiling rather than grinning, and smiling somehow sadly, regretfully, pityingly—yet beyond doubt, loonies!

"Good night!" he whispered. "Do you see, Lee? This must once have been a loony city. The steps, the doors, the buildings, all are on their scale of size. Somehow, some time, they must have achieved civilization, and the loonies we know are the degenerate residue of a great race."

"And," put in Lee, "the reason those four blocked the way when the slinkers tried to come through is that they still remember. Or probably they don't actually remember, but they have a tradition of past glories, or more likely still, just a superstitious feeling that this place is in some way sacred. They let us pass because, after all, we look more like loonies than like slinkers. But the amazing thing is that they still possess even that dim memory, because this city must have been in ruins for centuries. Or perhaps even for thousands of years."

"But to think that loonies could ever have had the intelligence to create a culture of their own," said Grant, waving away the purple one bobbing and giggling at his side. Suddenly he paused, turning a gaze of new respect on the creature. "This one's been following me for days. All right, old chap, what is it?"

The purple one extended a sorely bedraggled bundle of bleeding-grass and twigs, giggling idiotically. His ridiculous mouth twisted; his eyes popped in an agony of effort at mental concentration.

"Canny!" he giggled triumphantly.

"The imbecile!" flared Grant. "Nitwit! Idiot!" He broke off, then laughed. "Never mind. I guess you deserve it." He tossed his package of chocolate to the three delighted loonies. "Here's your candy."

A scream from Lee startled him. She was waving her arms wildly, and over the crest of Idiots' Hills a rocket plane roared, circled, and nosed its way into the valley.

The door opened. Oliver stalked gravely out, remarking casually. "I'm real and you're real." A man followed the parcat— two men.

"Father!" screamed Lee.

*   *   *   *   *

It was some time later that Gustavus Neilan turned to Grant. "I can't thank you," he said. "If there's ever any way I can show my appreciation for——"

"There is. You can cancel my contract."

"Oh, you work for me?"

"I'm Grant Calthorpe, one of your traders, and I'm about sick of this crazy planet."

"Of course, if you wish," said Neilan. "If it's a question of pay—"

"You can pay me for the six months I've worked."

"If you'd care to stay," said the older man, "there won't be trading much longer. We've been able to grow ferva near the polar cities, and I prefer plantations to the uncertainties of relying on loonies. If you'd work out your year, we might be able to put you in charge of a plantation by the end of that time."

Grant met Lee Neilan's gray eyes, and hesitated. "Thanks," he said slowly, "but I'm sick of it." He smiled at the girl, then turned back to her father. "Would you mind telling me how you happened to find us? This is the most unlikely place on the planet."

"That's just the reason," said Neilan. "When Lee didn't get back, I thought things over pretty carefully. At last I decided, knowing her as I did, to search the least likely places first. We tried the shores of the Fever Sea, and then the White Desert, and finally Idiots' Hills. We spotted the ruins of a shack, and on the debris was this chap"—he indicated Oliver—"remarking that Ten loonies make one half-wit.' Well, the half-wit part sounded very much like a reference to my daughter, and we cruised about until the roar of your flame pistol attracted our attention."

Lee pouted, then turned her serious gray eyes on Grant. "Do you remember," she said softly, "what I told you there in the jungle?"

"I wouldn't even have mentioned that," he replied. "I knew you were delirious."

"But—perhaps I wasn't. Would companionship make it any easier to work out your year? I mean if—for instance—you were to fly back with us to Junopolis and return with a wife?"

"Lee," he said huskily, "you know what a difference that would make, though I can't understand why you'd ever dream of it."

"It must," suggested Oliver, "be the fever."

REDEMPTION CAIRN

ORIGINALLY PUBLISHED IN *ASTOUNDING STORIES*
MARCH 1936

REDEMPTION CAIRN

Have you ever been flat broke, hungry as the very devil, and yet so down and out that you didn't even care? Looking back now, after a couple of months, it's hard to put it into words, but I think the low point was the evening old Captain Harris Henshaw dropped into my room—my room, that is, until the twenty-four-hour notice to move or pay up expired.

There I sat, Jack Sands, ex-rocket pilot. Yeah, the same Jack Sands you're thinking of, the one who cracked up the Gunderson Europa expedition trying to land at Young's Field, Long Island, in March, 2110. Just a year and a half ago! It seemed like ten and a half. Five hundred idle days. Eighteen months of having your friends look the other way when you happened to pass on the street, partly because they're ashamed to nod to a pilot that's been tagged yellow, and partly because they feel maybe it's kinder to just let you drop out of sight peacefully.

I didn't even look up when a knock sounded on my door, because I knew it could only be the landlady. "Haven't got it," I growled. "I've got a right to stay out my notice."

"You got a right to make a damn fool of yourself," said Henshaw's voice. "Why don't you tell your friends your address?"

"Harris!" I yelled. It was "Captain" only aboard ship. Then I caught myself. "What's the matter?" I asked, grinning bitterly. "Did you crack up, too? Coming to join me on the dust heap, eh?"

"Coming to offer you a job," he growled.

"Yeah? It must be a swell one, then. Carting sand to fill up the blast pits on a field, huh? And I'm damn near hungry enough to take it—but not quite."

"It's a piloting job," said Henshaw quietly.

"Who wants a pilot who's been smeared with yellow paint? What outfit will trust its ships to a coward? Don't you know that Jack Sands is tagged forever?"

"Shut up, Jack," he said briefly. "I'm offering you the job as pilot under me on Interplanetary's new Europa expedition."

I started to burn up then. You see, it was returning from Jupiter's third moon, Europa, that I'd smashed up the Gunderson outfit, and now I got a wild idea that Henshaw was taunting me about that. "By Heaven!" I screeched. "If you're trying to be funny—"

But he wasn't. I quieted down when I saw he was serious, and he went on slowly, "I want a pilot I can trust, Jack. I don't know anything about your cracking up the Hera; I was on the Venus run when it happened. All I know is that I can depend on you."

After a while I began to believe him. When I got over the shock a little, I figured Henshaw was friend enough to be entitled to the facts.

"Listen, Harris," I said. "You're taking me on, reputation and all, and it looks to me as if you deserve an explanation. I haven't been whining about the bump I got, and I'm not now. I cracked up Gunderson and his outfit all right, only—" I hesitated; it's kind of tough to feel that maybe you're squirming in the pinch— "only my co-pilot, that fellow Kratska, forgot to mention a few things, and mentioned a few others that weren't true. Oh, it was my shift, right enough, but he neglected to tell the investigating committee that I'd stood his shift and my own before it. I'd been on for two long shifts, and this was my short one."

"Two long ones!" echoed Henshaw. "You mean you were on sixteen hours before the landing shift?"

"That's what I mean. I'll tell you just what I told the committee, and maybe you'll believe me. They didn't. But when Kratska showed up to relieve me he was hopped. He had a regular hexylamine jag, and he couldn't have piloted a tricycle. So I did the only possible thing to do; I sent him back to sleep it off, and I reported it to Gunderson, but that still left me the job of getting us down.

"It wouldn't have been so bad if it had happened in space, because there isn't much for a pilot to do out there except follow the course laid out by the captain, and maybe dodge a meteor if the alarm buzzes. But I had sixteen solid hours of teetering down through a gravitational field, and by the time my four-hour spell came around I was bleary."

"I don't wonder," said the captain. "Two long shifts!"

Maybe I'd better explain a rocket's pilot system. On short runs like Venus or Mars, a vessel could carry three pilots, and then it's a simple matter of three eight-hour shifts. But on any longer run, because air and weight and fuel and food are all precious, no rocket ever carries more than two pilots.

So a day's run is divided into four shifts, and each pilot has one long spell of eight hours, then four hours off, then four hours on again for his short shift, and then eight hours to sleep. He eats two of his meals right at the control desk, and the third during his short free period. It's a queer life, and sometimes men have been co-pilots for years without really seeing each other except at the beginning and the end of their run.

I went on with my story, still wondering whether Henshaw would feel as if I were whining. "I was bleary," I repeated, "but Kratska showed up still foggy, and I didn't dare trust a hexylamine dope with the job of landing. Anyway, I'd reported to Gunderson, and that seemed to shift some of the responsibility to him. So I let Kratska sit in the control cabin, and I began to put down."

Telling the story made me mad all over. "Those lousy reporters!" I blazed. "All of them seemed to think landing a rocket is like settling down in bed; you just cushion down on your underblast. Yeah; they don't realize that you have to land blind, because three hundred feet down from the ground the blast begins to splash against it.

"You watch the leveling poles at the edge of the field and try to judge your altitude from them, but you don't see the ground; what you see under you are the flames of Hell. And another thing they don't realize: lowering a ship is like bringing down a dinner plate balanced on a fishing rod. If she starts to roll sideways—blooey! The underjets only hold you up when they're pointing down, you know."

Henshaw let me vent my temper without interruption, and I returned to my story. "Well, I was getting down as well as could be expected. The Hera always did have a tendency to roll a little, but she wasn't the worst ship I've put to ground.

"But every time she slid over a little, Kratska let out a yell; he was nervous from his dope jag, and he knew he was due to lose his license, and on top of that he was just plain scared by the side roll. We got to seventy feet on the leveling poles when she gave a pretty sharp roll, and Kratska went plain daffy."

I hesitated. "I don't know exactly how to tell what happened. It went quick, and I didn't see all of it, of course. But suddenly Kratska, who had been fumbling with the air lock for ten minutes, shrieked something like 'She's going over!' and grabbed the throttle. He shut off the blast before I could lift an eyelash, shut it off and flung himself out. Yeah; he'd opened the air lock.

"Well, we were only seventy feet—less than that—above the field. We dropped like an overripe apple off a tree. I didn't have time even to move before we hit, and when we hit, all the fuel in all the jets must have let go. And for what happened after that you'd better read the newspapers."

"Not me," said Henshaw. "You spill it."

"I can't, not all of it, because I was laid out. But I can guess, all right. It seems that when the jets blew off, Kratska was just picked up in a couple of cubic yards of the soft sand he had landed in, and tossed clear. He had nothing but a broken wrist. And as for me, apparently I was shot out of the control room, and banged up considerably. And as for Gunderson, his professors, and everyone else on the Hera—well, they were just stains on the pool of molten ferralumin that was left."

"Then how," asked Henshaw, "did they hang it on you?"

I tried to control my voice. "Kratska," I said grimly. "The field was clear for landing; nobody can stand in close with the blast splashing in a six-hundred-foot circle. Of course, they saw someone jump from the nose of the ship after the jets cut off, but how could they tell which of us? And the explosion shuffled the whole field around, and nobody knew which was what."

"Then it should have been his word against yours."

"Yeah; it should have been. But the field knew it was my shift because I'd been talking over the landing beam, and besides, Kratska got to the reporters first. I never even knew of the mess until I woke up at Grand Mercy Hospital thirteen days later. By that time Kratska had talked and I was the goat."

"But the investigating committee?"

I grunted. "Sure, the investigating committee. I'd reported to Gunderson, but he made a swell witness, being just an impurity in a mass of ferralumin alloy. And Kratska had disappeared anyway."

"Couldn't they find him?"

"Not on what I knew about him. We picked him up at Junopolis on Io, because Briggs was down with white fever. I didn't see him at all except when we were relieving each other, and you know what that's like, seeing somebody in a control cabin with the sun shields up. And on Europa we kept to space routine, so I couldn't even give you a good description of him. He had a beard, but so have ninety per cent of us after a long hop, and he said when we took him on that he'd just come over from the Earth." I paused. "I'll find him some day."

"Hope you do," said Henshaw briskly. "About this present run, now. There'll be you and me, and then there'll be Stefan Coretti, a physical chemist, and an Ivor Gogrol, a biologist. That's the scientific personnel of the expedition."

"Yeah, but who's my co-pilot? That's what interests me."

"Oh, sure," said Henshaw, and coughed. "Your co-pilot. Well, I've been meaning to tell you. It's Claire Avery."

"Claire Avery!"

"That's right," agreed the captain gloomily. "The Golden Flash herself. The only woman pilot to have her name on the Curry cup, winner of this year's Apogee race."

"She's no pilot!" I snapped. "She's a rich publicity hound with brass nerves. I was just curious enough to blow ten bucks rental on a 'scope to watch that race. She was ninth rounding the Moon. Ninth! Do you know how she won? She gunned her rocket under full acceleration practically all the way back, and then fell into a braking orbit.

"Any sophomore in Astronautics II knows that you can't calculate a braking orbit without knowing the density of the stratosphere and ionosphere, and even then it's a gamble. That's what she did—simply gambled, and happened to be lucky. Why do you pick a rich moron with a taste for thrills on a job like this?"

"I didn't pick her, Jack. Interplanetary picked her for publicity purposes. To tell the truth, I think this whole expedition is an attempt to get a little favorable advertising to offset that shady stock investigation this spring. Interplanetary wants to show itself as the noble patron of exploration. So Claire Avery will take off for the television and papers, and you'll be politely ignored."

"And that suits me! I wouldn't even take the job if things were a little different, and—" I broke off suddenly, frozen "Say," I said weakly, "did you know they'd revoked my license?"

"You don't say," said Henshaw. "And after all the trouble I had talking Interplanetary into permission to take you on, too." Then he grinned. "Here," he said, tossing me an envelope. "See how long it'll take you to lose this one."

But the very sight of the familiar blue paper was enough to make me forget a lot of things—Kratska, Claire Avery, even hunger.

*   *   *   *   *

The take-off was worse than I had expected. I had sense enough to wear my pilot's goggles to the field, but of course I was recognized as soon as I joined the group at the rocket. They'd given us the Minos, an old ship, but she looked as if she'd handle well.

The newsmen must have had orders to ignore me, but I could hear plenty of comments from the crowd. And to finish things up, there was Claire Avery, a lot prettier than she looked on the television screens, but with the same unmistakable cobalt-blue eyes, and hair closer to the actual shade of metallic gold than any I'd ever seen. The "Golden Flash," the newsmen called her. Blah!

She accepted her introduction to me with the coolest possible nod, as if to say to the scanners and cameras that it wasn't her choice she was teamed with yellow Jack Sands. But for that matter, Coretti's black Latin eyes were not especially cordial either, nor were Gogrol's broad features. I'd met Gogrol somewhere before, but couldn't place him at the moment.

Well, at last the speeches were over, and the photographers and broadcast men let the Golden Flash stop posing, and she and I got into the control cabin for the take-off. I still wore my goggles, and huddled down low besides, because there were a dozen telescopic cameras and scanners recording us from the field's edge. Claire Avery simply ate it up, though, smiling and waving before she cut in the underblast. But finally we were rising over the flame.

She was worse than I'd dreamed. The Minos was a sweetly balanced ship, but she rolled it like a baby's cradle. She had the radio on the field broadcast, and I could hear the description of the take-off: "—heavily laden. There—she rolls again. But she's making altitude. The blast has stopped splashing now, and is coming down in a beautiful fan of fire. A difficult take-off, even for the Golden Flash." A difficult take-off! Bunk!

I was watching the red bubble in the level, but I stole a glance to Claire Avery's face, and it wasn't so cool and stand-offish now. And just then the bubble in the level bobbed way over, and I heard the girl at my side give a frightened little gasp. This wasn't cradle rocking any more—we were in a real roll!

I slapped her hands hard and grabbed the U-bar. I cut the underjets completely off, letting the ship fall free, then shot the full blast through the right laterals. It was damn close, I'm ready to swear, but we leveled, and I snapped on the under-blast before we lost a hundred feet of altitude. And there was that inane radio still talking: "They're over! No—they've leveled again, but what a roll! She's a real pilot, this Golden Flash—"

I looked at her; she was pale and shaken, but her eyes were angry. "Golden Flash, eh?" I jeered. "The gold must refer to your money, but what's the flash? It can't have much to do with your ability as a pilot." But at that time I had no idea how pitifully little she really knew about rocketry.

She flared. "Anyway," she hissed, her lips actually quivering with rage, "the gold doesn't refer to color, Mr. Malaria Sands!" She knew that would hurt; the "Malaria" was some bright columnist's idea of a pun on my name. You see, malaria's popularly called Yellow Jack. "Besides," she went on defiantly, "I could have pulled out of that roll myself, and you know it."

"Sure," I said, with the meanest possible sarcasm. We had considerable upward velocity now, and plenty of altitude, both of which tend toward safety because they give one more time to pull out of a roll. "You can take over again now. The hard part's over."

She gave me a look from those electric blue eyes, and I began to realize just what sort of trip I was in for. Coretti and Gogrol had indicated their unfriendliness plainly enough, and heaven knows I couldn't mistake the hatred in Claire Avery's eyes, so that left just Captain Henshaw. But the captain of the ship dare not show favoritism; so all in all I saw myself doomed to a lonely trip.

*   *   *   *   *

Lonely isn't the word for it. Henshaw was decent enough, but since Claire Avery had started with a long shift and so had the captain, they were having their free spells and meals on the same schedule, along with Gogrol, and that left me with Coretti. He was pretty cool, and I had pride enough left not to make any unwanted advances.

Gogrol was worse; I saw him seldom enough, but he never addressed a word to me except on routine. Yet there was something familiar about him—As for Claire Avery, I simply wasn't in her scheme of things at all; she even relieved me in silence.

Offhand, I'd have said it was the wildest sort of stupidity to send a girl with four men on a trip like this. Well, I had to hand it to Claire Avery; in that way she was a splendid rocketrix. She took the inconveniences of space routine without a murmur, and she was so companionable—that is, with the others—that it was like having a young and unusually entertaining man aboard.

And, after all, Gogrol was twice her age and Henshaw almost three times; Coretti was younger, but I was the only one who was really of her generation. But as I say, she hated me; Coretti seemed to stand best with her.

So the weary weeks of the journey dragged along. The Sun shrunk up to a disk only a fifth the diameter of the terrestrial Sun, but Jupiter grew to an enormous moon-like orb with its bands and spots gloriously tinted. It was an exquisite sight, and sometimes, since eight hours' sleep is more than I can use, I used to slip into the control room while Claire Avery was on duty, just to watch the giant planet and its moons. The girl and I never said a word to each other.

We weren't to stop at Io, but were landing directly on Europa, our destination, the third moon outward from the vast molten globe of Jupiter. In some ways Europa is the queerest little sphere in the Solar System, and for many years it was believed to be quite uninhabitable. It is, too, as far as seventy per cent of its surface goes, but the remaining area is a wild and weird region.

This is the mountainous hollow in the face toward Jupiter, for Europa, like the Moon, keeps one face always toward its primary. Here in this vast depression, all of the tiny world's scanty atmosphere is collected, gathered like little lakes and puddles into the valleys between mountain ranges that often pierce through the low-lying air into the emptiness of space.

Often enough a single valley forms a microcosm sundered by nothingness from the rest of the planet, generating its own little rainstorms under pygmy cloud banks, inhabited by its indigenous life, untouched by, and unaware of, all else.

In the ephemeris, Europa is dismissed prosaically with a string of figures: diameter, 2099 M.—period, 3 days, 13 hours, 14 seconds—distance from primary, 425,160 M. For an astronomical ephemeris isn't concerned with the thin film of life that occasionally blurs a planet's surface; it has nothing to say of the slow libration of Europa that sends intermittent tides of air washing against the mountain slopes under the tidal drag of Jupiter, nor of the waves that sometimes spill air from valley to valley, and sometimes spill alien life as well.

Least of all is the ephemeris concerned with the queer forms that crawl now and then right up out of the air pools, to lie on the vacuum-bathed peaks exactly as strange fishes flopped their way out of the Earthly seas to bask on the sands at the close of the Devonian age.

*   *   *   *   *

Of the five of us, I was the only one who had ever visited Europa—or so I thought at the time. Indeed, there were few men in the world who had actually set foot on the inhospitable little planet; Gunderson and his men were dead, save me and perhaps Kratska, and we had been the first organized expedition.

Only a few stray adventurers from Io had preceded us. So it was to me that Captain Henshaw directed his orders when he said, "Take us as close as possible to Gunderson's landing."

It began to be evident that we'd make ground toward the end of Claire's long shift, so I crawled out of the coffinlike niche I called my cabin an hour early, and went up to the control room to guide her down. We were seventy or eighty miles up, but there were no clouds or air distortion here, and the valleys crisscrossed under us like a relief map.

It was infernally hard to pick Gunderson's valley; the burned spot from the blast was long since grown over, and I had only memory to rely on, for, of course, all charts were lost with the Hera. But I knew the general region, and it really made less difference than it might have, for practically all the valleys in that vicinity were connected by passes; one could walk between them in breathable air.

After a while I picked one of a series of narrow parallel valleys, one with what I knew was a salt pool in the center—though most of them had that; they'd be desert without it—and pointed it out to Claire. "That one," I said, adding maliciously, "and I'd better warn you that it's narrow and deep—a ticklish landing place."

She flashed me an unfriendly glance from sapphire eyes, but said nothing. But a voice behind me sounded unexpectedly: "To the left! The one to the left. It—it looks easier."

Gogrol! I was startled for a moment, then turned coldly on him. "Keep out of the control room during landings," I snapped.

He glared, muttered something, and retired. But he left me a trifle worried; not that his valley to the left was any easier to land in—that was pure bunk—but it looked a little familiar! Actually, I wasn't sure but that Gogrol had pointed out Gunderson's valley.

But I stuck to my first guess. The irritation I felt I took out on Claire. "Take it slow!" I said gruffly. "This isn't a landing field. Nobody's put up leveling poles in these valleys. You're going to have to land completely blind from about four hundred feet, because the blast begins to splash sooner in this thin air. You go down by level and guess, and Heaven help us if you roll her! There's no room for rolling between those cliffs."

She bit her lip nervously. The Minos was already rolling under the girl's inexpert hand, though that wasn't dangerous while we still had ten or twelve miles of altitude. But the ground was coming up steadily.

I was in a cruel mood. I watched the strain grow in her lovely features, and if I felt any pity, I lost it when I thought of the way she had treated me. So I taunted her.

"This shouldn't be a hard landing for the Golden Flash. Or maybe you'd rather be landing at full speed, so you could fall into a braking ellipse—only that wouldn't work here, because the air doesn't stick up high enough to act as a brake."

And a few minutes later, when her lips were quivering with tension, I said, "It takes more than publicity and gambler's luck to make a pilot, doesn't it?"

She broke. She screamed suddenly, "Oh, take it! Take it, then!" and slammed the U-bar into my hands. Then she huddled back in her corner sobbing, with her golden hair streaming over her face.

I took over; I had no choice. I pulled the Minos out of the roll Claire's gesture had put her in, and then started teetering down on the underjets. It was pitifully easy because of Europa's low gravitation and the resulting low falling acceleration; it gave the pilot so much time to compensate for side sway.

I began to realize how miserably little the Golden Flash really knew about rocketry, and, despite myself, I felt a surge of pity for her. But why pity her? Everyone knew that Claire Avery was simply a wealthy, thrill-intoxicated daredevil, with more than her share of money, of beauty, of adulation. The despised Jack Sands pitying her? That's a laugh!

The underblast hit and splashed, turning the brown-clad valley into black ashes and flame. I inched down very slowly now, for there was nothing to see below save the fiery sheet of the blast, and I watched the bubble on the level as if my life depended on it—which it did.

I knew the splash began at about four hundred feet in this density of air, but from then on it was guesswork, and a question of settling down so slowly that when we hit we wouldn't damage the underjets. And if I do say it, we grounded so gently that I don't think Claire Avery knew it until I cut off the blast.

She rubbed the tears away with her sleeve and glared blue-eyed defiance at me, but before she could speak, Henshaw opened the door. "Nice landing, Miss Avery," he said.

"Wasn't it?" I echoed, with a grin at the girl.

She stood up. She was trembling and I think that under Earthly gravitation she would have fallen back into the pilot's seat, for I saw her knees shaking below her trim, black shorts.

"I didn't land us," she said grimly. "Mr. Sands put us to ground."

Somehow my pity got the best of me then. "Sure," I said. "It's into my shift. Look." It was; the chronometer showed three minutes in. "Miss Avery had all the hard part—"

But she was gone. And try as I would, I could not bring myself to see her as the hard, brilliant thrill-seeker which the papers and broadcasts portrayed her. Instead, she left me with a strange and by no means logical impression of—wistfulness.

*   *   *   *   *

Life on Europa began uneventfully. Little by little we reduced the atmospheric pressure in the Minos to conform to that outside. First Coretti and then Claire Avery had a spell of altitude sickness, but by the end of twenty hours we were all acclimated enough to be comfortable outside.

Henshaw and I were first to venture into the open. I scanned the valley carefully for familiar landmarks, but it was hard to be sure; all these canyonlike ditches were much alike. I know that a copse of song-bushes had grown high on the cliff when the Hera had landed, but our blast had splashed higher, and if the bushes had been there, they were only a patch of ashes now.

At the far end of the valley there should have been a cleft in the hills, a pass leading to the right into the next valley. That wasn't there; all I could distinguish was a narrow ravine cutting the hills to the left.

"I'm afraid I've missed Gunderson's valley," I told Henshaw. "I think it's the next one to our left; it's connected to this one by a pass, if I'm right, and this is one I came in several times to hunt." It recurred to me suddenly that Gogrol had said the left one.

"You say there's a pass?" mused Henshaw. "Then we'll stay here rather than chance another take-off and another landing. We can work in Gunderson's valley through the pass. You're sure it's low enough so we won't have to use oxygen helmets?"

"If it's the right pass, I am. But work at what in Gunderson's valley? I thought this was an exploring expedition."

Henshaw gave me a queer, sharp look, and turned away. Right then I saw Gogrol standing in the port of the Minos, and I didn't know whether Henshaw's reticence was due to his presence or mine. I moved a step to follow him, but at that moment the outer door of the air lock opened and Claire Avery came out.

It was the first time I had seen her in a fair light since the take-off at Young's Field, and I had rather forgotten the loveliness of her coloring. Of course, her skin had paled from the weeks in semidarkness, but her cadmium-yellow hair and sapphire-blue eyes were really startling, especially when she moved into the sun shadow of the cliff and stood bathed only in the golden Jupiter light.

Like Henshaw and myself, she had slipped on the all-enveloping ski suit one wore on chilly little Europa. The small world received only a fourth as much heat as steamy Io, and would not have been habitable at all, except for the fact that it kept its face always toward its primary, and therefore received heat intermittently from the Sun, but eternally from Jupiter.

The girl cast an eager look over the valley; I knew this was her first experience on an uninhabited world, and there is always a sense of strangeness and the fascination of the unknown in one's first step on an alien planet.

She looked at Henshaw, who was methodically examining the scorched soil on which the Minos rested, and then her glance crossed mine. There was an electric moment of tension, but then the anger in her blue eyes—if it had been anger—died away, and she strode deliberately to my side.

She faced me squarely. "Jack Sands," she said with an undertone of defiance, "I owe you an apology. Don't think I'm apologizing for my opinion of you, but only for the way I've been acting toward you. In a small company like this there isn't room for enmity, and as far as I'm concerned, your past is yours from now on. What's more, I want to thank you for helping me during the take-off, and"—her defiance was cracking a bit—"d-during the—the landing."

I stared at her. That apology must have cost her an effort, for the Golden Flash was a proud young lady, and I saw her wink back her tears. I choked back the vicious reply I had been about to make, and said only, "O.K. You keep your opinion of me to yourself and I'll do the same with my opinion of you."

She flushed, then smiled. "I guess I'm a rotten pilot," she admitted ruefully. "I hate take-offs and landings. To tell the truth, I'm simply scared of the Minos. Up to the time we left Young's Field, I'd never handled anything larger than my little racing rocket, the Golden Flash."

I gasped. That wouldn't have been credible if I hadn't seen with my own eyes how utterly unpracticed she was. "But why?" I asked in perplexity. "If you hate piloting so, why do it? Just for publicity? With your money you don't have to, you know."

"Oh, my money!" she echoed irritably. She stared away over the narrow valley, and started suddenly. "Look!" she cried. "There's something moving on the peaks—like a big ball. And way up where there's no air at all!"

I glanced over. "It's just a bladder bird," I said indifferently. I'd seen plenty of them; they were the commonest mobile form of life on Europa. But of course Claire hadn't, and she was eagerly curious.

I explained. I threw stones into a tinkling grove of song-bushes until I flushed up another, and it went gliding over our heads with its membrane stretched taut.

I told her that the three-foot creature that had sailed like a flying squirrel was the same sort as the giant ball she had glimpsed among the airless peaks, only the one on the peaks had inflated its bladder. The creatures were able to cross from valley to valley by carrying their air with them in their big, balloonlike bladders. And, of course, bladder birds weren't really birds at all; they didn't fly, but glided like the lemurs and flying squirrels of Earth, and naturally, couldn't even do that when they were up on the airless heights.

Claire was so eager and interested and wide-eyed that I quite forgot my grudge. I started to show her my knowledge of things Europan; I led her close to the copse of song-bushes so that she could listen to the sweet and plaintive melody of their breathing leaves, and I took her down to the salt pool in the center of the valley to find some of the primitive creatures which Gunderson's men had called "nutsies," because they looked very much like walnuts with the hulls on. But within was a small mouthful of delicious meat, neither animal nor vegetable, which was quite safe to eat raw, since bacterial life did not exist on Europa.

I guess I was pretty exuberant, for after all, this was the first chance at companionship I'd had for many weeks. We wandered down the valley and I talked, talked about anything. I told her of the various forms life assumed on the planets, how on Mars and Titan and Europa sex was unknown, though Venus and Earth and Io all possessed it; and how on Mars and Europa vegetable and animal life had never differentiated, so that even the vastly intelligent beaked Martians had a tinge of vegetable nature, while conversely the song-bushes on the hills of Europa had a vaguely animal content. And meanwhile we wandered aimlessly along until we stood below the narrow pass or ravine that led presumably into Gunderson's valley to our left.

Far up the slope a movement caught my eye. A bladder bird, I thought idly, though it was a low altitude for one to inflate; they usually expanded their bladders just below the point where breathing became impossible. Then I saw that it wasn't a bladder bird; it was a man. In fact, it was Gogrol.

He was emerging from the pass, and his collar was turned up about his throat against the cold of the altitude. He hadn't seen us, apparently, as he angled down what mountaineers call a col, a ledge or neck of rock that slanted from the mouth of the ravine along the hillside toward the Minos. But Claire, following the direction of my gaze, saw him in the moment before brush hid him from view.

"Gogrol!" she exclaimed. "He must have been in the next valley. Stefan will want—" She caught herself sharply.

"Why," I asked grimly, "should your friend Coretti be interested in Gogrol's actions? After all, Gogrol's supposed to be a biologist, isn't he? Why shouldn't he take a look in the next valley?"

Her lips tightened. "Why shouldn't he?" she echoed. "I didn't say he shouldn't. I didn't say anything like that."

And thenceforward she maintained a stubborn silence. Indeed, something of the old enmity and coolness seemed to have settled between us as we walked back through the valley toward the Minos.

. . . . .

That night Henshaw rearranged our schedule to a more convenient plan than the requirements of space. We divided our time into days and nights, or rather into sleeping and waking periods, for, of course, there is no true night on Europa. The shifts of light are almost as puzzling as those on its neighbor Io, but not quite, because Io has its own rotation to complicate matters.

On Europa, the nearest approach to true night is during the eclipse that occurs every three days or so, when the landscape is illuminated only by the golden twilight of Jupiter, or at the most, only by Jupiter and Io light. So we set our own night time by arbitrary Earth reckoning, so that we might all work and sleep during the same periods.

There was no need for any sort of watch to be kept; no one had ever reported life dangerous to man on little Europa. The only danger came from the meteors that swarm about the giant Jupiter's orbit, and sometimes came crashing down through the shallow air of his satellites; we couldn't dodge them here as we could in space. But that was a danger against which a guard was unavailing.

It was the next morning that I cornered Henshaw and forced him to listen to my questions.

"Listen to me, Harris," I said determinedly. "What is there about this expedition that everybody knows but me? If this is an exploring party, I'm the Ameer of Yarkand. Now I want to know what it's all about."

Henshaw looked miserably embarrassed. He kept his eyes away from mine, and muttered unhappily, "I can't tell you, Jack. I'm damned sorry, but I can't tell you."

"Why not?"

He hesitated. "Because I'm under orders not to, Jack."

"Whose orders?"

Henshaw shook his head. "Damn it!" he said vehemently. "I trust you. If it were my choice, you'd be the one I'd pick for honesty. But it isn't my choice." He paused. "Do you understand that? All right"—he stiffened into his captain's manner—"no more questions, then. I'll ask the questions and give the orders."

Well, put on that basis, I couldn't argue. I'm a pilot, first, last, and always, and I don't disobey my superior's orders even when he happens to be as close a friend as Henshaw. But I began to kick myself for not seeing something queer in the business as soon as Henshaw offered me the job.

If Interplanetary was looking for favorable publicity, they wouldn't get it by signing me on. Moreover, the government wasn't in the habit of reissuing a revoked pilot's license without good and sufficient reason, and I knew I hadn't supplied any such reason by loafing around brooding over my troubles. That alone should have tipped me off that something was screwy.

And there were plenty of hints during the voyage itself. True, Gogrol seemed to talk the language of biology, but I'll be dogged if Coretti talked like a chemist. And there was that haunting sense of familiarity about Gogrol, too. And to cap the climax was the incongruity of calling this jaunt an exploring expedition; for all the exploring we were doing we might as well have landed on Staten Island or Buffalo. Better, as far as I was concerned, because I'd seen Europa but had never been to Buffalo.

Well, there was nothing to be done about it now. I suppressed my disgust and tried as hard as I could to cooperate with the others in whatever project we were supposed to be pursuing. That was rather difficult, too, because suspicious-appearing incidents kept cropping up to make me feel like a stranger or an outcast.

There was, for instance, the time Henshaw decided that a change in diet would be welcome. The native life of Europa was perfectly edible, though not all as tasty as the tiny shell creatures of the salt pools. However, I knew of one variety that had served the men of the Hera, a plantlike growth consisting of a single fleshy hand-sized member, that we had called liver-leaf because of its taste.

The captain detailed Coretti and myself to gather a supply of this delicacy, and I found a specimen, showed it to him, and then set off dutifully along the north—that is, the left—wall of the valley.

Coretti appeared to take the opposite side, but I had not gone far before I glimpsed him skirting my edge of the salt pool. That meant nothing; he was free to search anywhere for liver-leaf, but it was soon evident to me that he was not searching. He was following me; he was shadowing my movements.

I was thoroughly irritated, but determined not to show it. I plodded methodically along, gathering the fat leaves in my basket, until I reached the valley's far end and the slopes back and succeeded in running square into Coretti before he could maneuver himself out of a copse of song-bushes.

He grinned at me. "Any luck?" he asked.

"More than you, it seems," I retorted, with a contemptuous look at his all but empty basket.

"I had no luck at all. I thought maybe in the next valley, through the pass there, we might find some."

"I've found my share," I grunted.

I thought I noticed a flicker of surprise in his black eyes. "You're not going over?" he asked sharply. "You're going back?"

"You guessed it," I said sharply. "My basket's full and I'm going back."

I knew that he watched me most of the way back, because halfway to the Minos I turned around, and I could see him standing there on the slope below the pass.

Along toward what we called evening the Sun went into our first eclipse. The landscape was bathed in the aureate light of Jupiter alone, and I realized that I'd forgotten how beautiful that golden twilight could be.

I was feeling particularly lonesome, too; so I wandered out to stare at the glowing peaks against the black sky, and the immense, bulging sphere of Jupiter with Ganymede swinging like a luminous pearl close beside it. The scene was so lovely that I forgot my loneliness, until I was suddenly reminded of it.

A glint of more brilliant gold caught my eye, up near the grove of song-bushes. It was Claire's head; she was standing there watching the display, and beside her was Coretti. While I looked, he suddenly turned and drew her into his arms; she put her hands against his chest, but she wasn't struggling; she was perfectly passive and content. It was none of my business, of course, but—well, if I'd disliked Coretti before, I hated him now, because I was lonely again.

*   *   *   *   *

I think it was the next day that things came to a head, and trouble really began. Henshaw had been pleased with our meal of indigenous life, and decided to try it again. This time Claire was assigned to accompany me, and we set off in silence. A sort of echo of the coolness that had attended our last parting survived, and besides, what I had seen last night in the eclipse light seemed to make a difference to me. So I simply stalked along at her side, wondering what to choose for the day's menu.

We didn't want liver-leaves again. The little nutsies from the salt pool were all right, but it was a half-day's job to gather enough, and besides, they were almost too salty to be pleasant fare for a whole meal. Bladder birds were hopeless; they consisted of practically nothing except thin skin stretched over a framework of bones. I remembered that once we had tried a brown, fungoid lump that grew in the shade under the song-bushes; some of Gunderson's men had liked it.

Claire finally broke the silence. "If I'm going to help you look," she suggested, "I ought to know what we're looking for."

I described the lumpy growths. "I'm not so sure all of us will like them. Near as I can remember, they tasted something like truffles, with a faint flavor of meat added. We tried them both raw and cooked, and cooked was best."

"I like truffles," said the girl. "They're—"

A shot! There was no mistaking the sharp crack of a .38, though it sounded queerly thin in the rare atmosphere. But it sounded again, and a third time, and then a regular fusillade!

"Keep back of me!" I snapped as we turned and raced for the Minos. The warning was needless; Claire was unaccustomed to the difficulties of running on a small planet. Her weight on Europa must have been no more than twelve or fifteen pounds, one eighth Earth normal, and though she had learned to walk easily enough—one learned that on any space journey—she had had no opportunity to learn to run. Her first step sent her half a dozen feet in the air; I sped away from her with the long, sliding stride one had to use on such planets as Europa.

I burst out of the brush into the area cleared by the blast, where already growth had begun. For a moment I saw only the Minos resting peacefully in the clearing, then I reeled with shock. At the air lock lay a man—Henshaw—with his face a bloody pulp, his head split by two bullets.

There was a burst of sound, voices, another shot. Out of the open air lock reeled Coretti; he staggered backward for ten steps, then dropped on his side, while blood welled up out of the collar of his suit. And standing grimly in the opening, an automatic smoking in his right hand, a charged flame-pistol in his left, was Gogrol!

I had no weapon; why should one carry arms on airless Europa? For an instant I stood frozen, appalled, uncomprehending, and in that moment Gogrol glimpsed me. I saw his hand tighten on his automatic, then he shrugged and strode toward me.

"Well," he said with a snarl in his voice, "I had to do it. They went crazy. Anerosis. It struck both of them at once, and they went clean mad. Self-defense, it was."

I didn't believe him, of course. People don't get anerosis in air no rarer than Europa's; one could live his whole life out there without ever suffering from air starvation. But I couldn't argue those points with a panting murderer armed with the most deadly weapon ever devised, and with a girl coming up behind me. So I said nothing at all.

Claire came up; I heard her shocked intake of breath, and her almost inaudible wail, "Stefan!" Then she saw Gogrol holding his guns, and she flared out, "So you did it! I knew they suspected you! But you'll never get away with it, you—"

She broke off under the sudden menace of Gogrol's eyes, and I stepped in front of her as he raised the automatic. For an instant death looked squarely at both of us, then the man shrugged and the evil light in his eyes dimmed.

"A while yet," he muttered. "If Coretti dies—" He backed to the air lock and pulled a helmet from within the Minos, an air helmet that we had thought might serve should we ever need to cross the heights about a blind valley.

Then Gogrol advanced toward us, and I felt Claire quiver against my shoulder. But the man only glared at us and spat out a single word. "Back!" he rasped. "Back!"

We backed. Under the menace of that deadly flame-pistol he herded us along the narrow valley, eastward to the slope whence angled the ravine that led toward Gunderson's valley. And up the slope, into the dim shadows of the pass itself, so narrow in places that my outstretched hands could have spanned the gap between the walls. A grim, dark, echo-haunted, and forbidding place; I did not wonder that the girl shrank against me. The air was thin to the point of insufficiency, and all three of us were gasping for breath.

There was nothing I could do, for Gogrol's weapons bore too steadily on Claire Avery. So I slipped my arm about her to hearten her and inched warily along that shadowy canyon, until at last it widened, and a thousand feet below stretched a valley—Gunderson's valley, I knew at once. Far away was the slope where the *Hera* had rested, and down in the lower end was the heart-shaped pool of brine.

Gogrol had slipped on the helmet, leaving the visor open, and his flat features peered out at us like a gargoyle's. On he drove us, and down into the valley. But as he passed the mouth of the ravine, which by now was no more than a narrow gorge between colossal escarpments that loomed heavenward like the battlements of Atlantis, he stooped momentarily into the shadows, and when he rose again I fancied that a small sound like the singing of a teakettle followed us down the slope. It meant nothing to me then.

He waved the automatic. "Faster!" he ordered threateningly. We were down in the talus now, and we scrambled doggedly among the rocks and fallen debris. On he drove us, until we stumbled among the boulders around the central pond. Then, suddenly, he halted.

"If you follow," he said with a cold intensity, "I shoot!" He strode away not toward the pass, but toward the ridge itself, back along the slopes that lay nearest the *Minos*, hidden from view in the other valley. Of course, Gogrol could cross those airless heights, secure in this helmet, carrying his air supply like the bladder birds.

He seemed to seek the shelter of an ascending ridge. As the jutting rock concealed him, I leaped to a boulder.

"Come on!" I said. "Perhaps we can beat him through the pass to the ship!"

"No!" screamed Claire, so frantically that I halted. "My Lord, no! Didn't you see the blaster he left?"

The singing teakettle noise! I had barely time to throw myself beside the girl crouching behind a rock when the little atomic bomb let go.

I suppose everybody has seen, either by eye or television, the effect of atomic explosions. All of us, by one means or the other, have watched old buildings demolished, road grades or canals blasted, and those over forty may even remember the havoc-spreading bombs of the Pacific War. But none of you could have seen anything like this, for this explosion had a low air pressure and a gravitation only one-eighth normal as the sole checks to its fury.

It seemed to me that the whole mountain lifted. Vast masses of crumbling rock hurtled toward the black sky. Bits of stone, whistling like bullets and incandescent like meteors, shot past us, and the very ground we clung to heaved like the deck of a rolling rocket.

When the wild turmoil had subsided, when the debris no longer sang about us, when the upheaved masses had either fallen again or had spun beyond Europa's gravitation to crash on indifferent Jupiter, the pass had vanished. Mountain and vacuum hemmed us into a prison.

Both of us were slightly stunned by the concussion, although the thin atmosphere transmitted a strangely high-pitched sound instead of the resounding b-o-o-m one would have heard on the Earth. When my head stopped ringing, I looked around for Gogrol, and saw him at last seven or eight hundred feet up the slope of the mountain. Anger surged in me; I seized a stone from the margin of the pool, and flung it viciously at him. One can throw amazing distances on small worlds like Europa; I watched the missile raise dust at his very feet.

He turned; very deliberately he raised the automatic, and stone splinters from the boulder beside me stung my face. I dragged Claire down behind the shelter, knowing beyond doubt that he had meant that bullet to kill. In silence we watched him climb until he was but a tiny black speck, nearing the crest.

He approached a bladder bird crawling its slow way along the airless heights. Up there the creatures were slow as snails, for their flight membranes were useless in the near vacuum. But they had normally no enemies on the peaks.

I saw Gogrol change his course purposely to intercept the thing. Intentionally, maliciously, he kicked a hole in the inflated bladder, collapsing it like a child's balloon. He stood watching while the miserable creature flopped in the agonies of suffocation, then moved methodically on. It was the coldest exhibition of wanton cruelty I had ever witnessed.

Claire shuddered; still in silence we watched the man's leisurely progress along the ridge. There was something in his attitude that suggested searching, seeking, hunting. Suddenly he quickened his pace and then halted abruptly, stooping over what looked to me like a waist-high heap of stones, or perhaps merely a hummock on the ridge.

But he was burrowing in it, digging, flinging stones and dirt aside. And at last he stood up; if he held anything, distance hid it, but he seemed to wave some small object at us in derisive triumph. Then he moved over the crest of the hills and disappeared.

Claire sighed despondently; she seemed very little like the proud and rather arrogant Golden Flash. "That settles it," she murmured disconsolately. "He's got it, and he's got us trapped; so we're quite helpless."

"Got what?" I asked. "What was he digging for up there?"

Her blue eyes widened in amazement. "Don't you know?"

"I certainly don't. I seem to know less about this damn trip than anybody else on it."

She gazed steadily at me. "I knew Stefan was wrong," she said softly. "I don't care what you were when you wrecked the Hera, Jack Sands; on this trip you've been decent and brave and a gentleman."

"Thanks," I said dryly, but I was a little touched for all that because, after all, the Golden Flash was a very beautiful girl. "Then suppose you let me in on a few of the secrets. For instance, what was Coretti wrong about? And what did Gogrol dig for?"

"Gogrol," she said, watching me, "was digging in Gunderson's cairn."

I looked blank. "Gunderson's what? This is news to me."

She was silent for a moment. "Jack Sands," she said at last, "I don't care what Stefan or the government or anybody thinks of you. I think you're honest, and I think you've had an injustice done you somehow, and I don't believe you were to blame in the Hera crash. And I'm going to tell you all I know about this matter. But first, do you know the object of Gunderson's expedition to Europa?"

"I never knew it. I'm a pilot; I took no interest in their scientific gibberish."

She nodded. "Well, you know how a rocket motor works, of course. How they use a minute amount of uranium or radium as catalyst to release the energy in the fuel. Uranium has low activity; it will set off only metals like the alkalis, and ships using uranium motors burn salt. And radium, being more active, will set off the metals from iron to copper; so ships using a radium initiator usually burn one of the commoner iron or copper ores."

"I know all that," I grunted. "And the heavier the metal, the greater the power from its disintegration."

"Exactly." She paused a moment. "Well, Gunderson wanted to use still heavier elements. That required a source of rays more penetrating than those from radium, and he knew of only one available source—Element 91, protactinium. And it happens that the richest deposits of protactinium so far discovered are those in the rocks of Europa; so to Europa he came for his experiments."

"Well?" I asked. "Where do I fit in this mess?"

"I don't quite know, Jack. Let me finish what I know, which is all Stefan would tell me. Gunderson succeeded, they think; he's supposed to have worked out the formula by which protactinium could be made to set off lead, which would give much more power than any present type of initiator. But if he did succeed, his formula and notes were destroyed when the Hera crashed!"

I began to see. "But what—what about that cairn?"

"You really don't know?"

"I'll be double damned if I do! If Gunderson built a cairn, it must have been that last day. I had the take-off, so I slept through most of it. But—why, they did have some sort of ceremony!"

"Yes. Gunderson mentioned something about it when your ship touched at Junopolis on Io. What the government hopes is that he buried a copy of his formula in that cairn. They do, you know. Well, nobody could possibly know of the location except you and a man named Kratska, who had disappeared.

"So Interplanetary, which is in bad anyway because of some stock transactions, was ordered to back this expedition with you as pilot—or at least, that's what Stefan told me. I guess I was taken along just to give the corporation a little more publicity, and, of course, Stefan was sent to watch you, in hopes you'd give away the location. The formula's immensely valuable, you see."

"Yeah, I see. And how about Gogrol?"

She frowned. "I don't know. Stefan hinted that he had some connections with Harrick of Interplanetary, or perhaps some hold over him. Harrick insisted on his being a member."

"The devil!" I exploded suddenly. "He knew about the cairn! He knew where to look!"

Her eyes grew wide. "Why, he did! He's—could he be the representative of some foreign government? If we could stop him! But he's left us absolutely helpless here. Why didn't he kill us?"

"I can guess that," I said grimly. "He can't fly the Minos alone. Henshaw's dead, and if Coretti dies—well, one of us is due for the job of pilot."

A tremor shook her. "I'd rather be dead, too," she murmured, "than to travel with him alone."

"And I'd rather see you so," I agreed glumly. "I wish to heaven you had stayed out of this. You could be home enjoying your money."

"My money!" she flashed. "I haven't any money. Do you think I take these chances for publicity or thrills or admiration?"

I gaped; of course, I'd thought exactly that.

She was literally blazing. "Listen to me, Jack Sands. There's just one reason for the fool things I do—money! There isn't any Avery fortune, and hasn't been since my father died. I've needed money desperately these last two years, to keep the Connecticut place for my mother, because she'd die if she had to leave it. It's been our family home for two hundred years, since 1910, and I won't be the one to lose it!"

It took a moment to adjust myself to what she was saying. "But a racing rocket isn't a poor man's toy," I said feebly. "And surely a girl like you could find—"

"A girl like me!" she cut in bitterly. "Oh, I know I have a good figure and a passable voice, and perhaps I could have found work in a television chorus, but I needed real money. I had my choice of two ways to get it: I could marry it, or I could gamble my neck against it. You see which way I chose. As the Golden Flash, I can get big prices for endorsing breakfast foods and beauty preparations. That's why I gambled in that race; my racing rocket was all I had left to gamble with. And it worked, only"—her voice broke a little—"I wish I could stop gambling. I— I hate it!"

It wasn't only pity I felt for her then. Her confession of poverty had changed things; she was no longer the wealthy, unattainable being I had always imagined the Golden Flash to be. She was simply a forlorn and unhappy girl; one who needed to be loved and comforted. And then I remembered the evening of the eclipse, and Coretti's arms about her. So I gazed for an instant at the sunlight on her hair, and then turned slowly away.

After a while we gathered some liver-leaves and cooked them, and I tried to tell Claire that we were certain to be rescued. Neither of us believed it; we knew very well that Gogrol would carry no living companion to Io; whoever helped him run the Minos would certainly be dead and cast into space before landing. And we knew that Gogrol's story, whatever it might be, would not be one likely to encourage a rescue party. He'd simply report us all dead somehow or other.

"I don't care," said Claire. "I'm glad I'm with you."

I thought of Coretti and said nothing. We were just sitting in glum silence near the fire when Gogrol came over the hills again.

Claire saw him first and cried out. Despite his helmet, neither of us could mistake his broad, squat figure. But there was nothing we could do except wait, though we did draw closer to the area of wild and tumbled boulders about the central pool.

"What do you suppose—" asked Claire nervously. "Coretti may have died, or may be too injured to help." Pain twisted her features. "Yes, or—Oh, I know, Jack! It's that Gogrol can't plot a course. He can pilot; he can follow a course already laid out, but he can't plot one—and neither can Stefan!"

Instantly I knew she must be right. Piloting a ship is just a question of following directions, but plotting a course involves the calculus of function, and that, let me tell you, takes a mathematician. I could do it, and Claire handled a simple route well enough—one had to in rocket racing—but astrogators were not common even among pilots.

You see, the difficulty is that you don't just point the ship at your destination, because that destination is moving; you head for where the planet will be when you arrive. And in this case, assuming Gogrol meant to make for Io, a journey from Europa to that world meant speeding in the direction of the colossal mass of Jupiter, and if a rocket once passed the critical velocity in that direction—good night!

A hundred feet away Gogrol halted. "Listen, you two," he yelled, "I'm offering Miss Avery the chance to join the crew of the Minos."

"You're the crew," I retorted. "She's not taking your offer."

Without warning he leveled his revolver and fired, and a shock numbed my left leg. I fell within the shelter of a boulder, thrusting Claire before me, while Gogrol's bellow followed the crash of his shot: "I'll shut your mouth for you!"

There began the weirdest game of hide and seek I've ever played, with Claire and me crawling among the tumbled boulders, scarcely daring to breathe. Gogrol had all the advantage, and he used it. I couldn't stand upright, and my legs began to hurt so excruciatingly that I was afraid each minute of an involuntary groan forcing its way through my lips. Claire suffered with me; her eyes were agonized blue pools of torment, but she dared not even whisper to me.

Gogrol took to leaping atop the boulders. He glimpsed me, and a second bullet struck that same burning leg. He was deliberately hunting me down, and I saw it was the end.

We had a momentary shelter. Claire whispered to me, "I'm going to him. He'll kill you otherwise, and take me anyway."

"No!" I croaked. "No!"

Gogrol heard, and was coming. Claire said hastily. "He's—bestial. At least I can plot a course that will—kill us!" Then she called, "Gogrol! I'll surrender."

I snatched at her ankle—too late. I went crawling after her as she strode into the open, but her steps were too rapid. I heard her say, "I give up, if you won't—shoot him again."

Gogrol mumbled, and then Claire's voice again, "Yes, I'll plot your course, but how can I cross the peaks?"

"Walk," he said, and laughed.

"I can't breathe up there."

"Walk as far as you can. You won't die while I take you the rest of the way."

There was no reply. When I finally crept into the open, they were a hundred feet up the slope.

Helpless, raging, pain-maddened, I seized a stone and flung it. It struck Gogrol in the back, but it struck with no more force than if I'd tossed it a dozen feet on Earth. He spun in fury, thrust the screaming Claire aside, and sent another bullet at me. Missed me, I thought, though I wasn't sure, for pain had numbed me. I couldn't be sure of anything.

Claire saw that I still retained some semblance of consciousness. "Goodbye!" she called, and added something that I could not hear because of the red waves of pain, but I knew Gogrol laughed at it. Thereafter, for what seemed like a long time, I knew only that I was crawling doggedly through an inferno of torture.

When the red mist lifted, I was only at the base of the rise. Far above I could see the figures of Claire and Gogrol, and I perceived that though he strode with easy steps, protected by his helmet, the girl was already staggering from breathlessness. While I watched, she stumbled, and then began to struggle frantically and spasmodically to jerk away from him. It wasn't that she meant to break her promise, but merely that the agonies of suffocation drove her to attempt any means of regaining breathable air.

But the struggle was brief. It was less than a minute before she fainted, passed out from air starvation, and Gogrol slung her carelessly under one arm—as I said, she weighed about twelve pounds on Europa—and pressed on. At the very crest he paused and looked back, and in that thin, clear air I could see every detail with telescopic distinctness, even to the shadow he cast across Claire's drooping golden head.

He raised the revolver to his temple, waved it at me with a derisive gesture, and then flung it far down the mountainside toward me. His meaning was unmistakable; he was advising me to commit suicide. When I reached the revolver, there was a single unused catridge in the clip; I looked up, tempted to try it on Gogrol himself, but he was gone across the ridge.

Now I knew all hope was gone. Perhaps I was dying from that last bullet anyway, but whether I were or not, Claire was lost, and all that remained for me was the madness of solitude, forever imprisoned by empty space in this valley. That or—suicide.

I don't know how many times I thought of that single cartridge, but I know the thought grew very tempting after a few more hours of pain. By that time, for all I knew, the Minos might have taken off on its dash to death, for the roar of its blast could not carry over the airless heights, and it would be so high and small by the time I could see it above the hills that I might have missed it.

If only I could cross those hills! I began to realize that more important than my own life was Claire's safety, even if it meant saving her for Coretti. But I couldn't save her; I couldn't even get to her unless I could walk along the hills like a bladder bird.

Like a bladder bird! I was sure that it was only the delirium of fever that suggested that wild thought. Would it work? I answered myself that whether it worked or failed it was better than dying here without ever trying.

I stalked that bladder bird like a cat. Time after time I spent long minutes creeping toward a copse of song-bushes only to have the creature sail blithely over my head and across the valley. But at last I saw the thing crouched for flight above me; I dared not delay longer lest my wounds weaken me too much for the trial of my plan, and I fired. There went my single cartridge.

The bladder bird dropped! But that was only the beginning of my task. Carefully—so very carefully—I removed the creature's bladder, leaving the vent tube intact. Then, through the opening that connects to the bird's single lung, I slipped my head, letting the bloody rim contract about my throat.

I knew that wouldn't be air-tight, so I bound it with strips torn from my clothing, so closely that it all but choked me. Then I took the slimy vent tube in my mouth and began an endless routine. Breathe in through the vent tube, pinch it shut, breathe out into the bladder—over and over and over. But gradually the bladder expanded with filthy, vitiated, stinking, and once-breathed air.

I had it half filled when I saw that I was going to have to start if I were to have a chance of living long enough for a test. Breathing through the vent tube as long as there was air enough, peering dully through the semitransparent walls of the bladder, I started crawling up the hill.

I won't describe that incredible journey. On Earth it would have been utterly impossible; here, since I weighed but eighteen pounds, it was barely within the bounds of possibility. As I ascended, the bladder swelled against the reduced pressure; by the time I had to start breathing the fearful stuff, I could feel it escaping and bubbling through the blood around my neck.

Somehow I made the crest, almost directly above the Minos. It was still there, anyway. Gogrol hadn't come this way, and now I saw why. There was a sheer drop here of four hundred feet. Well, that only equaled fifty on Earth, but even fifty—But I had to try it, because I was dying here on the peaks. I jumped.

I landed with a wrench of pain on my wounded leg, but much more lightly than I had feared. Of course! Jumping down into denser air, the great bladder had acted like a parachute, and, after all, my weight here was but eighteen pounds. I crawled onward, in agony for the moment when I could cast off the stinking, choking bladder.

That moment came. I had crossed the peaks, and before me lay the Minos. I crawled on, around to the side where the air lock was. It was open, and a voice bellowed out of it. Gogrol!

"You'll trick me, eh!" he screeched. "You'll lay a course that will crash us! We'll see! We'll see!" There came the unmistakable sound of a blow, and a faint whimper of pain.

Somewhere I found the strength to stand up. Brandishing the empty automatic, I swayed into the air lock, sliding along the walls to the control room.

There was something about the figure that bent in the dusk above a sobbing girl that aroused a flash of recognition. Seeing him thus in a shadowed control room with the sun shields up—I knew what I should have known weeks ago. Gogrol was—Kratska!

"Kratska!" I croaked, and he whirled. Both he and Claire were frozen into utter rigidity by surprise and disbelief. I really think they were both convinced that I was a ghost.

"How—how—" squeaked Gogrol, or rather Kratska.

"I walked across. I'd walk across hell to find you, Kratska." I brandished the gun. "Get out and get away quick, if you expect to escape the blast. We're leaving you here until police from Io can pick you up—on that Hera matter among others." I spoke to the dazed Claire. "Close the air lock after him. We're taking off."

"Jack!" she cried, comprehending at last. "But Stefan's wired to a tree out there. The blast will incinerate him!"

"Then loose him, and for Heaven's sake, quickly!"

But no sooner had she vanished than Kratska took his chance. He saw how weak I was, and he gambled on the one shot he thought remained in the magazine of my weapon. He rushed me.

I think he was mad. He was screaming curses. "Damn you!" he screeched. "You can't beat me! I made you the goat on the Hera, and I can do it here."

And I knew he could, too, if he could overcome me before Claire released Coretti. She couldn't handle him, and we'd all be at his mercy. So I fought with all the life I had left, and felt it draining out of me like acid out of burette. And after a while it was all drained, and darkness filled up the emptiness.

I heard curious sounds. Some one was saying, "No, I'll take off first and lay out the course after we reach escape velocity. Saves time. We've got to get him to Io." And a little later, "Oh, Lord, Stefan! If I roll her now—Why am I such a rotten pilot?" And then there was the roar of the blast for hours upon hours.

A long time later I realized that I was lying on the chart room table, and Coretti was looking down at me. He said, "How you feel, Jack!" It was the first time he had used my name.

"O.K.," I said, and then memory came back. "Gogrol! He's Kratska!"

"He was," said Coretti. "He's dead."

"Dead!" There went any chance of squaring that Hera mess.

"Yep. You killed him, smashed in his head with that automatic before we could pull you off. But he had it coming."

"Yeah, maybe, but the Hera—"

"Never mind the Hera, Jack. Both Claire and I heard Kratska admit his responsibility. We'll clear you of that, all right." He paused. "And it might make you feel a little more chipper it I tell you that we got the formula, too, and that there's a reward for it that will leave us sitting in the clover field, even split three ways. That is, Claire keeps insisting on three ways; I know I don't deserve a split."

"Three ways is right," I said. "It'll give you and Claire a good send-off."

"Me and Claire?'

"Listen, Coretti. I didn't mean to, but I saw you the evening of the eclipse. Claire didn't look as if she was fighting you."

He smiled. "So you saw that," he said slowly. "Then you listen. A fellow who's asking a girl to marry him is apt to hold the girl a little close. And if she's got any heart, she doesn't push him away. She just says no as gently as possible."

"She says no?"

"She did that time. I'd bet different with you."

"She—she—" Something about the familiar sound of the blast caught my attention. "We're landing!"

"Yeah, on Io. We've been landing for two hours."

"Who took off?"

"Claire did. She took off and kept going. She's been sitting there fifty hours. She thinks you need a doctor, and I don't know a damn thing about running a rocket. She's taken it clear from Europa."

I sat up. "Take me in there," I said grimly. "Don't argue. Take me in there!"

Claire barely raised her eyes when Coretti slid me down beside her. She was all but exhausted, sitting there all those weary hours, and now up against her old terror of landing.

"Jack, Jack!" she whispered as if to herself. "I'm glad you're better."

"Honey," I said—her hair did look like honey—"I'm taking half the U-bar. Just let me guide you."

We came down without a roll, and landed like a canary feather. But I hadn't a thing to do with it; I was so weak I couldn't even move the U-bar, but she didn't know that. Confidence was all she needed; she had the makings of a damn good pilot. Yeah; I've proved that. She is a damn good pilot. But all the same, she went to sleep in the middle of our first kiss.

OTHER STORIES
BY
STANLEY WEINBAUM

Pygmalion's Spectacles

Originally Published in *Wonder Stories*
June 1935

PYGMALION'S SPECTACLES

"But what is reality?" asked the gnomelike man. He gestured at the tall banks of buildings that loomed around Central Park, with their countless windows glowing like the cave fires of a city of Cro-Magnon people. "All is dream, all is illusion; I am your vision as you are mine."

Dan Burke, struggling for clarity of thought through the fumes of liquor, stared without comprehension at the tiny figure of his companion. He began to regret the impulse that had driven him to leave the party to seek fresh air in the park, and to fall by chance into the company of this diminutive old madman. But he had needed escape; this was one party too many, and not even the presence of Claire with her trim ankles could hold him there. He felt an angry desire to go home—not to his hotel, but home to Chicago and to the comparative peace of the Board of Trade. But he was leaving tomorrow anyway.

"You drink," said the elfin, bearded face, "to make real a dream. Is it not so? Either to dream that what you seek is yours, or else to dream that what you hate is conquered. You drink to escape reality, and the irony is that even reality is a dream."

"Cracked!" thought Dan again.

"Or so," concluded the other, "says the philosopher Berkeley."

"Berkeley?" echoed Dan. His head was clearing; memories of a Sophomore course in Elementary Philosophy drifted back. "Bishop Berkeley, eh?"

"You know him, then? The philosopher of Idealism—no?—the one who argues that we do not see, feel, hear, taste the object, but that we have only the sensation of seeing, feeling, hearing, tasting."

"I—sort of recall it."

"Hah! But sensations are *mental* phenomena. They exist in our minds. How, then, do we know that the objects themselves do not exist only in our minds?" He waved again at the light-flecked buildings. "You do not see that wall of masonry; you perceive only a *sensation*, a feeling of sight. The rest you interpret."

"You see the same thing," retorted Dan.

"How do you know I do? Even if you knew that what I call red would not be green could you see through my eyes—even if you knew that, how do you know that I too am not a dream of yours?"

Dan laughed. "Of course nobody *knows* anything. You just get what information you can through the windows of your five senses, and then make your guesses. When they're wrong, you pay the penalty." His mind was clear now save for a mild headache. "Listen," he said suddenly. "You can argue a reality away to an illusion; that's easy. But if your friend Berkeley is right, why can't you take a dream and make it real? If it works one way, it must work the other."

The beard waggled; elf-bright eyes glittered queerly at him. "All artists do that," said the old man softly. Dan felt that something more quivered on the verge of utterance.

"That's an evasion," he grunted. "Anybody can tell the difference between a picture and the real thing, or between a movie and life."

"But," whispered the other, "the realer the better, no? And if one could make a—a movie—*very* real indeed, what would you say then?"

"Nobody can, though."

The eyes glittered strangely again. "I can!" he whispered. "I *did*!"

"Did what?"

"Made real a dream." The voice turned angry. "Fools! I bring it here to sell to Westman, the camera people, and what do they say? 'It isn't clear. Only one person can use it at a time. It's too expensive.' Fools! Fools!"

"Huh?"

"Listen! I'm Albert Ludwig—*Professor* Ludwig." As Dan was silent, he continued, "It means nothing to you, eh? But listen—a movie that gives one sight and sound. Suppose now I add taste, smell, even touch, if your interest is taken by the story. Suppose I make it so that you are in the story, you speak to the shadows, and the shadows reply, and instead of being on a screen, the story is all about you, and you are in it. Would that be to make real a dream?"

"How the devil could you do that?"

"How? How? But simply! First my liquid positive, then my magic spectacles. I photograph the story in a liquid with light-sensitive chromates. I build up a complex solution—do you see? I add taste chemically and sound electrically. And when the story is recorded, then I put the solution in my spectacle—my movie projector. I electrolyze the solution, break it down; the older chromates go first, and out comes the story, sight, sound, smell, taste—all!"

"Touch?"

"If your interest is taken, your mind supplies that." Eagerness crept into his voice. "You will look at it, Mr.——?"

"Burke," said Dan. "A swindle!" he thought. Then a spark of recklessness glowed out of the vanishing fumes of alcohol. "Why not?" he grunted.

He rose; Ludwig, standing, came scarcely to his shoulder. A queer gnomelike old man, Dan thought as he followed him across the park and into one of the scores of apartment hotels in the vicinity.

In his room Ludwig fumbled in a bag, producing a device vaguely reminiscent of a gas mask. There were goggles and a rubber mouthpiece; Dan examined it curiously, while the little bearded professor brandished a bottle of watery liquid.

"Here it is!" he gloated. "My liquid positive, the story. Hard photography—infernally hard, therefore the simplest story. A Utopia—just two characters and you, the audience. Now, put the spectacles on. Put them on and tell me what fools the Westman people are!" He decanted some of the liquid into the mask, and trailed a twisted wire to a device on the table. "A rectifier," he explained. "For the electrolysis."

"Must you use all the liquid?" asked Dan. "If you use part, do you see only part of the story? And which part?"

"Every drop has all of it, but you must fill the eye-pieces." Then as Dan slipped the device gingerly on, "So! Now what do you see?"

"Not a damn' thing. Just the windows and the lights across the street."

"Of course. But now I start the electrolysis. Now!"

*   *   *   *   *

There was a moment of chaos. The liquid before Dan's eyes clouded suddenly white, and formless sounds buzzed. He moved to tear the device from his head, but emerging forms in the mistiness caught his interest. Giant things were writhing there.

The scene steadied; the whiteness was dissipating like mist in summer. Unbelieving, still gripping the arms of that unseen chair, he was staring at a forest. But what a forest! Incredible, unearthly, beautiful! Smooth boles ascended inconceivably toward a brightening sky, trees bizarre as the forests of the Carboniferous age. Infinitely overhead swayed misty fronds, and the verdure showed brown and green in the heights. And there were birds—at least, curiously lovely pipings and twitterings were all about him though he saw no creatures—thin elfin whistlings like fairy bugles sounded softly.

He sat frozen, entranced. A louder fragment of melody drifted down to him, mounting in exquisite, ecstatic bursts, now clear as sounding metal, now soft as remembered music. For a moment he forgot the chair whose arms he gripped, the miserable hotel room invisibly about him, old Ludwig, his aching head. He imagined himself alone in the midst of that lovely glade. "Eden!" he muttered, and the swelling music of unseen voices answered.

Some measure of reason returned. "Illusion!" he told himself. Clever optical devices, not reality. He groped for the chair's arm, found it, and clung to it; he scraped his feet and found again an inconsistency. To his eyes the ground was mossy verdure; to his touch it was merely a thin hotel carpet.

The elfin buglings sounded gently. A faint, deliciously sweet perfume breathed against him; he glanced up to watch the opening of a great crimson blossom on the nearest tree, and a tiny reddish sun edged into the circle of sky above him. The fairy orchestra swelled louder in its light, and the notes sent a thrill of wistfulness through him. Illusion? If it were, it made reality almost unbearable; he wanted to believe that somewhere— somewhere this side of dreams, there actually existed this region of loveliness. An outpost of Paradise? Perhaps.

And then—far through the softening mists, he caught a movement that was not the swaying of verdure, a shimmer of silver more solid than mist. Something approached. He watched the figure as it moved, now visible, now hidden by trees; very soon he perceived that it was human, but it was almost upon him before he realized that it was a girl.

She wore a robe of silvery, half-translucent stuff, luminous as starbeams; a thin band of silver bound glowing black hair about her forehead, and other garment or ornament she had none. Her tiny white feet were bare to the mossy forest floor as she stood no more than a pace from him, staring dark-eyed. The thin music sounded again; she smiled.

Dan summoned stumbling thoughts. Was this being also—illusion? Had she no more reality than the loveliness of the forest? He opened his lips to speak, but a strained excited voice sounded in his ears. "Who are you?" Had he spoken? The voice had come as if from another, like the sound of one's words in fever.

The girl smiled again. "English!" she said in queer soft tones. "I can speak a little English." She spoke slowly, carefully. "I learned it from"—she hesitated—"my mother's father, whom they call the Grey Weaver."

Again came the voice in Dan's ears. "Who are you?"

"I am called Galatea," she said. "I came to find you."

"To find me?" echoed the voice that was Dan's.

"Leucon, who is called the Grey Weaver, told me," she explained smiling. "He said you will stay with us until the second noon from this." She cast a quick slanting glance at the pale sun now full above the clearing, then stepped closer. "What are you called?"

"Dan," he muttered. His voice sounded oddly different.

"What a strange name!" said the girl. She stretched out her bare arm. "Come," she smiled.

Dan touched her extended hand, feeling without any surprise the living warmth of her fingers. He had forgotten the paradoxes of illusion; this was no longer illusion to him, but reality itself. It seemed to him that he followed her, walking over the shadowed turf that gave with springy crunch beneath his tread, though Galatea left hardly an imprint. He glanced down, noting that he himself wore a silver garment, and that his feet were bare; with the glance he felt a feathery breeze on his body and a sense of mossy earth on his feet.

"Galatea," said his voice. "Galatea, what place is this? What language do you speak?"

She glanced back laughing. "Why, this is Paracosma, of course, and this is our language."

"Paracosma," muttered Dan. "Para—cosma!" A fragment of Greek that had survived somehow from a Sophomore course a decade in the past came strangely back to him. Paracosma! Land-beyond-the-world!

Galatea cast a smiling glance at him. "Does the real world seem strange," she queried, "after that shadow land of yours?"

"Shadow land?" echoed Dan, bewildered. "*This* is shadow, not my world."

The girl's smile turned quizzical. "Poof!" she retorted with an impudently lovely pout. "And I suppose, then, that *I* am the phantom instead of you!" She laughed. "Do I seem ghostlike?"

Dan made no reply; he was puzzling over unanswerable questions as he trod behind the lithe figure of his guide. The aisle between the unearthly trees widened, and the giants were fewer. It seemed a mile, perhaps, before a sound of tinkling water obscured that other strange music; they emerged on the bank of a little river, swift and crystalline, that rippled and gurgled its way from glowing pool to flashing rapids, sparkling under the pale sun. Galatea bent over the brink and cupped her hands, raising a few mouthfuls of water to her lips; Dan followed her example, finding the liquid stinging cold.

"How do we cross?" he asked.

"You can wade up there,"—the dryad who led him gestured to a sun-lit shallows above a tiny falls—"but I always cross here." She poised herself for a moment on the green bank, then dove like a silver arrow into the pool. Dan followed; the water stung his body like champagne, but a stroke or two carried him across to where Galatea had already emerged with a glistening of creamy bare limbs. Her garment clung tight as a metal sheath to her wet body; he felt a breath-taking thrill at the sight of her. And then, miraculously, the silver cloth was dry, the droplets rolled off as if from oiled silk, and they moved briskly on.

The incredible forest had ended with the river; they walked over a meadow studded with little, many-hued, star-shaped flowers, whose fronds underfoot were soft as a lawn. Yet still the sweet pipings followed them, now loud, now whisper-soft, in a tenuous web of melody.

"Galatea!" said Dan suddenly. "Where is the music coming from?"

She looked back amazed. "You silly one!" she laughed. "From the flowers, of course. See!" she plucked a purple star and held it to his ear; true enough, a faint and plaintive melody hummed out of the blossom. She tossed it in his startled face and skipped on.

A little copse appeared ahead, not of the gigantic forest trees, but of lesser growths, bearing flowers and fruits of iridescent colors, and a tiny brook bubbled through. And there stood the objective of their journey—a building of white, marble-like stone, single-storied and vine covered, with broad glassless windows. They trod upon a path of bright pebbles to the arched entrance, and here, on an intricate stone bench, sat a grey-bearded patriarchal individual. Galatea addressed him in a liquid language that reminded Dan of the flower-pipings; then she turned. "This is Leucon," she said, as the ancient rose from his seat and spoke in English.

"We are happy, Galatea and I, to welcome you, since visitors are a rare pleasure here, and those from your shadowy country most rare."

Dan uttered puzzled words of thanks, and the old man nodded, reseating himself on the carven bench; Galatea skipped through the arched entrance, and Dan, after an irresolute moment, dropped to the remaining bench. Once more his thoughts were whirling in perplexed turbulence. Was all this indeed but illusion? Was he sitting, in actuality, in a prosaic hotel room, peering through magic spectacles that pictured this world about him, or was he, transported by some miracle, really sitting here in this land of loveliness? He touched the bench; stone, hard and unyielding, met his fingers.

"Leucon," said his voice, "how did you know I was coming?"

"I was told," said the other.

"By whom?"

"By no one."

"Why—*someone* must have told you!"

The Grey Weaver shook his solemn head. "I was just told."

Dan ceased his questioning, content for the moment to drink in the beauty about him and then Galatea returned bearing a crystal bowl of the strange fruits. They were piled in colorful disorder, red, purple, orange and yellow, pear-shaped, egg-shaped, and clustered spheroids—fantastic, unearthly. He selected a pale, transparent ovoid, bit into it, and was deluged by a flood of sweet liquid, to the amusement of the girl. She laughed and chose a similar morsel; biting a tiny puncture in the end, she squeezed the contents into her mouth. Dan took a different sort, purple and tart as Rhenish wine, and then another, filled with edible, almond-like seeds. Galatea laughed delightedly at his surprises, and even Leucon smiled a grey smile. Finally Dan tossed the last husk into the brook beside them, where it danced briskly toward the river.

"Galatea," he said, "do you ever go to a city? What cities are in Paracosma?"

"Cities? What are cities?"

"Places where many people live close together."

"Oh," said the girl frowning. "No. There are no cities here."

"Then where are the people of Paracosma? You must have neighbors."

The girl looked puzzled. "A man and a woman live off there," she said, gesturing toward a distant blue range of hills dim on the horizon. "Far away over there. I went there once, but Leucon and I prefer the valley."

"But Galatea!" protested Dan. "Are you and Leucon alone in this valley? Where—what happened to your parents—your father and mother?"

"They went away. That way—toward the sunrise. They'll return some day."

"And if they don't?"

"Why, foolish one! What could hinder them?"

"Wild beasts," said Dan. "Poisonous insects, disease, flood, storm, lawless people, death!"

"I never heard those words," said Galatea. "There are no such things here." She sniffed contemptuously. "Lawless people!"

"Not—death?"

"What is death?"

"It's—" Dan paused helplessly. "It's like falling asleep and never waking. It's what happens to everyone at the end of life."

"I never heard of such a thing as the end of life!" said the girl decidedly. "There isn't such a thing."

"What happens, then," queried Dan desperately, "when one grows old?"

"Nothing, silly! No one grows old unless he wants to, like Leucon. A person grows to the age he likes best and then stops. It's a law!"

Dan gathered his chaotic thoughts. He stared into Galatea's dark, lovely eyes. "Have you stopped yet?"

The dark eyes dropped; he was amazed to see a deep, embarrassed flush spread over her cheeks. She looked at Leucon nodding reflectively on his bench, then back to Dan, meeting his gaze.

"Not yet," he said.

"And when will you, Galatea?"

"When I have had the one child permitted me. You see"—she stared down at her dainty toes—"one cannot—bear children—afterwards."

"Permitted? Permitted by whom?"

"By a law."

"Laws! Is everything here governed by laws? What of chance and accidents?"

"What are those—chance and accidents?"

"Things unexpected—things unforeseen."

"Nothing is unforeseen," said Galatea, still soberly. She repeated slowly, "Nothing is unforeseen." He fancied her voice was wistful.

Leucon looked up. "Enough of this," he said abruptly. He turned to Dan, "I know these words of yours—chance, disease, death. They are not for Paracosma. Keep them in your unreal country."

"Where did you hear them, then?"

"From Galatea's mother," said the Grey Weaver, "who had them from your predecessor—a phantom who visited here before Galatea was born."

Dan had a vision of Ludwig's face. "What was he like?"

"Much like you."

"But his name?"

The old man's mouth was suddenly grim. "We do not speak of him," he said and rose, entering the dwelling in cold silence.

"He goes to weave," said Galatea after a moment. Her lovely, piquant face was still troubled.

"What does he weave?"

"This," She fingered the silver cloth of her gown. "He weaves it out of metal bars on a very clever machine. I do not know the method."

"Who made the machine?"

"It was here."

"But—Galatea! Who built the house? Who planted these fruit trees?"

"They were here. The house and trees were always here." She lifted her eyes. "I told you everything had been foreseen, from the beginning until eternity—everything. The house and trees and machine were ready for Leucon and my parents and me. There is a place for my child, who will be a girl, and a place for her child—and so on forever."

Dan thought a moment. "Were you born here?"

"I don't know." He noted in sudden concern that her eyes were glistening with tears.

"Galatea, dear! Why are you unhappy? What's wrong?"

"Why, nothing!" She shook her black curls, smiled suddenly at him. "What could be wrong? How can one be unhappy in Paracosma?" She sprang erect and seized his hand. "Come! Let's gather fruit for tomorrow."

She darted off in a whirl of flashing silver, and Dan followed her around the wing of the edifice. Graceful as a dancer she leaped for a branch above her head, caught it laughingly, and tossed a great golden globe to him. She loaded his arms with the bright prizes and sent him back to the bench, and when he returned, she piled it so full of fruit that a deluge of colorful spheres dropped around him. She laughed again, and sent them spinning into the brook with thrusts of her rosy toes, while Dan watched her with an aching wistfulness. Then suddenly she was facing him; for a long, tense instant they stood motionless, eyes upon eyes, and then she turned away and walked slowly around to the arched portal. He followed her with his burden of fruit; his mind was once more in a turmoil of doubt and perplexity.

The little sun was losing itself behind the trees of that colossal forest to the west, and a coolness stirred among long shadows. The brook was purple-hued in the dusk, but its cheery notes mingled still with the flower music. Then the sun was hidden; the shadow fingers darkened the meadow; of a sudden the flowers were still, and the brook gurgled alone in a world of silence. In silence too, Dan entered the doorway.

The chamber within was a spacious one, floored with large black and white squares; exquisite benches of carved marble were here and there. Old Leucon, in a far corner, bent over an intricate, glistening mechanism, and as Dan entered he drew a shining length of silver cloth from it, folded it, and placed it carefully aside. There was a curious, unearthly fact that Dan noted; despite windows open to the evening, no night insects circled the globes that glowed at intervals from niches in the walls.

Galatea stood in a doorway to his left, leaning half-wearily against the frame; he placed the bowl of fruit on a bench at the entrance and moved to her side.

"This is yours," she said, indicating the room beyond. He looked in upon a pleasant, smaller chamber; a window framed a starry square, and a thin, swift, nearly silent stream of water gushed from the mouth of a carved human head on the left wall, curving into a six-foot basin sunk in the floor. Another of the graceful benches covered with the silver cloth completed the furnishings; a single glowing sphere, pendant by a chain from the ceiling, illuminated the room. Dan turned to the girl, whose eyes were still unwontedly serious.

"This is ideal," he said, "but, Galatea, how am I to turn out the light?"

"Turn it out?" she said. "You must cap it—so!" A faint smile showed again on her lips as she dropped a metal covering over the shining sphere. They stood tense in the darkness; Dan sensed her nearness achingly, and then the light was on once more. She moved toward the door, and there paused, taking his hand.

"Dear shadow," she said softly, "I hope your dreams are music." She was gone.

Dan stood irresolute in his chamber; he glanced into the large room where Leucon still bent over his work, and the Grey Weaver raised a hand in a solemn salutation, but said nothing. He felt no urge for the old man's silent company and turned back into his room to prepare for slumber.

*   *   *   *   *

Almost instantly, it seemed, the dawn was upon him and bright elfin pipings were all about him, while the odd ruddy sun sent a broad slanting plane of light across the room. He rose as fully aware of his surroundings as if he had not slept at all; the pool tempted him and he bathed in stinging water. Thereafter he emerged into the central chamber, noting curiously that the globes still glowed in dim rivalry to the daylight. He touched one casually; it was cool as metal to his fingers, and lifted freely from its standard. For a moment he held the cold flaming thing in his hands, then replaced it and wandered into the dawn.

Galatea was dancing up the path, eating a strange fruit as rosy as her lips. She was merry again, once more the happy nymph who had greeted him, and she gave him a bright smile as he chose a sweet green ovoid for his breakfast.

"Come on!" she called. "To the river!"

She skipped away toward the unbelievable forest; Dan followed, marveling that her lithe speed was so easy a match for his stronger muscles. Then they were laughing in the pool, splashing about until Galatea drew herself to the bank, glowing and panting. He followed her as she lay relaxed; strangely, he was neither tired nor breathless, with no sense of exertion. A question recurred to him, as yet unasked.

"Galatea," said his voice, "Whom will you take as mate?"

Her eyes went serious. "I don't know," she said. "At the proper time he will come. That is a law."

"And will you be happy?"

"Of course." She seemed troubled. "Isn't everyone happy?"

"Not where I live, Galatea."

"Then that must be a strange place—that ghostly world of yours. A rather terrible place."

"It is, often enough," Dan agreed. "I wish—" He paused. What did he wish? Was he not talking to an illusion, a dream, an apparition? He looked at the girl, at her glistening black hair, her eyes, her soft white skin, and then, for a tragic moment, he tried to feel the arms of that drab hotel chair beneath his hands—and failed. He smiled; he reached out his fingers to touch her bare arm, and for an instant she looked back at him with startled, sober eyes, and sprang to her feet.

"Come on! I want to show you my country." She set off down the stream, and Dan rose reluctantly to follow.

What a day that was! They traced the little river from still pool to singing rapids, and ever about them were the strange twitterings and pipings that were the voices of the flowers. Every turn brought a new vista of beauty; every moment brought a new sense of delight. They talked or were silent; when they were thirsty, the cool river was at hand; when they were hungry, fruit offered itself. When they were tired, there was always a deep pool and a mossy bank; and when they were rested, a new beauty beckoned. The incredible trees towered in numberless forms of fantasy, but on their own side of the river was still the flower-starred meadow. Galatea twisted him a bright-blossomed garland for his head, and thereafter he moved always with a sweet singing about him. But little by little the red sun slanted toward the forest, and the hours dripped away. It was Dan who pointed it out, and reluctantly they turned homeward.

As they returned, Galatea sang a strange song, plaintive and sweet as the medley of river and flower music. And again her eyes were sad.

"What song is that?" he asked.

"It is a song sung by another Galatea," she answered, "who is my mother." She laid her hand on his arm. "I will make it into English for you." She sang:

"The River lies in flower and fern,
In flower and fern it breathes a song.
It breathes a song of your return,
Of your return in years too long.
In years too long its murmurs bring
Its murmurs bring their vain replies,
Their vain replies the flowers sing,
The flowers sing, 'The River lies!'"

Her voice quavered on the final notes; there was silence save for the tinkle of water and the flower bugles. Dan said, "Galatea—" and paused. The girl was again somber-eyed, tearful. He said huskily, "That's a sad song, Galatea. Why was your mother sad? You said everyone was happy in Paracosma."

"She broke a law," replied the girl tonelessly. "It is the inevitable way to sorrow." She faced him. "She fell in love with a phantom!" Galatea said. "One of your shadowy race, who came and stayed and then had to go back. So when her appointed lover came, it was too late; do you understand? But she yielded finally to the law, and is forever unhappy, and goes wandering from place to place about the world." She paused. "I shall never break a law," she said defiantly.

Dan took her hand. "I would not have you unhappy, Galatea. I want you always happy."

She shook her head. "I *am* happy," she said, and smiled a tender, wistful smile.

They were silent a long time as they trudged the way homeward. The shadows of the forest giants reached out across the river as the sun slipped behind them. For a distance they walked hand in hand, but as they reached the path of pebbly brightness near the house, Galatea drew away and sped swiftly before him. Dan followed as quickly as he might; when he arrived, Leucon sat on his bench by the portal, and Galatea had paused on the threshold. She watched his approach with eyes in which he again fancied the glint of tears.

"I am very tired," she said, and slipped within.

Dan moved to follow, but the old man raised a staying hand.

"Friend from the shadows," he said, "will you hear me a moment?"

Dan paused, acquiesced, and dropped to the opposite bench. He felt a sense of foreboding; nothing pleasant awaited him.

"There is something to be said," Leucon continued, "and I say it without desire to pain you, if phantoms feel pain. It is this: Galatea loves you, though I think she has not yet realized it."

"I love her too," said Dan.

The Grey Weaver stared at him. "I do not understand. Substance, indeed, may love shadow, but how can shadow love substance?"

"I love her," insisted Dan.

"Then woe to both of you! For this is impossible in Paracosma; it is a confliction with the laws. Galatea's mate is appointed, perhaps even now approaching."

"Laws! Laws!" muttered Dan. "Whose laws are they? Not Galatea's nor mine!"

"But they are," said the Grey Weaver. "It is not for you nor for me to criticize them—though I yet wonder what power could annul them to permit your presence here!"

"I had no voice in your laws."

The old man peered at him in the dusk. "Has anyone, anywhere, a voice in the laws?" he queried.

"In my country we have," retorted Dan.

"Madness!" growled Leucon. "Man-made laws! Of what use are man-made laws with only man-made penalties, or none at all? If you shadows make a law that the wind shall blow only from the east, does the west wind obey it?"

"We do pass such laws," acknowledged Dan bitterly. "They may be stupid, but they're no more unjust than yours."

"Ours," said the Grey Weaver, "are the unalterable laws of the world, the laws of Nature. Violation is always unhappiness. I have seen it; I have known it in another, in Galatea's mother, though Galatea is stronger than she." He paused. "Now," he continued, "I ask only for mercy; your stay is short, and I ask that you do no more harm than is already done. Be merciful; give her no more to regret."

He rose and moved through the archway; when Dan followed a moment later, he was already removing a square of silver from his device in the corner. Dan turned silent and unhappy to his own chamber, where the jet of water tinkled faintly as a distant bell.

Again he rose at the glow of dawn, and again Galatea was before him, meeting him at the door with her bowl of fruit. She deposited her burden, giving him a wan little smile of greeting, and stood facing him as if waiting.

"Come with me, Galatea," he said.

"Where?"

"To the river bank. To talk."

They trudged in silence to the brink of Galatea's pool. Dan noted a subtle difference in the world about him; outlines were vague, the thin flower pipings less audible, and the very landscape was queerly unstable, shifting like smoke when he wasn't looking at it directly. And strangely, though he had brought the girl here to talk to her, he had now nothing to say, but sat in aching silence with his eyes on the loveliness of her face.

Galatea pointed at the red ascending sun. "So short a time," she said, "before you go back to your phantom world. I shall be sorry, very sorry." She touched his cheek with her fingers. "Dear shadow!"

"Suppose," said Dan huskily, "that I won't go. What if I won't leave here?" His voice grew fiercer. "I'll not go! I'm going to stay!"

The calm mournfulness of the girl's face checked him; he felt the irony of struggling against the inevitable progress of a dream. She spoke. "Had I the making of the laws, you should stay. But you can't, dear one. You can't!"

Forgotten now were the words of the Grey Weaver. "I love you, Galatea," he said.

"And I you," she whispered. "See, dearest shadow, how I break the same law my mother broke, and am glad to face the sorrow it will bring." She placed her hand tenderly over his. "Leucon is very wise and I am bound to obey him, but this is beyond his wisdom because he let himself grow old." She paused. "He let himself grow old," she repeated slowly. A strange light gleamed in her dark eyes as she turned suddenly to Dan.

"Dear one!" she said tensely. "That thing that happens to the old—that death of yours! What follows it?"

"What follows death?" he echoed. "Who knows?"

"But—" Her voice was quivering. "But one can't simply—vanish! There must be an awakening."

"Who knows?" said Dan again. "There are those who believe we wake to a happier world, but—" He shook his head hopelessly.

"It must be true! Oh, it must be!" Galatea cried. "There must be more for you than the mad world you speak of!" She leaned very close. "Suppose, dear," she said, "that when my appointed lover arrives, I send him away. Suppose I bear no child, but let myself grow old, older than Leucon, old until death. Would I join you in your happier world?"

"Galatea!" he cried distractedly. "Oh, my dearest—what a terrible thought!"

"More terrible than you know," she whispered, still very close to him. "It is more than violation of a law; it is rebellion! Everything is planned, everything was foreseen, except this; and if I bear no child, her place will be left unfilled, and the places of her children, and of *their* children, and so on until some day the whole great plan of Paracosma fails of whatever its destiny was to be." Her whisper grew very faint and fearful. "It is destruction, but I love you more than I fear—death!"

Dan's arms were about her. "No, Galatea! No! Promise me!"

She murmured, "I can promise and then break my promise." She drew his head down; their lips touched, and he felt a fragrance and a taste like honey in her kiss. "At least," she breathed. "I can give you a name by which to love you. Philometros! Measure of my love!"

"A name?" muttered Dan. A fantastic idea shot through his mind—a way of proving to himself that all this was reality, and not just a page that any one could read who wore old Ludwig's magic spectacles. If Galatea would speak his name! Perhaps, he thought daringly, perhaps then he could stay! He thrust her away.

"Galatea!" he cried. "Do you remember my name?"

She nodded silently, her unhappy eyes on his.

"Then say it! Say it, dear!"

She stared at him dumbly, miserably, but made no sound.

"Say it, Galatea!" he pleaded desperately. "My name, dear— just my name!" Her mouth moved; she grew pale with effort and Dan could have sworn that his name trembled on her quivering lips, though no sound came.

At last she spoke. "I can't, dearest one! Oh, I can't! A law forbids it!" She stood suddenly erect, pallid as an ivory carving. "Leucon calls!" she said, and darted away. Dan followed along the pebbled path, but her speed was beyond his powers; at the portal he found only the Grey Weaver standing cold and stern. He raised his hand as Dan appeared.

"Your time is short," he said. "Go, thinking of the havoc you have done."

"Where's Galatea?" gasped Dan.

"I have sent her away." The old man blocked the entrance; for a moment Dan would have struck him aside, but something withheld him. He stared wildly about the meadow—there! A flash of silver beyond the river, at the edge of the forest. He turned and raced toward it, while motionless and cold the Grey Weaver watched him go.

"Galatea!" he called. "Galatea!"

He was over the river now, on the forest bank, running through columned vistas that whirled about him like mist. The world had gone cloudy; fine flakes danced like snow before his eyes; Paracosma was dissolving around him. Through the chaos he fancied a glimpse of the girl, but closer approach left him still voicing his hopeless cry of "Galatea!"

After an endless time, he paused; something familiar about the spot struck him, and just as the red sun edged above him, he recognized the place—the very point at which he had entered Paracosma! A sense of futility overwhelmed him as for a moment he gazed at an unbelievable apparition—a dark window hung in midair before him through which glowed rows of electric lights. Ludwig's window!

It vanished. But the trees writhed and the sky darkened, and he swayed dizzily in turmoil. He realized suddenly that he was no longer standing, but sitting in the midst of the crazy glade, and his hands clutched something smooth and hard—the arms of that miserable hotel chair. Then at last he saw her, close before him—Galatea, with sorrow-stricken features, her tear-filled eyes on his. He made a terrific effort to rise, stood erect, and fell sprawling in a blaze of coruscating lights.

He struggled to his knees; walls—Ludwig's room—encompassed him; he must have slipped from the chair. The magic spectacles lay before him, one lens splintered and spilling a fluid no longer water-clear, but white as milk.

"God!" he muttered. He felt shaken, sick, exhausted, with a bitter sense of bereavement, and his head ached fiercely. The room was drab, disgusting; he wanted to get out of it. He glanced automatically at his watch: four o'clock—he must have sat here nearly five hours. For the first time he noticed Ludwig's absence; he was glad of it and walked dully out of the door to an automatic elevator. There was no response to his ring; someone was using the thing. He walked three flights to the street and back to his own room.

In love with a vision! Worse—in love with a girl who had never lived, in a fantastic Utopia that was literally nowhere! He threw himself on his bed with a groan that was half a sob.

He saw finally the implication of the name Galatea. Galatea—Pygmalion's statue, given life by Venus in the ancient Grecian myth. But *his* Galatea, warm and lovely and vital, must remain forever without the gift of life, since he was neither Pygmalion nor God.

* * * * *

He woke late in the morning, staring uncomprehendingly about for the fountain and pool of Paracosma. Slow comprehension dawned; how much—*how much*—of last night's experience had been real? How much was the product of alcohol? Or had old Ludwig been right, and was there no difference between reality and dream?

He changed his rumpled attire and wandered despondently to the street. He found Ludwig's hotel at last; inquiry revealed that the diminutive professor had checked out, leaving no forwarding address.

What of it? Even Ludwig couldn't give what he sought, a living Galatea. Dan was glad that he had disappeared; he hated the little professor. Professor? Hypnotists called themselves "professors." He dragged through a weary day and then a sleepless night back to Chicago.

It was mid-winter when he saw a suggestively tiny figure ahead of him in the Loop. Ludwig! Yet what use to hail him? His cry was automatic. "Professor Ludwig!"

The elfin figure turned, recognized him, smiled. They stepped into the shelter of a building.

"I'm sorry about your machine, Professor. I'd be glad to pay for the damage."

"*Ach*, that was nothing—a cracked glass. But you—have you been ill? You look much the worse."

"It's nothing," said Dan. "Your show was marvelous, Professor—marvelous! I'd have told you so, but you were gone when it ended."

Ludwig shrugged. "I went to the lobby for a cigar. Five hours with a wax dummy, you know!"

"It was marvelous!" repeated Dan.

"So real?" smiled the other. "Only because you co-operated, then. It takes self-hypnosis."

"It was real, all right," agreed Dan glumly. "I don't understand it—that strange beautiful country."

"The trees were club-mosses enlarged by a lens," said Ludwig. "All was trick photography, but stereoscopic, as I told you—three dimensional. The fruits were rubber; the house is a summer building on our campus—Northern University. And the voice was mine; you didn't speak at all, except your name at the first, and I left a blank for that. I played your part, you see; I went around with the photographic apparatus strapped on my head, to keep the viewpoint always that of the observer. See?" He grinned wryly. "Luckily I'm rather short, or you'd have seemed a giant."

"Wait a minute!" said Dan, his mind whirling. "You say you played my part. Then Galatea—is *she* real too?"

"Tea's real enough," said the Professor. "My niece, a senior at Northern, and likes dramatics. She helped me out with the thing. Why? Want to meet her?"

Dan answered vaguely, happily. An ache had vanished; a pain was eased. Paracosma was attainable at last!

THE ADAPTIVE ULTIMATE

ORIGINALLY PUBLISHED IN *ASTOUNDING STORIES*
NOVEMBER 1935

The Adaptive Ultimate

Dr. Daniel Scott, his dark and brilliant eyes alight with the fire of enthusiasm, paused at last and stared out over the city, or that portion of it visible from the office windows of Herman Bach—the Dr. Herman Bach of Grand Mercy Hospital. There was a moment of silence; the old man smiled a little indulgently, a little wistfully, at the face of the youthful biochemist.

"Go on, Dan," he said. "So it occurred to you that getting well of a disease or injury is merely a form of adaptation—then what?"

"Then," flashed the other, "I began to look for the most adaptive of living organisms. And what are they? Insects! Insects, of course. Cut off a wing, and it grows back. Cut off a head, stick it to the headless body of another of the same species, and that grows back on. And what's the secret of their great adaptability?"

Dr. Bach shrugged. "What is?"

Scott was suddenly gloomy. "I'm not sure," he muttered. "It's glandular, of course—a matter of hormones." He brightened again. "But I'm off the track. So then I looked around for the most adaptive insect. And which is that?"

"Ants?" suggested Dr. Bach. "Bees? Termites?"

"Bah! They're the most highly evolved, not the most adaptable. No; there's one insect that is known to produce a higher percentage of mutants than any other, more freaks, more biological sports. The one Morgan used in his experiments on the effect of hard X-rays on heredity—the fruit fly, the ordinary fruit fly. Remember? They have reddish eyes, but under X-rays they produced white-eyed offspring—and that was a true mutation, because the white eyes bred true! Acquired characteristics can't be inherited, but these were. Therefore—"

"I know," interrupted Dr. Bach.

Scott caught his breath. "So I used fruit flies," he resumed. "I putrefied their bodies, injected a cow, and got a serum at last, after weeks of clarifying with albumen, evaporating in vacuo, rectifying with—But you're not interested in the technique. I got a serum. I tried it on tubercular guinea pigs, and"—he paused dramatically—"it cured! They adapted themselves to the tubercle bacillus. I tried it on a rabid dog. He adapted. I tried it on a cat with a broken spine. That knit. And now, I'm asking you for the chance to try it on a human being!"

Dr. Bach frowned. "You're not ready," he grunted. "You're not ready by two years. Try it on an anthropoid. Then try it on yourself. I can't risk a human life in an experiment that's as raw as this."

"Yes, but I haven't got anything that needs curing, and as for an anthropoid, you get the board to allow funds to buy an ape—if you can. I've tried."

"Take it up with the Stoneman Foundation, then."

"And have Grand Mercy lose the credit? Listen, Dr. Bach, I'm asking for just one chance—a charity case—anything."

"Charity cases are human beings." The old man scowled down at his hands. "See here, Dan. I shouldn't even offer this much, because it's against all medical ethics, but if I find a hopeless case—utterly hopeless, you understand—where the patient himself consents, I'll do it. And that's the final word."

Scott groaned. "And try to find a case like that. If the patient's conscious, you think there's hope, and if he isn't how can he consent? That settles it!"

But it didn't. Less than a week later Scott looked suddenly up at the annunciator in the corner of his tiny laboratory. "Dr. Scott," it rasped. "Dr. Scott. Dr. Scott. To Dr. Bach's office."

He finished his titration, noted the figures, and hurried out. The old man was pacing the floor nervously as Scott entered.

"I've got your case, Dan," he muttered. "It's against all ethics—yet I'll be damned if I can see how you can do this one any harm. But you'd better hurry. Come on—isolation ward."

They hurried. In the tiny cubical room Scott stared appalled. "A girl!" he muttered.

She could never have been other than drab and plain, but lying there with the pallor of death already on her cheeks, she had an appearance of somber sweetness. Yet that was all the charm she could ever have possessed; her dark, cropped, oily hair was unkempt and stringy, her features flat and unattractive. She breathed with an almost inaudible rasp, and her eyes were closed.

"Do you," asked Scott, "consider this a test? She's all but dead now."

Dr. Bach nodded. "Tuberculosis," he said, "final stage. Her lungs are hemorrhaging—a matter of hours."

The girl coughed; flecks of blood appeared on her pallid lips. She opened dull, watery blue eyes.

"So!" said Bach, "conscious, eh? This is Dr. Scott. Dan, this is—uh"—he peered at the card at the foot of the bed—"Miss—uh—Kyra Zelas. Dr. Scott has an injection, Miss Zelas. As I warned you, it probably won't help, but I can't see how it can hurt. Are you willing?"

She spoke in faint, gurgling tones. "Sure, I'm through anyway. What's the odds?"

"All right. Got the hypo, Dan?" Bach took the tube of water-clear serum. "Any particular point of injection? No? Give me the cubital, then."

He thrust the needle into the girl's arm. Dan noted that she did not even wince at the bite of the steel point, but lay stoical and passive as thirty cc. of liquid flowed into her veins. She coughed again, then closed her eyes.

"Come out of here," ordered Bach gruffly, as they moved into the hall, "I'm damned if I like this. I feel like a dirty dog."

He seemed to feel less canine, however, the following day. "That Zelas case is still alive," he reported to Scott. "If I dared trust my eyes, I'd say she's improved a little. A very little. I'd still call it hopeless."

But the following day Scott found himself seated in his office with a puzzled expression in his old gray eyes. "Zelas is better," he muttered. "No question of it. But you keep your head, Dan. Such miracles have happened before, and without serums. You wait until we've had her under long observation."

By the end of the week it became evident that the observation was not to be long. Kyra Zelas flourished under their gaze like some swift-blooming tropical weed. Queerly, she lost none of her pallor, but flesh softened the angular features, and a trace of light grew in her eyes.

"The spots on her lungs are going," muttered Bach. "She's stopped coughing, and there's no sign of bugs in her culture. But the queerest thing, Dan—and I can't figure it out, either—is the way she reacts to abrasions and skin punctures. Yesterday I took a blood specimen for a Wasserman, and—this sounds utterly mad—the puncture closed almost before I had a c.c.! Closed and healed!"

And in another week, "Dan, I can't see any reason for keeping Kyra here. She's well. Yet I want her where we can keep her under observation. There's a queer mystery about this serum of yours. And besides, I hate to turn her out to the sort of life that brought her here."

"What did she do?"

"Sewed. Piece work in some sweatshop, when she could work at all. Drab, ugly, uneducated girl, but there's something appealing about her. She adapts quickly."

Scott gave him a strange look. "Yes," he said, "she adapts quickly."

"So," resumed Bach, "it occurred to me that she could stay at my place. We could keep her under observation, you see, and she could help the housekeeper. I'm interested—damn' interested. I think I'll offer her the chance."

Scott was present when Dr. Bach made his suggestion. The girl Kyra smiled. "Sure," she said. Her pallid, plain face lighted up. "Thanks."

Bach gave her the address. "Mrs. Getz will let you in. Don't do anything this afternoon. In fact, it might not hurt you to simply walk in the park for a few hours."

Scott watched the girl as she walked down the hall toward the elevator. She had filled out, but she was still spare to the point of emaciation, and her worn black suit hung on her as if it were on a frame of sticks. As she disappeared, he moved thoughtfully about his duties, and a quarter hour later descended to his laboratory.

On the first floor, turmoil met him. Two officers were carrying in the body of a nondescript old man, whose head was a bloody ruin. There was a babble of excited voices, and he saw a crowd on the steps outside.

"What's up?" he called. "Accident?"

"Accident!" snapped an officer. "Murder, you mean. Woman steps up to this old guy, picks a hefty stone from the park border, slugs him, and takes his wallet. Just like that!"

Scott peered out of the window. The Black Maria was backing toward a crowd on the park side of the street.

A pair of hulking policemen flanked a thin figure in black, thrusting it toward the doors of the vehicle. Scott gasped. It was Kyra Zelas!

A week later Dr. Bach stared into the dark fireplace of his living room. "It's not our business," he repeated. "My God!" blazed Scott. "Not our business! How do we know we're not responsible? How do we know that our injection didn't unsettle her mind? Glands can do that; look at Mongoloid idiots and cretins. Our stuff was glandular. Maybe we drove her crazy!"

"All right," said Bach. "Listen. We'll attend the trial tomorrow, and if it looks bad for her, we'll get hold of her lawyer and let him put us on the stand. We'll testify that she's just been released after a long and dangerous illness, and may not be fully responsible. That's entirely true."

Mid-morning of the next day found them hunched tensely on benches in the crowded courtroom. The prosecution was opening; three witnesses testified to the event.

"This old guy buys peanuts for the pigeons. Yeah, I sell 'em to him every day—or did. So this time he hasn't any change, and he pulls out his wallet, and I see it's stuffed with bills. And one minute later I see the dame pick up the rock and conk him. Then she grabs the dough—"

"Describe her, please."

"She's skinny, and dressed in black. She ain't no beauty, neither. Brownish hair, dark eyes, I don't know whether dark-blue or brown."

"Your witness!" snapped the prosecutor.

A young and nervous individual—appointed by the court, the paper said—rose. "You say," he squeaked, "that the assailant had brown hair and dark eyes?"

"Yeah."

"Will the defendant please rise?"

Her back was toward Scott and Bach as Kyra Zelas arose, but Scott stiffened. Something strangely different about her appearance; surely her worn black suit no longer hung so loosely about her. What he could see of her figure seemed—well, magnificent.

"Take off your hat, Miss Zelas," squeaked the attorney.

Scott gasped. Radiant as aluminum glowed the mass of hair she revealed!

"I submit, your honor, that this defendant does not possess dark hair, nor, if you will observe, dark eyes. It is, I suppose, conceivable that she could somehow have bleached her hair while in custody, and I therefore"—he brandished a pair of scissors—"submit a lock to be tested by any chemist the court appoints. The pigmentation is entirely natural. And as for her eyes—does my esteemed opponent suggest that they, too, are bleached?"

He swung on the gaping witness. "Is this lady the one you claim to have seen committing the crime?"

The man goggled. "Uh—I can't—say."

"Is she?"

"N-no!"

The speaker smiled. "That's all. Will you take the stand, Miss Zelas?"

The girl moved lithe as a panther. Slowly she turned, facing the court. Scott's brain whirled, and his fingers dug into Bach's arm. Silver-eyed, aluminum-haired, alabaster pale, the girl on the stand was beyond doubt the most beautiful woman he had ever seen!

The attorney was speaking again. "Tell the court in your own words what happened, Miss Zelas."

Quite casually the girl crossed her trim ankles and began to speak. Her voice was low, resonant, and thrilling; Scott had to fight to keep his attention on the sense of her words rather than the sound.

"I had just left Grand Mercy Hospital," she said, "where I had been ill for some months. I had crossed the park when suddenly a woman in black rushed at me, thrust an empty wallet into my hands, and vanished. A moment later I was surrounded by a screaming crowd, and—well, that's all."

"An empty wallet, you say?" asked the defense lawyer. "What of the money found in your own bag, which my eminent colleague believes stolen?"

"It was mine," said the girl, "about seven hundred dollars."

Bach hissed, "That's a lie! She had two dollars and thirty-three cents on her when we took her in."

"Do you mean you think she's the same Kyra Zelas we had at the hospital?" gasped Scott.

"I don't know. I don't know anything, but if I ever touch that damned serum of yours—Look! Look, Dan!" This last was a tense whisper.

"What?"

"Her hair! When the sun strikes it!"

Scott peered more closely. A vagrant ray of noon sunlight filtered through a high window, and now and again the swaying of a shade permitted it to touch the metallic radiance of the girl's hair. Scott stared and saw; slightly but unmistakable, whenever the light touched that glowing aureole, her hair darkened from bright aluminum to golden blond!

Something clicked in his brain. There was a clue somewhere—if he could but find it. The pieces of the puzzle were there, but they were woefully hard to fit together. The girl in the hospital and her reaction to incisions; this girl and her reaction to light.

"I've got to see her," he whispered. "There's something I have to find—Listen!"

The speaker was orating. "And we ask the dismissal of the whole case, your honor, on the grounds that the prosecution has utterly failed even to identify the defendant."

The judge's gavel crashed. For a moment his aging eyes rested on the girl with the silver eyes and, incredible hair, then: "Case dismissed!" he snapped. "Jury discharged!"

There was a tumult of voices. Flashlights shot instantaneous sheets of lightning. The girl on the witness stand rose with perfect poise, smiled with lovely, innocent lips, and moved away. Scott waited until she passed close at hand then:

"Miss Zelas!" he called.

She paused. Her strange silver eyes lighted with unmistakable recognition. "Dr. Scott!" said the voice of tinkling metal. "And Dr. Bach!"

She was, then. She was the same girl. This was the drab sloven of the isolation ward, this weirdly beautiful creature of exotic coloring. Staring, Scott could trace now the very identity of her features, but changed as by a miracle.

He pushed through the mob of photographers, press men, and curiosity seekers. "Have you a place to stay?" he asked. "Dr. Bach's offer still stands."

She smiled. "I am very grateful," she murmured, and then, to the crowd of reporters. "The doctor is an old friend of mine." She was completely at ease, unruffled, poised.

Something caught Scott's eye, and he purchased a paper, glancing quickly at the photograph, the one taken at the moment the girl had removed her hat. He started; her hair showed raven black! There was a comment below the picture, too, to the effect that "her striking hair photographs much darker than it appears to the eye."

He frowned. "This way," he said to the girl, then goggled in surprise again. For in the broad light of noon her complexion was no longer the white of alabaster; it was creamy tan, the skin of one exposed to long hours of sunlight; her eyes were deep violet, and her hair—that tiny wisp unconcealed by her hat— was as black as the basalt columns of hell!

Kyra had insisted on stopping to purchase a substitute for the worn black suit, and had ended by acquiring an entire outfit. She sat now curled in the deep davenport before the fireplace in Dr. Bach's library, sheathed in silken black from her white throat to the tiny black pumps on her feet. She was almost unearthly in her weird beauty, with her aluminum hair, silver eyes, and marble-pale skin against the jet silk covering.

She gazed innocently at Scott. "But why shouldn't I?" she asked. "The court returned my money; I can buy what I please with it."

"Your money?" he muttered. "You had less than three dollars when you left the hospital."

"But this is mine now."

"Kyra," he said abruptly, "where did you get that money?"

Her face was saintlike in its purity. "From the old man."

"You—you did murder him!"

"Why, of course I did."

He choked. "My Lord!" he gasped. "Don't you realize we'll have to tell?"

She shook her head, smiling, gently from one to the other of them. "No, Dan. You won't tell, for it wouldn't do any good. I can't be tried twice for the same crime. Not in America."

"But why, Kyra? Why did you—"

"Would you have me resume the life that sent me into your hands? I needed money; money was there; I took it."

"But murder!"

"It was the most direct way."

"Not if you happened to be punished for it," he returned grimly.

"But I wasn't," she reminded him gently.

He groaned. "Kyra," he said, shifting the subject suddenly, "why do your eyes and skin and hair darken in sunlight or when exposed to flashlight?"

She smiled. "Do they?" she asked. "I hadn't noticed." She yawned, stretched her arms above her head and her slim legs before her. "I think I shall sleep now," she announced. She swept her magnificent eyes over them, rose, and disappeared into the room Dr. Bach had given her—his own.

Scott faced the older man, his features working in emotion. "Do you see?" he hissed. "Good Lord, do you see?"

"Do you, Dan?"

"Part of it. Part of it, anyway."

"And I see part as well."

"Well," said Scott, "here it is as I see it. That serum—that accursed serum of mine—has somehow accentuated this girl's adaptability to an impossible degree. What is it that differentiates life from non-living matter? Two things, irritation and adaptation. Life adapts itself to its environment, and the greater the adaptability, the more successful the organism.

"Now," he proceeded, "all human beings show a very considerable adaptivity. When we expose ourselves to sunlight, our skin shows pigmentation—we tan. That's adaptation to an environment containing sunlight. When a man loses his right hand, he learns to use his left. That's another adaptation. When a person's skin is punctured, it heals and rebuilds, and that's another angle of the same thing. Sunny regions produce dark-skinned, dark-haired people; northern lands produce blonds— and that's adaptation again.

"So what's happened to Kyra Zelas, by some mad twist I don't understand, is that her adaptive powers have been increased to an extreme. She adapts instantly to her environment; when sun strikes her, she tans at once, and in shade she fades immediately. In sunlight her hair and eyes are those of a tropical race; in shadow, those of a Northerner. And— good Lord, I see it now—when she was faced with danger there in the courtroom, faced by a jury and judge who were men, she adapted to that! She met that danger, not only by changed appearance, but by a beauty so great, that she couldn't have been convicted!" He paused. "But how? How?"

"Perhaps medicine can tell how," said Bach. "Undoubtedly man is the creature of his glands. The differences between races—white, red, black, yellow—is doubtless glandular. And perhaps the most effective agent of adaptation is the human brain and neural system, which in itself is controlled partly by a little greasy mass on the floor of the brain's third ventricle, before the cerebellum, and supposed by the ancients to be the seat of the soul.

"I mean, of course, the pineal gland. I suspect that what your serum contains is the long-sought hormone pinealin, and that it has caused hypertrophy of Kyra's pineal gland. And Dan, do you realize that if her adaptability is perfect, she's not only invincible, but invulnerable?"

"That's true!" gulped Scott. "Why, she couldn't be electrocuted, because she'd adapt instantly to an environment containing an electric current, and she couldn't be killed by a shot, because she'd adapt to that as quickly as to your needle pricks. And poison—but there must be a limit somewhere!"

"There doubtless is," observed Bach. "I hardly believe she could adapt herself to an environment containing a fifty-ton locomotive passing over her body. And yet there's an important point we haven't considered. Adaptation itself is of two kinds."

"Two kinds?"

"Yes. One kind is biological; the other, human. Naturally a biochemist like you would deal only with the first, and equally naturally a brain surgeon like me has to consider the second as well. Biological adaptation is what all life—plant, animal, and human—possesses, and it is merely conforming to one's environment. A chameleon, for instance, shows much the same ability as Kyra herself, and so, in lesser degree, does the arctic fox, white in winter, brown in summer; or the snowshoe rabbit, for that matter, or the weasel. All life conforms to its environment to a great extent, because if it doesn't, it dies. But human life does more."

"More?"

"Much more. Human adaptation is not only conformity to environment, but also the actual changing of environment to fit human needs! The first cave man who left his cave to build a grass hut changed his environment, and so, in exactly the same sense, did Steinmetz, Edison, and as far as that goes, Julius Caesar and Napoleon. In fact, Dan, all human invention, genius, and military leadership boils down to that one fact—changing the environment instead of conforming to it."

He paused, then continued, "Now we know that Kyra possesses the biological adaptivity. Her hair and eyes prove that. But what if she possesses the other to the same degree? If she does, God knows what the result will be. We can only watch to see what direction she takes—watch and hope."

"But I don't see," muttered Scott, "how that could be glandular."

"Anything can be glandular. In a mutant—and Kyra's as much a mutant as your white-eyed fruit flies—anything is possible." He frowned reflectively. "If I dared phrase a philosophical interpretation, I'd say that Kyra—perhaps—represents a stage in human evolution. A mutation. If one ventured to believe that, then de Vries and Weissman are justified."

"The mutation theory of evolution, you mean?"

"Exactly. You see, Dan, while it is very obvious from fossil remains that evolution occurred, yet it is very easy to prove it couldn't possibly have occurred!"

"How?"

"Well, it couldn't have occurred slowly, as Darwin believed, for many reasons. Take the eye, for instance. He thought that very gradually, over thousands of generations, some sea creature developed a spot on its skin that was sensitive to light, and that this gave it an advantage over its blind fellows. Therefore its kind survived and others perished. But see here. If this eye developed slowly, why did the very first ones, the ones that couldn't yet see, have any better chance than the others? And take a wing. What good is a wing until you can fly with it? Just because a jumping lizard had a tiny fold of skin between foreleg and breast wouldn't mean that that lizard could survive where others died. What kept the wing developing to a point where it could actually have value?"

"What did?"

"De Vries and Weissman say nothing did. They answer that evolution must have progressed in jumps, so that when the eye appeared, it was already efficient enough to have survival value, and likewise the wing. Those jumps they named mutations. And in that sense, Dan, Kyra's a mutation, a jump from the human to—something else. Perhaps the superhuman."

Scott shook his head in perplexity. He was thoroughly puzzled, completely baffled, and more than a little unnerved. In a few moments more he bade Bach good night, wandered home, and lay for hours in sleepless thought.

The next day Bach managed a leave of absence for both of them from Grand Mercy, and Scott moved in. This was in part simply out of his fascinated interest in the case of Kyra Zelas, but in part it was altruistic. She had confessedly murdered one man; it occurred to Scott that she might with no more compunction murder Dr. Bach, and he meant to be at hand to prevent it.

He had been in her company no more than a few hours before Bach's words on evolution and mutations took on new meaning. It was not only Kyra's chameleon-like coloring, nor her strangely pure and saintlike features, nor even her incredible beauty. There was something more; he could not at once identify it, but decidedly the girl Kyra was not quite human.

The event that impressed this on him occurred in the late afternoon. Bach was away somewhere on personal business, and Scott had been questioning the girl about her own impressions of her experience.

"But don't you know you've changed?" he asked. "Can't you see the difference in yourself?"

"Not I. It is the world that has changed."

"But your hair was black. Now it's light as ashes."

"Was it?" she asked. "Is it?"

He groaned in exasperation. "Kyra," he said, "you must know something about yourself."

Her exquisite eyes turned their silver on him. "I do," she said. "I know that what I want is mine, and"—her pure lips smiled—"I think I want you, Dan."

It seemed to him, that she changed at that moment. Her beauty was not quite as it had been, but somehow more wildly intoxicating than before. He realized what it meant; her environment now contained a man she loved, or thought she loved, and she was adapting to that, too. She was becoming—he shivered slightly—irresistible!

Bach must have realized the situation, but he said nothing. As for Scott, it was sheer torture, for he realized only too well that the girl he loved was a freak, a biological sport, and worse than that, a cold murderess and a creature not exactly human. Yet for the next several days things went smoothly. Kyra slipped easily into the routine; she was ever a willing subject for their inquiries and investigations.

Then Scott had an idea. He produced one of the guinea pigs that he had injected, and they found that the creature evinced the same reaction as Kyra to cuts. They killed the thing by literally cutting it in half with an ax, and Bach examined its brain.

"Right!" he said at last. "It's hypertrophy of the pineal." He stared intently at Scott. "Suppose," he said, "that we could reach Kyra's pineal and correct the hypertrophy. Do you suppose that might return her to normal?"

Scott suppressed a pang of fear. "But why? She can't do any harm as long as we guard her here. Why do we have to gamble with her life like that?"

Bach laughed shortly. "For the first time in my life I'm glad I'm an old man," he said. "Don't you see we have to do something? She's a menace. She's dangerous. Heaven only knows how dangerous. We'll have to try."

Scott groaned and assented. An hour later, under the pretext of experiment, he watched the old man inject five grains of morphia into the girl's arm, watched her frown and blink—and adjust. The drug was powerless.

It was at night that Bach got his next idea. "Ethyl chloride!" he whispered. "The instantaneous anaesthetic. Perhaps she can't adjust to lack of oxygen. We'll try."

Kyra was asleep. Silently, carefully, the two crept in, and Scott stared down in utter fascination at the weird beauty of her features, paler than ever in the faint light of midnight. Carefully, so carefully, Bach held the cone above her sleeping face, drop by drop he poured the volatile, sweet-scented liquid into it. Minutes passed.

"That should anaesthetize an elephant," he whispered at last, and jammed the cone full upon her face.

She awoke. Fingers like slim steel rods closed on his wrist, forcing his hand away. Scott seized the cone, and her hand clutched his wrist as well, and he felt the strength of her grasp.

"Stupid," she said quietly, sitting erect. "This is quite useless—look!"

She snatched a paper knife from the table beside the bed. She bared her pale throat to the moonlight, and then, suddenly, drove the knife to its hilt into her bosom!

Scott gulped in horror as she withdrew it. A single spot of blood showed on her flesh, she wiped it away, and displayed her skin, pale, unscarred, beautiful.

"Go away," she said softly, and they departed.

The next day she made no reference to the incident. Scott and Bach spent a worried morning in the laboratory, doing no work, but simply talking. It was a mistake, for when they returned to the library, she was gone, having, according to Mrs. Getz, simply strolled out of the door and away. A hectic and hasty search of the adjacent blocks brought no sign of her.

At dusk she was back, pausing hatless in the doorway to permit Scott, who was there alone, to watch the miraculous change as she passed from sunset to chamber, and her hair faded from mahogany to aluminum.

"Hello," she said smiling. "I killed a child."

"What? My Lord, Kyra!"

"It was an accident. Surely you don't feel that I should be punished for an accident, Dan, do you?"

He was staring in utter horror. "How—"

"Oh, I decided to walk a bit. After a block or two, it occurred to me that I should like to ride. There was a car parked there with the keys in it, and the driver was talking on the sidewalk, so I slipped in, started it, and drove away. Naturally I drove rather fast, since he was shouting, and at the second corner I hit a little boy."

"And—you didn't stop?"

"Of course not. I drove around the corner, turned another corner or two, and then parked the car and walked back. The boy was gone, but the crowd was still there. Not one of them noticed me." She smiled her saintlike smile. "We're quite safe. They can't possibly trace me."

Scott dropped his head on his hands and groaned. "I don't know what to do!" he muttered. "Kyra, you're going to have to report this to the police."

"But it was an accident," she said gently, her luminous silver eyes pityingly on Scott.

"No matter. You'll have to."

She placed her white hand on his head. "Perhaps tomorrow," she said. "Dan, I have learned something. What one needs in this world is power. As long as there are people in the world with more power than I, I run afoul of them. They keep trying to punish me with their laws—and why? Their laws are not for me. They cannot punish me."

He did not answer.

"Therefore," she said softly, "tomorrow I go out of here to seek power. I will be more powerful than any laws."

That shocked him to action. "Kyra!" he cried. "You're not to try to leave here again." He gripped her shoulders. "Promise me! Swear that you'll not step beyond that door without me!"

"Why, if you wish," she said quietly.

"But swear it! Swear it by everything sacred!"

Her silver eyes looked steadily into his from a face like that of a marble angel. "I swear it," she murmured. "By anything you name, I swear it, Dan."

And in the morning she was gone, taking what cash and bills had been in Scott's wallet, and in Bach's as well. And, they discovered later, in Mrs. Getz's also.

"But if you could have seen her!" muttered Scott. "She looked straight into my eyes and promised, and her face was pure as a madonna's. I can't believe she was lying."

"The lie as an adaptive mechanism," said Bach, "deserves more attention than it has received. Probably the original liars are those plants and animals that use protective mimicry—

harmless snakes imitating poisonous ones, stingless flies that look like bees. Those are living lies."

"But she couldn't—"

"She has, however. What you've told me about her desire for power is proof enough. She's entered the second adaptive phase—that of adapting her environment to herself instead of herself to her environment. How far will her madness—or her genius—carry her? There is very little difference between the two, Dan. And what is left now for us to do but watch?"

"Watch? How? Where is she?"

"Unless I'm badly mistaken, watching her will be easy once she begins to achieve. Wherever she is, I think we—and the rest of the world—will know of it soon enough."

But weeks dropped away without sign of Kyra Zelas. Scott and Bach returned to their duties at Grand Mercy, and down in his laboratory the biochemist disposed grimly of the remains of three guinea pigs, a cat, and a dog, whose killing had been an exhausting and sickening task. In the crematory as well went a tube of water-clear serum.

Then one day the annunciator summoned him to Bach's office, where he found the old man hunched over a copy of the Post Record.

"Look here!" he said, indicating a political gossip column called "Whirls of Washington."

Scott read, "And the surprise of the evening was the soi disant confirmed bachelor of the cabinet, upright John Callan, who fluttered none other than the gorgeous Kyra Zelas, the lady who affects a dark wig by day and a white by night. Some of us remember her as the acquittee of a murder trial."

Scott looked up. "Callan, eh? Secretary of the treasury, no less! When she said power she meant power, apparently."

"But will she stop there?" mused Bach gloomily. "I have a premonition that she's just beginning."

"Well, actually, how far can a woman go?"

The old man looked at him. "A woman? This is Kyra Zelas, Dan. Don't set your limits yet. There will be more of her."

Bach was right. Her name began to appear with increasing frequency, first in social connections, then with veiled references to secret intrigues and influences.

Thus: "Whom do the press boys mean by the tenth cabineteer?" Or later: "Why not a secretary of personal relations? She has the powers; give her the name." And still later: "One has to go back to Egypt for another instance of a country whose exchequer was run by a woman. And Cleopatra busted that one."

Scott grinned a little ruefully to himself as he realized that the thrusts were becoming more indirect, as if the press itself were beginning to grow cautious. It was a sign of increasing power, for nowhere are people as sensitive to such trends as among the Washington correspondents. Kyra's appearance in the public prints began to be more largely restrained to purely social affairs, and usually in connection with John Callan, the forty-five-year-old bachelor secretary of the treasury.

Waking or sleeping, Scott never for a moment quite forgot her, for there was something mystical about her, whether she were mad or a woman of genius, whether freak or superwoman. The only thing he did forget was a thin girl with drab features and greasy black hair who had lain on a pallet in the isolation ward and coughed up flecks of blood.

It was no surprise to either Scott or Dr. Bach to return one evening to Bach's residence for a few hours' conversation, and find there, seated as comfortably as if she had never left it, Kyra Zelas. Outwardly she had changed but little; Scott gazed once more in fascination on her incredible hair and wide, innocent silver eyes. She was smoking a cigarette, and she exhaled a long, blue plume of smoke and smiled up at him.

He hardened himself. "Nice of you to honor us," he said coldly. "What's the reason for this visit? Did you run out of money?"

"Money? Of course not. How could I run out of money?"

"You couldn't, not as long as you replenished your funds the way you did when you left."

"Oh, that!" she said contemptuously. She opened her hand bag, indicating a green mass of bills. "I'll give that back, Dan. How much was it?"

"To hell with the money!" he blazed. "What hurts me is the way you lied. Staring into my eyes as innocent as a baby, and lying all the time!"

"Was I?" she asked. "I won't lie to you again, Dan. I promise."

"I don't believe you," he said bitterly. "Tell us what you're doing here, then."

"I wanted to see you. I haven't forgotten what I said to you, Dan." With the words she seemed to grow more beautiful than ever, and this time poignantly wistful as well.

"And have you," asked Bach suddenly, "abandoned your idea of power?"

"Why should I want power?" she rejoined innocently, flashing her magnificent eyes to him.

"But you said," began Scott impatiently, "that you—"

"Did I?" There was a ghost of a smile on her perfect lips. "I won't lie to you, Dan," she went on, laughing a little. "If I want power, it is mine for the taking—more power than you dream."

"Through John Callan?" he rasped.

"He offers a simple way," she said impassively. "Suppose, for instance, that in a day or so he were to issue a statement—a supremely insulting statement—about the war debts. The administration couldn't afford to reprimand him openly, because most of the voters feel that a supremely insulting statement is called for. And if it were insulting enough—and I assure you it would be—you would see the animosity of Europe directed westward.

"Now, if the statement were one that no national government could ignore and yet keep its dignity in the eyes of its people, it would provoke counter-insults. And there are three nations—you know their names as well as I—who await only such a diversion of interest. Don't you see?" She frowned.

"How stupid you both are!" she murmured, and then, stretching her glorious figure and yawning, "I wonder what sort of empress I would make. A good one, doubtless."

But Scott was aghast. "Kyra, do you mean you'd urge Callan into such a colossal blunder as that?"

"Urge him!" she echoed contemptuously. "I'd force him."

"Do you mean you'd do it?"

"I haven't said so," she smiled. She yawned again, and snapped her cigarette into the dark fireplace. "I'll stay here a day or two," she added pleasantly, rising. "Good night."

Scott faced Dr. Bach as she vanished into the old man's chamber. "Damn her!" he grated, his lips white. "If I believed she meant all of that—"

"You'd better believe it," said Bach.

"Empress, eh! Empress of what?"

"Of the world, perhaps. You can't set limits to madness or genius."

"We've got to stop her!"

"How? We can't keep her locked up here. In the first place, she'd doubtless develop strength enough in her wrists to break the locks on the doors, and if she didn't, all she'd need to do is shout for help from a window."

"We can have her adjudged insane!" flared Scott. "We can have her locked up where she can't break out or call for help."

"Yes, we could. We could if we could get her committed by the Sanity Commission. And if we got her before them, what chance do you think we'd have?"

"All right, then," said Scott grimly, "we're going to have to find her weakness. Her adaptability can't be infinite. She's immune to drugs and immune to wounds, but she can't be above the fundamental laws of biology. What we have to do is to find the law we need."

"You find it then," said Bach gloomily.

"But we've got to do something. At least we can warn people—" He broke off, realizing the utter absurdity of the idea.

"Warn people!" scoffed Bach. "Against what? We'd be the ones to go before the Sanity Commission then. Callan would ignore us with dignity, and Kyra would laugh her pretty little laugh of contempt, and that would be that."

Scott shrugged helplessly. "I'm staying here to-night," he said. "At least we can talk to her again tomorrow."

"If she's still here," remarked Bach ironically.

But she was. She came out as Scott was reading the morning papers alone in the library, and sat silently opposite him, garbed in black silk lounging pajamas against which her alabaster skin and incredible hair glowed in startling contrast. He watched skin and hair turn faintly golden as the morning sun lightened the chamber. Somehow it angered him that she should be so beautiful and at the same time deadly with an inhuman deadliness.

He spoke first. "You haven't committed any murders since our last meeting, I hope." He said it spitefully, viciously.

She was quite indifferent. "Why should I? It has not been necessary."

"You know, Kyra," he said evenly, "that you ought to be killed."

"But not by you, Dan. You love me."

He said nothing. The fact was too obvious to deny.

"Dan," she said softly, "if you only had my courage, there is no height we might not reach together. No height—if you had the courage to try. That is why I came back here, but—" She shrugged. "I go back to Washington tomorrow."

Later in the day Scott got Bach alone. "She's going tomorrow!" he said tensely. "Whatever we can do has to be done to-night."

The old man gestured helplessly. "What can we do? Can you think of any law that limits adaptability?"

"No, but—" He paused suddenly. "By Heaven!" he cried. "I can! I've got it!"

"What?"

"The law! A fundamental biological law that must be Kyra's weakness!"

"But what?"

"This! No organism can live in its own waste products! Its own waste is poison to any living thing!"

"But—"

"Listen. Carbon dioxide is a human waste product. Kyra can't adapt to an atmosphere of carbon dioxide!"

Bach stared. "By Heaven!" he cried. "But even if you're right, how—"

"Wait a minute. You can get a couple of cylinders of carbonic acid gas from Grand Mercy. Can you think of any way of getting the gas into her room?"

"Why—this is an old house. There's a hole from her room to the one I'm using, where the radiator connection goes through. It's not tight; we could get a rubber tube past the pipe."

"Good!"

"But the windows! She'll have the windows open." "Never mind that," said Scott. "See that they're soaped so they'll close easily, that's all."

"But even if it works, what good—Dan! You don't mean to kill her?"

He shook his head. "I—couldn't," he whispered. "But once she's helpless, once she's overcome—if she is—you'll operate. That operation on the pineal you suggested before. And may Heaven forgive me!"

Scott suffered the tortures of the damned that evening. Kyra was, if possible, lovelier than ever, and for the first time she seemed to exert herself to be charming. Her conversation was literally brilliant; she sparkled, and over and over Scott found himself so fascinated that the thought of the treachery he planned was an excruciating pain. It seemed almost a blasphemy to attempt violence against one whose outward appearance was so pure, so innocent, so saintlike.

"But she isn't quite—human!" he told himself. "She's not an angel but a female demon, a—what were they called?—an incubus!"

Despite himself, when at last Kyra yawned luxuriously and dropped her dainty feet to the floor to depart, he pleaded for a few moments more.

"But it's early," he said, "and tomorrow you leave."

"I will return, Dan. This is not the end for us."

"I hope not," he muttered miserably, watching the door of her room as it clicked shut.

He gazed at Bach. The older man, after a moment's silence, whispered, "It is likely that she sleeps almost at once. That's also a matter of adaptability."

In tense silence they watched the thin line of light below the closed door. Scott started violently when, after a brief interval, her shadow crossed it and it disappeared with a faint click.

"Now, then," he said grimly. "Let's get it over."

He followed Bach into the adjacent room. There, cold, metallic, stood the gray cylinders of compressed gas. He watched as the old man attached a length of tubing, ran it to the opening around the steam pipe, and began to pack the remaining space with wet cotton.

Scott turned to his own task. He moved quietly into the library. With utmost stealth he tried the door of Kyra's room; it was unlocked as he had known it would be, for the girl was supremely confident of her own invulnerability.

For a long moment he gazed across at the mass of radiant silver hair on her pillow, then, very cautiously, he placed a tiny candle on the chair by the window, so that it should be at about the level of the bed, lighted it with a snap of his cigarette lighter, withdrew the door key, and departed.

He locked the door on the outside, and set about stuffing the crack below it with cotton. It was far from airtight, but that mattered little, he mused, since one had to allow for the escape of the replaced atmosphere.

He returned to Bach's room. "Give me a minute," he whispered. "Then turn it on."

He stepped to a window. Outside was a two-foot ledge of stone, and he crept to this precarious perch. He was visible from the street below, but not markedly noticeable, for he was directly above an areaway between Bach's house and its neighbor. He prayed fervently that he might escape attention.

He crept along the ledge. The two windows of Kyra's chamber were wide, but Bach had done his work. They slid downward, without a creak, and he pressed close against the glass to peer in.

Across the room glowed the faint and steady flame of his little taper. Close beside him, within a short arm's length had no pane intervened, lay Kyra, quite visible in the dusk. She lay on her back, with one arm thrown above her unbelievable hair, and she had drawn only a single sheet over her. He could watch her breathing, quiet, calm, peaceful.

It seemed as if a long time passed. He fancied at last that he could hear the gentle hiss of gas from Bach's window, but he knew that that must be fancy. In the chamber he watched there was no sign of anything unusual; the glorious Kyra slept as she did everything else—easily, quietly, and confidently.

Then there was a sign. The little candle flame, burning steadily in the draughtless air, flickered suddenly. He watched it, certain now that its color was changing. Again it flickered, flared for a moment, then died. A red spark glowed on the wick for a bare instant, then that was gone.

The candle flame was smothered. That meant a concentration of eight or ten per cent of carbon dioxide in the room's temperature—far too high to support ordinary life. Yet Kyra was living. Except that her quiet breathing seemed to have deepened, she gave not even a sign of inconvenience. She had adapted to the decreased oxygen supply.

But there must be limits to her powers. He blinked into the darkness. Surely—surely her breathing was quickening. He was positive now; her breast rose and fell in convulsive gasps, and somewhere in his turbulent mind the scientist in him recorded the fact.

"Cheyne-Stokes breathing," he muttered. In a moment the violence of it would waken her.

It did. Suddenly the silver eyes started open. She brushed her hand across her mouth, then clutched at her throat. Aware instantly of danger, she thrust herself erect, and her bare legs flashed as she pushed herself from the bed. But she must have been dazed, for she turned first to the door.

He saw the unsteadiness in her movements. She twisted the doorknob, tugged frantically, then whirled toward the window. He could see her swaying as she staggered through the vitiated air, but she reached it. Her face was close to his, but he doubted if she saw him, for her eyes were wide and frightened, and her mouth and throat were straining violently for breath. She raised her hand to smash the pane; the blow landed, but weakly, and the window shook but did not shatter.

Again her arm rose, but that blow was never delivered. For a moment she stood poised, swaying slowly, then her magnificent eyes misted and closed, she dropped to her knees, and at last collapsed limply on the floor.

Scott waited a long, torturing moment, then thrust up the window. The rush of lifeless air sent him whirling dizzily on his dangerous perch, and he clutched the casement. Then a slow breeze moved between the buildings, and his head cleared.

He stepped gingerly into the chamber. It was stifling, but near the open window he could breathe. He kicked thrice against Bach's wall.

The hiss of gas ceased. He gathered Kyra's form in his arms, waited until he heard the key turn, then dashed across the room and into the library.

Bach stared as if fascinated at the pure features of the girl. "A goddess overcome," he said. "There is something sinful about our part in this."

"Be quick!" snapped Scott. "She's unconscious, not anaesthetized. God knows how quickly she'll readjust."

But she had not yet recovered when Scott laid her on the operating table in Bach's office, and drew the straps about her arms and body and slim bare legs. He looked down on her still, white face and bright hair, and he felt his heart contract with pain to see them darken ever so faintly and beautifully under the brilliant operating light, rich in actinic rays.

"You were right," he whispered to the unhearing girl. "Had I your courage there is nothing we might not have attained together."

Bach spoke brusquely. "Nasal?" he asked. "Or shall I trephine her?"

"Nasal."

"But I should like a chance to observe the pineal gland. This case is unique, and—"

"Nasal!" blazed Scott. "I won't have her scarred!"

Bach sighed and began. Scott, despite his long hospital experience, found himself quite unable to watch this operation; he passed the old man his instruments as needed, but kept his eyes averted from the girl's passive and lovely face.

"So!" said Bach at last. "It is done." For the first time he himself had a moment's leisure to survey Kyra's features.

Bach started violently. Gone was the exquisite aluminum hair, replaced by the stringy, dark, and oily locks of the girl in the hospital! He pried open her eye, silver no longer, but pallid blue. Of all her loveliness, there remained—what? A trace, perhaps; a trace in the saintlike purity of her pale face, and in the molding of her features. But a flame had died; she was a goddess no longer, but a mortal—a human being. The superwoman had become no more than a suffering girl.

An ejaculation had almost burst from his lips when Scott's voice stopped him.

"How beautiful she is!" he whispered. Bach stared. He realized suddenly that Scott was not seeing her as she was, but as she once had been. To his eyes, colored by love, she was still Kyra the magnificent.

Proteus Island

Originally Published in *Astounding Stories*
August 1936

PROTEUS ISLAND

The brown Maori in the bow of the outrigger stared hard at Austin Island slowly swimming nearer; then he twisted to fix his anxious brown eyes on Carver. "Taboo!" he exclaimed. "Taboo! Aussitan taboo!"

Carver regarded him without change of expression. He lifted his gaze to the island. With an air of sullen brooding the Maori returned to his stroke. The second Polynesian threw the zoologist a pleading look.

"Taboo," he said. "Aussitan taboo!"

The white man studied him briefly, but said nothing. The soft brown eyes fell and the two bent to their work. But as Carver stared eagerly shoreward there was a mute, significant exchange between the natives.

The proa slid over green combers toward the foam-skirted island, then began to sheer off as if reluctant to approach. Carver's jaw squared. "Malloa! Put in, you chocolate pig. Put in, do you hear?"

He looked again at the land. Austin Island was not traditionally sacred, but these natives had a fear of it for some reason. It was not the concern of a zoologist to discover why. The island was uninhabited and had been charted only recently. He noted the fern forests ahead, like those of New Zealand, the Kauri pine and dammar—dark wood hills, a curve of white beach, and between them a moving dot—an apteryx mantelli, thought Carver—a kiwi.

The proa worked cautiously shoreward.

"Taboo," Malloa kept whispering. "Him plenty bunyip!"

"Hope there is," the white man grunted. "I'd hate to go back to Jameson and the others at Macquarie without at least one little bunyip, or anyway a ghost of a fairy." He grinned. "Bunyip Carveris. Not bad, eh? Look good in natural-history books with pictures."

On the approaching beach the kiwi scuttled for the forest—if it was a kiwi after all. It looked queer, somehow, and Carver squinted after it. Of course, it had to be an apteryx; these islands of the New Zealand group were too deficient in fauna for it to be anything else. One variety of dog, one sort of rat, and two species of bat—that covered the mammalian life of New Zealand.

Of course, there were the imported cats, pigs and rabbits that ran wild on the North and Middle Islands, but not here. Not on the Aucklands, not on Macquarie, least of all here on Austin, out in the lonely sea between Macquarie and the desolate Balleny Islands, far down on the edge of Antarctica. No; the scuttling dot must have been a kiwi.

The craft grounded. Kolu, in the bow, leaped like a brown flash to the beach and drew the proa above the gentle inwash of the waves. Carver stood up and stepped out, then paused sharply at a moan from Malloa in the stern.

"See!" he gulped. "The trees, wahi! The bunyip trees!"

Carver followed his pointing figure. The trees—what about them? There they were beyond the beach as they had fringed the sands of Macquarie and of the Aucklands. Then he frowned. He was no botanist; that was Halburton's field, back with Jameson and the Fortune at Macquarie Island. He was a zoologist, aware only generally of the variations of flora. Yet he frowned.

The trees were vaguely queer. In the distance they had resembled the giant ferns and towering kauri pine that one would expect. Yet here, close at hand, they had a different aspect—not a markedly different one, it is true, but none the less, a strangeness. The kauri pines were not exactly kauri, nor were the tree ferns quite the same Cryptogamia that flourished on the Aucklands and Macquarie. Of course, those islands were many miles away to the north, and certain local variations might be expected. All the same—

"Mutants," he muttered, frowning. "Tends to substantiate Darwin's isolation theories. I'll have to take a couple of specimens back to Halburton."

"Wahi," said Kolu nervously, "we go back now?"

"Now!" exploded Carver. "We just got here! Do you think we came all the way from Macquarie for one look? We stay here a day or two, so I have a chance to take a look at this place's animal life. What's the matter, anyway?"

"The trees, wahi!" wailed Malloa. "Bunyip!—the walking trees, the talking trees!"

"Bah! Walking and talking, eh?" He seized a stone from the pebbled beach and sent it spinning into the nearest mass of dusky green. "Let's hear 'em say a few cuss words, then."

The stone tore through leaves and creepers, and the gentle crash died into motionless silence. Or not entirely motionless; for a moment something dark and tiny fluttered there, and then soared briefly into black silhouette against the sky. It was small as a sparrow, but bat-like, with membranous wings. Yet Carver stared at it amazed, for it trailed a twelve-inch tail, thin as a pencil, but certainly an appendage no normal bat ought to possess.

For a moment or two the creature fluttered awkwardly in the sunlight, its strange tail lashing, and then it swooped again into the dusk of the forest whence his missile had frightened it. There was only an echo of its wild, shrill cry remaining, something that sounded like "Wheer! Whe-e-e-r!"

"What the devil!" said Carver. "There are two species of Chiroptera in New Zealand and neighboring islands, and that was neither of them! No bat has a tail like that!"

Kolu and Malloa were wailing in chorus. The creature had been too small to induce outright panic, but it had flashed against the sky with a sinister appearance of abnormality. It was a monstrosity, an aberration, and the minds of Polynesians were not such as to face unknown strangeness without fear. Nor for that matter, reflected Carver, were the minds of whites; he shrugged away a queer feeling of apprehension. It would be sheer stupidity to permit the fears of Kolu and Malloa to influence a perfectly sane zoologist.

"Shut up!" he snapped. "We'll have to trap that fellow, or one of his cousins. I'll want a specimen of his tribe. Rhimolophidae, I'll bet a trade dollar, but a brand-new species. We'll net one tonight."

The voices of the two brown islanders rose in terror. Carver cut in sharply on the protests and expostulations and fragmentary descriptions of the horrors of bunyips, walking and talking trees, and the bat-winged spirits of evil.

"Come on," he said gruffly. "Turn out the stuff in the proa. I'll look along the beach for a stream of fresh water. Mawson reported water on the north side of the island."

Malloa and Kolu were muttering as he turned away. Before him the beach stretched white in the late afternoon sun; at his left rolled the blue Pacific and at his right slumbered the strange, dark, dusky quarter; he noted curiously the all but infinite variety of the vegetable forms, marveling that there was scarcely a tree or shrub that he could identify with any variety common on Macquarie or the Aucklands, or far-away New Zealand. But, of course, he mused, he was no botanist.

Anyway, remote islands often produced their own particular varieties of flora and fauna. That was part of Darwin's original evolution theory, this idea of isolation. Look at Mauritius and its dodo, and the Galapagos turtles, or for that matter, the kiwi of New Zealand, or the gigantic, extinct moa. And yet—he frowned over the thought—one never found an island that was entirely covered by its own unique forms of plant life. Windblown seeds of ocean borne debris always caused an interchange of vegetation among islands; birds carried seeds clinging to their feathers, and even the occasional human visitors aided in the exchange.

Besides, a careful observer like Mawson in 1911 would certainly have reported the peculiarities of Austin Island. He hadn't; nor, for that matter, had the whalers, who touched here at intervals as they headed into the antarctic, brought back any reports. Of course, whalers had become very rare of late years; it might have been a decade or more since one had made anchorage at Austin. Yet what change could have occurred in ten or fifteen years?

Carver came suddenly upon a narrow tidal arm into which dropped a tinkling trickle of water from a granite ledge at the verge of the jungle. He stooped, moistened his finger, and tasted it. It was brackish but drinkable, and therefore quite satisfactory. He could hardly expect to find a larger stream on Austin, since the watershed was too small on an island only seven miles by three. With his eyes he followed the course of the brook up into the tangle of fern forest, and a flash of movement arrested his eyes. For a moment he gazed in complete incredulity, knowing that he couldn't possibly be seeing—what he was seeing!

The creature had apparently been drinking at the brink of the stream, for Carver glimpsed it first in kneeling position. That was part of the surprise—the fact that it was kneeling—for no animal save man ever assumes that attitude, and this being, whatever it might be, was not human.

Wild, yellow eyes glared back at him, and the thing rose to an erect posture. It was a biped, a small travesty of man, standing no more than twenty inches in height. Little clawed fingers clutched at hanging creepers. Carver had a shocked glimpse of a body covered in patches with ragged gray fur, of an agile tail, of needle-sharp teeth in a little red mouth. But mostly he saw only malevolent yellow eyes and a face that was not human, yet had a hideous suggestion of humanity gone wild, a stunning miniature synthesis of manlike and feline characteristics. Carver had spent much time in the wastelands of the planet. His reaction was almost in the nature of a reflex, without thought or volition; his blue-barreled gun leaped and flashed as if it moved of itself. This automatism was a valuable quality in the wilder portions of the earth; more than once he had saved his life by shooting first when startled, and reflecting afterward. But the quickness of the reaction did not lend itself to accuracy.

His bullet tore a leaf at the very cheek of the creature. The thing snarled, and then, with a final flash of yellow flame from its wild eyes, leaped headlong into the tangle of foliage and vanished.

Carver whistled. "What in Heaven's name," he muttered aloud, "was that?" But he had small time for reflection; long shadows and an orange tint to the afternoon light warned that darkness—sudden, twilightless darkness—was near. He turned back along the curving beach toward the outrigger.

A low coral spit hid the craft and the two Maoris, and the ridge jutted like a bar squarely across the face of the descending sun. Carver squinted against the light and trudged thoughtfully onward—to freeze into sudden immobility at the sound of a terrified scream from the direction of the proa!

He broke into a run. It was no more than a hundred yards to the coral ridge, but so swiftly did the sun drop in these latitudes that dusk seemed to race him to the crest. Shadows skittered along the beach as he leaped to the top and stared frantically toward the spot where his craft had been beached.

Something was there. A box—part of the provisions from the proa. But the proa itself—was gone!

Then he saw it, already a half dozen cables' lengths out in the bay. Malloa was crouching in the stern, Kolu was partly hidden by the sail, as the craft moved swiftly and steadily out toward the darkness gathering in the north.

His first impulse was to shout, and shout he did. Then he realized that they were beyond earshot, and very deliberately, he fired his revolver three times. Twice he shot into the air, but since Malloa cast not even a glance backward, the third bullet he sent carefully in the direction of the fleeing pair. Whether or not it took effect he could not tell, but the proa only slid more swiftly into the black distance.

He stared in hot rage after the deserters until even the white sail had vanished; then he ceased to swear, sat glumly on the single box they had unloaded, and fell to wondering what had frightened them. But that was something he never discovered.

Full darkness settled. In the sky appeared the strange constellations of the heaven's under hemisphere; southeast glowed the glorious Southern Cross, and south the mystic Clouds of Magellan. But Carver had no eyes for these beauties; he was already long familiar with the aspect of the Southern skies.

He mused over his situation. It was irritating rather than desperate, for he was armed, and even had he not been, there was no dangerous animal life on these tiny islands south of the Aucklands, nor, excepting man, on New Zealand itself. But not even man lived in the Aucklands, or on Macquarie, or here on remote Austin. Malloa and Kolu had been terrifically frightened, beyond doubt; but it took very little to rouse the superstitious fears of a Polynesian. A strange species of bat was enough, or even a kiwi passing in the shadows of the brush, or merely their own fancies, stimulated by whatever wild tales had ringed lonely Austin Island with taboos.

And as for rescue, that too was certain. Malloa and Kolu might recover their courage and return for him. If they didn't, they still might make for Macquarie Island and the Fortune expedition. Even if they did what he supposed they naturally would do—head for the Aucklands, and then to their home on the Chathams—still Jameson would begin to worry in three or four days, and there'd be a search made.

There was no danger, he told himself—nothing to worry about. Best thing to do was simply to go about his work. Luckily, the box on which he sat was the one that contained his cyanide jar for insect specimens, nets, traps, and snares. He could proceed just as planned, except that he'd have to devote some of his time to hunting and preparing food.

Carver lighted his pipe, set about building a fire of the plentiful driftwood, and prepared for the night. He delivered himself of a few choice epithets descriptive of the two Maoris as he realized that his comfortable sleeping bag was gone with the proa, but the fire would serve against the chill of the high Southern latitude. He puffed his pipe reflectively to its end, lay down near his driftwood blaze, and prepared to sleep.

When, seven hours and fifty minutes later, the edge of the sun dented the eastern horizon, he was ready to admit that the night was something other than a success. He was hardened to the tiny, persistent fleas that skipped out of the sand, and his skin had long been toughened to the bloodthirsty night insects of the islands. Yet he had made a decided failure at the attempt to sleep.

Why? It surely couldn't be nervousness over the fact of strange surroundings and loneliness. Alan Carver had spent too many nights in wild and solitary places for that. Yet the night sounds had kept him in a perpetual state of half-wakeful apprehension, and at least a dozen times he had started to full consciousness in a sweat of nervousness. Why?

He knew why. It was the night sounds themselves. Not their loudness nor their menace, but their—well, their variety. He knew what darkness ought to bring forth in the way of noises; he knew every bird call and bat squeak indigenous to these islands. But the noises of night here on Austin Island had refused to conform to his pattern of knowledge. They were strange, unclassified, and far more varied than they should have been; and yet, even through the wildest cry, he fancied a disturbing note of familiarity.

Carver shrugged. In the clear daylight his memories of the night seemed like foolish and perverse notions, quite inexcusable in the mind of one as accustomed to lonely places as himself. He heaved his powerful form erect, stretched, and gazed toward the matted tangle of plant life under the tree ferns.

He was hungry, and somewhere in there was breakfast, either fruit or bird. Those represented the entire range of choice, since he was not at present hungry enough to consider any of the other possible variations—rat, bat, or dog. That covered the fauna of these islands.

Did it, indeed? He frowned as sudden remembrance struck him. What of the wild, yellow-eyed imp that had snarled at him from the brookside? He had forgotten that in the excitement of the desertion of Kolu and Malloa. That was certainly neither bat, rat, nor dog. What was it?

Still frowning, he felt his gun, glancing to assure himself of its readiness The two Maoris might have been frightened away by an imaginary menace, but the thing by the brook was something he could not ascribe to superstition. He had seen that. He frowned more deeply as he recalled the tailed bat of earlier in the preceding evening. That was no native fancy either.

He strode toward the fern forest. Suppose Austin Island did harbor a few mutants, freaks, and individual species. What of it? So much the better; it justified the Fortune expedition. It might contribute to the fame of one Alan Carver, zoologist, if he were the first to report this strange, insular animal world. And yet—it was queer that Mawson had said nothing of it, nor had the whalers.

At the edge of the forest he stopped short. Suddenly he perceived what was responsible for its aspect of queerness. He saw what Malloa had meant when he gestured toward the trees. He gazed incredulously, peering from tree to tree. It was true. There were no related species. There were no two trees alike. Not two alike. Each was individual in leaf, bark, stem. There were no two the same. No two trees were alike!

But that was impossible. Botanist or not, he knew the impossibility of it. It was all the more impossible on a remote islet where inbreeding must of necessity take place. The living forms might differ from those of other islands, but not from each other—at least, not in such incredible profusion. The number of species must be limited by the very intensity of competition on an island. Must be!

Carver stepped back a half dozen paces, surveying the forest wall. It was true. There were ferns innumerable; there were pines; there were deciduous trees—but there were, in the hundred yard stretch he could scan accurately, no two alike! No two, even, with enough similarity to be assigned to the same species, perhaps not even to the same genus.

He stood frozen in uncomprehending bewilderment. What was the meaning of it? What was the origin of this unnatural plenitude of species and genera? How could any one of the numberless forms reproduce unless there were somewhere others of its kind to fertilize it? It was true, of course, that blossoms on the same tree could cross-fertilize each other, but where, then, were the offspring? It is a fundamental aspect of nature that from acorns spring oaks, and from kauri cones spring kauri pines.

In utter perplexity, he turned along the beach, edging away from the wash of the waves into which he had almost backed. The solid wall of forest was immobile save where the sea breeze ruffled its leaves, but all that Carver saw was the unbelievable variety of those leaves. Nowhere—nowhere—was there a single tree that resembled any he had seen before.

There were compound leaves, and digitate, palmate, cordate, acuminate, bipinnate, and ensiform ones. There were specimens of every variety he could name, and even a zoologist can name a number if he has worked with a botanist like Halburton. But there were no specimens that looked as if they might be related, however distantly, to any one of the others. It was as if, on Austin Island, the walls between the genera had dissolved, and only the grand divisions remained.

Carver had covered nearly a mile along the beach before the pangs of hunger recalled his original mission to his mind. He had to have food of some sort, animal or vegetable. With a feeling of distinct relief, he eyed the beach birds quarreling raucously up and down the sand; at least, they were perfectly normal representatives of the genus Larus. But they made, at best, but tough and oily fare, and his glance returned again to the mysterious woodlands.

He saw now a trail or path, or perhaps just a chance thinning of the vegetation along a subsoil ridge of rock, that led into the green shades, slanting toward the forested hill at the western end of the island. That offered the first convenient means of penetration he had encountered, and in a moment he was slipping through the dusky aisle, watching sharply for either fruit or bird.

He saw fruit in plenty. Many of the trees bore globes and ovoids of various sizes, but the difficulty, so far as Carver was concerned, was that he saw none he could recognize as edible. He dared not chance biting into some poisonous variety, and Heaven alone knew what wild and deadly alkaloids this queer island might produce.

Birds fluttered and called in the branches, but for the moment he saw none large enough to warrant a bullet. And besides, another queer fact had caught his attention; he noticed that the farther he proceeded from the sea, the more bizarre became the infinite forms of the trees of the forest. Along the beach he had been able at least to assign an individual growth to its family, if not its genus, but here even those distinctions began to vanish.

He knew why. "The coastal growths are crossed with strays from other islands," he muttered. "But in here they've run wild. The whole island's run wild."

The movement of a dark mass against the leaf-sprinkled sky caught his attention. A bird? If it were, it was a much larger one than the inconsiderable passerine songsters that fluttered about him. He raised his revolver carefully, and fired.

The weird forest echoed to the report. A body large as a duck crashed with a long, strange cry, thrashed briefly among the grasses of the forest floor, and was still. Carver hurried forward to stare in perplexity at his victim.

It was not a bird. It was a climbing creature of some sort, armed with viciously sharp claws and wicked, needle-pointed white teeth in a triangular little red mouth. It resembled quite closely a small dog—if one could imagine a tree-climbing dog— and for a moment Carver froze in surprise at the thought that he had inadvertently shot somebody's mongrel terrier, or at least some specimen of Canis.

But the creature was no dog. Even disregarding its plunge from the treetops, Carver could see that. The retractile claws, five on the forefeet, four on the hind, were evidence enough, but stronger still was the evidence of those needle teeth. This was one of the Felidae. He could see further proof in the yellow, slitted eyes that glared at him in moribund hate, to lose their fire now in death. This was no dog, but a cat!

His mind flashed to that other apparition on the bank of the stream. That had borne a wild aspect of feline nature, too. What was the meaning of it? Cats that looked like monkeys; cats that looked like dogs!

He had lost his hunger. After a moment he picked up the furry body and set off toward the beach. The zoologist had superseded the man; this dangling bit of disintegrating protoplasm was no longer food, but a rare specimen. He had to get to the beach to do what he could to preserve it. It would be named after him—Felis Carveri—doubtless.

A sound behind him brought him to an abrupt halt. He peered cautiously back through the branch-roofed tunnel. He was being trailed. Something, bestial or human, lurked back there in the forest shadows. He saw it —or them—dimly, as formless as darker shades in the shifting array that marked the wind-stirred leaves.

For the first time, the successive mysteries began to induce a sense of menace. He increased his pace. The shadows slid and skittered behind him, and, lest he ascribe the thing to fancy, a low cry of some sort, a subdued howl, rose in the dusk of the forest at his left, and was answered at his right.

He dared not run, knowing that the appearance of fear too often brought a charge from both beasts and primitive humans. He moved as quickly as he could without the effect of flight from danger, and at last saw the beach. There in the opening he would at least distinguish his pursuers, if they chose to attack.

But they didn't. He backed away from the wall of vegetation, but no forms followed him. Yet they were there. All the way back to the box and the remains of his fire, he knew that just within the cover of the leaves lurked wild forms.

The situation began to prey on his mind. He couldn't simply remain on the beach indefinitely, waiting for an attack. Sooner or later he'd have to sleep, and then—Better to provoke the attack at once, see what sort of creatures he faced, and try to drive them off or exterminate them. He had, after all, plenty of ammunition.

He raised his gun, aimed at the skittering shadow, and fired. There was a howl that was indubitably bestial; before it had quivered into silence, others answered. Then Carver started violently backward, as the bushes quivered to the passage of bodies, and he saw what sort of beings had lurked there.

A line of perhaps a dozen forms leaped from the fringe of underbrush to the sand. For the space of a breath they were motionless, and Carver knew that he was in the grip of a zoologist's nightmare, for no other explanation was at all adequate.

The pack was vaguely doglike; but by no means did its members resemble the indigenous hunting dogs of New Zealand, nor the dingoes of Australia. Nor, for that matter, did they resemble any other dogs in his experience, nor, if the truth be told, any dogs at all, except perhaps in their lupine method of attack, their subdued yelps, their slavering mouths, and the arrangement of their teeth—what Carver could see of that arrangement.

But the fact that bore home to him now was another stunning repetition of all his observations of Austin Island—they did not resemble each other! Indeed, it occurred to Carver with the devastating force of a blow that, so far on this mad island, he had seen no two living creatures, animal or vegetable, that appeared to belong to related species!

The nondescript pack inched forward. He saw the wildest extremes among the creatures—beings with long hind legs and short forelimbs; a creature with hairless, thorn-scarred skin and a face like the half-human visage of a werewolf; a tiny, rat-sized thing that yelped with a shrill, yapping voice; and a mighty, barrel-chested creature whose body seemed almost designed for erect posture, and who loped on its hinder limbs with its fore-paws touching the ground at intervals like the knuckles of an orangutan. That particular being was a horrible, yellow-fanged monstrosity, and Carver chose it for his first bullet.

The thing dropped without a sound; the slug had split its skull. As the report echoed back and forth between the hills on the east and west extremities of Austin, the pack answered with a threatening chorus of bays, howls, growls, and shrieks. They shrank back momentarily from their companion's body, then came menacingly forward.

Again Carver fired. A red-eyed hopping creature yelped and crumpled. The line halted nervously, divided now by two dead forms. Their cries were no more than a muffled growling as they eyed him with red and yellowish orbs.

He started suddenly as a different sound rose, a cry whose nature he could not determine, though it seemed to come from a point where the forested bank rose sharply in a little cliff. It was as if some watcher urged on the nondescript pack, for they gathered courage again to advance. And it was at this moment that a viciously flung stone caught the man painfully on the shoulder.

He staggered, then scanned the line of brush. A missile meant humankind. The mad island harbored something more than aberrant beasts.

A second cry sounded, and another stone hummed past his ear. But this time he had caught the flash of movement at the top of the cliff, and he fired instantly.

There was a scream. A human figure reeled from the cover of foliage, swayed, and pitched headlong into the brush at the base, ten feet below. The pack of creatures broke howling, as if their courage had vanished before this evidence of power. They fled like shadows into the forest.

But something about the figure that had fallen from the cliff struck Carver as strange. He frowned, waiting a moment to assure himself that the nondescript pack had fled, and that no other menace lurked in the brush, then he darted toward the place where his assailant had fallen.

The figure was human, beyond doubt—or was it? Here on this mad island where species seemed to take any form, Carver hesitated to make even that assumption. He bent over his fallen foe, who lay face down, then turned the body over. He stared.

It was a girl. Her face, still as the features of the Buddha of Nikko, was young and lovely as a Venetian bronze figurine, with delicate features that even in unconsciousness had a wildness apparent in them. Her eyes, closed though they were, betrayed a slight, dryadlike slant.

The girl was white, though her skin was sun-darkened almost to a golden hue. Carver was certain of her color, nevertheless, for at the edges of her single garment—an untanned hide of leopard-like fur, already stiffening and cracking—her skin showed whiter.

Had he killed her? Curiously perturbed, he sought for the wound, and found it, at last, in a scarcely bleeding graze above her right knee. His shot had merely spun her off balance; it was the ten-foot fall from the cliff that had done the damage, of which the visible evidence was a reddening bruise of her left temple. But she was living. He swung her hastily into his arms and bore her across the beach, away from the brush in which her motley pack was doubtless still lurking.

He shook his nearly empty canteen, then tilted her head to pour water between her lips. Instantly her eyes flickered open, and for a moment she stared quite uncomprehendingly into Carver's eyes, not twelve inches from her own. Then her eyes widened, not so much in terror as in startled bewilderment; she twisted violently from his arms, tried twice to rise, and twice fell back as her legs refused to support her. At last she lay quite passive, keeping her fascinated gaze on his face.

But Carver received a shock as well. As her lids lifted, he started at the sight of the eyes behind them. They were unexpected, despite the hint given by their ever-so-faint Oriental cast, for they flamed upon him in a tawny hue. They were amber, almost golden, and wild as the eyes of a votary of Pan. She watched the zoologist with the intentness of a captive bird, but not with a bird's timidity, for he saw her hand fumbling for the pointed stick or wooden knife in the thong about her waist.

He proffered the canteen, and she shrank away from his extended hand. He shook the container, and at the sound of gurgling liquid, she took it gingerly, tilted a trickle into her hand, and then, to Carver's surprise, smelled it, her dainty nostrils flaring as widely as her diminutive, uptilted nose permitted. After a moment she drank from her cupped palm, poured another trickle, and drank that. It did not occur to her, apparently, to drink from the canteen.

Her mind cleared. She saw the two motionless bodies of the slain creatures, and murmured a low sound of sorrow. When she moved as if to rise, her gashed knee pained her, and she turned her strange eyes on Carver with a renewed expression of fear. She indicated the red streak of the injury.

"C'm on?" she said with a questioning inflection. Carver realized that the sound resembled English words through accident only. "Where to?" He grinned.

She shook a puzzled head. "Bu-r-r-o-o-on!" she said "Zee-e-e!"

He understood that. It was her attempt to imitate the sound of his shot and the hum of the bullet. He tapped the revolver. "Magic!" he said warningly. "Bad medicine. Better be good girl, see?" It was obvious that she didn't understand. "Thumbi?" he tried. "You Maori?" No result save a long look from slanting, golden eyes. "Well," he grunted, "Sprechen zie Deutsch, then? Or Kanaka? Or—what the devil! That's all I know—Latinum intelligisne?"

"C'm on?" she said faintly, her eyes on the gun. She rubbed the scratch on her leg and the bruise on her temple, apparently ascribing both to the weapon.

"All right," Carver acceded grimly. He reflected that it could do no harm to impress the girl with his powers. "I'll come on. Watch this!"

He leveled his weapon at the first target he saw—a dead branch that jutted from a drifted log at the end of the coral spit. It was thick as his arm, but it must have been thoroughly rotted, for instead of stripping a bit of bark as he expected, the heavy slug shattered the entire branch.

"O-o-oh!" gasped the girl, clapping her hands over her ears. Her eyes flickered sidewise at him; then she scrambled wildly to her feet. She was in sheer panic.

"No, you don't!" he snapped. He caught her arm. "You stay right here!"

For a moment he was amazed at the lithe strength of her. Her free arm flashed upward with the wooden dagger, and he caught that wrist as well. Her muscles were like tempered steel wires. She twisted frantically; then, with sudden yielding, stood quietly in his grasp, as if she thought, "What use to struggle with a god?"

He released her. "Sit down!" he growled.

She obeyed his gesture rather than his voice. She sat on the sand before him, gazing up with a trace of fear but more of wariness in her honey-hued eyes.

"Where are your people?" he asked sharply, pointing at her and then waving in an inclusive gesture at the forest.

She stared without comprehension, and he varied his symbolism. "Your home, then?" he pantomimed the act of sleeping.

The result was the same, simply a troubled look from her glorious eyes.

"Now what the devil!" he muttered. "You have a name, haven't you? A name? Look!" He tapped his chest. "Alan. Get it? Alan. Alan."

That she understood instantly. "Alan," she repeated dutifully, looking up at him.

But when he attempted to make her assign a name to herself, he failed utterly. The only effect of his efforts was a deepening of the perplexity in her features. He reverted, at last, to the effort to make her indicate in some fashion the place of her home and people, varying his gestures in every way he could devise. And at last she seemed to comprehend.

She rose doubtfully to her feet and uttered a strange, low, mournful cry. It was answered instantly from the brush, and Carver stiffened as he saw the emergence of that same motley pack of nondescript beings. They must have been watching, lurking just beyond view. Again they circled the two slain members as they advanced.

Carver whipped out his revolver. His movement was followed by a wail of anguish from the girl, who flung herself before him, arms outspread as if to shield the wild pack from the menace of the weapon. She faced him fearfully, yet defiantly, and there was puzzled questioning in her face as well. It was as if she accused the man of ordering her to summon her companions only to threaten them with death.

He stared. "O.K.," he said at last. "What's a couple of rare specimens on an island that's covered with 'em? Send 'em away."

She obeyed his gesture of command. The weird pack slunk silently from view, and the girl backed hesitantly away as if to follow them, but halted abruptly at Carver's word. Her attitude was a curious one, partly fear, but more largely composed, it seemed, of a sort of fascination, as if she did not quite understand the zoologist's nature.

This was a feeling he shared to a certain extent, for there was certainly something mysterious in encountering a white girl on this mad Austin Island. It was as if there were one specimen, and only one, of every species in the world here on this tiny islet, and she were the representative of humanity. But still he frowned perplexedly into her wild, amber eyes.

It occurred to him again that on the part of Austin he had traversed he had seen no two creatures alike. Was this girl, too, a mutant, a variant of some species other than human, who had through mere chance adopted a perfect human form? As, for instance, the doglike cat whose body still lay on the sand where he had flung it. Was she, perhaps, the sole representative of the human form on the island, Eve before Adam, in the garden? There had been a woman before Adam, he mused.

"We'll call you Lilith," he said thoughtfully. The name fitted her wild, perfect features and her flame-hued eyes. Lilith, the mysterious being whom Adam found before him in Paradise, before Eve was created. "Lilith," he repeated. "Alan—Lilith. See?"

She echoed the sounds and the gesture. Without question she accepted the name he had given her, and that she understood the sound as a name was evident by her response to it. For when he uttered it a few minutes later, her amber eyes flashed instantly to his face and remained in a silent question.

Carver laughed and resumed his puzzled thoughts. Reflectively, he produced his pipe and packed it, then struck a match and lighted it. He was startled by a low cry from the girl Lilith, and looked up to see her extended hand. For a moment he failed to perceive what she sought, and then her fingers closed around the hissing stem of the match! She had tried to seize the flame as one takes a fluttering bit of cloth.

She screamed in pain and fright. At once the pack of nondescripts appeared at the edge of the forest, voicing their howls of anger, and Carver whirled again to meet them. But again Lilith, recovering from the surprise of the burn, halted the pack with her voice, and sent them slinking away into the shadows. She sucked her scorched fingers and turned widened eyes to his face. He realized with a start of disbelief that the girl did not comprehend fire!

There was a bottle of alcohol in the box of equipment; he produced it and, taking Lilith's hand, bound a moistened strip of handkerchief about her two blistered fingers, though he knew well enough that alcohol was a poor remedy for burns. He applied the disinfectant to the bullet graze on her knee; she moaned softly at the sting, then smiled as it lessened, while her strange amber eyes followed fixedly the puffs of smoke from his pipe, and her nostrils quivered to the pungent tobacco odor.

"Now what," queried Carver, smoking reflectively, "am I going to do with you?"

Lilith had apparently no suggestion. She simply continued her wide-eyed regard.

"At least," he resumed, "you ought to know what's good to eat on this crazy island. You do eat, don't you?" He pantomimed the act.

The girl understood instantly. She rose, stepped to the spot where the body of the doglike cat lay, and seemed for an instant to sniff its scent. Then she removed the wooden knife from her girdle, placed one bare foot upon the body, and hacked and tore a strip of flesh from it. She extended the bloody chunk to him, and was obviously surprised at his gesture of refusal.

After a moment she withdrew it, glanced again at his face, and set her own small white teeth in the meat. Carver noted with interest how daintily she managed even that difficult maneuver, so that her soft lips were not stained by the slightest drop of blood.

But his own hunger was unappeased. He frowned over the problem of conveying his meaning, but at last hit upon a means. "Lilith!" he said sharply. Her eyes flashed at once to him. He indicated the meat she held, then waved at the mysterious line of trees. "Fruit," he said. "Tree meat. See?" He went through the motions of eating.

Again the girl understood instantly. It was odd, he mused, how readily she comprehended some things, while others equally simple seemed utterly beyond her. Queer, as everything on Austin Island was queer. Was Lilith, after all, entirely human? He followed her to the tree line, stealing a sidelong look at her wild, flame-colored eyes, and her features, beautiful, but untamed, dryadlike, elfin—wild.

She scrambled up the crumbling embankment and seemed to vanish magically into the shadows. For a moment Carver felt a surge of alarm as he clambered desperately after her; she could elude him here as easily as if she were indeed a shadow herself. True, he had no moral right to restrain her, save the hardly tenable one given by her attack; but he did not want to lose her—not yet. Or perhaps not at all.

"Lilith!" he shouted as he topped the cliff.

She appeared almost at his elbow. Above them twined a curious vine like a creeping conifer of some kind, bearing white-greenish fruits the size and shape of a pullet's egg. Lilith seized one, halved it with agile fingers, and raised a portion to her nostrils. She sniffed carefully, daintily, then flung the fruit away.

"Pah bo!" she said, wrinkling her nose distastefully.

She found another sort of queerly unprepossessing fruit composed of five finger-like protuberances from a fibrous disk, so that the whole bore the appearance of a large, malformed hand. This she sniffed as carefully as she had the other, then smiled sidewise up at him.

"Bo!" she said, extending it.

Carver hesitated. After all, it was not much more than an hour ago that the girl had been trying to kill him. Was it not entirely possible that she was now pursuing the same end, offering him a poisonous fruit?

She shook the unpleasantly bulbous object. "Bo!" she repeated, and then, exactly as if she understood his hesitancy, she broke off one of the fingers and thrust it into her own mouth. She smiled at him.

"Good enough, Lilith." He grinned, taking the remainder.

It was much pleasanter to the tongue than to the eye. The pulp had a tart sweetness that was vaguely familiar to him, but he could not quite identify the taste. Nevertheless, encouraged by Lilith's example, he ate until his hunger was appeased.

The encounter with Lilith and her wild pack had wiped out thoughts of his mission. Striding back toward the beach he frowned, remembering that he was here as Alan Carver, zoologist, and in no other role. Yet—where could he begin? He was here to classify and to take specimens, but what was he to do on a mad island where every creature was of an unknown variety? There was no possibility of classification here, because there were no classes. There was only one of everything—or so it appeared.

Rather than set about a task futile on the very face of it, Carver turned his thoughts another way. Somewhere on Austin was the secret of this riotous disorder, and it seemed better to seek the ultimate key than to fritter away his time at the endless task of classifying. He would explore the island. Some strange volcanic gas, he mused vaguely, or some queer radioactive deposit—analogous to Morgan's experiments with X-rays on germ plasm. Or—or something else. There must be some answer.

"Come on, Lilith," he ordered, and set off toward the west, where the hill seemed to be higher than the opposing eminence at the island's eastern extremity.

The girl followed with her accustomed obedience, with her honey-hued eyes fastened on Carver in that curious mixture of fear, wonder, and—perhaps—a dawning light of worship.

The zoologist was not too preoccupied with the accumulation of mysteries to glance occasionally at the wild beauty of her face, and once he caught himself trying to picture her in civilized attire—her mahogany hair confined under one of the current tiny hats, her lithe body sheathed in finer textile than the dried and cracking skin she wore, her feet in dainty leather, and her ankles in chiffon. He scowled and thrust the visualization away, but whether because it seemed too anomalous or too attractive he did not trouble to analyze.

He turned up the slope. Austin was heavily wooded, like the Aucklands, but progress was easy, for it was through a forest, not a jungle. A mad forest, true enough, but still comparatively clear of underbrush.

A shadow flickered, then another. But the first was only a queen's pigeon, erecting its glorious feather crest, and the second only an owl parrot. The birds on Austin were normal; they were simply the ordinary feathered life of the southern seas. Why? Because they were mobile; they traveled, or were blown by storms, from island to island.

It was mid-afternoon before Carver reached the peak, where a solemn outcropping of black basalt rose treeless, like a forester's watchtower. He clambered up its eroded sides and stood with Lilith beside him, gazing out across the central valley of Austin Island to the hill at the eastern point, rising until its peak nearly matched their own.

Between sprawled the wild forest, in whose depths blue-green shadows shifted in the breeze like squalls visible here and there on the surface of a calm lake. Some sort of soaring bird circled below, and far away, in the very center of the valley, was the sparkle of water. That, he knew must be the rivulet he had already visited. But nowhere—nowhere at all—was there any sign of human occupation to account for the presence of Lilith—no smoke, no clearing, nothing.

The girl touched his arm timidly, and gestured toward the opposite hill.

"Pah bo!" she said tremulously. It must have been quite obvious to her that he failed to understand, for she amplified the phrase. "R-r-r-r!" she growled, drawing her perfect lips into an imitation of a snarl. "Pah bo, lay shot." She pointed again toward the east.

Was she trying to tell him that some fierce beasts dwelt in that region? Carver could not interpret her symbolism in any other way, and the phrase she had used was the same she had applied to the poisonous fruit.

He narrowed his eyes as he gazed intently toward the eastern eminence, then started. There was something, not on the opposing hill, but down near the flash of water midway between.

At his side hung the prism binoculars he used for identifying birds. He swung the instrument to his eyes. What he saw, still not clearly enough for certainty, was a mound or structure, vine-grown and irregular. But it might be the roofless walls of a ruined cottage.

The sun was sliding westward. Too late in the day now for exploration, but to-morrow would do. He marked the place of the mound in his memory, then scrambled down.

As darkness approached, Lilith began to evince a curious reluctance to move eastward, hanging back, sometimes dragging timidly at his arm. Twice she said "No, no!" and Carver wondered whether the word was part of her vocabulary or whether she had acquired it from him. Heaven knew, he reflected amusedly, that he had used the word often enough, as one might use it to a child.

He was hungry again, despite the occasional fruits Lilith had plucked for him. On the beach he shot a magnificent Cygnus Atratus, a black Australian swan, and carried it with its head dragging, while Lilith, awed by the shot, followed him now without objection.

He strode along the beach to his box; not that that stretch was any more desirable than the next, but if Kolu and Malloa were to return, or were to guide a rescue expedition from the Fortune, that was the spot they'd seek first.

He gathered driftwood, and, just as darkness fell, lighted a fire.

He grinned at Lilith's start of panic and her low "O-o-oh!" of sheer terror as the blaze of the match caught and spread. She remembered her scorched fingers, doubtless, and she circled warily around the flames, to crouch behind him where he sat plucking and cleaning the great bird.

She was obviously quite uncomprehending as he pierced the fowl with a spit and set about roasting it, but he smiled at the manner in which her sensitive nostrils twitched at the combined odor of burning wood and cooking meat.

When it was done, he cut her a portion of the flesh, rich and fat like roast goose, and he smiled again at her bewilderment. She ate it, but very gingerly, puzzled alike by the heat and the altered taste; beyond question she would have preferred it raw and bleeding. When she had finished, she scrubbed the grease very daintily from her fingers with wet sand at a tidal pool.

Carver was puzzling again over what to do with her. He didn't want to lose her, yet he could hardly stay awake all night to guard her. There were the ropes that had lashed his case of supplies; he could, he supposed, tie her wrists and ankles; but somehow the idea appealed to him not at all. She was too naive, too trusting, too awe-struck and worshipful. And besides, savage or not, she was a white girl over whom he had no conceivable rightful authority.

At last he shrugged and grinned across the dying fire at Lilith, who had lost some of her fear of the leaping flames. "It's up to you," he remarked amiably. "I'd like you to stick around, but I won't insist on it."

She answered his smile with her own quick, flashing one, and the gleam of eyes exactly the color of the flames they mirrored, but she said nothing. Carver sprawled in the sand; it was cool enough to dull the activities of the troublesome sand fleas, and after a while he slept.

His rest was decidedly intermittent. The wild chorus of night sounds disturbed him again with its strangeness, and he woke to see Lilith staring fixedly into the fire's dying embers. Some time later he awakened again; now the fire was quite extinct, but Lilith was standing. While he watched her silently, she turned toward the forest. His heart sank; she was leaving.

But she paused. She bent over something dark—the body of one of the creatures he had shot. The big one, it was; he saw her struggle to lift it, and, finding the weight too great, drag it laboriously to the coral spit and roll it into the sea.

Slowly she returned; she gathered the smaller body into her arms and repeated the act, standing motionless for long minutes over the black water. When she returned once more she faced the rising moon for a moment, and he saw her eyes glistening with tears. He knew he had witnessed a burial.

He watched her in silence. She dropped to the sand near the black smear of ashes; but she seemed in no need of sleep. She stared so fixedly and so apprehensively toward the east that Carver felt a sense of foreboding. He was about to raise himself to sitting position when Lilith, as if arriving at a decision after long pondering, suddenly sprang to her feet and darted across the sand to the trees.

Startled, he stared into the shadows, and out of them drifted that same odd call he had heard before. He strained his ears, and was certain he heard a faint yelping among the trees. She had summoned her pack. Carver drew his revolver quietly from its holster and half rose on his arm.

Lilith reappeared. Behind her, darker shadows against the shadowy growths, lurked wild forms, and Carver's hand tightened on the grip of his revolver.

But there was no attack. The girl uttered a low command of some sort, the slinking shadows vanished, and she returned alone to her place on the sand.

The zoologist could see her face, silver-pale in the moonlight, as she glanced at him, but he lay still in apparent slumber, and Lilith, after a moment, seemed ready to imitate him. The apprehension had vanished from her features; she was calmer, more confident. Carver realized why, suddenly; she had set her pack to guard against whatever danger threatened from the east.

Dawn roused him. Lilith was still sleeping, curled like a child on the sand, and for some time he stood gazing down at her. She was very beautiful, and now, with her tawny eyes closed, she seemed much less mysterious; she seemed no island nymph or dryad, but simply a lovely, savage, primitive girl. Yet he knew— or he was beginning to suspect—the mad truth about Austin Island. If the truth were what he feared, then he might as well fall in love with a sphinx, or a mermaid, or a female centaur, as with Lilith.

He steeled himself. "Lilith!" he called gruffly.

She awoke with a start of terror. For a moment she faced him with sheer panic in her eyes; then she remembered, gasped, and smiled tremulously. Her smile made it very hard for him to remember what it was that he feared in her, for she looked beautifully and appealingly human save for her wild, flame-colored eyes, and even what he fancied he saw in those might be but his own imagining.

She followed him toward the trees. There was no sign of her bestial bodyguards, though Carver suspected their nearness. He breakfasted again on fruits chosen by Lilith, selected unerringly, from the almost infinite variety, by her delicate nostrils. Carver mused interestedly that smell seemed to be the one means of identifying genera on this insane island.

Smell is chemical in nature. Chemical differences meant glandular ones, and glandular differences, in the last analysis, probably accounted for racial ones. Very likely the differences between a cat, say, and a dog was, in the ultimate sense, a glandular difference. He scowled at the thought and stared narrowly at Lilith; but, peer as he might, she seemed neither more nor less than an unusually lovely little savage—except for her eyes.

He was moving toward the eastern part of the island, intending to follow the brook to the site of the ruined cabin, if it was a ruined cabin. Again he noted the girl's nervousness as they approached the stream that nearly bisected this part of the valley. Certainly, unless her fears were sheer superstition, there was something dangerous there. He examined his gun again, then strode on.

At the bank of the brook Lilith began to present difficulties. She snatched his arm and tugged him back, wailing, "No, no, no!" in frightened repetition.

When he glanced at her in impatient questioning, she could only repeat her phrase of yesterday. "Lay shot" she said, anxiously and fearfully. "Lay shot!"

"Humph!" he growled. "A cannon's the only bird I ever heard of that could—" He turned to follow the watercourse into the forest.

Lilith hung back. She could not bring herself to follow him there. For an instant he paused, looking back at her slim loveliness, then turned and strode on. Better that she remained where she was. Better if he never saw her again, for she was too beautiful for close proximity. Yet Heaven knew, he mused, that she looked human enough. But Lilith rebelled. Once she was certain that he was determined to go on, she gave a frightened cry. "Alan!" she called. "Al-an!"

He turned, astonished that she remembered his name, and found her darting to his side. She was pallid, horribly frightened, but she would not let him go alone.

Yet there was nothing to indicate that this region of the island was more dangerous than the rest. There was the same mad profusion of varieties of vegetation, the same unclassifiable leaves, fruits, and flowers. Only—or he imagined this—there were fewer birds.

One thing slowed their progress. At times the eastern bank of the rivulet seemed more open than their side, but Lilith steadfastly refused to permit him to cross. When he tried it, she clung so desperately and so violently to his arms that he at last yielded, and plowed his way through the underbrush on his own bank. It was as if the watercourse were a dividing line, a frontier, or—he frowned—a border.

By noon they had reached a point which Carver knew must be close indeed to the spot he sought. He peered through the tunnel that arched over the course of the brook, and there ahead, so overgrown that it blended perfectly with the forest wall, he saw it.

It was a cabin, or the remains of one. The log walls still stood, but the roof, doubtless of thatch, had long ago disintegrated. But what struck Carver first was the certainty, evident in design, in window openings, in doorway, that this was no native hut. It had been a white man's cabin of perhaps three rooms.

It stood on the eastern bank; but by now the brook had narrowed to a mere rill, gurgling from pool to tiny rapids. He sprang across, disregarding Lilith's anguished cry. But at a glimpse of her face he did pause. Her magnificent honey-hued eyes were wide with fear, while her lips were set in a tense little line of grimmest determination. She looked as an ancient martyr must have looked marching out to face the lions, as she stepped deliberately across to his side. It was almost as if she said, "If you are bound to die, then I will die beside you."

Yet within the crumbling walls there was nothing to inspire fear. There was no animal life at all, except a tiny, ratlike being that skittered out between the logs at their approach. Carver stared around him at the grassy and fern grown interior, at the remnants of decaying furniture and the fallen debris. It had been years since this place had known human occupants, a decade at the very least.

His foot struck something. He glanced down to see a human skull and a human femur in the grass. And then other bones, though none of them were in a natural position. Their former owner must have died there where the ruined cot sagged, and been dragged here by—well, by whatever it was that had feasted on human carrion.

He glanced sidewise at Lilith, but she was simply staring affrightedly toward the east. She had not noticed the bones, or if she had, they had meant nothing to her. Carver poked gingerly among them for some clue to the identity of the remains, but there was nothing save a corroded belt buckle. That, of course, was a little; it had been a man, and most probably a white man.

Most of the debris was inches deep in the accumulation of loam. He kicked among the fragments of what must once have been a cupboard, and again his foot struck something hard and round—no skull this time, but an ordinary jar.

He picked it up. It was sealed, and there was something in it. The cap was hopelessly stuck by the corrosion of years; Carver smashed the glass against a log. What he picked from the fragments was a notebook, yellowedged and brittle with time. He swore softly as a dozen leaves disintegrated in his hands, but what remained seemed stronger. He hunched down on the log and scanned the all-but-obliterated ink.

There was a date and a name. The name was Ambrose Callan, and the date was October 25th, 1921. He frowned. In 1921 he had been—let's see, he mused; fifteen years ago—he had been in grade school. Yet the name Ambrose Callan had a familiar ring to it.

He read more of the faded, written lines, then stared thoughtfully into space. That was the man, then. He remembered the Callan expedition because as a youngster he had been interested in far places, exploration, and adventure, as what youngster isn't? Professor Ambrose Callan of Northern; he began to remember that Morgan had based some of his work with artificial species—synthetic evolution—on Callan's observations.

But Morgan had only succeeded in creating a few new species of fruit fly, of Drosophila, by exposing germ plasm to hard X-rays. Nothing like this—this madhouse of Austin Island. He stole a look at the tense and fearful Lilith, and shuddered, for she seemed so lovely—and so human. He turned his eyes to the crumbling pages and read on, for here at last he was close to the secret.

He was startled by Lilith's sudden wail of terror. "Lay shot!" she cried. "Alan, lay shot!"

He followed her gesture, but saw nothing. Her eyes were doubtless sharper than his, yet—There! In the deep afternoon shadows of the forest something moved. For an instant he saw it clearly—a malevolent pygmy like the cat-eyed horror he had glimpsed drinking from the stream. Like it? No, the same; it must be the same, for here on Austin no creature resembled another, nor ever could, save by the wildest of chances.

The creature vanished before he could draw his weapon, but in the shadows lurked other figures, other eyes that seemed alight with nonhuman intelligence. He fired, and a curious squawling cry came back, and it seemed to him that the forms receded for a time. But they came again, and he saw without surprise the nightmare horde of creatures.

He stuffed the notebook in his pocket and seized Lilith's wrist, for she stood as if paralyzed by horror. He backed away out of the doorless entrance, over the narrow brook. The girl seemed dazed, half hypnotized by the glimpses of the things that followed them. Her eyes were wide with fear, and she stumbled after him unseeing. He sent another shot into the shadows.

That seemed to rouse Lilith. "Lay shot!" she whimpered, then gathered her self-control. She uttered her curious call, and somewhere it was answered, and yet further off, answered again.

Her pack was gathering for her defense, and Carver felt a surge of apprehension for his own position. Might he not be caught between two enemies?

He never forgot that retreat down the course of the little stream. Only delirium itself could duplicate the wild battles he witnessed, the unearthly screaming, the death grips of creatures not quite natural, things that fought with the mad frenzy of freaks and outcasts. He and Lilith must have been slain immediately save for the intervention of her pack; they slunk out of the shadows with low, bestial noises, circling Carver cautiously, but betraying no scrap of caution against—the other things.

He saw or sensed something that had almost escaped him before. Despite their forms, whatever their appearance happened to be, Lilith's pack was doglike. Not in looks, certainly; it was far deeper than that. In nature, in character; that was it.

And their enemies, wild creatures of nightmare though they were, had something feline about them. Not in appearance, no more than the others, but in character and actions. Their method of fighting, for instance—all but silent, with deadly claw and needle teeth, none of the fencing of canine nature, but with the leap and talons of feline. But their aspect, their—their catness was more submerged by their outward appearance, for they ranged from the semi-human form of the little demon of the brook to ophidian-headed things as heavy and lithe as a panther. And they fought with a ferocity and intelligence that was itself abnormal.

Carver's gun helped. He fired when he had any visible target, which was none too often; but his occasional hits seemed to instill respect into his adversaries.

Lilith, weaponless save for stones and her wooden knife, simply huddled at his side as they backed slowly toward the beach. Their progress was maddeningly slow, and Carver began to note apprehensively that the shadows were stretching toward the east, as if to welcome the night that was sliding around from that half of the world. Night meant—destruction.

If they could attain the beach, and if Lilith's pack could hold the others at bay until Carver could build a fire, they might survive. But the creatures that were allied with Lilith were being overcome. They were hopelessly outnumbered. They were being slain more rapidly with each one that fell, as ice melts more swiftly as its size decreases.

Carver stumbled backward into orange-tinted sunlight. The beach! The sun was already touching the coral spit, and darkness was a matter of minutes—-brief minutes.

Out of the brush came the remnants of Lilith's pack, a half dozen nondescripts, snarling, bloody, panting, and exhausted. For the moment they were free of their attackers, since the catlike fiends chose to lurk among the shadows. Carver backed farther away, feeling a sense of doom as his own shadow lengthened in the brief instant of twilight that divided day from night in these latitudes. And then swift darkness came just as he dragged Lilith to the ridge of the coral spit.

He saw the charge impending. Weird shadows detached themselves from the deeper shadows of the trees. Below, one of the nondescripts whined softly. Across the sand, clear for an instant against the white ground coral of the beach, the figure of the small devil with the half-human posture showed, and a malevolent sputtering snarl sounded. It was exactly as if the creature had leaped forward like a leader to exhort his troops to charge.

Carver chose that figure as his target. His gun flashed; the snarl became a squawl of agony, and the charge came.

Lilith's pack crouched; but Carver knew that this was the end. He fired. The flickering shadows came on. The magazine emptied; there was no time now to reload, so he reversed the weapon, clubbed it. He felt Lilith grow tense beside him.

And then the charge halted. In unison, as if at command, the shadows were motionless, silent save for the low snarling of the dying creature on the sand. When they moved again, it was away—toward the trees!

Carver gulped. A faint shimmering light on the wall of the forest caught his eye, and he spun. It was true! Down the beach, down there where he had left his box of supplies, a fire burned, and rigid against the light, facing toward them in the darkness, were human figures. The unknown peril of fire had frightened off the attack. He stared. There in the sea, dark against the faint glow of the West, was a familiar outline. The Fortune! The men there were his associates; they had heard his shots and lighted the fire as a guide.

"Lilith!" he choked. "Look there. Come on!"

But the girl held back. The remnant of her pack slunk behind the shelter of the ridge of coral, away from the dread fire. It was no longer the fire that frightened Lilith, but the black figures around it, and Alan Carver found himself suddenly face to face with the hardest decision of his life.

He could leave her here. He knew she would not follow, knew it from the tragic light in her honey-hued eyes. And beyond all doubt that was the best thing to do; for he could not marry her. Nobody could ever marry her, and she was too lovely to take among men who might love her—as Carver did. But he shuddered a little as a picture flashed in his mind. Children! What sort of children would Lilith bear? No man could dare chance the possibility that Lilith, too, was touched by the curse of Austin Island.

He turned sadly away—a step, two steps, toward the fire. Then he turned.

"Come, Lilith," he said gently, and added mournfully, "other people have married, lived, and died without children. I suppose we can, too."

*   *   *   *   *

The Fortune slid over the green swells, northward toward New Zealand. Carver grinned as he sprawled in a deck chair. Halburton was still gazing reluctantly at the line of blue that was Austin Island.

"Buck up, Vance," Carver chuckled. "You couldn't classify that flora in a hundred years, and if you could, what'd be the good of it? There's just one of each, anyway."

"I'd give two toes and a finger to try," said Halburton. "You had the better part of three days there, and might have had more if you hadn't winged Malloa. They'd have gone home to the

Chathams sure, if your shot hadn't got his arm. That's the only reason they made for Macquarie."

"And lucky for me they did. Your fire scared off the cats."

"The cats, eh? Would you mind going over the thing again, Alan? It's so crazy that I haven't got it all yet."

"Sure. Just pay attention to teacher and you'll catch on." He grinned. "Frankly, at first I hadn't a glimmering of an idea myself. The whole island seemed insane. No two living things alike! Just one of each genus, and all unknown genera at that. I didn't get a single clue until after I met Lilith. Then I noticed that she differentiated by smell. She told good fruits from poisonous ones by the smell, and she even identified that first cat-thing I shot by smell. She'd eat that because it was an enemy, but she wouldn't touch the dog-things I shot from her pack."

"So what?" asked Halburton, frowning.

"Well, smell is a chemical sense. It's much more fundamental than outward form, because the chemical functioning of an organism depends on its glands. I began to suspect right then that the fundamental nature of all living things on Austin Island was just the same as anywhere else. It wasn't the nature that was changed, but just the form. See?"

"Not a bit."

"You will. You know what chromosomes are, of course. They're the carriers of heredity, or rather, according to Weissman, they carry the genes that carry the determinants that carry heredity. A human being has forty-eight chromosomes, of which he gets twenty-four from each parent."

"So," said Halburton, "has a tomato."

"Yes, but a tomato's forty-eight chromosomes carry a different heredity, else one could cross a human being with a tomato. But to return to the subject, all variations in individuals come about from the manner in which chance shuffles these forty-eight chromosomes with their load of determinants. That puts a pretty definite limit on the possible variations.

"For instance, eye color has been located on one of the genes on the third pair of chromosomes. Assuming that this gene contains twice as many brown-eye determinants as blue-eye ones, the chances are two to one that the child of whatever man or woman owns that particular chromosome will be brown-eyed—if his mate has no marked bias either way. See?"

"I know all that. Get along to Ambrose Callan and his notebook."

"Coming to it. Now remember that these determinants carry all heredity, and that includes shape, size, intelligence, character, coloring—everything. People—or plants and animals—can vary in the vast number of ways in which it is possible to combine forty-eight chromosomes with their cargo of genes and determinants. But that number is not infinite. There are limits, limits to size, to coloring, to intelligence. Nobody ever saw a human race with sky-blue hair, for instance."

"Nobody'd ever want to!" grunted Halburton.

"And," proceeded Carver, "that is because there are no blue-hair determinants in human chromosomes. But—and here comes Callan's idea—suppose we could increase the number of chromosomes in a given ovum. What then? In humans or tomatoes, if, instead of forty-eight, there were four hundred eighty, the possible range of variation would be ten times as great as it is now.

"In size, for instance, instead of the present possible variation of about two and a half feet, they might vary twenty-five feet! And in shape—a man might resemble almost anything! That is, almost anything within the range of the mammalian orders. And in intelligence—" He paused thoughtfully.

"But how," cut in Halburton, "did Callan propose to accomplish the feat of inserting extra chromosomes? Chromosomes themselves are microscopic; genes are barely visible under the highest magnification, and nobody ever saw a determinant."

"I don't know how," said Carver gravely. "Part of his notes crumbled to dust, and the description of his method must have gone with those pages. Morgan uses hard radiations, but his object and his results are both different. He doesn't change the number of chromosomes."

He hesitated. "I think Callan used a combination of radiation and injection," he resumed. "I don't know. All I know is that he stayed on Austin four or five years, and that he came with only his wife. That part of his notes is clear enough. He began treating the vegetation near his shack, and some cats and dogs he had brought. Then he discovered that the thing was spreading like a disease."

"Spreading?" echoed Halburton.

"Of course. Every tree he treated strewed multi-chromosomed pollen to the wind, and as for the cats—Anyway, the aberrant pollen fertilized normal seeds, and the result was another freak, a seed with the normal number of chromosomes from one parent and ten times as many from the other. The variations were endless. You know how swiftly kauri and tree ferns grow, and these had a possible speed of growth ten times as great.

"The freaks overran the island, smothering out the normal growths. And Callan's radiations, and perhaps his injections, too, affected Austin Island's indigenous life—the rats, the bats. They began to produce mutants. He came in 1918, and by the time he realized his own tragedy, Austin was an island of freaks where no child resembled its parents save by the merest chance."

"His own tragedy? What do you mean?"

"Well, Callan was a biologist, not an expert in radiation. I don't know exactly what happened. Exposure to X-rays for long periods produces burns, ulcers, malignancies. Maybe Callan didn't take proper precautions to shield his device, or maybe he was using a radiation of peculiarly irritating quality. Anyway, his wife sickened first—an ulcer that turned cancerous.

"He had a radio—a wireless, rather, in 1921—and he summoned his sloop from the Chathams. It sank off that coral spit, and Callan, growing desperate, succeeded somehow in breaking his wireless. He was no electrician, you see.

"Those were troubled days, after the close of the War. With Callan's sloop sunk, no one knew exactly what had become of him, and after a while he was forgotten. When his wife died, he buried her; but when he died there was no one to bury him. The descendants of what had been his cats took care of him, and that was that."

"Yeah? What about Lilith?"

"Yes," said Carver soberly. "What about her? When I began to suspect the secret of Austin Island, that worried me. Was Lilith really quite human? Was she, too, infected by the taint of variation, so that her children might vary as widely as the offspring of the—cats? She spoke not a word of any language I knew—or I thought so, anyway—and I simply couldn't fit her in. But Callan's diary and notes did it for me."

"How?"

"She's the daughter of the captain of Callan's sloop, whom he rescued when it was wrecked on the coral point. She was five years old then, which makes her almost twenty now. As for language—well, perhaps I should have recognized the few halting words she recalled. C'm on, for instance, was comment— that is, 'how?' And pah bo was simply pas bon, not good. That's what she said about the poisonous fruit. And lay shot was les chats, for somehow she remembered, or sensed, that the creatures from the eastern end were cats.

"About her, for fifteen years, centered the dog creatures, who despite their form were, after all, dogs by nature, and loyal to their mistress. And between the two groups was eternal warfare."

"But are you sure Lilith escaped the taint?"

"Her name's Lucienne," mused Carver, "but I think I prefer Lilith." He smiled at the slim figure clad in a pair of Jameson's trousers and his own shirt, standing there in the stern looking back at Austin. "Yes, I'm sure. When she was cast on the island, Callan had already destroyed the device that had slain his wife and was about to kill him. He wrecked his equipment completely, knowing that in the course of time the freaks he had created were doomed."

"Doomed?"

"Yes. The normal strains, hardened by evolution, are stronger. They're already appearing around the edges of the island, and some day Austin will betray no more peculiarities than any other remote islet. Nature always reclaims her own."

THE CIRCLE OF ZERO

ORIGINALLY PUBLISHED IN *THRILLING WONDER STORIES*
OCTOBER 1936

THE CIRCLE OF ZERO

Chapter I.

If there were a mountain a thousand miles high and every thousand years a bird flew over it, just brushing the peak with the tip of its wing, in the course of inconceivable eons the mountain would be worn away. Yet all those ages would not be one second to the length of eternity.

I don't know what philosophical mind penned the foregoing, but the words keep recurring to me since last I saw old Aurore de Neant, erstwhile professor of psychology at Tulane. When, back in '24, I took that course in Morbid Psychology from him, I think the only reason for taking it at all was that I needed an eleven o'clock on Tuesdays and Thursdays to round out a lazy program.

I was gay Jack Anders, twenty-two years old, and the reason seemed sufficient. At least, I'm sure that dark and lovely Yvonne de Neant had nothing to do with it. She was but a slim child of sixteen.

Old de Neant liked me, Lord knows why, for I was a poor enough student. Perhaps it was because I never, to his knowledge, punned on his name. Aurore de Neant translates to Dawn of Nothingness, you see; you can imagine what students did to such a name. 'Rising Zero'—'Empty Morning'—those were two of the milder soubriquets.

That was in '24. Five years later I was a bond salesman in New York and Professor Aurore de Neant was fired. I learned about it when he called me up. I had drifted quite out of touch with University days.

He was a thrifty sort. He had saved a comfortable sum, and had moved to New York and that's when I started seeing Yvonne again, now darkly beautiful as a Tanagra figurine. I was doing pretty well and was piling up a surplus against the day when Yvonne and I...

At least that was the situation in August, 1929. In October of the same year I was as clean as a gnawed bone and old de Neant had but little more meat. I was young and could afford to laugh—he was old and he turned bitter. Indeed, Yvonne and I did little enough laughing when we thought of our own future—but we didn't brood like the professor.

I remember the evening he broached the subject of the Circle of Zero. It was a rainy, blustering fall night and his beard waggled in the dim lamplight like a wisp of grey mist. Yvonne and I had been staying in evenings of late. Shows cost money and I felt that she appreciated my talking to her father, and—after all—he retired early.

She was sitting on the davenport at his side when he suddenly stabbed a gnarled finger at me and snapped, 'Happiness depends on money!'

I was startled. 'Well, it helps,' I agreed.

His pale blue eyes glittered. 'We must recover ours!' he rasped.

'How?'

'I know how. Yes, I know how,' he grinned thinly. 'They think I'm mad. You think I'm mad. Even Yvonne thinks so.'

The girl said softly, reproachfully, 'Father!'

'But I'm not,' he continued. 'You and Yvonne and all the fools holding chairs at universities—yes! But not I.'

'I will be all right, if conditions don't get better soon,' I murmured. I was used to the old man's outbursts.

'They will be better for us,' he said, calming. 'Money! We will do anything for money, won't we, Anders?'

'Anything honest.'

'Yes, anything honest. Time is honest, isn't it? An honest cheat, because it takes everything human and turns it into dust.' He peered at my puzzled face. I will explain,' he said, 'how we can cheat time.'

'Cheat—'

'Yes. Listen, Jack. Have you ever stood in a strange place and felt a sense of having been there before? Have you ever taken a trip and sensed that sometime, somehow, you had done exactly the same thing—when you know you hadn't?'

'Of course. Everyone has. A memory of the present, Bergson calls it.'

'Bergson is a fool! Philosophy without science. Listen to me.' He leaned forward. 'Did you ever hear of the Law of Chance?'

I laughed. 'My business is stocks and bonds. I ought to know of it.'

'Ah,' he said, 'but not enough of it. Suppose I have a barrel with a million trillion white grains of sand in it and one black grain. You stand and draw single grains, one after the other, look at each one and throw it back into the barrel. What are the odds against drawing the black grain?'

'A million trillion to one, on each draw.'

'And if you draw half of the million trillion grains?'

'Then the odds are even.'

'So!' he said. 'In other words, if you draw long enough, even though you return each grain to the barrel and draw again, some day you will draw the black one—if you try long enough!'

'Yes,' I said.

He half smiled.

'Suppose now you tried for eternity?'

'Eh?

'Don't you see, Jack? In eternity the Law of Chance functions perfectly. In eternity, sooner or later, every possible combination of things and events must happen. Must happen, if it's a possible combination. I say, therefore, that in eternity, whatever can happen, will happen!' His blue eyes blazed in pale fire.

I was a trifle dazed. 'I guess you're right,' I muttered.

'Right! Of course I'm right. Mathematics is infallible. Now do you see the conclusion?'

'Why—that sooner or later everything will happen.'

'Bah! It is true that there is eternity in the future; we cannot imagine time ending. But Flammarion, before he died, pointed out that there is also an eternity in the past. Since in eternity everything possible must happen, it follows that everything must already have happened!'

I gasped. 'Wait a minute! I don't see—'

'Stupidity!' he hissed. 'It is but to say with Einstein that not only space is curved, but time. To say that, after untold eons of millennia, the same things repeat themselves because they must! The Law of Chance says they must, given time enough. The past and the future are the same thing, because everything that will happen must already have happened. Can't you follow so simple a chain of logic?'

'Why—yes. But where does it lead?'

To our money! To our money!'

'What?'

'Listen. Do not interrupt. In the past all possible combinations of atoms and circumstances must have occurred.' He paused then stabbed that bony finger of his at me. 'Jack Anders, you are a possible combination of atoms and circumstances! Possible because you exist at this moment!'

'You mean—that I have happened before?'

'How apt you are! Yes, you have happened before and will again.'

'Transmigration!' I gulped. 'That's unscientific.'

'Indeed?' He frowned as if in effort to gather his thoughts. 'The poet Robert Burns was buried under an apple tree. When, years after his death, he was to be removed to rest among the great men of Westminster Abbey, do you know what they found? Do you know?'

'I'm sorry, but I don't.'

'They found a root! A root with a bulge for a head, branch roots for arms and legs and little rootlets for fingers and toes. The apple tree had eaten Bobby Burns—but who had eaten the apples?'

'Who—what?'

'Exactly. Who and what? The substance that had been Burns was in the bodies of Scotch countrymen and children, in the bodies of caterpillars who had eaten the leaves and become butterflies and been eaten by birds, in the wood of the tree. Where is Bobby Burns? Transmigration, I tell you! Isn't that transmigration?'

'Yes—but not what you meant about me. His body may be living, but in a thousand different forms.'

'Ah! And when some day, eons and eternities in the future, the Laws of Chance form another nebula that will cool to another sun and another earth, is there not the same chance that those scattered atoms may reassemble another Bobby Burns?'

'But what a chance! Trillions and trillions to one!'

'But eternity, Jack! In eternity that one chance out of all those trillions must happen—must happen!'

I was floored. I stared at Yvonne's pale and lovely features, then at the glistening old eyes of Aurore de Neant.

'You win,' I said with a long sigh. 'But what of it? This is still nineteen twenty-nine, and our money's still sunk in a very sick securities market.'

'Money!' he groaned. 'Don't you see? That memory we started from—that sense of having done a thing before—that's a memory out of the infinitely remote future. If only—if only one could remember clearly! But I have a way.' His voice rose suddenly to a shrill scream. 'Yes, I have a way!'

Wild eyes glared at me. I said, 'A way to remember our former incarnations?' One had to humour the old professor. 'To remember—the future?'

'Yes! Reincarnation!' His voice crackled wildly. Re-in-carnatione, which is Latin for "by the thing in the carnation", but it wasn't a carnation—it was an apple tree. The carnation is dianthus carophyllus, which proved that the Hottentots plant carnations on the graves of their ancestors, whence the expression "nipped in the bud". If carnations grow on apple trees—'

'Father!' cut in Yvonne sharply. 'You're tired!' Her voice softened. 'Come. You're going to bed.'

'Yes,' he cackled. 'To a bed of carnations.'

CHAPTER II: Memory of Things Past

Some evenings later Aurore de Neant reverted to the same topic. He was clear enough as to where he had left off.

'So in this millennially dead past,' he began suddenly, 'there was a year nineteen twenty-nine and two fools named Anders and de Neant, who invested their money in what are sarcastically called securities. There was a clown's panic, and their money vanished.' He leered fantastically at me.

'Wouldn't it be nice if they could remember what happened in, say, the months from December, nineteen twenty-nine, to June, nineteen thirty—next year?' His voice was suddenly whining. 'They could get their money back then!'

I humoured him. 'If they could remember.'

They can!' he blazed. 'They can!'

'How?'

His voice dropped to a confidential softness. 'Hypnotism! You studied Morbid Psychology under me, didn't you, Jack? Yes—I remember.'

'But, hypnotism!' I objected. 'Every psychiatrist uses that in his treatments and no one has remembered a previous incarnation or anything like it.'

'No. They're fools, these doctors and psychiatrists. Listen—do you remember the three stages of the hypnotic state as you learned them?'

'Yes. Somnambulism, lethargy, catalepsy.'

'Right. In the first the subject speaks, answers questions. In the second he sleeps deeply. In the third, catalepsy, he is rigid, stiff, so that he can be laid across two chairs, sat on—all that nonsense.'

'I remember. What of it?'

He grinned bleakly. 'In the first stage the subject remembers everything that ever happened during his life. His subconscious mind is dominant and that never forgets. Correct?'

'So we were taught.'

He leaned tensely forward. 'In the second stage, lethargy, my theory is that he remembers everything that happened in his other lives! He remembers the future!'

'Huh? Why doesn't someone do it, then?'   ·

'He remembers while he sleeps. He forgets when he wakes. That's why. But I believe that with proper training he can learn to remember.'

'And you're going to try?'

'Not I. I know too little of finance. I wouldn't know how to interpret my memories.'

'Who, then?'

'You!' He jabbed that long finger against me.

I was thoroughly startled. 'Me? Oh, no! Not a chance of it!'

'Jack,' he said querulously, 'didn't you study hypnotism in my course? Didn't you learn how harmless it is? You know what tommy-rot the idea is of one mind dominating another. You know the subject really hypnotizes himself, that no one can hypnotize an unwilling person. Then what are you afraid of?'

'I—well,' I didn't know what to answer.

I'm not afraid,' I said grimly. 'I just don't like it.'

'You're afraid!'

'I'm not!'

'You are!' He was growing excited.

It was at that moment that Yvonne's footsteps sounded in the hall. His eyes glittered. He looked at me with a sinister hint of cunning.

'I dislike cowards,' he whispered. His voice rose. 'So does Yvonne!'

The girl entered, perceiving his excitement. 'Oh!' she frowned. 'Why do you have to take these theories so to heart, father?'

'Theories?' he screeched. 'Yes! I have a theory that when you walk you stand still and the sidewalk moves back. No—then the sidewalk moves back. No—then the sidewalk would split if two people walked towards each other—or maybe it's elastic. Of course it's elastic! That's why the last mile is the longest. It's been stretched!'

Yvonne got him to bed.

Well, he talked me into it. I don't know how much was due to my own credulity and how much to Yvonne's solemn dark eyes. I half-believed the professor by the time he'd spent another evening in argument but I think the clincher was his veiled threat to forbid Yvonne my company. She'd have obeyed him if it killed her. She was from New Orleans too, you see, and of Creole blood.

I won't describe that troublesome course of training. One has to develop the hypnotic habit. It's like any other habit, and must be formed slowly. Contrary to the popular opinion morons and people of low intelligence can't ever do it. It takes real concentration—the whole knack of it is the ability to concentrate one's attention—and I don't mean the hypnotist, either.

I mean the subject. The hypnotist hasn't a thing to do with it except to furnish the necessary suggestion by murmuring, 'Sleep—sleep—sleep—sleep ...' And even that isn't necessary once you learn the trick of it.

I spent half-an-hour or more nearly every evening, learning that trick. It was tedious and a dozen times I became thoroughly disgusted and swore to have no more to do with the farce. But always, after the half-hour's humouring of de Neant, there was

Yvonne, and boredom vanished. As a sort of reward, I suppose, the old man took to leaving us alone. And we used our time, I'll wager, to better purpose than he used his.

But I began to learn, little by little. Came a time, after three weeks of tedium, when I was able to cast myself into a light somnambulistic state. I remember how the glitter of the cheap stone in Professor de Neant's ring grew until it filled the world and how his voice, mechanically dull, murmured like the waves in my ears. I remember everything that transpired during those minutes, even his query, 'Are you sleeping?' and my automatic reply, 'Yes.'

By the end of November we had mastered the second state of lethargy and then—I don't know why, but a sort of enthusiasm for the madness took hold of me. Business was at a standstill. I grew tired of facing customers to whom I had sold bonds at a par that were now worth fifty or less and trying to explain why. After a while I began to drop in on the professor during the afternoon and we went through the insane routine again and again.

Yvonne comprehended only a part of the bizarre scheme. She was never in the room during our half-hour trials and knew only vaguely that we were involved in some sort of experiment which was to restore our lost money. I don't suppose she had much faith in it but she always indulged her father.

It was early in December that I began to remember things. Dim and formless things at first—sensations that utterly eluded the rigities of words. I tried to express them to de Neant but it was hopeless.

'A circular feeling,' I'd say. 'No—not exactly—a sense of spiral—not that, either. Roundness—I can't recall it now. It slips away.'

He was jubilant. 'It comes!' he whispered, grey beard awaggle and pale eyes glittering. 'You begin to remember!'

'But what good is a memory like that?'

'Wait! It will come clearer. Of course not all your memories will be of the sort we can use. They will be scattered. Through all the multifold eternities of the past-future circle you can't have been always Jack Anders, securities salesman.

'There will be fragmentary memories, recollections of times when your personality was partially existent, when the Laws of

Chance had assembled a being who was not quite Jack Anders, in some period of the infinite worlds that must have risen and died in the span of eternities.

'But somewhere, too, the same atoms, the same conditions, must have made you. You're the black grain among the trillions of white grains and, with all eternity to draw in from, you must have been drawn before—many, many times.'

'Do you suppose,' I asked suddenly, 'that anyone exists twice on the same earth? Reincarnation in the sense of the Hindus?'

He laughed scornfully. 'The age of the earth is somewhere between a thousand million and three thousand million years. What proportion of eternity is that?'

'Why—no proportion at all. Zero.'

'Exactly. And zero represents the chance of the same atoms combining to form the same person twice in one cycle of a planet. But I have shown that trillions, or trillions of trillions of years ago, there must have been another earth, another Jack Anders, and'—his voice took on that whining note—'another crash that ruined Jack Anders and old de Neant. That is the time you must remember out of lethargy.'

'Catalepsy!' I said. 'What would one remember in that?'

'God knows.'

'What a mad scheme!' I said suddenly. 'What a crazy pair of fools we are!' The adjectives were a mistake.

'Mad? Crazy?' His voice became a screech. 'Old de Neant is mad, eh? Old Dawn of Nothingness is crazy! You think time doesn't go in a circle, don't you? Do you know what a circle represents? I'll tell you!

'A circle is the mathematical symbol for zero! Time is zero— time is a circle. I have a theory that the hands of a clock are really the noses, because they're on the clock's face, and since time is a circle they go round and round and round ...'

Yvonne slipped quietly into the room and patted her father's furrowed forehead. She must have been listening.

CHAPTER III: Nightmare or Truth?

'Look here,' I said at a later time to de Neant. 'If the past and future are the same thing, then the future's as unchangeable as the past. How, then, can we expect to change it by recovering our money?'

'Change it?' he snorted. 'How do you know we're changing it? How do you know that this same thing wasn't done by that Jack Anders and de Neant back on the other side of eternity? I say it was!'

I subsided, and the weird business went on. My memories—if they were memories—were becoming clearer now. Often and often I saw things out of my own immediate past of twenty-seven years, though of course de Neant assured me that these were visions from the past of that other self on the far side of time.

I saw other things too, incidents that I couldn't place in my experience, though I couldn't be quite sure they didn't belong there. I might have forgotten, you see, since they were of no particular importance. I recounted everything dutifully to the old man immediately upon awakening and sometimes that was difficult—like trying to find words for a half-remembered dream.

There were other memories as well—bizarre, outlandish dreams that had little parallel in human history. These were always vague and sometimes very horrible and only their inchoate and formless character kept them from being utterly nerve-racking and terrifying.

At one time, I recall, I was gazing through a little crystalline window into a red fog through which moved indescribable faces—not human, not even associable with anything I had ever seen. On another occasion I was wandering, clad in furs, across a cold grey desert and at my side was a woman who was not quite Yvonne.

I remember calling her Pyroniva, and knowing that the name meant 'Snowy-fire'. And here and there in the air about us floated fungoid things, bobbing around like potatoes in a water-bucket. And once we stood very quiet while a menacing form that was only remotely like the small fungi droned purposefully far overhead, toward some unknown objective.

At still another time I was peering, fascinated, into a spinning pool of mercury, watching an image therein of two wild winged figures playing in a roseate glade—not at all human in form but transcendently beautiful, bright and iridescent.

I felt a strange kinship between these two creatures and myself and Yvonne but I had no inkling of what they were, nor upon what world, nor at what time in eternity, nor even of what nature was the room that held the spinning pool that pictured them.

Old Aurore de Neant listened carefully to the wild word-pictures I drew.

'Fascinating!' he muttered. 'Glimpses of an infinitely distant future caught from a ten-fold infinitely remote past. These things you describe are not earthly; it means that somewhere, sometime, men are actually to burst the prison of space and visit other worlds. Some day ...'

'If these glimpses aren't simply nightmares,' I said.

They're not nightmares,' he snapped, 'but they might as well be for all the value they are to us.' I could see him struggle to calm himself. 'Our money is still gone. We must try, keep trying for years, for centuries, until we get the black grain of sand, because black sand is a sign of gold-bearing ore ...' He paused. 'What am I talking about?' he said querously.

Well, we kept trying. Interspersed with the wild, all but indescribable visions came others almost rational. The thing became a fascinating game. I was neglecting my business—though that was small loss—to chase dreams with old Professor Aurore de Neant.

I spent evenings, afternoons and finally mornings, too, living in the slumber of the lethargic state or telling the old man what fantastic things I had dreamed—or, as he said, remembered. Reality became dim to me. I was living in an outlandish world of fancy and only the dark, tragic eyes of Yvonne tugged at me, pulled me back into the daylight world of sanity.

I have mentioned more nearly rational visions. I recall one a city—but what a city! Sky-piercing, white and beautiful and the people of it were grave with the wisdom of gods, pale and lovely people, but solemn, wistful, sad. There was the aura of brilliance and wickedness that hovers about all great cities, that was born, I suppose, in Babylon and will remain until great cities are no more.

But that was something else, something intangible. I don't know exactly what to call it but perhaps the word decadence is as close as any word we have. As I stood at the base of a colossal structure there was the whir of quiet machinery but it seemed to me, nevertheless, that the city was dying.

It might have been the moss that grew green on the north walls of the buildings. It might have been the grass that pierced here and there through the cracks of the marble pavements. Or it might have been only the grave and sad demeanor of the pale inhabitants. There was something that hinted of a doomed city and a dying race.

A strange thing happened when I tried to describe this particular memory to old de Neant. I stumbled over the details, of course—these visions from the unplumbed depths of eternity were curiously hard to fix between the rigid walls of words. They tended to grow vague, to elude the waking memory. Thus, in this description I had forgotten the name of the city.

'It was called,' I said hesitatingly, Termis or Termoplia, or ...'

'Termopolis!' cried de Neant impatiently. 'City of the End!'

I stared amazed. 'That's it! But how did you know?' In the sleep of lethargy, I was sure, one never speaks.

A queer, cunning look flashed in his pale eyes. 'I knew,' he muttered. 'I knew.' He would say no more.

But I think I saw that city once again. It was when I wandered over a brown and treeless plain, not like that cold grey desert but apparently an arid and barren region of the earth. Dim on the western horizon was the circle of a great cool reddish sun. It had always been there, I remembered, and knew with some other part of my mind that the vast brake of the tides had at last slowed the earth's rotation to a stop, that day and night no longer chased each other around the planet.

The air was biting cold and my companions and I—there were half a dozen of us—moved in a huddled group as if to lend each other warmth from our half-naked bodies. We were all of us thin-legged, skinny creatures with oddly deep chests and enormous, luminous eyes, and the one nearest me was again a woman who had something of Yvonne in her but very little. And I was not quite Jack Anders, either. But some remote fragment of me survived in that barbaric brain.

Beyond a hill was the surge of an oily sea. We crept circling about the mound and suddenly I perceived that sometime in the infinite past that hill had been a city. A few Gargantuan blocks of stone lay crumbling on it and one lonely fragment of a ruined wall rose gauntly to four or five times a man's height. It was at this spectral remnant that the leader of our miserable crew gestured then spoke in sombre tones—not English words but I understood.

'The Gods,' he said—'the Gods who piled stones upon stones are dead and harm us not who pass the place of their dwelling.'

I knew what that was meant to be. It was an incantation, a ritual—to protect us from the spirits that lurked among the ruins—the ruins, I believe, of a city built by our own ancestors thousands of generations before.

As we passed the wall I looked back at a flicker of movement and saw something hideously like a black rubber doormat flop itself around the angle of the wall. I drew closer to the woman beside me and we crept on down to the sea for water—yes, water, for with the cessation of the planet's rotation rainfall had vanished also, and all life huddled near the edge of the undying sea and learned to drink its bitter brine.

I didn't glance again at the hill which had been Termopolis, the City of the End. But I knew that some chance-born fragment of Jack Anders had been—or will be (what difference, if time is a circle?)—witness of an age close to the day of humanity's doom.

It was early in December that I had the first memory of something that might have been suggestive of success. It was a simple and very sweet memory, just Yvonne and I in a garden that I knew was the inner grounds on one of the New Orleans' old homes—one of those built in the Continental fashion about a court.

We sat on a stone bench beneath the oleanders and I slipped my arm very tenderly about her and murmured, 'Are you happy, Yvonne?'

She looked at me with those tragic eyes of hers and smiled, and then answered, 'As happy as I have ever been.'

And I kissed her.

That was all, but it was important. It was vastly important because it was definitely not a memory out of my own personal past. You see, I had never sat beside Yvonne in a garden sweet with oleanders in the Old Town of New Orleans and I had never kissed her until we met in New York.

Aurore de Neant was elated when I described this vision.

'You see!' he gloated. 'There is evidence. You have remembered the future! Not your own future, of course, but that of another ghostly Jack Anders, who died trillions and quadrillions of years ago.'

'But it doesn't help us, does it?' I asked.

'Oh, it will come now! You wait. The thing we want will come.'

And it did, within a week. This memory was curiously bright and clear, and familiar in every detail. I remember the day. It was the eighth of December, 1929, and I had wandered aimlessly about in search of business during the morning. In the grip of that fascination I mentioned I drifted to de Neant's apartment after lunch. Yvonne left us to ourselves, as was her custom, and we began.

This was, as I said, a sharply outlined memory—or dream. I was leaning over my desk in the company's office, that too-seldom visited office. One of the other salesmen—Summers was his name—was leaning over my shoulder.

We were engaged in the quite customary pastime of scanning the final market reports in the evening paper. The print stood out, clear as reality itself. I glanced without surprise at the dateline. It was Thursday, April 27th, 1930—almost five months in the future!

Not that I realised that during the vision, of course. The day was merely the present to me. I was simply looking over the list of the day's trading. Figures—familiar names. Telephone 210¾—US Steel—161; Paramount, 68½.

I jabbed a finger at Steel. 'I bought that at 72,' I said over my shoulder to Summers. 'I sold out everything today. Every stock I own. I'm getting out before there's a secondary crash.'

'Lucky stiff!' he murmured. 'Buy at the December lows and sell out now! Wish I'd had money to do it.' He paused, 'What you gonna do? Stay with the company?'

'No, I've enough to live on. I'm going to stick it in Governments and paid-up insurance and live on the income. I've had enough of gambling.'

'You lucky stiff!' he said again. 'I'm sick of the Street too. Staying in New York?'

'For a while. Just till I get my stuff invested properly; Yvonne and I are going to New Orleans for the winter.' I paused. 'She's had a tough time of it. I'm glad we're where we are.'

'Who wouldn't be?' asked Summers, and then again, 'You lucky stiff!'

De Neant was frantically excited when I described this to him.

That's it!' he screamed. 'We buy! We buy tomorrow! We sell on the twenty-seventh of May and then—New Orleans!'

Of course I was nearly equally enthusiastic. 'By heaven!' I said. 'It's worth the risk! We'll do it!' And then a sudden hopeless thought. 'Do it? Do it with what? I have less than a hundred dollars to my name. And you ...'

The old man groaned. 'I have nothing,' he said in abrupt gloom. 'Only the annuity we live on. One can't borrow on that.' Again a gleam of hope. 'The banks. We'll borrow from them!'

I had to laugh, although it was a bitter laugh. 'What bank would lend us money on a story like this? They wouldn't lend Rockefeller himself money to play this sick market, not without security. We're sunk, that's all.'

I looked at his pale, worried eyes. 'Sunk,' he echoed dully. Then again that wild gleam. 'Not sunk!' he yelled. 'How can we be? We did do it! You remembered our doing it! We must have found the way!'

I gazed speechless. Suddenly a queer, mad thought flashed over me. This other Jack Anders, this ghost of quadrillions of centuries past—or future—he too must be watching, or had watched, or yet would watch, me—the Jack Anders of this cycle of eternity.

He must be watching as anxiously as I to discover the means. Each of us watching the other—neither of us knowing the answer. The blind leading the blind! I laughed at the irony.

But old de Neant was not laughing. The strangest expression I have ever seen in a man's eyes was in his as he repeated very softly, 'We must have found the way because it was done. At least you and Yvonne found the way.'

'Then all of us must,' I answered sourly.

'Yes. Oh, yes. Listen to me, Jack. I am an old man, old Aurore de Neant. I am old Dawn of Nothingness and my mind is cracking. Don't shake your head!' he snapped. 'I am not mad. I am simply misunderstood. None of you understand.

'Why, I have a theory that trees, grass and people do not grow taller at all. They grow by pushing the earth away from them, which is why you keep hearing that the earth is getting smaller every day. But you don't understand—Yvonne doesn't understand.'

The girl must have been listening. Without my seeing her, she had slipped into the room and put her arms gently about her father's shoulders, while she gazed across at me with anxious eyes.

CHAPTER IV: The Bitter Fruit

There was one more vision, irrelevant in a way, yet vitally important in another way. It was the next evening. An early December snowfall was dropping its silent white beyond the windows and the ill-heated apartment of the de Neants was draughty and chill.

I saw Yvonne shiver as she greeted me and again as she left the room. I noticed that old de Neant followed her to the door with his thin arms about her and that he returned with very worried eyes.

'She is New Orleans born,' he murmured. 'This dreadful Arctic climate will destroy her. We must find a way at once.'

That vision was a sombre one. I stood on a cold, wet, snowy ground—just myself and Yvonne and one who stood beside an open grave. Behind us stretched rows of crosses and white tomb stones, but in our corner the place was ragged, untended, unconsecrated. The priest was saying, 'And these are things that only God understands.'

I slipped a comforting arm about Yvonne. She raised her dark, tragic eyes and whispered, 'It was yesterday, Jack—just yesterday—that he said to me, "Next winter you shall spend in New Orleans, Yvonne." Just yesterday!'

I tried a wretched smile, but I could only stare mournfully at her forlorn face, watching a tear that rolled slowly down her right cheek, hung glistening there a moment, then was joined by another to splash unregarded on the black bosom of her dress.

That was all but how could I describe that vision to old de Neant? I tried to evade. He kept insisting.

'There wasn't any hint of the way,' I told him. Useless—at last I had to tell anyway.

He was very silent for a full minute. 'Jack,' he said finally, 'do you know when I said that to her about New Orleans? This morning when we watched the snow. This morning!'

I didn't know what to do. Suddenly this whole concept of remembering the future seemed mad, insane. In all my memories there had been not a single spark of real proof, not a single hint of prophecy.

So I did nothing at all but simply gazed silently as old Aurore de Neant walked out of the room. And when, two hours later, while Yvonne and I talked, he finished writing a certain letter and then shot himself through the heart—why, that proved nothing either.

It was the following day that Yvonne and I, his only mourners, followed old Dawn of Nothingness to his suicide's grave. I stood beside her and tried as best I could to console her, and roused myself from a dark reverie to hear her words.

'It was yesterday, Jack—just yesterday—that he said to me, "Next winter you shall spend in New Orleans, Yvonne". Just yesterday!'

I watched the tear that rolled slowly down her right cheek hung glistening there a moment, then was joined by another to splash on the black bosom of her dress.

But it was later, during the evening, that the most ironic revelation of all occurred. I was gloomily blaming myself for the weakness of indulging old de Neant in the mad experiment that had led, in a way, to his death.

It was as if Yvonne read my thoughts, for she said suddenly:

'He was breaking, Jack. His mind was going. I heard all those strange things he kept murmuring to you.'

'What?'

'I listened, of course, behind the door there. I never left him alone. I heard him whisper the queerest things—faces in a red fog, words about a cold grey desert, the name Pyronive, the word Termopolis. He leaned over you as you sat with closed eyes and he whispered, whispered all the time.'

Irony of ironies! It was old de Neant's mad mind that had suggested the visions! He had described them to me as I sat in the sleep of lethargy!

Later we found the letter he had written and again I was deeply moved. The old man had carried a little insurance. Just a week before he had borrowed on one of the policies to pay the premiums on it and the others. But the letter—well, he had made me beneficiary of half the amount! And the instructions were—

'You, Jack Anders, will take both your money and Yvonne's and carry out the plan as you know I wish.'

Lunacy! De Neant had found the way to provide the money but—I couldn't gamble Yvonne's last dollar on the scheme of a disordered mind.

'What will we do?' I asked her. 'Of course the money's all yours. I won't touch it.'

'Mine?' she echoed. 'Why, no. We'll do as he wished. Do you think I'd not respect his last request?'

Well, we did. I took those miserable few thousands and spread them around in that sick December market. You remember what happened, how during the spring the prices skyrocketed as if they were heading back toward 1929, when actually the depression was just gathering breath.

I rode that market like a circus performer. I took profits and pyramided them back and, on April 27th, with our money multiplied fifty times, I sold out and watched the market slide back.

Coincidence? Very likely. After all, Aurore de Neant's mind was clear enough most of the time. Other economists predicted that spring rise. Perhaps he foresaw it too. Perhaps he staged this whole affair just to trick us into the gamble, one which we'd never have dared risk otherwise. And then when he saw we were going to fail from lack of money he took the only means he had of providing it.

Perhaps. That's the rational explanation, and yet—that vision of ruined Termopolis keeps haunting me. I see again the grey cold desert of the floating fungi. I wonder often about the immutable Law of Chance and about a ghostly Jack Anders somewhere beyond eternity.

For perhaps he does—did—will exist. Otherwise, how to explain that final vision? What of Yvonne's words beside her father's grave? Could he have foreseen those words and whispered them to me? Possibly. But what, then, of those two tears that hung glistening, merged and dropped from her cheeks?

What of them?

THE BRINK OF INFINITY

ORIGINALLY PUBLISHED IN *THRILLING WONDER STORIES*
DECEMBER 1936

THE BRINK OF INFINITY

One would hardly choose the life of an assistant professor of mathematics at an Eastern University as an adventurous one. Professors in general are reputed to drone out in a quiet, scholarly existence, and an instructor of mathematics might seem the driest and least lively of men, since his subject is perhaps the most desiccated. And yet—even the lifeless science of figures has had its dreamers—Clerk Maxwell, Lobachewski, Einstein and the rest. The latter, the great Albert Einstein himself who is forging the only chain that ever tied a philosophers' dream to experimental science, is pounding his links of tenuous mathematical symbols, shadowy as thought, but unbreakable.

And don't forget that "Alice in Wonderland" was written by a dreamer who happened also to be a mathematician. Not that I class myself with them; I'm practical enough to leave fantasies alone. Teaching is my business.

At least, teaching is my main business. I do a little statistical work for industrial corporations when the occasion presents itself—in fact, you'll find my name in the classified section: Abner Aarons, Statistician and Consulting Mathematician. I eke out my professional salary, and I do at times strike something interesting. Of course, in the main such work consists of graphing trends of consumption for manufacturers, or population increase for public utilities.

And occasionally some up-and-coming advertising agency will consult me on how many sardine cans would be needed to fill the Panama Canal, or some such material to use as catchy advertising copy. Not exactly exciting work, but it helps financially.

Thus I was not particularly surprised that July morning to receive a call. The university had been closed for some weeks; the summer session was about to open, without however, the benefit of my presence. I was taking a vacation, leaving in two or three days for a Vermont village I knew, where the brook trout cared not a bit whether a prizefighter, president, or professor was on the hither end of the line. And I was going alone; three-quarters of the year before a classroom full of the tadpoles called college students had thoroughly wearied me of any further desire for human companionship; my social instincts were temporarily in abeyance.

Nevertheless, I'm not unthrifty enough to disregard an opportunity to turn an honest penny, and the call was far from unwelcome. Even the modest holiday I planned can bite deeply enough into the financial foundation of an assistant professor's pittance. And the work sounded like one of these fairly lucrative and rather simple propositions.

"This is Court Strawn," the telephone announced. "I'm an experimental chemist, and I've completed a rather long series of experiments. I want them tabulated and the results analyzed; do you do that sort of work?"

I did, and acknowledged as much.

"It will be necessary for you to call here for your data," the voice continued. Strangely unctuous, that voice. "It is impossible for me to leave." There followed an address on West Seventieth Street.

Well, I had called for data before. Generally the stuff was delivered or mailed to me, but his request wasn't extraordinary, I agreed, and added that I'd be over shortly. No use delaying my vacation if I could help it.

I took the subway. Taxis are a needless luxury to a professor, and a car of my own was an unrealized ambition. It wasn't long before I entered one of the nondescript brown houses that still survive west of the Avenue. Strawn let me in, and I perceived the reason for his request. The man was horribly crippled; his whole left side was warped like a gnarled oak, and he was hard put to hobble about the house. For the rest—stringy dark hair, and little tense eyes.

He greeted me pleasantly enough, and I entered a small library, while my host hobbled over to a littered desk, seating himself facing me. The deep-set eyes looked me over, and he chuckled.

"Are you a good mathematician, Dr. Aarons?" he asked. There was more than a hint of a sneer in his voice.

"My work has been satisfactory," I answered, somewhat nettled. "I've been doing statistical work for several years."

He waved a shriveled left hand.

"Of course—of course! I don't doubt your practical ability. Are you, however, well versed in the more abstract branches—the theory of numbers, for instance, or the hyper-spatial mathematics?"

I was feeling rather irritated. There was something about the man—

"I don't see that any of this is necessary in statistical analysis of experimental results," I said. "If you'll give me your data, I'll be going."

He chuckled again, seemingly hugely amused. "As a matter of fact, Dr. Aarons," he said smirking, "the experiment isn't completed yet. Indeed, to tell the truth, it is just beginning."

"What!" I was really angry. "If this is your idea of a joke—" I started to rise, thoroughly aroused.

"Just a moment," said Strawn coolly. He leveled a very effective-looking blue-barreled automatic at me. I sat down again open-mouthed; I confess to a feeling of panic at the sight of the cripple's beady little eyes peering along the ugly weapon.

"Common politeness dictates that you at least hear me out, Dr. Aarons." I didn't like the oily smoothness of his voice, but what was I to do? "As I was saying, the experiment is just beginning. As a matter of fact, you are the experiment!"

"Eh?" I said, wondering again if the whole thing might not be a joke of some sort.

"You're a mathematician, aren't you?" Strawn continued. "Well, that makes you fair game for me. A mathematician, my good friend, is no more to me than something to be hunted down. And I'm doing it!"

The man was crazy! The realization dawned on me as I strove to hold myself calm. Best to reason with him, I thought.

"But why?" I asked. "We're a harmless lot."

His eyes blazed up with a fierce light.

"Harmless, eh, harmless! Well, it was one of your colleagues that did—this!" He indicated his withered leg with his withered arm. "He did this with his lying calculations!" He leaned forward confidentially. "Listen to me, Dr. Aarons. I am a chemist, or was once. I used to work with explosives, and was pretty good, too.

And then one of you damned calculators figured out a formula for me! A misplaced decimal point—bah! You're all fair game to me!" He paused, and the sneer came back to his lips. "That's simple justice, now, isn't it?"

Well, you can imagine how thoroughly horrified I was, sitting there facing a homicidal maniac with a loaded gun in his hand. Humor him! I'd heard that was the best treatment. Use persuasion, reason!

"Now, Mr. Strawn," I said, "you're certainly entitled to justice. Yes, you certainly are! But surely, Mr. Strawn, you are not serving the ends of justice by venting your anger on me! Surely that isn't justice."

He laughed wildly and continued. "A very specious argument, Dr. Aarons. You are simply unfortunate in that your name is the first in the classified section of the directory. Had your colleague given me a chance—any slightest chance to save my body from this that you see, I might be forgiving. But I trusted that fool's calculations!" He twisted his face again into that bitter leer. "As it is, I am giving you far more of a chance than I had. If, as you claim, you are a good mathematician, you shall have your opportunity to escape. I have no quarrel with the real students of figures, but only"—his leer became a very sinister scowl—"only with the dullards, the fakes and the blunderers. Yes, you'll have your chance!" The grin returned to his lips, but his eyes behind the blue automatic never wavered.

I saw no other alternative but to continue the ghastly farce. Certainly open opposition to any of his suggestions might only inflame the maniac to violence, so I merely questioned. "And what is the proposition, Mr. Strawn?"

The scowl became a sneer again.

"A very fair one, sir. A very fair proposition, indeed." He chuckled.

"I should like to hear it," I said, hoping for an interruption of some sort.

"You shall. It is just this: You are a mathematician, and you say, a good one. Very well. We shall put your claim to the test. I am thinking of a mathematical quantity, a numerical expression, if you prefer. You have ten questions to discover it. If you do so you are free as far as I am concerned. But if you fail"—his scowl reappeared—"well, if you fail I shall recognize you as one of the tribe of blunderers against whom I war, and the outcome will not be pleasant!"

Well! It was several moments before I found my voice, and began to babble protests. "But, Mr. Strawn! That's an utter impossibility! The range of numbers is infinite; how can I identify one with ten questions? Give me a fair test, man! This one offers not a chance in a million! In a billion!"

He silenced me with a wave of the blue barrel of his weapon.

"Remember, Dr. Aarons, I did not say it was a number. I said a numerical expression, which is a vastly wider field. I am giving you this hint without deducting a question; you must appreciate my magnanimity!" He laughed. "The rules of our little game are as follows: You may ask me any questions except the direct question, 'What is the expression?' I am bound to answer you in full and to the best of my knowledge any question except the direct inquiry. You may ask me as many questions at a time as you wish up to your limit of ten, but in any event I will answer not less than two per day. That should give you sufficient time for reflection"—again that horrible chuckle—"and my time too is limited."

"But, Mr. Strawn," I argued, "that may keep me here five days. Don't you know that by tomorrow my wife will have the police searching for me?"

A glint of anger flashed in the mad eyes. "You are not being fair, Dr. Aarons! I know you are not married! I checked up on you before you came here. I know you will not be missed. Do not attempt to lie to me; rather help me serve the ends of justice! You should be more than willing to prove your worth to survive as one of the true mathematicians." He rose suddenly. "And now, sir, you will please precede me through the door and up those stairs!"

Nothing to do but obey! The stubby gun in his hand was enough authority, at least to an unadventurous soul like myself. I rose and stalked out of the room at his direction, up the stairs and through a door he indicated. Beyond was a windowless little cell ventilated by a skylight, and the first glance revealed that this was barred. A piece of furniture of the type known as a day-bed, a straight chair, a deep overstuffed chair, and a desk made up the furnishings.

"Here," said the self-appointed host, "is your student's cell. On the desk is a carafe of water, and, as you see, an unabridged dictionary. That is the only reference allowed in our little game." He glanced at his watch. "It is ten minutes to four. By four tomorrow you must have asked me two questions, and have them well thought out! The ten minutes over are a gift from me, lest you doubt my generosity!" He moved toward the door. "I will see that your meals are on time," he added. "My best wishes, Dr. Aarons."

The door clicked shut and I at once commenced a survey of the room. The skylight was hopeless, and the door even more so; I was securely and ingloriously imprisoned. I spent perhaps half an hour in painstaking and fruitless inspection, but the room had been well designed or adapted to its purpose; the massive door was barred on the outside, the skylight was guarded by a heavy iron grating, and the walls offered no slightest hope. Abner Aarons was most certainly a prisoner!

My mind turned to Strawn's insane game. Perhaps I could solve his mad mystery; at least, I could keep him from violence for five days, and something might occur in the interim. I found cigars on the desk, and, forcing myself to a degree of calm, I lit one and sat down to think.

Certainly there was no use in getting at his lunatic concept from a quantitative angle, I could waste all ten questions too easily by asking, "Is it greater or less than a million? Is it greater or less than a thousand? Is it greater or less than a hundred?" Impossible to pin the thing by that sort of elimination when it might be a negative number, a fraction or a decimal, or even an imaginary number like the square root of minus one— or, for that matter, any possible combination of these. And that reflection gave me my impulse for the first question; by the time my cigar had been consumed to a tattered stub I had formulated my initial inquiry. Nor had I very long to wait; it was just past six when the door opened. "Stand away from the door, Dr. Aarons," came the voice of my host. I complied perforce; the madman entered, pushing before him a tea caddy bearing a really respectable meal, complete from bouillon to a bottle of wine. He propelled the cart with his withered left hand; the right brandished the evil automatic.

"I trust you have used your time well," he sneered.

"At least I have my first question," I responded.

"Good, Dr. Aarons! Very good! Let us hear it."

"Well," I continued, "among numbers, expressions of quantity, mathematicians recognize two broad distinctions—two fields in which every possible numerical expression may be classified. These two classifications are known as real numbers on the one hand, including every number both positive and negative, all fractions, decimals, and multiples of these numbers, and on the other hand the class of imaginary numbers, which include all products of operations on the quantity called 'e,' otherwise expressed as the square root of minus one."

"Of course, Dr. Aarons. That is elementary!"

"Now then—is this quantity of yours real or imaginary?"

He beamed with a sinister satisfaction.

"A very fair question, sir! Very fair! And the answer—may it assist you—is that it is either!"

A light seemed to burst in my brain! Any student of numbers knows that only one figure is both real and imaginary, the one that marks the point of intersection between the real and imaginary numbergraphs. "I've got it!" The phrase kept running through my mind like a crazy drumbeat! With an effort I kept an appearance of calm.

"Mr. Strawn," I said, "is the quantity you have in mind zero?"

He laughed—a nasty, superior laugh that rasped in my ears.

"It is not, Dr. Aarons! I know as well as you that zero is both a real and imaginary number! Let me call your attention to my answer: I did not say that my concept was both real and imaginary; I said it was either!" He was backing toward the door. "Let me further remind you that you have eight guesses remaining, since I am forced to consider this premature shot in the dark as one chance! Good evening!"

He was gone; I heard the bar outside the door settle into its socket with a thump. I stood in the throes of despair, and cast scarcely a glance at the rather sumptuous repast he had served me, but slumped back into my chair.

It seemed hours before my thoughts were coherent again; actually I never knew the interval, since I did not glance at my watch. However, sooner or later I recovered enough to pour a tumbler of wine and eat a bit of the roast beef; the bouillon was hopelessly cold. And then I settled down to the consideration of my third question. From Strawn's several hints in the wording of his terms and the answers to my first and second queries, I tabulated what information I could glean. He had specifically designated a numerical expression; that eliminated the x's and y's of algebraic usage. The quantity was either real or imaginary and was not zero; well, the square of any imaginary is a real number. If the quantity contained more than one figure, or if an exponent was used, then I felt sure his expression was merely the square of an imaginary; one could consider such a quantity either real or imaginary. A means of determining this by a single question occurred to me. I scribbled a few symbols on a sheet of paper, and then, feeling a sudden and thorough exhaustion, I threw myself on the daybed and slept. I dreamed Strawn was pushing me into a nightmarish sea of grinning mathematical monsters.

The creaking of the door aroused me. Sunbeams illumined the skylight; I had slept out the night. Strawn entered balancing a tray on his left arm, holding the ever-present weapon in his free hand. He placed a half dozen covered dishes on the tea-cart, removing the remains of the evening meal to his tray.

"A poor appetite, Dr. Aarons," he commented. "You should not permit your anxiety to serve the ends of justice to upset you!" He chuckled with enjoyment of his sarcasm. "No questions yet? No matter; you have until four tomorrow for your next two."

"I have a question," I said, more thoroughly awakened. I rose and spread the sheet of paper on the desk.

"A numerical quantity, Mr. Strawn, can be expressed as an operation on numbers. Thus, instead of writing the numeral '4' one may prefer to express it as a product, such as '2×2,' or as a sum, as '3+1,' or as a quotient, as '8÷2' or 8/2 or as a remainder, as '5−1.' Or even in other ways—as a square, such as 22, or as a root, such as $\sqrt{16}$ or $3\sqrt{64}$. All different methods of expressing the single quantity '4.' Now here I have written out the various mathematical symbols of operations; my question is this: Which if any of these symbols is used in the expression you have in mind?"

"Very neatly put, Dr. Aarons! You have succeeded in combining several questions in one." He took the paper from me, spreading it on the desk before him. "This symbol, sir, is the one used." He indicated the first one in my list—the subtraction sign, a simple dash!

And my hopes, to use the triviality of a pun, were dashed as well! For that sign eliminated my carefully thought-out theory of a product or square of imaginaries to form a real number. You can't change imaginary to real by addition or subtraction; it takes multiplication, squaring or division to perform that mathematical magic! Once more I was thoroughly at sea, and for a long time I was unable to marshal my thoughts.

And so the hours dragged into days with the tantalizing slow swiftness that tortures the condemned in a prison death house. I seemed checkmated at every turn; curious paradoxical answers defeated my questions.

My fourth query, "Are there any imaginaries in your quantity?" elicited a cool, definite "No," My fifth, "How many digits are used in this expression?" brought forth an equally definite "Two."

Now there you are! What two digits connected by a minus sign can you name whose remainder is either real or imaginary? "An impossibility," I thought. "This maniac's merely torturing me!" And yet—somehow Strawn's madness seemed too ingenious, too clever, for such an answer. He was sincere in his perverted search for justice. I'd have sworn to that.

On my sixth question, I had an inspiration! By the terms of our game, Strawn was to answer any question save the direct one, "What is this expression?" I saw a way out! On his next appearance I met him with feverish excitement, barely waiting for his entrance to begin my query.

"Mr. Strawn! Here is a question you are bound by your own rules to answer. Suppose we place an equal sign after your quantity, what number or numbers will complete the equation: What is the quantity equal to?"

Why was the fiend laughing? Could he squirm out of that poser?

"Very clever, Dr. Aarons. A very clever question. And the answer is—anything!"

I suppose I shouted. "Anything! Anything! Then you're a fraud, and your game's a damnable trickery. There's no such expression!"

"But there is, Doctor! A good mathematician could find it!" And he departed, still laughing.

I spent a sleepless night. Hour after hour I sat at that hateful desk, checking my scraps of information, thinking, trying to remember fragments of all-but-forgotten theories. And I found solutions! Not one, but several. Lord, how I sweated over them! With four questions—two days—left to me, the solution of the problem began to loom very close. The things dinned in my brain; my judgment counseled me to proceed slowly, to check my progress with another question, but my nature was rebelling against the incessant strain. "Stake it all on your last four questions! Ask them all at once, and end this agony one way or the other!"

I thought I saw the answer. Oh, the fiendish, insane cleverness of the man! He had pointed to the minus sign of my list, deliberately misled me, for all the time the symbol had meant the bar of a fraction. Do you see? The two symbols are identical—just a simple dash—but one use means subtraction and the other division!"1–1" means zero, but "1/1" means one! And by division his problem could be solved. For there is a quantity that means literally anything, real number or imaginary, and that quantity is "0/0"! Yes, zero divided by zero. You'd think offhand that the answer'd be zero, or perhaps one, but it isn't, not necessarily. Look at it like this: take the equation "2×3 = 6." See? That's another way of saying that two goes into six three times. Now take "0×6 = 0." Perfectly correct, isn't it? Well, in that equation zero goes into zero six times! Or "0/0 = 6"! And so on for any number, real or imaginary—zero divided by zero equals anything!

And that's what I figured the fiend had done. Pointed to the minus sign when he meant the bar of a fraction, or division!

He came in grinning at dawn.

"Are your questions ready, Dr. Aarons? I believe you have four remaining."

I looked at him. "Mr. Strawn, is your concept zero divided by zero?"

He grinned, "No, sir, it is not!"

I wasn't disheartened. There was just one other symbol I had been thinking of that would meet the requirement—one other possibility. My eighth question followed. "Then is it infinity divided by infinity?"

The grin widened. "It is not, Dr. Aarons."

I was a little panicky then! The end loomed awfully near! There was one way to find out if the thing was fraudulent or not; I used my ninth question:

"Mr. Strawn, when you designated the dash as the mathematical symbol used in your expression, did you mean it as the bar of a fraction or as the sign of subtraction?"

"As the subtraction sign, Dr. Aarons, You have one more question. Will you wait until tomorrow to ask it?"'

The fiend was grinning in huge enjoyment. Thoroughly confident, he was, in the intricacies of his insane game. I hesitated in a torture of frenzied indecision. The appalling prospect of another agonized night of doubts decided me.

"I'll ask it now, Mr. Strawn!"

It had to be right! There weren't any other possibilities; I'd exhausted all of them in hour after hour of miserable conjecture!

"Is the expression—the one you're thinking of—infinity minus infinity?"

It was! I knew it by the madman's glare of amazed disappointment.

"The devil must have told you!" he shrieked. I think there were flecks of froth on his lips. He lowered the gun in his hand as I edged toward the door; he made no move to stop me, but stood in a sort of desolate silence, until I gained the top of the stairway. Then—

"Wait a minute!" he screamed. "You'll tell them! Wait just a minute, Dr. Aarons!"

I was down the stairs in two leaps, and tugging at the door. Strawn came after me, his gun leveled. I heard it crash as the door opened and I slipped out into a welcome daylight.

Yes, I reported him. The police got him as he was slipping away and dragged him before an alienist. Crazy, but his story was true; he had been mangled in an experimental laboratory explosion.

Oh, the problem? Don't you see? Infinity is the greatest expression of number possible—a number greater than any conceivable. Figure it out like this:

The mathematician's symbol for infinity is a tipsy eight—so:
∞

Well, take the question, ∞+6=∞. That's true, because you can't add anything to infinity that will make it any greater than it is. See? It's the greatest possible number already. Well then, just by transposition, ∞−∞=6. And so on; the same system applies to any conceivable number, real or imaginary.

There you are! Infinity minus itself may equal any quantity, absolutely any number, real or imaginary, from zero to infinity. No, there was nothing wrong with Court Strawn's mathematics.

SHIFTING SEAS

ORIGINALLY PUBLISHED IN *AMAZING STORIES*
APRIL 1937

Shifting Seas

It developed later that Ted Welling was one of the very few eye-witnesses of the catastrophe, or rather, that among the million and a half eye-witnesses, he was among the half dozen that survived. At the time, he was completely unaware of the extent of the disaster, although it looked bad enough to him in all truth!

He was in a Colquist gyro, just north of the spot where Lake Nicaragua drains its brown overflow into the San Juan, and was bound for Managua, seventy-five miles north and west across the great inland sea. Below him, quite audible above the muffled whir of his motor, sounded the intermittent clicking of his tripanoramic camera, adjusted delicately to his speed so that its pictures could be assembled into a beautiful relief map of the terrain over which he passed. That, in fact, was the sole purpose of his flight; he had left San Juan del Norte early that morning to traverse the route of the proposed Nicaragua Canal, flying for the Topographical branch of the U. S. Geological Survey. The United States, of course, had owned the rights to the route since early in the century—a safeguard against any other nation's aspirations to construct a competitor for the Panama Canal.

Now, however, the Nicaragua Canal was actually under consideration. The over-burdened ditch that crossed the Isthmus was groaning under vastly increased traffic, and it became a question of either cutting the vast trench another eighty-five feet to sea-level or opening an alternate passage. The Nicaragua route was feasible enough; there was the San Juan emptying from the great lake into the Atlantic, and there was Lake Managua a dozen miles or so from the Pacific. It was simply a matter of choice, and Ted Welling, of the Topographical Service of the Geological Survey, was doing his part to aid the choice.

At precisely 10:40 it happened. Ted was gazing idly through a faintly misty morning toward Ometepec, its cone of a peak plumed by dusky smoke. A hundred miles away, across both

Lake Nicaragua and Lake Managua, the fiery mountain was easily visible from his altitude. All week, he knew, it had been rumbling and smoking, but now, as he watched it, it burst like a mighty Roman candle.

There was a flash of white fire not less brilliant than the sun. There was a column of smoke with a red core that spouted upward like a fountain and then mushroomed out. There was a moment of utter silence in which the camera clicked methodically, and then there was a roar as if the very roof of Hell had blown away to let out the bellows of the damned!

Ted had one amazed thought—the sound had followed too quickly on the eruption! It should have taken minutes to reach him at that distance—and then his thoughts were forcibly diverted as the Colquist tossed and skittered like a leaf in a hurricane. He caught an astonished glimpse of the terrain below, of Lake Nicaragua heaving and boiling as if it were the seas that lash through the Straits of Magellan instead of a body of landlocked fresh water. On the shore to the east a colossal wave was breaking, and there in a banana grove frightened figures were scampering away. And then, exactly as if by magic, a white mist condensed about him, shutting out all view of the world below.

He fought grimly for altitude. He had had three thousand feet, but now, tossed in this wild ocean of fog, of up-drafts and down-drafts, of pockets and humps, he had no idea at all of his position. His altimeter needle quivered and jumped in the changing pressure, his compass spun, and he had not the vaguest conception of the direction of the ground. So he struggled as best he could, listening anxiously to the changing whine of his blades as strain grew and lessened. And below, deep as thunder, came intermittent rumblings that were, unless he imagined it, accompanied by the flash of jagged fires.

Suddenly he was out of it. He burst abruptly into clear air, and for a horrible instant it seemed to him that he was actually flying inverted. Apparently below him was the white sea of mist, and above was what looked at first glance like dark ground, but a moment's scrutiny revealed it as a world-blanketing canopy of smoke or dust, through which the sun shone with a fantastic blue light. He had heard of blue suns, he recalled; they were one of the rarer phenomena of volcanic eruptions.

His altimeter showed ten thousand. The vast plain of mist heaved in gigantic ridges like rolling waves, and he fought upward away from it. At twenty thousand the air was steadier, but still infinitely above was the sullen ceiling of smoke. Ted leveled out, turning at random north-east, and relaxed.

"Whew!" he breathed. "What—what happened?"

He couldn't land, of course, in that impenetrable fog. He flew doggedly north and east, because there was an airport at Bluefields, if this heaving sea of white didn't blanket it.

But it did. He had still half a tank of fuel, and, he bored grimly north. Far away was a pillar of fire, and beyond it to the right, another and a third. The first, of course, was Ometepec, but what were the others? Fuego and Tajumulco? It seemed impossible.

Three hours later the fog was still below him, and the grim roof of smoke was dropping as if to crush him between. He was going to have to land soon; even now he must have spanned Nicaragua and be somewhere over Honduras. With a sort of desperate calm he slanted down toward the fog and plunged in. He expected to crash; curiously, the only thing he really regretted was dying without a chance to say goodbye to Kay Lovell, who was far off in Washington with her father, old Sir Joshua Lovell, Ambassador from Great Britain.

When the needle read two hundred, he leveled off—and then, like a train bursting out of a tunnel, he came clear again! But under him was wild and raging ocean, whose waves seemed almost to graze the ship. He spun along at a low level, wondering savagely how he could possibly have wandered out to sea. It must, he supposed, be the gulf of Honduras.

He turned west. Within five minutes he had raised a storm-lashed coast, and then—miracle of all miracles!—a town! And a landing field, He pancaked over it, let his vanes idle, and dropped as vertically as he could in that volley of gusty winds.

It was Belize in British Honduras. He recognized the port even before the attendants had reached him.

"A Yankee!" yelled the first. "Ain't that Yankee luck for you!"

Ted grinned. "I needed it. What happened?"

"The roof over this part of Hell blew off. That's all."

"Yeah. I saw that much. I was over it."

"Then you know more'n any of us. Radio's dead and there ain't no bloomin' telegraph at all."

It began to rain suddenly, a fierce, pattering rain with drops as big as marbles. The men broke for the shelter of a hangar, where Ted's information, meager as it was, was avidly seized upon, for sensational news is rare below the Tropic of Cancer. But none of them yet realized just how sensational it was.

*   *   *   *   *

It was three days before Ted, and the rest of the world as well, began to understand in part what had happened. This was after hours of effort at Belize had finally raised Havana on the beam, and Ted had reported through to old Asa Gaunt, his chief at Washington. He had been agreeably surprised by the promptness of the reply ordering him instantly to the Capital; that meant a taste of the pleasant life that Washington reserved for young departmentals, and most of all, it meant a glimpse of Kay Lovell after two months of letter-writing. So he had flown the Colquist gayly across Yucatan Channel, left it at Havana, and was now comfortably settled in a huge Caribbean plane bound for Washington, boring steadily north through a queerly misty mid-October morning.

At the moment, however, his thoughts were not of Kay. He was reading a grim newspaper account of the catastrophe, and wondering what thousand-to-one shot had brought him unscathed through the very midst of it. For the disaster overshadowed into insignificance such little disturbances as the Yellow River flood in China, the eruption of Krakatoa, the holocaust of Mount Pelee, or even the great Japanese earthquake of 1923, or any other terrible visitation ever inflicted on a civilized race.

For the Ring of Fire, that vast volcanic circle that surrounds the Pacific Ocean, perhaps the last unhealed scars of the birththroes of the Moon, had burst into flame. Aniakchak in Alaska had blown its top away, Fujiyama had vomited lava, on the Atlantic side La Soufriere and the terrible Pelee had awakened again.

But these were minor. It was at the two volcanic foci, in Java and Central America, that the fire-mountains had really shown their powers. What had happened in Java was still a mystery, but on the Isthmus—that was already too plain. From Mosquito Bay to the Rio Coco, there was—ocean! Half of Panama, seven-eighths of Nicaragua—and as for Costa Rica, that country was as if it had never been. The Canal was a wreck, but Ted grinned a wry grin at the thought that it was now as unnecessary as a pyramid. North and South America had been cut adrift, and the Isthmus, the land that had once known Atlantis, had gone to join it.

*　　*　　*　　*　　*

In Washington Ted reported at once to Asa Gaunt. That dry Texan questioned him closely concerning his experience, grunted disgustedly at the paucity of information, and then ordered him tersely to attend a meeting at his office in the evening. There remained a full afternoon to devote to Kay, and Ted lost little time in so devoting it.

He didn't see her alone. Washington, like the rest of the world, was full of excitement because of the earthquake, but in Washington more than elsewhere the talk was less of the million and a half deaths and more largely of the other consequences. After all, the bulk of the deaths had been among the natives, and it was a sort of remote tragedy, like the perishing of so many Chinese. It affected only those who had friends or relatives in the stricken region, and these were few in number.

But at Kay's home Ted encountered an excited group arguing physical results. Obviously, the removal of the bottleneck of the Canal strengthened the naval power of the United States enormously. No need now to guard the vulnerable Canal so intensively. The whole fleet could stream abreast through the four hundred mile gap left by the subsidence. Of course the country would lose the revenues of the toll-charges, but that was balanced by the cessation of the expense of fortifying and guarding.

Ted fumed until he managed a few moments of greeting with Kay alone. Once that was concluded to his satisfaction, he joined the discussion as eagerly as the rest. But no one even considered the one factor in the whole catastrophe that could change the entire history of the world.

At the evening meeting Ted stared around him in surprise. He recognized all those present, but the reasons for their presence were obscure. Of course there was Asa Gaunt, head of the Geological Survey, and of course there was Golsborough, Secretary of the Interior, because the Survey was one of his departments. But what was Maxwell, joint Secretary of War and the Navy, doing there? And why was silent John Parish, Secretary of State, frowning down at his shoes in the corner?

Asa Gaunt cleared his throat and began. "Do any of you like eels?" he asked soberly.

There was a murmur. "Why, I do," said Golsborough, who had once been Consul at Venice. "What about it?"

"This—that you'd better buy some and eat 'em tomorrow. There won't be any more eels."

"No more eels?"

"No more eels. You see, eels breed in the Sargasso Sea, and there won't be any Sargasso Sea."

"What is this?" growled Maxwell. "I'm a busy man. No more Sargasso Sea, huh!"

"You're likely to be busier soon," said Asa Gaunt dryly. He frowned. "Let me ask one other question. Does anyone here know what spot on the American continent is opposite London, England?"

Golsborough shifted impatiently, "I don't see the trend of this, Asa," he grunted, "but my guess is that New York City and London are nearly in the same latitude. Or maybe New York's a little to the north, since I know its climate is somewhat colder."

"Hah!" said Asa Gaunt. "Any disagreement?"

There was none. "Well," said the head of the Survey, "you're all wrong, then. London is about one thousand miles north of New York. It's in the latitude of southern Labrador!"

"Labrador! That's practically the Arctic!"

Asa Gaunt pulled down a large map on the wall behind him, a Mercator projection of the world.

"Look at it," he said. "New York's in the latitude of Rome, Italy. Washington's opposite Naples. Norfolk's level with Tunis in Africa, and Jacksonville with the Sahara Desert. And gentlemen, these facts lead to the conclusion that next summer is going to see the wildest war in the history of the world!"

Even Ted, who knew his superior well enough to swear to his sanity, could not resist a glance at the faces of the others, and met their eyes with full understanding of the suspicion in them.

Maxwell cleared his throat. "Of course, of course," he said gruffly. "So there'll be a war and no more eels. That's very easy to follow, but I believe I'll ask you gentlemen to excuse me. You see, I don't care for eels."

"Just a moment more," said Asa Gaunt. He began to speak, and little by little a grim understanding dawned on the four he faced.

*   *   *   *   *

Ted remained after the appalled and sobered group had departed. His mind was too chaotic as yet for other occupations, and it was already too late in the evening to find Kay, even had he dared with these oppressive revelations weighing on him.

"Are you sure?" he asked nervously. "Are you quite certain?"

"Well, let's go over it again," grunted Asa Gaunt, turning to the map. He swept his hand over the white lines drawn in the Pacific Ocean. "Look here. This is the Equatorial Counter Current, sweeping cast to wash the shores of Guatemala, Salvador, Honduras, Nicaragua, Costa Rica, and Panama."

"I know. I've flown over every square mile of that coast."

"Uh." The older man turned to the blue-mapped expanse of the Atlantic. "And here," he resumed, "is the North Equatorial Drift, coming west out of the Atlantic to sweep around Cuba into the Gulf, and to emerge as—the Gulf Stream. It flows at an average speed of three knots per hour, is sixty miles broad, a hundred fathoms deep, and possesses, to start with, an average temperature of 50°. And here—it meets the Labrador Current and turns east to carry warmth to all of Western Europe. That's why England is habitable; that's why southern France is semi-tropical; that's why men can live even in Norway and Sweden. Look at Scandinavia, Ted; it's in the latitude of central Greenland, level with Baffin Bay. Even Eskimos have difficulty scraping a living on Baffin Island."

"I know," said Ted in a voice like a groan. "But are you certain about—the rest of this?"

"See for yourself," growled Asa Gaunt. "The barrier's down now. The Equatorial Counter Current, moving two knots per hour, will sweep right over what used to be Central America and strike the North Equatorial Drift just south of Cuba. Do you see what will happen—is happening—to the Gulf Stream? Instead of moving north-east along the Atlantic coast, it will flow almost due east, across what used to be the Sargasso Sea. Instead of bathing the shores of Northern Europe, it will strike the Spanish peninsula, just as the current, called the West Wind Drift does now, and instead of veering north it will turn south, along the coast of Africa. At three knots an hour it will take less than three months for the Gulf Stream to deliver its last gallon of warm water to Europe. That brings us to January—and after January, what?"

Ted said nothing.

"Now," resumed Asa Gaunt grimly, "the part of Europe occupied by countries dependent on the Gulf Stream consists of Norway, Sweden, Denmark, Germany, the British Isles, the Netherlands, Belgium, France, and to a lesser extent, several others. Before six months have passed, Ted, you're going to see a realignment of Europe. The Gulf Stream countries are going to be driven together; Germany and France are suddenly going to become bosom friends, and France and Russia, friendly as they are today, are going to be bitter enemies. Do you see why?"

"N-no."

"Because the countries I've named now support over two hundred million inhabitants. Two hundred million, Ted! And without the Gulf Stream, when England and Germany have the climate of Labrador, and France of Newfoundland, and Scandinavia of Baffin Land—how many people can those regions support then? Three or four million, perhaps, and that with difficulty. Where will the others go?"

"Where?"

"I can tell you where they'll try to go. England will try to unload its surplus population on its colonies. India's hopelessly overcrowded, but South Africa, Canada, Australia, and New Zealand can absorb some. About twenty-five of its fifty millions, I should estimate, because Canada's a northern country and Australia desert in a vast part of it. France has Northern Africa, already nearly as populous as it can be. The others—well, you guess, Ted."

"I will. Siberia, South America, and—the United States!"

"A good guess. That's why Russia and France will no longer be the best of friends. South America is a skeleton continent, a shell. The interior is unfit for white men, and so—it leaves Siberia and North America. What a war's in the making!"

"It's almost unbelievable!" muttered Ted. "Just when the world seemed to be settling down, too."

"Oh, it's happened before," observed Asa Gaunt. "This isn't the only climatic change that brought on war. It was decreasing rainfall in central Asia that sent the Huns scouring Europe, and probably the Goths and Vandals as well. But it's never happened to two hundred million civilized people before!" He paused. "The newspapers are all shrieking about the million and a half deaths in Central America. By this time next year they'll have forgotten that a million and a half deaths ever rated a headline!"

"But good Lord!" Ted burst out. "Isn't there anything to be done about it?"

"Sure, sure," said Asa Gaunt. "Go find a nice tame earthquake that will raise back the forty thousand square miles the last one sunk. That's all you have to do, and if you can't do that, Maxwell's suggestion is the next best: build submarines and submarines. They can't invade a country if they can't get to it."

Asa Gaunt was beyond doubt the first man in the world to realize the full implications of the Central American disaster, but he was not very much ahead of the brilliant Sir Phineas Grey of the Royal Society. Fortunately (or unfortunately, depending on which shore of the Atlantic you call home), Sir Phineas was known to the world of journalism as somewhat of a sensationalist, and his warning was treated by the English and Continental newspapers as on a par with those recurrent predictions of the end of the world. Parliament noticed the warning just once, when Lord Rathmere rose in the Upper House to complain of the unseasonably warm weather and to suggest dryly that the Gulf Stream be turned off a month early this year. But now and again some oceanographer made the inside pages by agreeing with Sir Phineas.

So Christmas approached very quietly, and Ted, happy enough to be stationed in Washington, spent his days in routine topographical work in the office and his evenings, as many as she permitted, with Kay Lovell. And she did permit an increasing number, so that the round of gaiety during the holidays found them on the verge of engagement. They were engaged so far as the two of them were concerned, and only awaited a propitious moment to inform Sir Joshua, whose approval Kay felt, with true English conservatism, was a necessity.

Ted worried often enough about the dark picture Asa Gaunt had drawn, but an oath of secrecy kept him from ever mentioning it to Kay. Once, when she had casually brought up the subject of Sir Phineas Grey and his warning, Ted had stammered some inanity and hastily switched the subject. But with the turn of the year and January, things began to change.

It was on the fourteenth that the first taste of cold struck Europe. London shivered for twenty-four hours in the unheard-of temperature of twenty below zero, and Paris argued and gesticulated about its grands froids. Then the high pressure area moved eastward and normal temperatures returned.

But not for long. On the twenty-first another zone of frigid temperature came drifting in on the Westerlies, and the English and Continental papers, carefully filed at the Congressional Library, began to betray a note of panic. Ted read the editorial comments avidly: of course Sir Phineas Grey was crazy; of course he was—but just suppose he were right. Just suppose he were. Wasn't it unthinkable that the safety and majesty of Germany (or France or England or Belgium, depending on the particular capital whence the paper came) was subject to the disturbances of a little strip of land seven thousand miles away? Germany (or France, et al) must control its own destiny.

With the third wave of Arctic cold, the tone became openly fearful. Perhaps Sir Phineas was right. What then? What was to be done? There were rumblings and mutterings in Paris and Berlin, and even staid Oslo witnessed a riot, and conservative London as well. Ted began to realize that Asa Gaunt's predictions were founded on keen judgment; the German government made an openly friendly gesture toward France in a delicate border matter, and France reciprocated with an equally indulgent note. Russia protested and was politely ignored; Europe was definitely realigning itself, and in desperate haste.

But America, save for a harassed group in Washington, had only casual interest in the matter. When reports of suffering among the poor began to come during the first week in February, a drive was launched to provide relief funds, but it met with only nominal success. People just weren't interested; a cold winter lacked the dramatic power of a flood, a fire, or an earthquake. But the papers reported in increasing anxiety that the immigration quotas, unapproached for a half a dozen years, were full again; there was the beginning of an exodus from the Gulf Stream countries.

By the second week in February stark panic had gripped Europe, and echoes of it began to penetrate even self-sufficient America. The realignment of the Powers was definite and open now, and Spain, Italy, the Balkans, and Russia found themselves herded together, facing an ominous thunderhead on the north and west. Russia instantly forgot her longstanding quarrel with Japan, and Japan, oddly, was willing enough to forget her own grievances. There was a strange shifting of sympathies; the nations which possessed large and thinly populated areas—Russia, the United States, Mexico, and all of South America—were glaring back at a frantic Europe that awaited only the release of summer to launch a greater invasion than any history had recorded. Attila and his horde of Huns— the Mongol waves that beat down on China—even the vast movements of the white race into North and South America—all these were but minor migrations to that which threatened now. Two hundred million people, backed by colossal fighting power, glaring panic-stricken at the empty places of the world. No one knew where the thunderbolt would strike first, but that it would strike was beyond doubt.

*   *   *   *   *

While Europe shivered in the grip of an incredible winter, Ted shivered at the thought of certain personal problems of his own. The frantic world found an echo in his own situation, for here was he, America in miniature, and there was Kay Lovell, a small edition of Britannia. Their sympathies clashed like those of their respective nations.

The time for secrecy was over. Ted faced Kay before the fireplace in her home and stared from her face to the cheery fire, whose brightness merely accentuated his gloom.

"Yeah," he admitted. "I knew about it. I've known it since a couple of days after the Isthmus earthquake."

"Then why didn't you tell me? You should have."

"Couldn't. I swore not to tell."

"It isn't fair!" blazed Kay. "Why should it fall on England? I tell you it sickens me even to think of Merecroft standing there in snow, like some old Norse tower. It was born in Warwickshire, Ted, and so was my father, and his father, and his, and all of us back to the time of William the Conqueror. Do you think it's a pleasant thing to think of my mother's rose garden as barren as—as a tundra?"

"I'm sorry," said Ted gently, "but what can I—or anyone—do about it? I'm just glad you're here on this side of the Atlantic, where you're safe."

"Safe!" she flashed. "Yes, I'm safe, but what about my people? I'm safe because I'm in America, the lucky country, the chosen land! Why did this have to happen to England? The Gulf Stream washes your shores too. Why aren't Americans shivering and freezing and frightened and hopeless, instead of being warm and comfortable and indifferent? Is that fair?"

"The Gulf Stream," he explained miserably, "doesn't affect our climate so definitely because in the first place we're much farther south than Europe and in the second place our prevailing winds are from the west, just as England's. But our winds blow from the land to the Gulf Stream, and England's from the Gulf Stream to the land."

"But it's not fair! It's not fair!"

"Can I help it, Kay?"

"Oh, I suppose not," she agreed in suddenly weary tones, and then, with a resurgence of anger, "But you people can do something about it! Look here! Listen to this!"

She spied a week-old copy of the London Times, fingered rapidly through it, and turned on Ted. "Listen—just listen! 'And in the name of humanity it is not asking too much to insist that our sister nation open her gates to us. Let us settle the vast areas where now only Indian tribes hunt and buffalo range. We would not be the only ones to gain by such a settlement, for we would bring to the new country a sane, industrious, law-abiding citizenry, no harborers of highwaymen and gangsters—a point well worth considering. We would bring a great new purchasing public for American manufacturers, carrying with us all our portable wealth. And finally, we would provide a host of eager defenders in the war for territory, a war that now seems inevitable. Our language is one with theirs; surely this is the logical solution, especially when one remembers that the state of Texas alone contains land enough to supply two acres to every man, woman, and child on earth!" She paused and stared defiantly at Ted. "Well?"

He snorted. "Indians and buffalo!" he snapped. "Have you seen either one in the United States?"

"No, but—"

"And as for Texas, sure there's enough land there for two acres to everybody in the world, but why didn't your editor mention that two acres won't even support a cow over much of it? The Llano Estacado's nothing but an alkali desert, and there's a scarcity of water in lots of the rest of it. On that argument, you ought to move to Greenland; I'll bet there's land enough there for six acres per person!"

"That may be true, but—"

"And as for a great new purchasing public, your portable wealth is gold and paper money, isn't it? The gold's all right, but what good is a pound if there's no British credit to back it? Your great new public would simply swell the ranks of the unemployed until American industry could absorb them, which might take years! And meanwhile wages would go down to nothing because of an enormous surplus of labor, and food and rent would go skyhigh because of millions of extra stomachs to feed and bodies to shelter."

"All right!" said Kay bleakly. "Argue all you wish. I'll even concede that your arguments are right, but there's one thing I know is wrong, and that's leaving fifty million English people to starve and freeze and suffer in a country that's been moved, as far as climate goes, to the North Pole. Why, you even get excited over a newspaper story about one poor family in an unheated hovel! Then what about a whole nation whose furnace has gone out?"

"What," countered Ted grimly, "about the seven or eight other nations whose furnaces have also gone out?"

"But England deserves priority!" she blazed. "You took your language from us, your literature, your laws, your whole civilization. Why, even now you ought to be nothing but an English colony! That's all you are, if you want the truth!"

"We think differently. Anyway, you know as well as I that the United States can't open the door to one nation and exclude the others. It must be all or none, and that means—none!"

"And that means war," she said bitterly. "Oh, Ted! I can't help the way I feel. I have people over there—aunts, cousins, friends. Do you think I can stand indifferently aside while they're ruined? Although they're ruined already, as far as that goes. Land's already dropped to nothing there. You can't sell it at any price now."

"I know. I'm sorry, Kay, but it's no one's fault. No one's to blame."

"And so no one needs to do anything about it, I suppose. Is that your nice American theory?"

"You know that isn't fair! What can we do?"

"You could let us in! As it is we'll have to fight our way in, and you can't blame us!"

"Kay, no nation and no group of nations can invade this country. Even if our navy were utterly destroyed, how far from the sea do you think a hostile army could march? It would be Napoleon in Russia all over again; your army marches in and is swallowed up. And where is Europe going to find the food to support an invading army? Do you think it could live on the land as it moved? I tell you no sane nation would try that!"

"No sane nation, perhaps!" she retorted fiercely. "Do you think you're dealing with sane nations?"

He shrugged gloomily.

"They're desperate!" she went on. "I don't blame them. Whatever they do, you've brought it on yourselves. Now you'll be fighting all of Europe, when you could have the British navy on your side. It's stupid. It's worse than stupid; it's selfish!"

"Kay," he said miserably, "I can't argue with you. I know how you feel, and I know it's a hell of a situation. But even if I agreed with everything you've said—which I don't—what could I do about it? I'm not the President and I'm not Congress. Let's drop the argument for this evening, honey; it's just making you unhappy."

"Unhappy! As if I could ever be anything else when everything I value, everything I love, is doomed to be buried under Arctic snow."

"Everything, Kay?" he asked gently. "Haven't you forgotten that there's something for you on this side of the Atlantic as well?"

"I haven't forgotten anything," she said coldly. "I said everything, and I mean it. America! I hate America. Yes, and I hate Americans too!"

"Kay!"

"And what's more," she blazed, "I wouldn't marry an American if he—if he could rebuild the Isthmus! If England's to freeze, I'll freeze with her, and if England's to fight, her enemies are mine!"

She rose suddenly to her feet, deliberately averted her eyes from his troubled face, and stalked out of the room.

Sometimes, during those hectic weeks in February, Ted wormed his way into the Visitor's Gallery in one or the other Congressional house. The outgoing Congress, due to stand for re-election in the fall, was the focal point of the dawning hysteria in the nation, and was battling sensationally through its closing session. Routine matters were ignored, and day after day found both houses considering the unprecedented emergency with a sort of appalled inability to act in any effective unison. Freak bills of all description were read, considered, tabled, reconsidered, put to a second reading, and tabled again. The hard-money boom of a year earlier had swept in a Conservative majority in the off-year elections, but they had no real policy to offer, and the proposals of the minority group of Laborites and Leftists were voted down without substitutes being suggested.

Some of the weirdest bills in all the weird annals of Congress appeared at this time. Ted listened in fascination to the Leftist proposal that each American family adopt two Europeans, splitting its income into thirds; to a suggestion that Continentals be advised to undergo voluntary sterilization, thus restraining the emergency to the time of one generation; to a fantastic paper money scheme of the Senator from the new state of Alaska, that was to provide a magic formula to permit Europe to purchase its livelihood without impoverishing the rest of the world. There were suggestions of outright relief, but the problem of charity to two hundred million people was so obviously staggering that this proposal at least received little attention. But there were certain bills that passed both houses without debate, gaining the votes of Leftists, Laborites, and Conservatives alike; these were the grim appropriations for submarines, super-bombers and interceptors, and aircraft-carriers.

Those were strange, hectic days in Washington. Outwardly there was still the same gay society that gathers like froth around all great capitals, and Ted, of course, being young and decidedly not unattractive, received his full share of invitations. But not even the least sensitive could have overlooked the dark undercurrents of hysteria that flowed just beneath the surface. There was dancing, there was gay dinner conversation, there was laughter, but beneath all of it was fear. Ted was not the only one to notice that the diplomatic representatives of the Gulf Stream countries were conspicuous by their absence from all affairs save those of such importance that their presence was a matter of policy. And even then, incidents occurred; he was present when the Minister from France stalked angrily from the room because some hostess had betrayed the poor taste of permitting her dance orchestra to play a certain popular number called "The Gulf Stream Blues." Newspapers carefully refrained from mentioning the occurrence, but Washington buzzed with it for days.

Ted looked in vain for Kay. Her father appeared when appearance was necessary, but Ted had not seen the girl since her abrupt dismissal of him, and in reply to his inquiries, Sir Joshua granted only the gruff and double-edged explanation that she was "indisposed." So Ted worried and fumed about her in vain, until he scarcely knew whether his own situation or that of the world was more important. In the last analysis, of course, the two were one and the same.

The world was like a crystal of nitrogen iodide, waiting only the drying-out of summer to explode. Under its frozen surface Europe was seething like Mounts Erebus and Terror that blaze in the ice of Antarctica. Little Hungary had massed its army on the west, beyond doubt to oppose a similar massing on the part of the Anschluss. Of this particular report, Ted heard Maxwell say with an air of relief that it indicated that Germany had turned her face inland; it meant one less potential enemy for America.

But the maritime nations were another story, and especially mighty Britain, whose world-girdling fleet was gathering day by day in the Atlantic. That was a crowded ocean indeed, for on its westward shore was massed the American battle fleet, built at last to treaty strength, and building far beyond it, while north and south piled every vessel that could raise a pound of steam, bearing those fortunates who could leave their European homes to whatever lands hope called them. Africa and Australia, wherever Europe had colonies, were receiving an unheard of stream of immigrants. But this stream was actually only the merest trickle, composed of those who possessed sufficient liquid wealth to encompass the journey. Untold millions remained chained to their homes, bound by the possession of unsalable lands, or by investments in business, or by sentiment, or by the simple lack of sufficient funds to buy passage for families. And throughout all of the afflicted countries were those who clung stubbornly to hope, who believed even in the grip of that unbelievable winter that the danger would pass, and that things would come right in the end.

Blunt, straightforward little Holland was the first nation to propose openly a wholesale transfer of population. Ted read the note, or at least the version of it given the press on February 21st. In substance it simply repeated the arguments Kay had read from the London paper—the plea to humanity, the affirmation of an honest and industrious citizenry, and the appeal to the friendship that had always existed between the two nations; and the communication closed with a request for an immediate reply because of "the urgency of the situation." And an immediate reply was forthcoming.

This was also given to the press. In suave and very polished diplomatic language it pointed out that the United States could hardly admit nationals of one country while excluding those of others. Under the terms of the National Origins Act, Dutch immigrants would be welcomed to the full extent of their quota. It was even possible that the quota might be increased, but it was not conceivable that it could be removed entirely. The note was in effect a suave, dignified, diplomatic No.

March drifted in on a southwest wind. In the Southern states it brought spring, and in Washington a faint forerunner of balmy weather to come, but to the Gulf Stream countries it brought no release from the Arctic winter that had fallen on them with its icy mantle. Only in the Basque country of Southern France, where vagrant winds slipped at intervals across the Pyrenees with the warm breath of the deflected Stream, was there any sign of the relaxing of that frigid clutch. But that was a promise; April would come, and May—and the world flexed its steel muscles for war.

Everyone knew now that war threatened. After the first few notes and replies, no more were released to the press, but everyone knew that notes, representatives, and communiques were flying between the powers like a flurry of white doves, and everyone knew, at least in Washington, that the tenor of those notes was no longer dove-like. Now they carried brusque demands and blunt refusals.

Ted knew as much of the situation as any alert observer, but no more. He and Asa Gaunt discussed it endlessly, but the dry Texan, having made his predictions and seen them verified, was no longer in the middle of the turmoil, for his bureau had, of course, nothing to do with the affair now. So the Geological Survey staggered on under a woefully reduced appropriation, a handicap shared by every other governmental function that had no direct bearing on defense.

All the American countries, and for that matter, every nation save those in Western Europe, were enjoying a feverish, abnormal, hectic boom. The flight of capital from Europe, and the incessant, avid, frantic cry for food, had created a rush of business, and exports mounted unbelievably. In this emergency, France and the nations under her hegemony, those who had clung so stubbornly to gold ever since the second revaluation of the franc, were now at a marked advantage, since their money would buy more wheat, more cattle, and more coal. But the paper countries, especially Britain, shivered and froze in stone cottage and draughty manor alike.

On the eleventh of March, that memorable Tuesday when the thermometer touched twenty-eight below in London, Ted reached a decision toward which he had been struggling for six weeks. He was going to swallow his pride and see Kay again. Washington was buzzing with rumors that Sir Joshua was to be recalled, that diplomatic relations with England were to be broken as they had already been broken with France. The entire nation moved about its daily business in an air of tense expectancy, for the break with France meant little in view of that country's negligible sea power, but now, if the colossus of the British navy were to align itself with the French army—

But what troubled Ted was a much more personal problem. If Sir Joshua Lovell were recalled to London, that meant that Kay would accompany him, and once she were caught in the frozen Hell of Europe, he had a panicky feeling that she was lost to him forever. When war broke, as it surely must, there would go his last hope of ever seeing her again. Europe, apparently, was doomed, for it seemed impossible that any successful invasion could be carried on over thousands of miles of ocean, but if he could save the one fragment of Europe that meant everything to him, if he could somehow save Kay Lovell, it was worth the sacrifice of pride or of anything else. So he called one final time on the telephone, received the same response from an unfriendly maid, and then left the almost idle office and drove directly to her home.

The same maid answered his ring. "Miss Lovell is not in," she said coldly. "I told you that when you telephoned."

"I'll wait," returned Ted grimly, and thrust himself through the door. He seated himself stolidly in the hall, glared back at the maid, and waited. It was no more than five minutes before Kay herself appeared, coming wearily down the steps.

"I wish you'd leave," she said. She was pallid and troubled, and he felt a great surge of sympathy.

"I won't leave."

"What do I have to do to make you go away? I don't want to see you, Ted."

"If you'll talk to me just half an hour, I'll go." She yielded listlessly, leading the way into the living room where a fire still crackled in cheerful irony. "Well?" she asked.

"Kay, do you love me?"

"I—No, I don't!"

"Kay," he persisted gently, "do you love me enough to marry me and stay here where you're safe?"

Tears glistened suddenly in her brown eyes. "I hate you," she said. "I hate all of you. You're a nation of murderers. You're like the East Indian Thugs, only they call murder religion and you call it patriotism."

"I won't even argue with you, Kay. I can't blame you for your viewpoint, and I can't blame you for not understanding mine. But—do you love me?"

"All right," she said in sudden weariness. "I do."

"And will you marry me?"

"No. No, I won't marry you, Ted. I'm going back to England."

"Then will you marry me first? I'll let you go back, Kay, but afterwards—if there's any world left after what's coming—I could bring you back here. I'll have to fight for what I believe in, and I won't ask you to stay with me during the time our nations are enemies, but afterwards, Kay—if you're my wife I could bring you here. Don't you see?"

"I see, but—no."

"Why, Kay? You said you loved me."

"I do," she said almost bitterly. "I wish I didn't, because I can't marry you hating your people the way I do. If you were on my side, Ted, I swear I'd marry you tomorrow, or today, or five minutes from now—but as it is, I can't. It just wouldn't be fair."

"You'd not want me to turn traitor," he responded gloomily. "One thing I'm sure of, Kay, is that you couldn't love a traitor." He paused. "Is it goodbye, then?"

"Yes." There were tears in her eyes again. "It isn't public yet, but father has been recalled. Tomorrow he presents his recall to the Secretary of State, and the day after we leave for England. This is goodbye."

"That does mean war!" he muttered. "I've been hoping that in spite of everything—God knows I'm sorry, Kay. I don't blame you for the way you feel. You couldn't feel differently and still be Kay Lovell, but—it's damned hard. It's damned hard!"

She agreed silently. After a moment she said, "Think of my part of it, Ted—going back to a home that's like—well, the Rockefeller Mountains in Antarctica. I tell you, I'd rather it had been England that sunk into the sea! That would have been easier, much easier than this. If it had sunk until the waves rolled over the very peak of Ben Macduhl—" She broke off.

"The waves are rolling over higher peaks than Ben Macduhl," he responded drearily. "They're—" Suddenly he paused, staring at Kay with his jaw dropping and a wild light in his eyes!

"The Sierra Madre!" he bellowed, in such a roaring voice that the girl shrank away. "The Mother range! The Sierra Madre! The Sierra Madre!"

"Wh-what?" she gasped.

"The Sierra-! Listen to me, Kay! Listen to me! Do you trust me! Will you do something—something for both of us? Us? I mean for the world! Will you?"

"I know you will! Kay, keep your father from presenting his recall! Keep him here another ten days—even another week. Can you?"

"How? How can I?"

"I don't know. Any way at all. Get sick. Get too sick to travel, and beg him not to present his papers until you can leave. Or— or tell him that the United States will make his country an alternate proposal in a few days. That's the truth. I swear that's true, Kay."

"But—but he won't believe me!"

"He's got to! I don't care how you do it, but keep him here! And have him report to the Foreign Office that new developments—vastly important developments—have come up. That's true, Kay."

"True? Then what are they?"

"There isn't time to explain. Will you do what I ask?"

"I'll try!"

"You're—well you're marvelous!" he said huskily. He stared into her tragic brown eyes, kissed her lightly, and rushed away.

*   *   *   *   *

Asa Gaunt was scowling down at a map of the dead Salton Sea when Ted dashed unannounced into the office. The rangy Texan looked up with a dry smile at the unceremonious entry.

"I've got it!" yelled Ted.

"A bad case of it," agreed Asa Gaunt. "What's the diagnosis?"

"No, I mean—Say, has the Survey taken soundings over the Isthmus?"

"The Dolphin's been there for weeks," said the older man. "You know you can't map forty thousand square miles of ocean bed during the lunch hour."

"Where," shouted Ted, "are they sounding?"

"Over Pearl Cay Point, Bluefields, Monkey Point, and San Juan del Norte, of course. Naturally they'll sound the places where there were cities first of all."

"Oh, naturally!" said Ted, suppressing his voice to a tense quiver. "And where is the Marlin?"

"Idle at Newport News. We can't operate both of them under this year's budget."

"To hell with the budget!" flared Ted. "Get the Marlin there too, and any other vessel that can carry an electric plumb!"

"Yes, sir—right away, sir," said Asa Gaunt dryly. "When did you relieve Golsborough as Secretary of the Interior, Mr. Welling?"

"I'm sorry," replied Ted. "I'm not giving orders, but I've thought of something. Something that may get all of us out of this mess we're in."

"Indeed? Sounds mildly interesting. Is it another of these international fiat—money schemes?"

"No!" blazed Ted. "It's the Sierra Madre! Don't you see?"

"In words of one syllable, no."

"Then listen! I've flown over every square mile of the sunken territory. I've mapped and photographed it, and I've laid out the geodetics. I know that buried strip of land as well as I know the humps and hollows in my own bed."

"Congratulations, but what of it?"

"This!" snapped Ted. He turned to the wall, pulled down the topographical map of Central America, and began to speak. After a while Asa Gaunt leaned forward in his chair and a queer light gathered in his pale blue eyes.

What follows has been recorded and interpreted in a hundred ways by numberless historians. The story of the Dolphin and the Marlin, sounding in frantic haste the course of the submerged Cordilleras, is in itself romance of the first order. The secret story of diplomacy, the holding of Britain's neutrality so that the lesser sea powers dared not declare war across three thousand miles of ocean, is another romance that will never be told openly. But the most fascinating story of all, the building of the Cordilleran Inter-continental Wall, has been told so often that it needs little comment.

The soundings traced the irregular course of the sunken Sierra Madre mountains. Ted's guess was justified; the peaks of the range were not inaccessibly far below the surface. A route was found where the Equatorial Counter Current swept over them with a depth at no point greater than forty fathoms, and the building of the Wall began on March the 31st, began in frantic haste, for the task utterly dwarfed the digging of the abandoned Canal itself. By the end of September some two hundred miles had been raised to sea-level, a mighty rampart seventy-five feet broad at its narrowest point, and with an extreme height of two hundred and forty feet and an average of ninety.

There was still almost half to be completed when winter swept out of the north over a frightened Europe, but the half that had been built was the critical sector. On one side washed the Counter Current, on the other the Equatorial Drift, bound to join the Gulf Stream in its slow march toward Europe, And the mighty Stream, traced by a hundred oceanographic vessels, veered slowly northward again, and bathed first the shores of France, then of England, and finally of the high northern Scandinavian Peninsula. Winter came drifting in as mildly as of old, and a sigh of relief went up from every nation in the world.

Ostensibly the Cordilleran Inter-continental Wall was constructed by the United States. A good many of the more chauvinistic newspapers bewailed the appearance of Uncle Sam as a sucker again, paying for the five hundred million dollar project for the benefit of Europe. No one noticed that there was no Congressional appropriation for the purpose, nor has anyone since wondered why the British naval bases on Trinidad, Jamaica, and at Belize have harbored so large a portion of His Majesty's Atlantic Fleet. Nor, for that matter, has anyone inquired why the dead war debts were so suddenly exhumed and settled so cheerfully by the European powers.

A few historians and economists may suspect. The truth is that the Cordilleran Inter-continental Wall has given the United

States a world hegemony, in fact almost a world empire. From the south tip of Texas, from Florida, from Puerto Rico, and from the otherwise useless Canal Zone, a thousand American planes could bomb the Wall into ruin. No European nation dares risk that.

Moreover, no nation in the world, not even in the orient where the Gulf Stream has no climatic influence, dares threaten war on America. If Japan, for instance, should so much as speak a hostile word, the whole military might of Europe would turn against her. Europe simply cannot risk an attack on the Wall, and certainly the first effort of a nation at war with the United States would be to force a passage through the Wall.

In effect the United States can command the armies of Europe with a few bombing planes, though not even the most ardent pacifists have yet suggested that experiment. But such are the results of the barrier officially known as the Cordilleran Intercontinental Wall, but called by every newspaper after its originator, the Welling Wall.

*   *   *   *   *

It was mid-summer before Ted had time enough to consider marriage and a honeymoon. He and Kay spent the latter on the Caribbean, cruising that treacherous sea in a sturdy fifty-foot sloop lent for the occasion by Asa Gaunt and the Geological Survey. They spent a good share of the time watching the great dredges and construction vessels working desperately at the task of adding millions of cubic yards to the peaks of the submarine range that was once the Sierra Madre. And one day as they lay on the deck in swimming suits, bent on acquiring a tropical tan, Ted asked her a question.

"By the way," he began, "you've never told me how you managed to keep Sir Joshua in the States. That stalled off war just long enough for this thing to be worked out and presented. How'd you do it?"

Kay dimpled. "Oh, first I tried to tell him I was sick. I got desperately sick."

"I knew he'd fall for that."

"But he didn't. He said a sea voyage would help me."

"Then—what did you do?"

"Well, you see he has a sort of idiosyncrasy toward quinine. Ever since his service in India, where he had to take it day after day, he develops what doctors call a quinine rash, and he hasn't taken any for years."

"Well?"

"Don't you see? His before-dinner cocktail had a little quinine in it, and so did his wine, and so did his tea, and the sugar and the salt. He kept complaining that everything he ate tasted bitter to him, and I convinced him that it was due to his indigestion."

"And then?"

"Why, then I brought him one of his indigestion capsules, only it didn't have his medicine in it. It had a nice dose of quinine, and in two hours he was pink as a salmon, and so itchy he couldn't sit still!"

Ted began to laugh. "Don't tell me that kept him there!"

"Not that alone," said Kay demurely. "I made him call in a doctor, a friend of mine who—well, who kept asking me to marry him—and I sort of bribed him to tell father he had—I think it was erysipelas he called it. Something violently contagious, anyway.

"And so—?"

"And so we were quarantined for two weeks! And I kept feeding father quinine to keep up the bluff, and—well, we were very strictly quarantined. He just couldn't present his recall!"

Also From Resurrected Press
Science Fiction Authors Resurrected

Fyfe Resurrected - The Stories of H. B. Fyfe
Stories from the Golden Age of Science Fiction by the author of D-99. dealing with the interaction of humans and aliens on far off worlds in ways that were as creative as they were imaginative.

Schmitz Resurrected - Selected Stories of James H. Schmitz
Includes "An Incident on Route 12", "Watch the Sky", "The Other Likeness", "The Star Hyacinths", "Oneness", "The Winds of Time", "Ham Sandwich" and "Gone Fishing".

Sheckly Resurrected - The Early Stories of Robert Sheckley
Resurrected Press has collected some of the best of these from the 50's including "Warrior Race", "The Leech", "Watchbird", "Warm", "Diplomatic Immunity", "The Hour of Battle", "Besides Still Waters", "Keep Your Shape", "One Man's Poison", 'Ask a Foolish Question", "Cost of Living", "Death Wish Forever".

Dick Resurrected - The Early Stories of Philip K. Dick
Early stories from the author of the novels that inspired "Blade Runner," "Total Recall," and "A Scanner Darkly".

Hamilton Resurrected - Classic Stories of Edmond Hamilton
Edmond Hamilton was one of the most popular writers during the 30's and 40's, the period that saw the first flowering of modern science fiction.

Smith Resurrected - Selected Stories of Evelyn E. Smith ton
During an era when women rarely appeared in science fiction magazines, Evelyn E. Smith appeared regularly in the pages of Galaxy and Fantastic Universe. Resurrected Press is proud to return these stories to print.

OTHER CLASSIC SCIENCE FICTION NOVELS

TALENTS, INCORPORATED - BY MURRAY LEINSTER
When a Mekinese fleet conquers his home planet, Captain Bors turns to Talents, Incorporated for help using their collection of individuals with unusual abilities to defeat the enemy and save the galaxy.

THE PIRATES OF ERSATZ - BY MURRAY LEINSTER
Bran Hodden just wanted to be an electronic engineer and marry a delightful girl. But when he's framed by the powers on Walden he's forced to turn back to his family's trade, piracy. Also published as The Pirates of Zan.

EMPIRE - BY CLIFFORD SIMAK
Spencer Chambers and Interplanetary Power owned the Solar System because they controlled the source of power. It fell to Russell Page and Harry Wilson to challenge that control if they had to cross the universe to do it.

NIGHT OF THE LONG KNIVES - THE CREATURE FROM THE CLEVELAND DEPTHS - BY FRITZ LEIBER
Two classic novellas set in the not too distant future from a classic master of science fiction.

ARMAGEDDON - 2419 A.D. - THE AIR LORDS OF HAN - BY PHILLIP FRANCIS NOWLAN
The two novels that introduced the world to that intrepid hero of the 25th Century, Buck Rogers. Buck Rogers must save the world from the clutches of the insidious Han.

Resurrected Press Fiction by Randall Garrett

Anything You Can Do...

What do you do when an alien with exceptional physical abilities crash lands on Earth and leaves a path of death and destruction in its wake? You use biological modification to create an enhanced human able to match the alien in strength and speed. But is the result still human?

Unwise Child

After two unsuccessful and seemingly random attempts on his life in the space of as many hours, Michael Raphael Gabriel finds himself called on to act as engineering officer on a new type of spacecraft designed for one mission only, to carry a giant computer to a distant destination before it can destroy the Earth. But once under way he discovers there is a murderer on board and the computer has gone crazy.

By Randall Garrett and Laurence Janifer

Pagan Passions

The Gods and Goddesses of the Ancient Greece and Rome have returned to rule Earth. William Forrester, a mortal teacher, dedicated to the pleasures of the mind, finds himself caught up in the power struggles of the immortals and seduced by the pleasures of the flesh.

The Fictional Detective
by Greg Fowlkes

Who killed Ezekial O. Handler?

A beautiful dame, a hard-boiled private eye — and a dead body.

It started like any other case. When a famous writer dies in a mysterious car crash, private detective Frank Slade is called in to find answers, but all he finds is more questions. Who killed Ezekial Handler? Who is Janet Nielsen and why is she so interested in finding out? Who is leaving the neatly typed clues? And as Slade tries to find answers to these questions he starts to wonder if the ultimate answer will threaten his very existence.

Read about it in
The Fictional Detective

Visit www.thefictionaldetective.com

About Resurrected Press

A division of Intrepid Ink, LLC, Resurrected Press is dedicated to bringing high quality, vintage books back into publication. See our entire catalogue and find out more at www.ResurrectedPress.com.

About Intrepid Ink, LLC

Intrepid Ink, LLC provides full publishing services to authors of fiction and non-fiction books, eBooks and websites. From editing to formatting, from publishing to marketing, Intrepid Ink gets your creative works into the hands of the people who want to read them. Find out more at www.IntrepidInk.com.